THE DRUMCHESTER DIARIES

The Drumchester Diaries

The extraordinary in the ordinary
A story of friendship and hope

Tim Buckley

Contents

THE DRUMCHESTER DIARIES

INTRODUCTION

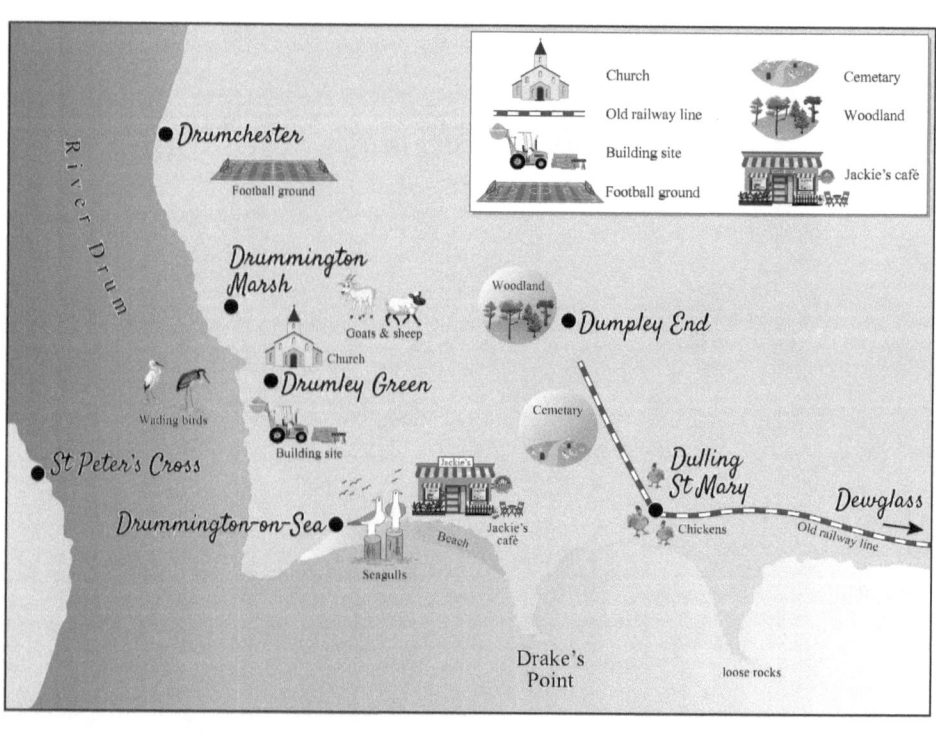

"So you kept a diary as well?"

Everyone, I reckon, has a box of childhood memories somewhere. It could be under the bed, or at the back of the wardrobe, or stuffed into a drawer somewhere. We don't exactly want to get rid of it, but we don't want to show it to anyone, either. So we hang on to it, until we finally decide either it's going out or we're going to show it to our nearest and dearest.

My husband found my diaries when we were unpacking into the first house we had just bought together. It was right there, among my memories of Mum, and my school photos, and all the other bits pieces at the bottom of the crate. He stood there embarrassed, not quite sure whether he should open them or not. I said nothing, but dived in amid his trophies and medals, and all the stuff to do with his Dad and Gran, and sure enough, there they were, carefully preserved - and yet unseen since the day they were written.

So for the next few hours we ignored the chaos all around us, and curled up in each other's arms, we shared memories, and laughter, and not a few tears.

"Your spelling was atrocious," I said.

"Your handwriting was terrible," he replied.

But we both found the words powerful, and we sat there transported to a very different time when so much happened, when it turned out that, one way or another the direction of our lives was set - even if we didn't realise it at the time.

Then Ally noticed the time. "Sorry, I have to dash," he said, "or I will be late for training." Then he gave me a kiss and brushed away a loose hair from my cheek. "I love you, KT."

"I know," I replied, thinking how this gangly, awkward schoolboy had grown into the man I was now proud to call my own.

~ * ~ * ~ * ~

We mentioned the diaries the next time we saw our best friends Alex and Daisy down in Drummington-on-Sea. We were sitting on the beach at Drake's point, our own special place, far away from the tourists, where we had spent so many hours together. As usual, Daisy was busy sketching, and mostly listening to what the three of us were saying.

"I kept a diary as well," said Alex. "I thought about burning it at one point, but then I found I couldn't do it."

"Well, you always said you were going to be a famous writer." I laughed and then blushed as I realised I had said something really stupid. Daisy just looked at me, and gently rested her hand on Alex's arm.

"So I did," admitted Alex, "but then we all had a headful of dreams, didn't we?"

There was an awkward silence for a while. The sun disappeared briefly behind a bank of cloud, and the sea turned from a brilliant blue into a more metallic grey. I am sure even now Alex was thinking of how to put the scene into a poem, and I bitterly regretted my foolish words.

I muttered an apology. "That's all right," said Alex, "what happened, happened, and I don't have too many regrets, not any more. Anyway," he went on, "I was thinking, what would it be like if we all read each other's diaries?"

"I dunno about that," said Ally, "wouldn't it be a bit like taking off our clothes in public?"

I smiled at Ally. I know to some people he is a bit of a celebrity, and he guards our privacy fiercely.

"It's just that, if we put our stories together, I think we'd have quite a tale to tell."

Ally and I were still considering Alex's proposal when the alarm on Daisy's phone went off. "Sorry," she said, "but we've got to go and get the children." She slipped her gorgeous straw-coloured hair into a bun and offered her hand to Alex who pulled her up. "But we won't be long, and they're dying to see you again."

"Make sure you buy them an ice cream from *Digby's*," I said. "That's on us."

While Alex and Daisy were gone, we looked at the sketch pad Daisy had left behind. She had drawn from memory the portraits of the three of us when we were younger. There was Ally, looking all sporty, and yet at the same time, surprisingly vulnerable; Alex in his serious intellectual phase apparently lost in thought; and me? Oh, I was wearing that smile I always wore as a defence against the world, when everything was, as usual, proving just too much.

Daisy, as always, had captured us perfectly. And although we hated to admit it, we reckoned Alex was right. Yeah, we may have been just a bunch of ordinary teenagers living somewhere no-one has ever heard of, but we went through so much, and somehow with our faith, with each other we survived.

~ * ~ * ~ * ~

That's how, a few months later, my lockdown project started. I spent ages reading, deciphering, praying, working out what do with our precious, irreplaceable books of secrets. Eventually I decided the best thing to do was for each of us to tell a separate part of the story, right until near the end. I ran this past Ally and Alex and they seemed cool with it. Alex said it was rather like composing a three-part fugue, and if Wikipedia is right, then I can sort of see what he means. Anyway, whatever it is, I showed the final result to our former vicar, John, who's still a great friend, and prays for us regularly.

He read everything through from start to finish, made a few suggestions, and even wrote the conclusion. "You know what to do with it," he said, smiling, as he handed the precious manuscript back to me.

So here they are - the Drumchester Diaries. As I have been putting together the final touches, I have at the same time slowly and wearily been approaching my due date. I can't help wondering whether our son will appreciate what we've written, if he will show any interest, or simply be embarrassed.

"Let's hope he'll have his own story to tell," said Ally, gently working his large hands up and down my aching back. "But for now, this is ours and that's all that matters."

THE DRUMCHESTER DIARIES: VOLUME 1
FINDING A FAITH
THE DIARY OF ALLY GREEN, AGED 11

January 1st

That has to have been the worst Christmas ever. I don't get on with my stepfather's relations at the best of times, and this certainly wasn't the best of times. His brother Bill came to stay - some kind of professional children's entertainer, apparently. The twins loved him - well they're only two years old - and the whole week was like one big children's party. His own children are only three and seven, so they joined in with the fun as well. But I'm eleven now, and I really don't want to make puppies out of balloons, or pin tails onto donkeys, or play pass the parcel. I spent most of the time in my bedroom on the DS my Mum gave me. She came up once or twice to check I was OK. I think she knew I was struggling, but she didn't say anything to my stepfather George. I wish she had.

Anyway Bill and his family have gone now, so we have a few days' peace before I head back to school. George is taking me to see Drumchester City play - their ground is just round the corner from where we live, and he's promised me a pizza afterwards.

January 4th

First day of school today, so that means a train ride down to Drummington-on-Sea where my Dad lives. Mum, Dad and me all used to live in Drummington-on-Sea when I was little. Dad owned a big shop in town, and we had a lovely house near the river. But then the supermarket came and Dad's shop went bust. We had to sell the house, and the furniture, and Mum moved up to Drumchester where she met and married George.

I wish sometimes we could still be all together but as Mum says it's no use living in the past. So every Monday morning I catch the early morning train down to

Drummington and spend the school week at Dad's. They've had the same arrangement for several years now. Me at Dad's during the term, and at Mum's for weekends and holidays. It's just how it is. I can't imagine life being any different, really.

Today's a beautiful morning. The line meets the river at Drummington Marsh, and then goes through the little station at Drumley Green before getting to its destination. As we pull away from Drummington Marsh I see the sun rise over the water and there are lots of birds feeding on the shoreline. I can't write poetry no matter how much my teacher Mr Crossley tries to make me, but I never get tired of this journey.

When I arrive at the station, it's a walk through the town square (where Dad used to have his shop), down the high street, over the roundabout, and then next right down the street to the school. My friend Steve is already in the playground. "Did you have a good Christmas?" he asks. Then he spots my expression and says, "OK, that was the wrong question. What was the match like?" "We won 3-0." "Brilliant - do you think we could be promoted this year?" "No chance. But we might avoid dropping out of the league." He laughs, and then tries to nick my rucksack. We have a friendly tussle, until we spot Mr Crossley coming through the gates and we walk away all innocent, giggling to ourselves.

January 5th

Now I'm eleven, I don't have to go to after-school club any more. Dad's given me a key to his tiny little flat so I can let myself in. Sometimes I go round to my friends, but mostly I do my homework so I can spend the evenings with Dad.

Dad got home just before 6. When I haven't seen him for a while, he always gives me a big hug and brings a pizza. I ask him how his Christmas has been. "Not too bad," he says, "except I had this tummy bug." And I notice he's looking tired and somehow older than usual. "But your Gran asked after you, and I said you were doing great."

"Dad," I ask, "Can I spend next Christmas with you?"

"Possibly," he replies in that kind of grown-up way which you know really means no. "But you know the one good thing about you spending Christmas with Mum?"

"What's that?"

"I get to give you your last Christmas present."

And Dad goes into his bedroom, and fishes out a small package wrapped in brown paper.

I open it excitedly. It's a new pair of goalkeeping gloves. Just what I've needed.

"Thanks, Dad," I say, and for once I give him a hug.

January 13th

Football practice today! It was too wet last week, but at last we have a chance to play after school. No-one wants to be goalkeeper apart from me. I really don't understand why. I love being able to dive around in the mud, and there's no better feeling than turning a shot round the post or over the crossbar. At the end of the session Mr Crossley tells me I'm in the team to play Drumley Green in a fortnight. I am not really that surprised. The only other option is 'Timmy' Timms, and while he's a great guy, he's big and fat and slow. He can block most things that come his way. But you can't expect him to get down on the ball in a hurry.

January 24th

Steve has asked me to his birthday sleepover on Saturday. Weekends are always awkward, so I text my Mum. She reminds me I'm seeing her at parents' evening tonight, which is just as well, because I always try to forget it's happening.

Mum and Dad used to argue who'd come to parents' evening, but Mum as usual won the argument. It's the only time she gets to see my school so she likes to thoroughly interrogate my teacher how I'm doing, whether I'm on target, what I should be doing to improve, whether my homework is in on time. I guess she's a bit pushy, but I don't mind that much. Ever since she left Dad, she's learnt to make her own way. Now she's a successful businesswoman selling mobile phones, and as she heads back to her car she's telling me how she and George are thinking about moving to a bigger house and would I like that?

I nod my head. I am thinking about Dad's tiny, damp, two-bedroom basement flat which he just about keeps up by working in a shop during the week and driving a taxi at weekends. It seems like more and more I am living in two different worlds. In fact, sometimes I can't even remember the three of us ever being together.

She's just about to drive off when I remember Steve's sleepover.

"Give George a ring," she says. "I think he's planning to take you to the football on Saturday."

So, as she turns into the street I ring George. The twins are rioting in the background, but George calmly says, "No problem. You tell me where to go, and I'll drop you off after the match." For a stepfather he isn't that bad. Or maybe he just wants to escape the terrible twins.

January 29th

A day of two halves. Drumchester City lost 4-1 at home today, so that was really bad. The team itself didn't play too badly, but the goalie got injured early on and they put some young lad between the sticks who had never played in the league before. I have to say, it showed. He was so nervous, the defence lost all its confidence, and we were 2-0 down by half-time. As we queued for our cup of tea and pasty, I told George how I'd been selected for the school team and how Dad had given me a new pair of goal-keeping gloves.

"Keep practising," he said. "The team will need you soon."

We laughed but as the third and fourth goals went in, it got beyond a joke. It began to rain heavily and we left the car park, wet and miserable.

But Steve's sleepover was a real laugh. His Dad's a fisherman, and he had done a deal with the local chippy, so we all ate fish and chips in front of some really cool action adventure. The next morning when we were all planning to leave, I had a text from Mum. Apparently, the twins had been out to a birthday party yesterday and were now throwing up, and could I stay with Dad?

I tried to ring Dad, but his mobile was switched off. He had probably been driving out late into the morning and was still fast asleep. I explained the situation to Steve's Mum and Dad, and they were brilliant. They let me stay until lunchtime, and I got to fly Steve's new kite on the beach with his older brother Paul. Then Dad picked me up and took me to the local Chinese for lunch, and having checked I'd be OK at home, went off to work.

February 3rd

I played a blinder against Drumley Green today! Steve gave away a penalty early on, although he swears blind he didn't mean to trip the forward. This big, ugly guy steps forward, lashes it to my right, and I just manage to finger-tip it round the post. From that point on, I knew nothing could get past me. No matter how hard they try, they're not going to score. We go on to win 3-0 and as usual it's the goalscorers who get all the credit.

But Mr Crossley gives me a big pat on the back as we walk off and says, "Well done. Keep it up, son," and that means a lot to me.

There's also an old guy in a tracksuit there who seems to be taking notes. Don't know what he's doing there, and he's gone by the end of the match.

February 5th

Mum explains why she and George are looking for a new house. Apparently, George's son, Mark, is coming down from London to work with his father in the car repair business, and he needs somewhere to live. I say nothing. The thing I've learnt about stepfamilies is that you keep on finding new relations you are supposed to get along with.

At least Mum has invited me to go house-hunting with her, so for once I have a Saturday on my own with her. Don't get me wrong, the twins - Carrie and Nina - are lovely as far as they go. But they're only two, and whenever I think I can have some quality time with my mother, one or both of them keep butting in.

The first house we look at is a square brick box on a new housing estate. It's exactly the same as the other square brick boxes on the street. It's brand new and it's even got curtains and carpets, but there's one problem. There's no garden to speak of, and Mum knows I need a garden. So we go out to the edge of Drumchester to look at a really old cottage with a massive garden attached. The front door is surrounded by tall, evil-looking weeds, and it's clear no-one has lived in the house for years. Neither Mum or George has the time to take on a building project, so that's definitely off the list.

It's getting near lunch time now, so Mum takes me to an Italian restaurant in town. I like the way she takes all the house details she's brought from the estate agents and goes through them with me. It's been so long since it's just been the two of us, I'd forgotten how much fun she can be. We make two lists - of "possibles" and "impossibles" and she writes rude comments on the impossibles.

In the end, as we finish our ice cream, we decide we are going to look at two more. The first one is OK - if you ignore the fact it's right next to the railway line, with an electricity pylon on the other side. But the second one is something else. I guess it's quite old, and Mum says we need to check out how much work the house needs. However, the owner has recently painted it and is looking to sell it quickly as he's moving to Australia. Mum rings George who soon joins us, and they end up ringing the estate agent. Meanwhile I try and stop Carrie and Nina from wrecking the garden and falling in the pond. I play a game of chase with them, until in the end Carrie falls over and bangs her knee. Why do my games with them always end like this?

February 9th

I don't get on with most of the girls in our class. They're into things that are pink, and make-up and fashion. But KT Lee is different. She's a bit of a tomboy really. Likes to join in with the football in the playground and is apparently learning the drums. I learnt today she actually lives just round the corner. I was walking to school when I saw her coming out of her gate.

"Hello," I said stupidly, "I didn't know you lived there."

"Well obviously I do."

"So why haven't I seen you walk to school before?"

"Because I normally cycle. But someone stole my bicycle last evening. Do you want to see a picture of it?"

She shows me a picture of her bicycle on her phone. It's not a usual girly affair. It's a proper bright red, ten-speed affair that she was given at Christmas.

"If I see it, I'll let you know."

"You can tell if it's mine because I painted 'KTL' in nail varnish underneath the saddle."

"I'll keep an eye out for it."

We walk on in silence. I think we are both a bit embarrassed walking together. We reach the town square where KT dives into a shop to get some sweets. If she hadn't done so, I would have gone in instead.

February 12th

We are definitely buying that house. Just as well, because Mark came down for the weekend. He's a younger version of George, except he has more hair, and a lot more spots. He came with us to the football even though he really supports Charlton Athletic. As George said, "If you're going to be with one of us, you've got to fit in."

"No worries," said Mark. "The chances of Charlton playing Drumchester are virtually nil."

I have to say I agree with him. Drumchester have borrowed another keeper as the regular one will be out for some time. He's OK, but not brilliant. It's a dull 0-0 draw in pouring rain. At the end it's hard to tell the players apart there's so much mud on their backs.

In the evening George takes Mark down the pub, so after the twins have finally gone to bed, Mum and I start to make plans for the new house. Mum explains Mark is only going to live with us for a few months before he gets a place of his own. Then the twins can have separate bedrooms. I suggest we paint his bedroom pink to start with. She's not sure it's such a good idea.

February 17th

There's only one problem playing in goal. If the other team are rubbish, then you get cold and bored standing at the other end. Today we played Drummington Marsh and we won 14-0. Even Steve who usually never crosses the halfway line scored twice. I only picked up the ball a few times and caught it once as it came into the penalty area. No-one was going to notice my contribution today!

At the end Mr Crossley asked me if I'd thought of joining Drummington Colts. I asked when they met, and he said Saturday morning. I knew this was going to be a problem before I phoned Mum. She said no but offered to find a team somewhere in Drumchester. That's no good to me. If I can't play for Drummington-on-Sea, then I'm not going to play for anyone else.

March 1st

Today we all learnt which school we are going to next year. Everybody is going to Drummington-on-Sea Comprehensive. Except me. Mum and Dad agreed long ago that I would go to Drumchester Academy so I would stay with Mum during the week and go to Dad at weekends and some holidays. I had known this all along, but I didn't want to tell anyone. It's been really hard explaining it to Steve and the gang.

Mr Crossley asked if anyone would stay in at break time and help tidy up the bookshelves. For the first time in my life I volunteered. When everyone else left the classroom, Mr Crossley asked me what was wrong. I didn't say anything at first, but eventually I told him.

"Well, I know what it's like," he said. "When I was your age, I was the only one in my class to go to grammar school. Back in those days you only kept in touch with your friends if you went round to their house or asked your parents to use the phone. At least nowadays you have text and e-mail."

I know he was trying to be helpful. But today has really been hard. At lunch time no-one sat with me until in the end KT Lee sat down next to me.

"Have you found my bike yet?" she asked.

"No," I said, "but I'll keep looking."

It was good of her to chat but I really didn't feel like chatting. Then Timmy Timms sat down on someone's yoghurt and the whole place erupted in laughter. For a few minutes I even stopped feeling sorry for myself.

March 12th

We are going to move during the Easter holidays, so Mum has made me go through all my stuff. I can think of lots of better things to do than sit in my bedroom looking at boxes. But it's a fairly easy job. There are lots of books and jigsaws and games I'm never going to need any more and we'll take them to the charity shop later. I also find a box of special memories I'd forgotten I ever had. There's a Bible my Gran (Dad's mother) gave me when I was born with lots of brightly coloured pictures. I haven't looked at it for ages, but I guess it might come in useful for RE lessons. There's also a photo of me as a baby with Mum and Dad together. I don't want to think about it too much, so I shove it inside the Bible. I know I'm not going to read it any time soon.

March 19th

Mark's come down from London again and wants to buy some stuff for his room. He offers to take me into town, and he turns out to be a real laugh. We end up in some second-hand place where he is looking for a cheap *PlayStation*. He is taking ages and I am getting bored. So I wander off to the back of the shop where there is a load of bicycles. I notice one of them is a red *Raleigh* 10-speed. I think about the picture on KT's phone and look under the saddle. Sure enough, there are her initials painted in nail-varnish.

I find Mark and take him to have a look. "That's my friend's bike," I whisper, "the one that was stolen last month."

"How do you know?" he replies.

So I show him the saddle. "OK, leave it with me," he says.

At that moment, the shop owner comes over, a thin, weedy-looking man with thick spectacles. "Can I help you, boys?"

"My younger brother here wants to buy this bicycle but needs to ask his Dad for the money. Can I put a deposit down on it?"

"Sure. £10 guarantees any bicycle."

So Mark gives him a note and takes me out of the shop. When we are clear of the entrance, he asks me if I know my friend's phone number. I say no, but explain she lives just round the corner from Dad. Mark tells me to ring Dad who happens to be in, and he says he will ring back in a few minutes.

We wait for what seems like ages. It begins to rain, and we huddle in a bus stop, counting the seconds.

At last my phone rings.

"Is that Ally?" says a deep voice I don't recognise.

"Yes."

"This is Trevor, KT's Dad. Can you tell me where you are?"

"I think so," and I give him directions.

"Your Dad's bringing us over. We'll be with you in about half an hour."

Mark goes over to a newsagent's and comes back with cans of *Cola* and some packets of crisps. Two old ladies waiting for a bus eye us nervously, as if we're going to mug them. I smile at one of them, but it only makes them more frightened. Fortunately, their bus arrives at that point, and they hurry on board while we carry on what my Dad calls "loitering."

A policeman walks down the street. Now he's looking at us. I think he's just about to speak to us, when Dad's taxi comes into view. He parks up outside the second-hand shop and out of the back of the car step KT and the biggest man I've ever seen. Seriously, he's huge. I learn later he moves furniture for a living, and I can believe it. He's wearing a cut-off denim jacket with tattoos down both arms, and he has an earring in his ear.

"You must be Ally?" he says.

I nod.

"Show us where the bike is then."

I don't argue. KT smiles at me and follows me and her father towards the back of the shop. Trevor looks at the saddle of the bicycle and gives KT the thumbs up. Then with a glare he fixes the shop manager who is coming over to see what's going on.

"Are you interested in the bicycle, sir?"

"You might say that. It belongs to my daughter, and it was stolen last month. Now you and I are going to have a little chat while my mate here," he jerks his head at my Dad "phones the police."

"I think we'll leave them to it," says my Dad. "It looks like Trevor has got the matter in hand."

Twenty minutes later the police turn up. The shopkeeper comes out to meet them, white and shaking, although Trevor swears he didn't touch him. Trevor picks up the bike and puts it in the back of Dad's taxi. Then to celebrate, he takes us all out to lunch at *KFC*. I don't really like greasy chicken, but for once I don't care. I'm happy. KT is happy. And it looks like Trevor, Mark and my Dad are getting on like a house a fire. It's just a shame I can't be a hero every day.

March 29th

We played Dumpley End today and won 5-1. I was really cross I let in a goal, but Steve says I should stop trying to be perfect. I'm not so sure. The old guy with the tracksuit was there, but this time he stayed to the end of the match making notes. As we came off the pitch, he spoke to Mr Crossley who then introduced him to me. Apparently, he is some kind of youth scout for Drumchester City, and would I like to do some football training there over the Easter holidays? Would I?? Of course I say yes, and I try to act all calm, although on the inside I am punching the air. I buy a huge bottle of lemonade on the way home to celebrate. It's only when I am about to reach home that I realise we're supposed to be moving home as well. But Mum's not going to say no, is she? I quickly text her and open the front door.

To my surprise, Dad is already there. He isn't looking very well. Apparently, he's come home early because he's got another tummy bug.

"You ought to go and see a doctor."

"Possibly," he says.

"No, seriously," I say.

"Yeah, you could be right. Anyway, how did you get on?"

At that moment there's a text back from my Mum. *No problem - it will keep you out of the way!*

Absolutely charming, but I know she's joking.

So I tell Dad all about it, and he gives me another one of his great big hugs. Even though he's feeling as rotten as they come, I can tell he's really proud of me.

April 5th

The local vicar came to school today to talk about Easter. I am sure he is a good man who tries his best, but honestly, he's so boring. I think he was saying Easter means we should be nice to other people, even if we don't like them. But I'm not sure we need an old man with a dog collar to tell us that. And then we had the head telling us year 6s off for an April Fool's joke we were supposed to have played last week. I know nothing about it. Well, apart from the fact Big Dave brought a bag of flour in that day...

When Dad gets home today, he tells me he's seen the doctor and he's been sent to Drumchester General for some tests. I ask if it's serious, and he says he doesn't know. But he doesn't want any of this to affect my training with Drumchester City next week.

"Look, Ally," he says, as he puts a pizza into the oven, "you can either worry about me and play badly, or you can do the very best you can to make your old man proud. You're a smart kid. You know what to do." Then with tea cooking he shows me a letter that's arrived that day from Drumchester City. Apparently, if the Easter camp goes well, I get invited back to their summer school.

I think about it all later as I am going to sleep. Yeah, I'm going to do the best I can. For my sake. For Dad's sake. And then I start thinking about Dad and I find myself praying that everything's going to be all right. I just hope God isn't old and boring like the vicar but is someone who can actually make a difference.

April 11th

Today was exhausting! The removal van turned up at 8 o'clock. Of course, the twins weren't ready. They were enjoying charging through the house, enjoying all the extra space we had created by packing up over the weekend. It took the four of us - Mum, George, Mark and myself - to get hold of them, get them washed and dressed, and give them something to eat. By this time it was half past eight, and I suddenly realised I had to be at the Drumchester City training ground by nine. I dashed out of the door, down the street and just caught the bus to the edge of town, to the Octopus and Trumpet training ground (apparently named after the local pub). And if I thought I was fit before, then I certainly am now! We spent most of the first day on fitness conditioning, and basic skills, and by the end of it I felt like I had run several marathons and climbed several mountains.

On the way back I looked forward to having a long shower, only to realise I had caught the bus back to our old house. Fortunately, I knew where to change buses, and arrived at our new place just in time to see the van pulling away from the street. Only it turns out the hot water doesn't work, and in any case Mum and George haven't yet found the box with all the bathroom bits in it. I go into my bedroom, and there's a bed in my new bedroom, but that's it. No mattress, no wardrobes, no chairs nothing. The only positive is that Mum has sent Carrie and Nina over to her friend's house for the night. We're going to need all the energy we've got to get this place ready to live in.

April 15th

The final day of camp! I actually got to meet the Drumchester City manager this afternoon and he stayed for our final practice match, even though it was tipping it down. It was hard work keeping goal in all the mud, and I did let a couple of goals in, but I felt I was playing well, and made a couple of really smart saves. As I came off, panting and dripping like a wet dog, the old man in the tracksuit (I never did find out his name) came up to me and said, "Well done. We'll see you in the summer."

I had made it! OK, I'm not living the dream yet, but maybe, just maybe one day I will become a professional footballer. When Mum asked me what I'd like to have for tea by way of celebration, I stunned her by asking for pasta with salad, and freshly squeezed orange juice. Well, I'm going to have to watch my diet from now on. Lots of carbohydrates and vitamins from now on - except, of course, on special occasions. Like at the match tomorrow when you've just got to have a pasty, like at Big Dave's party next week... But I will try to be good. Honest.

April 22nd

Just before I go off to Big Dave's party, there's a phone call from Dad to Mum. Dad doesn't usually phone Mum, and when he does, it's something serious. Dad's been to Drumchester Hospital today and they've decided he needs a small operation on this stomach some time during the summer. He might then need some powerful drugs afterwards that could make him quite unwell for some time. He would of course still like to have me as much as possible, but he'd have to take each week as it comes.

"He's not a bad man, your Dad," says Mum.

"Yeah, I know," I say.

"You will let me know how things go, won't you?"

"I promise."

And then Mum does something she very rarely does nowadays - she gives me a kiss. Normally I back away at this point, but for the moment I feel very little and very small, and I let her hold me tight, until Carrie comes into the room asking for a story. And for once, I tell her I will read to her, and she snuggles up to me on one side. Soon afterwards, Nina snuggles up on the other side, and we enjoy being a family together.

April 25th

First day back at school. Found it really hard to concentrate. Really anxious to know how Dad would be when I saw him tonight. I had texted and phoned him, of course, but it's not the same as actually seeing somebody in front of you, is it?

As usual, it was only KT who seemed to notice something was wrong, so I told her what was going on.

"I'll be praying for you," she says.

What does that mean? Haven't got a clue. But it sounds comforting, all the same.

Actually, when Dad comes in from work, he doesn't seem at all bad.

"Here I am," he says cheerfully as walks in through the door. "Now what does a future England goalkeeper want for tea?"

As we tuck into our jacket potatoes (I'm still trying to be good), we talk about the next few months. I think everything's going to be OK. We'll just have to wait and see.

May 3rd

Quite literally back to earth with a bang! I don't remember what happened, but we were playing away against Drumley Green in the reverse fixture. In their first attack of the game, the same big ugly boy whose penalty I saved in the first match, comes charging into the penalty area. He overruns the ball slightly and I dive at his feet. I have the ball safely in my grasp but he keeps on running. He swears later it's an accident, but I'm not too sure. All I know is that a bit later I am waking in hospital with a cracking headache and feeling rather sick. My Dad is sitting by my bed, holding my hand.

"Hey, big fella, you all right?"

I try to nod but it hurts too much. There's also a nurse in the room who tells me what has happened, and that I'm going to spend the night in hospital. At that precise moment I don't feel like going anywhere, so that suits me fine. It turns out the match was abandoned after the accident, and according to my Dad I'm not allowed to play football for the next month. A whole month without football? I groan out loud, but it's not because I'm in any kind of pain.

I don't sleep well that night. It's hard when you're in a strange place with people coming and going outside, and there are other boys sleeping in beds nearby. When I doze off, I have some really weird dreams that are all confused and mixed up, and at one point I have to wake myself up to check everything's OK. Still, when the doctor sees me in the morning, he seems happy with me and tells me I can go home. He tells me my Mum is going to pick me up in half an hour, and would I like the nurse to help me pack my stuff?

As I am waiting for Mum, the hospital chaplain comes into the ward. I can tell he's a vicar by the dog collar round his neck, but he's nothing like the vicar who came to the school assembly. For a start, he looks happy and there's a kind of twinkle in his eye. He is also wearing a Drumchester City badge on his jacket, and anyone who does that is OK as far as I'm concerned. He's here to see the lad next to me who's called

Ben and has a really nasty broken leg, but as we've made eye contact, he chats to me first. And for some reason I tell him all about Dad, and how he's coming to the hospital to have an operation, and the treatment he needs afterwards. The chaplain promises to keep an eye out for him and asks if I'd like him to say a prayer. I can't see it would do any harm, so he prays a very simple prayer in language I can actually understand. I didn't know you could speak to God like that. Maybe I'll try it some day.

I explain what's happened when Mum picks me up, but she just laughs and says, "A blow to the head can do funny things, can't it? I didn't know it would make you all religious."

May 17th

They've rearranged the match against Drumley Green for today. I go along to support the team, even though I'm not allowed to play. Timmy Timms is doing his best in goal, and he makes several good blocks, but he isn't really the diving sort. The big guy who kicked me in the head isn't to be seen - there's a rumour he's been suspended from school - but their star of the show is their right-winger. He doesn't have great ball control, but he's slight and quick, and twice cuts through our defence to score. When the final whistle goes, we have lost by three goals to two.

I go over to Timmy Timms and say, "Bad luck."

"Thanks," he says. And then he smiles and says, "Get well soon."

I'll do my best. My head is gradually getting better, but I do have headaches from time to time. Mostly when I'm thinking about the end of year tests next week...

May 21st

I am really, really mad with Mum. I knew something wasn't quite right when she actually sat down with me at breakfast time as I was eating my cornflakes. Mum never sits with me over breakfast, because usually she's doing something with the twins. But Carrie and Nina were nowhere to be seen, and the house was unusually quiet. (I learnt later George had taken them off to the park.)

I was just beginning to wonder what I was supposed to say to Mum when she said, "Ally, I have some fantastic news. You're going to have another brother or sister round about Christmas."

Fantastic news? It's bad enough having the terrible twins around, and the thought of having another baby in the house fills me with dread. In any case, after we had moved house, and after Mark had come to live with us, I thought life at Mum's would calm down a bit. Especially with Dad being ill. But no, Mum and George are going to have a baby. Marvellous.

Not only that, but the twins are having a birthday party at home next week and Mum insists I stick around and play the older brother. I said I wanted to go with Steve to see *Revenge of the Killer Hamsters* to celebrate the end of exams. But no, that's out of the question.

As I write these words, Mark comes into the room. I quickly shove my diary under the pillow so he can't see what I'm doing.

"You OK?" he asks. I shrug my shoulders. "I couldn't help hearing what you and your Mum were talking about downstairs," he goes on. "Families can be a real pain sometimes, can't they? My Mum is on her third boyfriend after George, and she's had a child by each of them. That's why I had to get away. Come down here for some peace and quiet at home." Mark smiles and I realise he really is like a brother to me. "Anyway," he continues, "Drumchester City are playing their final meaningless match of their mediocre season this afternoon. George has to work, but he says I can take you."

"Thanks," I say, and I mean it.

June 7th

My first match back in goal. We're playing our rivals from along the coast, from Dewglass School. Early on, their striker bursts past Steve into the penalty area and shoots low to the right. I throw myself down, and tip it round the corner. I don't even think about my head hitting the ground. Steve turns round and applauds me. I give him the thumbs up. Everything really is all right again. We end up winning 2-0, and Mr Crossley gives me a pat on the back as I walk off the pitch.

June 24th

We've had an activity week away this week and most of the time it's been fantastic fun. We stayed in an old farmhouse on Drum Moor at the edge of an enormous, scary forest. We've been orienteering, and gone on a death slide, and looked for postboxes, and even tried archery. I'm trying not to think too much about starting a new school in September without this crowd. I write a postcard to Dad telling him I'm going to miss him this week and hoping he's all right. When I saw him last week, he was in a good mood but very tired. He tells me he's trying to do as much work as possible before he has to go into hospital and start treatment.

Last night we had a talent show where we are supposed to show off our skills. It's not really my thing, but Big Dave persuades me to take part in one of his silly sketches. Most of the time I have to put up with the girls doing the dance moves from the latest TV show. They are all taking it very seriously, but I have to say I just find it boring. After about six of these routines it looks like the evening is finally over. But no, Mr Crossley comes to the front with a guitar, and KT Lee steps up to sing the old Bryan Adams song *Everything I do, I do for you*. I didn't know she had such a good voice. The girls are whispering to each other and giggling. But I think it's really brilliant, and my gang all clap her loudly as she finishes.

Next morning there is a bit of an incident. Apparently KT Lee wears a cross round her neck during the day and puts it under her pillow. But as we all pack up and get ready to leave, it turns out her cross is missing. Mr Crossley orders everyone to look for it, and in the end, someone finds it in the bin in the girls' washroom. I have never seen Mr Crossley look so, well, cross before. He tells us that none of us are getting on the bus home before the culprit is found.

Eventually, as we all get on the bus Mr Crossley stays behind for a few minutes with a girl called Maxine. When she finally comes on board, you can tell she's been crying because her make-up has run. Her friends have saved her a special seat at the back of the bus, and all give her a hug. KT Lee is sitting at the front on her own, behind the TA, Mrs Cook, just staring out of the window. I want to sit next to her and give her some of my sweets, but I know it wouldn't be a good move for me or for her. In the end it's Doris who sits next to her. She's a very quiet girl who doesn't speak much English, from Poland, I think. But she puts her arm on KT Lee's shoulder and as the coach pulls away, they begin to chat. I don't know why, but I have the funny feeling I ought to pray for her.

July 13th

Not a good day. Everyone else in my class has gone off to Drummington Comp to spend a day in their new school. And I am the odd one out. To be honest, the school don't know what to do with me. But I talked it over with Dad a few days ago and he suggested to Mr Crossley I spend a day with him in the shop. Mr Crossley wasn't sure, but he couldn't come up with a better idea.

So this morning I got up and walked with Dad to 'Marvin's Discount Furniture'. Dad's been working there ever since his own shop went bust. He still misses the hustle and bustle of the newsagents, and selling sweets to the kids after school, but, as Dad tells me, you're only going to survive in Drummington-on-Sea if you sell something the supermarket doesn't stock. Like beds and wardrobes and tables and chairs. The supermarket doesn't sell these. At least not yet.

But there's one big problem with working in a furniture shop, especially when like today it's a bright, sunny day in the middle of the week. You just don't get many customers. After all, nobody passing by looks in at the window and says, "I fancy popping in and buying a bed." And if folk aren't out at work today, the chances are they're down on the beach. In other words, today is totally dead. After the first couple of hours when I've helped Dad unpack some stuff, there isn't anything at all to do. And Dad is getting pretty bored as well.

In the end Marvin tells Dad he can have the afternoon off. So Dad and I join the crowds at the beach, and we do all the stuff we used to. We buy fish and chips from the van by the pier. We dig sandcastles. And when we've had enough of that, we start to dig an enormous hole so we can bury one another. As we dig, we start to chat about stuff, like what's going to happen over the summer. The big news is that he's going to have his operation first week in August. But he tells me not to worry. We're going to go camping for a week first. And after I've had my camp with Drumchester City and two weeks away with Mum and George, he's hoping he's going to be fit enough to have me for the last week of the holiday.

"You're going to be all right, aren't you, Dad?" I ask.

"Don't worry about me. Just make me proud," is his only reply.

From out of nowhere I say, "I'll be praying for you," and I immediately feel so stupid for saying it.

But he only smiles and says, "Thanks," and then he pushes me in the hole and tries to cover me right up with sand.

On the way home I bump into a lad from my class called Simon. I ask him how the visit went. "Fine," he says. "You'll hear all about it tomorrow."

But I won't. Tomorrow I have to visit Drumchester Academy. I am nervous about going. But I am glad I won't have to hear everyone else talking about their new school.

July 23rd

My last day ever at Drummington Primary! It's been pretty boring the last few days packing everything up and taking stuff home to put somewhere in Dad's tiny flat. I suggest putting it all in a skip but for some strange reason he wants to keep it all. I really don't understand grown-ups sometimes.

We finish the day with our last ever assembly which is as dull as ever. The vicar who did the Easter assembly came back but I don't think anyone of us listened to a word he said. We were all thinking about the disco we were going to have in the evening. Not a silly Key Stage 2 disco with lots of little kids, but a disco just for us. We'd been allowed to choose the music and the food and the theme, and we all knew it really was going to be the end of something special.

By the time I arrived in the evening, Maxine and her gang were already there. I reckon they were all trying to look like Disney princesses, with the long frocks and the high-heeled shoes and the fancy make-up. I ignored them, and they ignored me. That suited me just fine. Then I heard them giggling and whispering again, and I realised of course that KT Lee must have arrived. She was wearing an orange top, white jeans and trainers. I couldn't see what the problem was, but I could tell she was embarrassed. She went over to get a drink where Mr Crossley was serving. He said something to her I couldn't catch, and she suddenly started smiling. Then I think she noticed I was watching her, and I got all shy and went red. But she came over to me anyway and soon Steve and Timmy and Big Dave came and joined us, and we had a great time.

At one point we began chatting about our names. Obviously, Big Dave's real name was David, and Steve was Steven. But what about the rest of us?

"Promise you won't laugh," says Timmy. "But my real name is Rex."

"You think that's bad?" says KT. "My real name is Karen Tracy. Who's called Karen Tracy nowadays?"

We all laugh and then I get the question I dread. "What's Ally short for?" asks Steve.

Just before I was born, my grandfather on my Mum's side died. His name was Albert. But nobody, and I mean nobody, will ever know my real name is Albert. Apart from Mum and Dad, of course. "It's Alan," I say, lying.

"Boring," says Steve.

And then for the rest of evening we invent names for each other, and drink far too much lemonade, and laugh at Maxine and the girls as they go through their routines.

When it's time to go, I realise I'm walking home with KT Lee. She doesn't seem to mind, and we make up silly words for some of the songs we've been listening to. Then suddenly she says, "Goodnight," and runs up her street back home.

July 24th
Dad drops me off at Mum's briefly to pick up some stuff for our camping holiday.

Mum insists on me eating something because she reckons I won't be properly fed for the next seven days. I point out that Dad's waiting out in the car.

"Never mind," she says, passing me a sandwich. "Dad can wait." I don't think that's very fair on Dad, but I know I can't argue with her. "Besides which, I've got something to show you," And she produces from her handbag a fuzzy black and white photo of a strange blob. "This is the new member of the family. Isn't it wonderful?" she beams.

"I want a sister," says Carrie bouncing into the room.

"I want a dog," says Nina trailing after her.

"I want to go," I say stuffing the sandwich into my mouth.

On the way out I bump into Mark. "Has she shown you the photo?" he whispers just before Mum comes out to the front door. I nod. He rolls his eyes at me, in such a way that Mum can't see him. Then he punches me on the arm and says, "Have a great time. The weather forecast is awful, by the way."

But before I can reply, Carrie and Nina launch themselves at me, so I have to pick them up and kiss them goodbye. I hadn't really thought about it before, but maybe I would prefer a brother.

August 2nd

Mark was right. The weather was awful. And Dad really wasn't very well, although he tried not to show it. But we had a great time. Dad wanted to spoil me, so we spent a lot of our time at this amazing theme park with loads of rides and an enormous roller-coaster that turned your stomach inside out. We also were able to visit Gran who didn't live too far away. She made a fuss of me as she always does and told me how much I'd grown. Then she sent me out into the garden so she and Dad could have a chat about things. I don't know much about what they said except this Christmas Gran is coming to us. And I'm really looking forward to that. Usually she's so busy with her church Dad has to go up specially to see her. But not this year.

"Family must come first," she says, as she passes over to me the most enormous plate of buttered scones you'd ever seen.

But I do wish I hadn't had quite so many scones on holiday and eaten quite so much candyfloss. The fitness training today was ten times worse than the training at Easter. But I am going to stick with it. For Dad's sake. To do him proud.

When I come in all exhausted, Mum tells me Dad has rung and his operation went well. He'll be in for a few days and then he'll be able to come home.

"That's good news," I say and then I remember something. "Do you have the telephone number of the hospital?" I ask.

"Yes," says Mum. "But I don't think Dad will be able to speak to you."

"That's OK," I reply. "Just give it to me anyway." Then, later on when I'm on my own in my bedroom I phone the hospital and ask to be put through to the vicar. The line goes dead for a moment and I'm afraid I might have done something stupid.

But then I hear the voice of the vicar who saw me in hospital and as soon as he asks, "Can I help you?" I know he can help me. Not only does he remember who I am, he seems excited to hear about my training with Drumchester City and he says he will definitely see my Dad soon.

August 6th

The end of the most tiring week I've ever had. But I feel great. Because the season is about to start, we've had to use the pitches at Drumchester Academy this week and I have to say I am looking forward to using the facilities in September. There are real changing rooms, and a decent shower, and lockers aren't all bashed in, like down the swimming pool.

Today I met the Drumchester City goalkeeping coach and if I thought I knew all about goalkeeping before, I do now! I never knew there was so much to handling the ball, and positioning, and taking kicks. I'm going to be working on all this next week with his young assistant Lee. I can't wait. I know Mum doesn't really understand what football's all about, but I know George and Mark will be impressed.

On the way home I get a text from Dad, "*Home now. Sore, but doing OK. Thanks for ringing the chaplain. We had a good chat. You're a star! Love you, Dad.* I try not to cry on the bus because you don't see professional goalkeepers crying, but I have to wipe my eye before I get off. I'm sure I must have got something in it.

August 15th

For reasons I can't understand, Mum and George decided that this year we would go on a traditional seaside holiday. I mean, it's not as if we actually live by the sea at home, is it! So yesterday we went on a long, hot journey all along the coast to another seaside resort just like Drummington-on-Sea except we are staying in a hotel and there's a steam railway which George loves and a designer retail outlet which Mum loves. Carrie and Nina will play on a beach anywhere, so they're sorted. Which just leaves me. Fortunately, the hotel does have a gym and a swimming pool, but I keep being told this holiday is all about "family time" and "doing things together." I honestly wish I could be back home with Mark who's looking after the business while we're away. Maybe in a few years' time I'll be old enough to do this.

'Cos my great plan is to make it eventually into the youth academy so there won't be any time to go away on boring summer holidays. I actually met some of the players last week, and I got a shirt signed by the whole squad. I nearly screamed at Mum when I brought it home and she suggested it needed a wash. But maybe that's just it. Maybe she doesn't realise I'm serious about this football business and thinks a good holiday with a pair of squabbling toddlers will take my mind off it.

So tonight as we tuck into our evening meal, I tell her all about my plans to play for Drumchester City. Her reply? "You're only eleven. There are lots more important things in life. Don't make your mind up too soon."

At that point Nina knocks over her lemonade and Carrie decides she needs to go to the toilet, so that puts an end to the conversation. But at the end George puts his hand on my shoulder and says, "You go for it, Ally. Only if it doesn't work out, make sure you've got some exams behind you."

That sounds fair enough. Maybe if I can't play for a living, I could write about it instead? 'Ally Green, chief sports correspondent' has a certain ring about it. So long as I don't have to be the guy who reads the results out every Saturday at 5pm.

August 27th

The last day of the holiday. I've survived, just. I've been a good boy and read to Carrie and Nina most nights. So I hope that lets me off for the next few months. I've been on the steam engine and let George explain how the locomotive works. And I've trailed round the shops after Mum who keeps wanting to look at things like buggies and changing mats and blankets. What more could a dutiful son like me do?

The good news is that I've had a couple of texts. One from KT Lee wishing me good luck in my new school. The other from Dad who is asking whether I could look after my old man for a few days. Could I ever? It's started raining and we're stuck in a cafe trying to make our lunch last longer. Mum is cross with George because he's lost her sunglasses. George is cross with Nina who has been pulling Carrie's hair. And Nina is cross with me because I won't play I-spy with her any longer. But it's not my fault she thinks every word begins with N.

I turn my back on the lot of them and text Dad back at once.

August 31st

I hadn't realised Dad's treatment would make all his hair fall out. Now he's bald and got these big bags under his eyes he looks more like my grandfather than anything else. He's not up to very much so I am learning to help with the cooking and the washing. He's sorry this isn't much fun, but I don't mind. I like having time with Dad so much I could do almost anything with him.

Today Dad had to go to Drummington General for his next course of treatment. He wanted me to stay home, but I said no. We had to catch a couple of buses, and it was quite a long ride, so we made up stories about the other passengers on the bus. The guy with the beard and the dark glasses was definitely a spy, we decided. While the blonde opposite him with a large file of papers was a double agent with her secret plans.

When I pointed out to Dad that double agents wouldn't use the bus, he said, "Yes, but that's what everyone thinks. It's the perfect cover really." And for the first time since the operation I see him laugh out long and loud, until he starts coughing and has to take some time to recover his breath.

September 6th

First day at Drumchester Academy! Mum insisted on me getting my uniform and my bag ready the night before, and I got to school far too early. I felt really small and on my own, but in the end, I found my form room, down the end of a really long corridor that smelt of chemicals. When I got there, I discovered most of the students in my class already knew each other. There was someone there I knew from the football academy, a left-back called Lloyd but as he spent most of his free time there talking into his phone or listening to his I-pod I didn't get a chance to know him. And now in the middle of all his mates he wasn't going to start talking to me either. So I sat down and waited, wondering how the first day at Drummington Comp was going.

September 7th

At break I wandered along to the sports noticeboard as I heard I could sign up there for football training. That's where I bump into the speedy right-winger from Drumley Green. It turns out his name is Alex and he's even shorter than me (in fact, a lot shorter). I know from the moment I meet him we're going to be friends. He can even remember I didn't play in the last match against them because I had a head injury and is concerned to find out if I'm all right. Then I tell him about my summer training with

City and how I am going there on Thursday nights, and he says, "Cool." He's not in my form obviously but we make sure we meet up at lunch time and he introduces me to a couple of his friends from his old school. Not the same as the old crowd, but as Mum keeps on saying, "It's no use living in the past."

September 18th
Mum has gone out clothes shopping with Carrie and Nina, and George is at work. Dad isn't feeling up to having me, and Drumchester City are playing away from home. I'm trying to ignore the large pile of homework that's built up this week, and generally feeling bored, watching the rain trickle down the window, when Mark comes downstairs and says, "Do you want to come out with me for a bit?"

I need no second invitation. Mark has decided he better start looking for a flat now if he's going to move out before the baby comes, and he knows how I helped Mum find this house. So for the next couple of hours we trudge round the back streets of Drumchester looking at some fairly grotty places. There's nothing suitable that Mark can afford, but he's glad I'm with him. And at the end he buys me a burger and we sit and watch the football results in a tiny little cafe squashed between a bookmaker's and a shoe repair place. We're just in time to discover Drumchester City have lost 5-0.

"You're sure you want to play for them?" asks Mark.

"Yeah," I say.

"Eat up, then," he says. "You've got some growing to do."

September 21st
Football training this lunch time was a real laugh. The school sports teacher, Mr David, had us all doing some warming up exercises. I could have done them in my sleep, but I didn't do them too well, just in case anyone noticed, especially the years 8 and 9. Then we did some ball work and some heading practice, and at the end Mr David invited us all to take a penalty past him. After the first few shots had comfortably passed him, I asked politely if I might go in goal. That seemed to genuinely puzzle him, but he couldn't see any reason why not. So then this massive year 9 runs up and kicks the ball gently to my left, I think expecting me to simply let it roll into the net. I catch it cleanly and throw it back to him. He's not supposed to have another go, but this time he hits it a little harder, to my right. I make a fairly comfortable save, and his friends laugh at him. Then his mate decides he's going to take a penalty properly and goes for the long run-up. He blasts it with all his might,

and I simply reach up and tip it over the bar. This goes on for a while and no-one, but no-one, is able to score against me.

At the end Mr David comes up to me and says, "Where did you learn to keep goal like that?"

"Drumchester City," I reply. I can see all these big boys looking at me and I'm not sure if they are envious of me or want to beat me up.

As I get changed for lessons, Alex comes up to me and says, "Well done. That was a real David and Goliath moment."

"A what?" I say, pulling on my shirt.

"You know? When this big, huge giant comes out to face the Israelites and this little lad kills him with only a sling. It's a story I learnt down at church youth club," he adds, as if I needed some kind of explanation. A church with a youth club? Can't quite imagine that. The next lesson turns out to be RE, and I soon get lost as the teacher drones on about rites of passage in world religions. Why on earth am I learning this stuff??

October 11th

For some time Alex has been asking me if I can go round to his place. But it's been really tricky knowing when to fit it in. Schoolwork during the week, football training on Thursday evening, sometimes the match on Saturday, and of course seeing Dad at weekends. But today both George and Mark have to work, and I can't go on my own, and Dad has said he doesn't mind me coming on later. So around lunch time I turn up at Drumley Green station in my faded T-shirt and jeans. I see there's a huge posh car waiting outside, and I realise Alex is sitting in it with his Mum and Dad and kid brother. I've never done posh, and if it wasn't for Alex I certainly wouldn't be getting inside. It then turns out the family doesn't actually live in Drumley Green. They have the local manor house just outside, a massive affair with proper gates, and its own orchard and stables round the back. As soon as I see it, I wish this afternoon I was on the terraces with my pasty and my *Coke*, where I belong.

I think Alex's Dad can read my expression 'cos as soon as we get out, he says, "Don't worry, Ally. Might not be what you're used to, but we welcome anyone here, and if you're Alex's friend, that's good enough for us."

"I just wasn't expecting this place to be so big," I said stupidly.

"We weren't either," says Alex's Mum, "but we were left it by a great-uncle a couple of years back. It eats every penny we've got. And sometimes more. We'll give the guided tour after lunch. But first things first. What about lunch? You look like a pasty and *Coke* sort of lad."

How did she know??

We ate lunch in the kitchen because it was the warmest room in the house. As we ate and chatted, I realised that despite the size of their house Joe and Jackie – Alex's parents - were really quite ordinary folk I could just talk to. And so I told them about Dad and his illness. About Mum and the baby. I was going to tell them about the terrible twins when I had a text.

"Excuse me," I say. "It could be from my Dad."

It turns out in fact to be from Mark. He's gone to see another flat at lunch time and it's worse than all the others he's looked at so far. Well, not exactly the words he used, but I am in polite company at the time.

For some strange reason Joe and Jackie are at this point looking at each other. "We own a couple of flats in Drumchester," says Joe. "And one of them has just become empty. I could drive over this afternoon and meet Mark if you like?"

So in the end Joe goes to meet Mark, Jackie takes Mitch – Alex's kid brother - swimming, and Alex and I are left alone for a couple of hours to set up a football pitch in the orchard.

Later on I get a text from Mark to say thanks for the flat. Dad has finally got *Revenge of the Killer Hamsters* out on DVD and not only that, he's bought my favourite tub of ice cream. Oh, and Drumchester City won 3-1 at home. But maybe Mum's right. Maybe sometimes there are things more important than football.

October 21st

Something weird happened today. I was walking through the middle of Drumchester to catch a bus to football training when I saw a group of lads wearing Drummington Comp uniforms outside *McDonalds*. I recognised one of them as Steve. I was going to wave to him, but he didn't seem that pleased to see me. So instead I sent him a message, *Text me some time*. But I don't think he will. In fact I haven't really heard from anyone since September, except the odd message from KT Lee. It's all very strange really.

I was still thinking about it when I got to the ground. It might be why the coaches had to spend the first few minutes shouting at me to concentrate. But when I got it together, the session went superbly well. We had a practice match at the end, and I didn't let a single goal in! At the end Lee comes over to me and says there's a county under-13 match next Sunday, and as the regular goalie's injured, could I step in?

Could I ever? Even Mum is pleased when she comes to collect me. She's starting to have trouble fitting in behind the steering wheel now. She says that means she's going to have a boy. Sometimes I think grown-ups don't know what they're talking about.

October 31st

The end of a pretty boring half-term. One day I had to help Mark move his stuff into his new flat. Another day the childminder was off sick, so I had to look after Carrie and Nina by myself. "Well, you are nearly twelve," says Mum as she cheerfully goes off to work. And, oh yes, we have exams next week so I've done my best to get ready for these. If this is all that growing up's all about, I can't be bothered.

The one thing that's kept me going has been the thought of the match today. I OK'd it with Dad who said he didn't mind as he had to start driving his taxi again this weekend. So I got up early and met the rest of the team at the training ground. They were all twelve years old, and most of them were bigger than me. We got onto a rickety old coach that sounded more like a lawnmower as it trundled onto the motorway. And as we reached our destination somewhere in the middle of Somerset it began to drizzle, the slow, steady sort of drizzle that you think isn't too bad until you realise your clothes are soaked through and it's half an hour to the whistle.

The match itself was certainly a step up from playing Drummington Marsh or even Dumpley End. When the defenders slid in for the tackle, they really meant it. And the wingers were faster than I'd ever seen before. It didn't help that I didn't know the rest of my team that well, and I soon sussed that the boys in front of me were trying to protect me. So we soon got into trouble defending too deep, and I was completely unsighted for the first goal which took a wicked deflection off the centre-half's knee. As I retrieved the ball from the back of the net, I yelled at them to push up, But it was only when the second goal went it, again because the defender got in my way, that anyone paid any attention to what I was saying.

By this time it was nearly half-time. It was still drizzling, I was miles away from home, and we were 2-0 down. I wondered if the trip had in fact been worth it. But then their centre forward burst into the penalty area, hits the ball on the volley... and I somehow leap full stretch to my left to turn it away for a corner. Yeah, it's been worth it. And this time when the corner comes in, my team let me come out and catch it cleanly, without blocking me off. I then punt the ball down field, our centre-forward traps it cleanly and lays it off to his striking partner who belts it into the back of the net. We go in 2-1 down, but I suddenly have a feeling we're going to win this one.

The second half starts. We suddenly believe in ourselves. The second goal goes in, then the third, then the fourth. With ten minutes to go it is 4-2. And then that same central defender - a lad called Jay, I believe - gives away a penalty right on the edge of the area. He is having a 'mare of a game. But no time to feel sorry for him. The penalty is perfect and there's no way I can keep it out. It's now 4-3 and until the end of the game there's a tide of red shirts heading my way. A point-blank header straight at me. A long-range lob that I just tip over the bar. A wicked cross that I scramble away before the centre-forward taps it into the empty net. A snap shot that I smother gratefully on the goal-line. When the final whistle goes, I'm exhausted. But very, very happy. I notice Lee has turned up at some point during the game, and as I head to the changing rooms, he gives me a big thumbs up.

November 6th

Last night was Bonfire Night. Alex invited me to the firework display in his back garden, which on its own is probably bigger than the playing field at school. There are lots of boys our own age there and I know some of them from my year. There's also a large bunch of older students who are in their own group drinking and having a laugh. It turns out the tall blonde girl in the middle of them is Alex's older sister, Sophie. They of course, don't want anything to do with us, which suits us fine. And in any case, we're too busy watching the fireworks. Joe knows a local fireman who helps him do this every year, and there are all sorts of rockets and Catherine wheels and bangers and other things that fill the sky with all sorts of loud noises and bright colours. For once, Bonfire Night is dry so there's a big BBQ as well, and I find myself pigging out on beefburgers and sausages.

When 9 o'clock comes Dad arrives to take me over to his place. I am going to tell him all about the great evening I've had but I tell at once he's not in the mood. In fact, he's positively grumpy. He tells me he's not going to do this every Friday evening, and it's too late, and did I know I had ketchup on my jeans? We drive home in an awkward silence, and I take myself off to bed with only a brief, "Goodnight."

Dad's still like it today. In the end I have to ask him what's wrong.

"Nothing," he says in the way grown-ups say when they mean something. I find myself still looking at him, and he sighs, and says, "OK, well, there is. I had a letter from the landlord yesterday. He's going to throw me out if I don't pay up the rent."

"Oh," I say, not knowing what to say.

"Well, there's nothing you can do, Ally. I still have big debts from when the shop closed, and I haven't been able to work much these past few months. I'll just have to manage somehow."

And then I say something really stupid. "Alex's Dad's an accountant. He knows all about money. Perhaps he can help you."

And for once in his life Dad shouts at me and says, "Don't you ever, ever tell anyone else about my problems." Then he storms out the house and goes goodness where.

Much later Dad returns. I've been getting hungry, but I wasn't sure whether I should make myself some lunch or not. I've just been sitting there playing on my DS, wishing I had a Mum and Dad who still lived together, who had a big house, and didn't have lots of little children running around. When Dad comes in, I jump as if I've just been electrocuted.

"Sit down," says Dad. "I've been for a long walk. I don't want to admit it, but I do need some advice. Just ask Alex if his Dad could help me with a financial matter and leave it at that."

"OK," I say. Then Dad sits down heavily, and I can see the long walk has worn him out. He has some more treatment this Wednesday and I can guess he isn't feeling very well. "Let me make you some lunch," I say.

"Will it be edible?"

"There's only one way to find out," and for once I give Dad a hug, and he holds on to me all tight.

Then Dad starts to cheer up and over lunch he says, "By the way, there is some good news. Because the baby's coming, I have you over the Christmas holiday. And Gran's going to be here for a couple of weeks as well. We might have to take her to a church, but that's a small price to pay, isn't it?"

I nod, but I can't say anything as I am trying to eat a burnt piece of pizza.

November 16th

Difficult situation at football practice this lunchtime. Ever since I saved all those penalties, Mr David hasn't let me play in goal, so I've been practising my skills as a centre-forward. There's a lad called Barry who's been keeping goal instead and apart from the fact he can only dive to his right, he is actually pretty good. But now there is a school match coming up next week and Mr David wants me to take over. He calls us both over at the end of the session and explains the situation. I can see Barry's disappointed, so I say, "I don't mind if Barry plays. I've got another county match coming up soon, anyway." Big mistake. I didn't realise Barry had two older brothers at the school - at least not until they surrounded me at the end of school. I am not sure what they were planning to do, but at that point one of Sophie's friends walked past and told us boys, "To play nicely." I think I've learnt to keep my mouth shut in future.

November 20th

Went to see Dad again this weekend. This time he seems in a really good mood, and he actually takes me out to lunch. Turns out he's been to see Joe who is not only an accountant but also part of a Christian credit action team in the area, whatever that might be. The long and the short of it is that Dad can stay in his flat and he's worked out how to pay off some of his debts.

"All thanks to you, Ally," he says, raising his pint. "You know, maybe when Gran comes, perhaps we ought to go to Alex's church. What do you think?"

"Fine," I say. Then I notice it's nearly 2 o'clock and the FA cup will soon be on. "Come on," I say, "we've got a match to watch. Bet you a bottle of lemonade Drumchester City get knocked out today."

"You're on," he says, and as he gets up, I notice he's starting to get some of his old energy back.

November 23rd

My goalkeeping gloves went missing at school. I don't really need to take them in, but I always carry them, just in case. I think I know who took them, but what can I do? They were already starting to get tight, but I'll somehow need to get a new pair before Thursday night. So who do I tell? I don't want to ring Dad because he gave the old pair to me. George is busy at the garage. Mum is just getting bigger and bigger, and she's busy enough looking after the twins. In the end I decide to call round on Mark on the way back from school. He's off work today and I know he will understand the situation.

Only, when I get there, he takes ages to answer the door and there is a girl there I've never seen before. "What do you want?" says Mark sharply.

"Oh, nothing," I say, "well, nothing important anyway."

"You ring next time you want to come round," Mark says in a voice I've never heard him use before.

"OK," I say, and walk off. I can hear the two of them giggling as I make my way downstairs. I don't want to think what they are doing.

In the end I tell the whole story to George (about the gloves that is, not about Mark) when he gets in from work. "No worries," he says. "Only let me know if this keeps happening."

"What?" says Mum, waddling into the kitchen.

"Only boy trouble," says George. "We've got it under control," and the next day he slips out from work and buys a lime-green pair of gloves that seem to glow in the dark. There's no way I won't be noticed from now on.

December 17th

It's been ages since I wrote in my diary, but there's been so much going on, I haven't had time to stop and write. Lots of schoolwork, of course, and everyone seems quite pleased with the work I'm doing - apart from the RE teacher, that is. And the big Christmas production at school. I somehow ended up in the chorus line with a bunch of girls even though I can't sing and I don't really like girls, so that was really not cool. And then there have been all the Christmas presents to get. I'm off to Dad's tomorrow for a couple of weeks, maybe longer if the baby is late, and I've decided to leave everyone else's gift here. Some bubble bath for Mum, a book on steam engines for George, some dolls' clothes for Carrie and Nina.

And, oh yes, a Drumchester City scarf for Mark. I did make sure I rang before I delivered it yesterday evening. He did let me in briefly, but I couldn't stay, "'Cos Kylie was coming round later." With the amount of aftershave he was wearing I didn't really want to anyway.

So now I am basically packed to go down to Drummington-on-Sea tomorrow morning. I tried to work out today when was the last Christmas I had with Dad. I reckon it must have been eight years ago just before Mum and Dad split. In a funny kind of way I will miss Carrie and Nina tearing open all their presents in five minutes flat and then playing with all the wrapping paper. I will miss George's roast turkey which always turns out a treat. And I will miss Mum getting tipsy on the whisky and cheating at *Monopoly*. But then there's Dad to look forward to, and Gran, and maybe I'll see Alex too. It won't be the same this Christmas. It will just be different, that's all.

December 21st

Gran turned up today. She's really sorry she couldn't come sooner but one of the choir members dropped dead last week so she had to go to the funeral yesterday, and was that all right?

"Of course," I say, and I take her suitcase into the flat. She's going to have my bedroom for Christmas, so I will have to sleep in the lounge. But that's no real hardship. Gran doesn't see much of me, but when she does, she is so generous and so thoughtful. When she has finished unpacking, she gives Dad a new pair of slippers, and me a new pair of jeans which fit perfectly.

"Not your Christmas presents, you understand, just a little something to keep you going." And then she adds, "You never guess what? I had a Christmas card from Granpa this year. He's now living in Florida with wife number four who's half his age. You know, Ally," she says turning to me, "that's when I started going to church, when your grandfather ran off with the girl from *Boots*. Talking of which," she says, turning now to my Dad, "where are we going to church at Christmas?"

Dad looks at me with a big grin and says, "That's all sorted. There's a big carol service at Drumley Green on Christmas Eve, and maybe we'll go again on Sunday."

"Excellent," she says beaming. "Now tell me what's been happening. I want to hear all your news."

December 24th

I have often seen the church at Drumley Green and it's always looked grey and ordinary from the outside. But when we got to the church it was absolutely humming. Alex and his parents were looking out for us, and they got us a seat near the front. Which was just as well, because the place was soon packed out. I wondered as we sat down, where Mitch and Sophie were, but I soon spotted Mitch with a huddle of other boys in the corner, playing with a load of *K'nex*.

"Where's Sophie?" I whispered to Alex.

"Just wait and see," he said mysteriously.

Meanwhile, my Gran had spotted the drum kit and the guitars on stage and was asking if they did proper music here.

"Oh yes," said Joe. "We do all the old carols. I think you'll enjoy it."

My Gran took out a mint and started sucking on it quietly. I then looked at Dad who I could tell didn't know what to make of it. The two of us sat for a bit, not quite sure what we had got ourselves into, looking at our watches to see what time the service would begin. I thought churches were places where people were all boring and quiet. But no, there were folk greeting each other and chatting, and actually smiling. It was a most peculiar experience.

Then just before the service started, the door in front of us opened and a group of people came out. The vicar, of course, who was wearing some kind of dress, a young lad carrying a cross, and then... Sophie, and another girl I didn't know, and a huge bloke covered in tattoos and a girl with short, white hair and a scar under her left eye. It was Trevor and KT Lee! KT Lee caught my eye, and she gave me the most enormous smile as she took her place behind the drum kit. Sophie stood behind the microphone, while Trevor and the other girl picked up their guitars. I expected the vicar to be the one who would say something, but he had already sat down and in fact it was Trevor who spoke. "Welcome to y'all," he said. "'Specially if you're new today," and he looked at me and Dad with a broad grin. "We've come here to celebrate Jesus who I know changed my life, so what better way to start than to sing, 'O Come all Ye Faithful'?"

I never knew a church could rock before. It was even better than singing on the terraces at Drumchester City (who lost 2-1 today). Even Gran, who doesn't really approve of all this modern music, joined in, and I never realised she could sing like that. Of course, it wasn't all singing. There were Bible readings, and some prayers, and a sermon. But the thing was, I could actually understand what was going on. I thought of the Bible I had packed away so carefully when we moved house, and how I reckoned I was never going to look at it again. Maybe when no-one was looking, I'd get it out again when I got home.

At the end, Dad turned to Gran and said, "You know, Gran, we might just come here again."

"You do that, Pete," she says. "It'll be good for you. And don't forget to bring Ally with you."

"Come on," says Alex, "who's for a mince pie in the hall? The vicar's wife gets really cross if we don't eat them all up."

So we all troop out of church, round the back and into this old, run-down building that smells of damp and floor polish. But the atmosphere is great. I bump into KT Lee again and ask her what she's doing here.

"It's a long story to do with my Dad. One day, when I've got time, I'll tell you. And what about you?"

"Oh, Alex invited me," I say, "although there's a bit of a story behind that as well."

She laughs and says, "It is so good to see you. We all miss you at Drummington Comp. Well, I do anyway," and she blushes.

Fortunately, at this point Alex comes over and it's then I have my idea. "It's my birthday on New Year's Eve. Why don't the two of you come over?"

"And fit into our flat?" asks Dad, overhearing our conversation.

"It's OK," says Alex. "Bring your birthday party round to my place. I'm sure my Dad won't mind. At least not if I ask him nicely."

So that's sorted. Dad and I are going to start going to church. I have fixed up my birthday party. And I have met up with KT Lee again.

December 25th

Mum was planning to bring my present over this morning, but she doesn't feel up to it today. So I give her a ring.

"How are you?" I ask.

"Big and bored," she says. "Thanks for the bubble bath. It gives me an excuse to escape when Bill arrives this afternoon."

"With his whole family?" I ask.

"Yes," she says. "And they have a dog this time."

"Poor you," I say. "Happy Christmas anyway."

"Happy Christmas, love," she says. "What are you up to?"

So I tell her all about yesterday, but she doesn't really understand. "You had to be there to know what it was like," I say.

"Right," she says. "Oh, heck, Carrie is playing with Nina's new doll. I better stop her wrecking it before World War Three breaks out."

"Love you, Mum," I say.

"Love you too," she says.

As it turns out, I don't get my Gran's old Bible today because she's given me a new one, a really cool Manga version. As she sees me looking at it, she says, "You will read it, won't you?"

"Yes," I say, and I really mean it. A year ago I would have stuffed it into the back of a cupboard. But not now. Not after all that's happened. I haven't quite figured it all out yet, but I think the words in this book could be really important. The vicar in the hospital, the church at Drumley Green, KT Lee and Alex praying for me - they all must mean something. And I think it's time I started finding out what it is.

THE DRUMCHESTER DIARIES: VOLUME 2

FINDING A FAMILY

THE DIARY OF KT LEE, AGED 12

January 5th

The first day back at school. Great. I like school, I honestly do. It's just sometimes the other girls get me down. There's this girl, Maxine, who's had it in for me ever since primary school, and I don't know why. She sat down at lunch right next to me with her two friends Cherie and Cheryl, and they were having some silly argument about hairstyles. I wasn't really listening, then Maxine turns to me and says, "Of course, you're not interested in any of this. You cut your hair with a pair of scissors," And they all started laughing as if it was really funny. I finished my lunch and made my way to the library, 'cos I know it's the one place they'd never visit.

I bumped into Stacey there. Stacey's one of the few girls who didn't go to Drummington Primary, and she doesn't mix much with us lot. But she seemed to know I was upset, so I told her what had happened. "Don't worry about them," she said. "Be yourself," And with that she carried on reading an article about horse-riding.

"You like animals?" I asked.

"Mostly horses," she said. "They're a lot cleverer than most people round here."

I wasn't sure what she meant by that, so I got on with my homework instead.

January 8th

I went up Janine's today. Janine – Mrs Prout – used to be my MTA in years 3 and 4. Then she went and set up what she calls a smallholding just outside Drummington-on-Sea. She rang up last night and asked if I wanted to see the chicks that she'd just hatched in the barn. Dad had to work today, and Jacky was trying to get a leak fixed at the café, so I was glad to have somewhere to go. The bad news was it was pouring with rain. I took the cycle track next to the railway line and once I got past the houses, the wind almost blew me off my bike. Fortunately, Janine was looking out for me as I came down to the track to the funny little house her husband is sort of doing up, and she gave me a towel to dry myself down. And the chicks were so cute.

I offered to help tidy up the barn, and after we had changed the bedding for the hens, and topped up the feeders and the drinkers, and collected all the eggs, Janine made me lunch. She says I can come round most Saturdays if I want to. If I want to? Course I do. And when Dad came home, he said yes straightaway. So that's all right then. Maybe I could even become a vet. Mind you, when I said that to Dad, he pointed out that involves lots of exams, and no-one in our family as far as he knows has ever been near a university. "Still," he said, "there's no harm trying."

January 11th

I'm going to have my first drumming lesson after school tomorrow. I had to ring Jacky at lunch time to say I'd forgotten my money for the lessons, so she came round to the school office straightaway with the money. "Is that your mother?" asked a girl called Doris who'd seen her there.

"No, it's my aunt. My Dad and I live with her," I explained.

"Oh I see," said Doris and then the bell rang and it was time for lessons.

I've long ago stopped trying to make people understand who Jacky really is. The thing is, I don't know. I think she's Dad's second cousin, whatever that means. Or is she mine? All I know is that when Mum and Dad had to get out of Essex in a hurry, she was the only person who could take them in. She ran away from home when she was 16, and she's had a seaside café here for years. I keep thinking she's really old, but Dad says she isn't yet 40. Well, that seems old to me.

I went down to the café after school. Jacky doesn't like me going there in summer when it gets busy, but today there were just some ancient people slowly drinking cups of tea and talking about the weather. Apparently, it's going to snow next week. Except it never does down here.

"But what about the winter of 1963?" says a lady called Mavis to her friend Pearl.

"What about the winter of 1963?" says Pearl. "You weren't even here then."

"Oh no, so I wasn't. I came in 1965, I remember now," says Mavis. And Jacky and I exchange a smile with each other.

Whatever relation she is to me, I'm glad to be living with her. She makes me a hot chocolate, and as the last customers totter out of the door, she decides to close early.

While she shuts up the café for the night, she chats with me about school and although she's busy the whole time, I can tell she's paying attention. She's such a great listener. One day I may even tell her about Maxine. But not yet.

January 23rd

It snowed today! Sort of. It was that wet, heavy snow that turns to water as soon as it hits the ground. Church today was freezing. I had to wear my gloves to play the drums properly. At the end of the service I had a chance to catch up with Ally Green. Ally used to go to my primary school, but he now has to go to school in Drumchester. He wants to be an England goalkeeper, or something like that. I'm so pleased he and his Dad have started coming to church. I asked him about his Mum's new baby.

"It's a boy," he said.

"Sweet." I realised he didn't understand that word, so I asked, "What's he called?"

"Harry."

At that point, Alex came up and joined in the conversation. Alex is OK, but he can be a bit of a nerd sometimes. "So you now have a sister called Carrie and a brother called Harry?"

"So?"

"You've never heard of hari-kari?" We both looked blank. "It's a type of suicide they used to practise in Japan."

We moved away slowly. I could see Ally wanted to ask me something. It turns out he has extra football coaching coming up on Sundays so he wanted to find out if he could come to the youth club on Friday evenings. "Sure. It will be good to have you there." It will indeed. Apart from Alex, the only other children my age are Daisy who is learning to make her own clothes, and is rather wet, and, from time to time, a lad called Joe who wears a baseball cap the wrong way round and is always listening to the latest rap music.

By the time we got out of church, the wet snow had given way to driving rain. I was bored, so after lunch, I made a new baby card for Ally's Mum, then realised I didn't know where she lived. I'll have to give it to Ally on Friday, if I don't forget.

January 28th

Had an incident with Maxine at school. Again. We were doing PE in the hall. It was supposed to be 'expressive dance', but most of the boys saw it as a chance to muck around. While the teacher was dealing with them, Maxine tried to show off some of her latest moves. Only she fell over. I tried hard not to laugh. Mrs Percy came over to see what was wrong.

"Please, Miss," says Maxine, "KT pushed me over."

"Don't be stupid," says Stacey. "KT was nowhere near you."

"Stay out of it," says Mrs Percy, who clearly was having a bad lesson. "Did you push her over, KT Lee?"

"Course not."

"Then get up, Maxine and stop making excuses."

Maxine got up slowly, with Cherie and Cheryl making sure she was all right. As Mrs Percy went away to deal with the boys, Maxine glared at me. I think she means to make trouble, big time.

I forgot the card tonight. It wasn't very good anyway. But Ally was there. He's got lots of questions, and John the vicar got us doing a Bible chase to find some of the answers. Then just as we were getting tired of doing this, his wife, Helen, brought in a huge plate of fish and chips. Ally ate most of them. He said he needed to build himself up for the big match tomorrow. That was his excuse, anyway.

February 7th

I hate this day. I've been dreading it for weeks. Five years ago my mother was killed in a road accident. When I was at Drummington Primary, Dad and I used to take the day off and visit Drummington cemetery together. We had a long talk last week about what we should do. Dad reckoned I ought to be brave and go into school this year. I tried, but by break time I was struggling. Timmy Timms played some joke on the maths teacher, and everyone else thought it was hilarious. Me, I just couldn't help thinking how stupid he was. I went to the girls' toilets to hide at break time. I was feeling kind of sick. I was just about to head off home when I had a text message from Helen to say she was praying for me. She may be the vicar's wife, but she's a good friend as well.

I made it through to lunchtime, but I couldn't face anything to eat. Doris was in the library, and she noticed something was wrong. I told her briefly.

"So that's why you live with your aunt?"

"Yeah, kind of. It's a bit more complicated than that."

"OK, why don't you come over next week as it's half-term?"

"Thanks," I said and gave her a hug. I like people who don't ask too many questions.

When I got home, Dad was already there. "How did it go?"

"All right," and then I burst into tears, and he gave me one of his huge squeezes. Stupid really. I thought this year might be better.

Last thing at night I always take off the cross my mother gave me and put it under my pillow. Only tonight I hung it up over Mum's photo next to my bed. I don't believe people who say there is no heaven. I know there is, and I know Mum's there. Safe with Jesus. Forever.

February 8th

I lost it today. Silly I know, but there you go. I had just finished this cool bit of art work, when Cheryl 'accidentally' spilt paint all over it. I wanted so much to hit her. I knew if I told the teacher she would get her own back later. So I took a deep breath, tried to control myself... and then I screwed up her picture and walked out of the classroom. And I kept on walking. I found myself going through the school gates, out into town, down onto the beach. I guess I was still upset about yesterday.

I found my way to Jacky's café. She wasn't best pleased to see me, as she was about to start serving lunch. I told her what happened. "Oh, love," she said, "I'll ring the school."

I know I'll get a detention. I don't care. Dad came in late that night. He'd had a long day, helping with a removal somewhere in Dorset, and he was tired. Jacky had a long word with him. I thought he might be cross or something, but he simply said, "Well done. You're the first family member not to beat the living daylights out of your enemies. We'll get it sorted with school. I shouldn't have let you go in yesterday."

February 16th

Detention last week was sorting out the library at the end of term. I didn't mind doing that one bit. When I came back the following day, Maxine and her gang tried to do their level best to upset me again, but I wasn't going to let them get to me. I even found there were some people on my side. Stacey who told them where to get off, Doris who slipped me a note when no-one was looking, and most surprising of all, Timmy who diverted their attention with another one of his 'jokes' when things began to look nasty.

Today Doris invited me round. She lives on the edge of town, on the way to Prout's Farm. I thought she lived a quiet life in a quiet house with her Mum and Dad. I didn't realise she had four younger brothers and sisters who all ran screaming towards me when Doris opened the door. Her Mum, Agnieszka, ushered them away and I went upstairs with Doris. She might not say much, but when you get to know her, she's a good laugh. She tried to teach me a Polish folk song on the guitar. I got the tune, but I couldn't get my tongue round the words, no matter how much I tried.

When I got home, there was a letter from school suggesting that we all go for family counselling. Dad ripped it up and said, "It's not our heads that need examining." Then it turned out he was taking a couple of days off work, and he had tickets for Drumchester City on Saturday.

February 26th

I met David Prout today. I didn't like him. I had gone over to Janine's to look at the chicks. They have grown so much, and they make so much noise. Janine was explaining how they sorted out the roosters from the hens, and how they only kept the hens, when this man came up and put his arms around her waist. "Hello, love," he said. "Who do we have here, then?"

"This is KT, and she's 12."

Don't know why she told him my age.

"Pleased to meet you," he said with a nasty smile. "Must get on and check out the porkers. Liberty is due any day now."

Liberty? Who calls a pig Liberty? I was quite glad when Janine didn't invite me to stay for lunch.

March 4th

Ally was at youth club again last night. (He had a cold last week.) I told him I'd seen Drumchester City recently.

"Which match was that? ... The 2-2 draw against Mansfield Town? We should have won it. Goalkeeper went down too early for the first goal and shouldn't have got stuck on the line for the second."

"You know," I said, "you can be so boring, sometimes."

"You know," he said, "your Dad invited mine over for lunch on Sunday."

"What? Like, you're going to be there?"

"You could always come round my place," said Alex, interrupting as usual. "It's my birthday on Sunday. Going to have a film show in the afternoon. Everyone is invited."

Ally and I exchanged glances. "I might come over later," said Ally, trying not to hurt his feelings.

"Why would I want to spend time with a load of boys?" I said, not trying not to hurt his feelings.

March 6th

As usual, Jacky left us a superb Sunday lunch in the oven, before she headed off to the café. I couldn't help thinking the last time the four of us - Dad, me, Pete and Ally - had last had lunch together it was after Ally found my stolen bike in that shop in Drumchester. This time Ally clearly didn't feel comfortable being round my place, and I was busy going in and out of the kitchen, so it was the grown-ups who did most of the talking. Honestly, the things men talk about are so boring. We were about to finish pudding, and I was thinking how to escape, before the conversation got at all interesting.

"Tell me, Trevor," said Pete, "how you came to be part of the church at Drumley Green. I mean, if a year ago someone asked me what church was like, I would have said it was full of old women in hats and men in frocks."

"And I'm not an old woman, and I don't wear a frock," said Dad. "Hmm... there are obviously plenty of things you don't know about me."

They both laughed. "Seriously, I guess you can tell I've had an interesting life. That's a polite way of putting it. Never knew my Dad. Left school at 16, joined a gang. Started with a few muggings, moved on to the more organised stuff. Ended up doing – let's call it, security work in a few pubs in the area. Got busted for knocking a customer unconscious 'cos I didn't like the colour of his money. With my history, seven years in the nick. No-one thought I'd get time off for good behaviour.

"Like you," he continued, polishing off a slice of pie, "I thought the church was full of old women in hats and men in frocks. Never knew it was anything to do with Jesus. But one night in prison I had a dream about Him. Sounds strange. Maybe it was. I couldn't tell you what I'd been smoking that day. The next day I found this Bible lying around. I was bored, so I began to read it. Took me ages to find anything about Jesus. Sort of went on from there."

"So how come you ended up down in this part of the world?"

"The simple answer is a woman. Not any old woman – Susan, KT's Mum. KT, get the photo from the mantelpiece... quite a looker, wasn't she? I know what yer thinking – how did she end up with me? She came from a good home, had a good education, and she gave it all up to work with prisoners and help them settle back into society. Said it was what God wanted her to do. Only when she helped me, we fell in love. Her family were horrified. More to the point, my family were horrified. They expected me to go back to my old way of life. They thought I'd gone soft, made threats against me and Susan, God rest her soul. By this time, she was expecting KT, and we'd had enough. The only person who would take us in, and help us make a clean break, was Jacky. Best thing we ever done. The Lord saw fit to take Susan away five years ago, but I'm still here. I would never, ever go back to my old way of life. Trevor Lee, follower of Jesus and furniture mover of Drummington-on-Sea, that's me. The old Trevor don't exist no more."

There was a kind of silence. Dad helped himself to another slice of pie. Pete sipped his ginger beer slowly.

"I think I'll head over to Alex's," said Ally.

"I'll clear the table," I said.

"Good girl," said Dad. "I think Pete has some questions for me. Best leave the two old ones to set the world to rights."

Pete nodded, gave Ally a high five as he headed off, and I closed the door.

March 12th

The Prouts were having an argument when I arrived. The fox got a couple of hens last night, and they were each blaming the other. When David saw me coming, he slouched off. I asked Janine if everything was all right. "Well, no, but we'll kiss and make up later."

Something didn't feel right, though, so I left early and cycled on up the river to Drumley Green where there was a spring-cleaning morning in the church. By the time I arrived Helen was having a hard time with Emily, so I sat and played with her while her Mum sorted out the toys in the church hall. Most of them were ancient and went in the black sack. It makes me so cross people think they can give their leftovers to the church. I suggested to Helen we should raise some money for new toys.

"That's fine," she said. "You come up with the idea and we'll make it happen."

Me and my big mouth. Still, I'd better do something.

March 22nd

Doris invited me back to her place after school. I was surprised that Timmy Timms went most of the way with us. Turns out Timmy lives in the next street to Doris. Loud, clumsy Timmy walking with quiet, careful Doris – it was quite a combination. He chatted about the new game he had bought for the Wii, and Doris pretended to listen carefully. After he turned into his street, Doris whispered, "He's not all bad. It's his life at home that's difficult." I didn't ask any questions.

After tea, as I was about to go home, I asked Doris what she was doing at the weekend. "Sorry, I'm busy. It's little Maria's first communion."

"Big occasion?"

"With aunts and uncles and all the cousins, about 25 of us."

I couldn't imagine a family that big. I sometimes wish there were more than the 3 of us, but not 25.

March 28th

Helen reminded me over the weekend of my big idea. I ended up talking about it with Doris.

"You go to church?" she asked, surprised.

"Why not?" I said.

"In Poland, most of the boys and girls go to church. Here no English girls go to church."

"Yes, it can be hard sometimes. But we have a good crowd there."

"So you could have lots of people baking cakes, for example?"

A cake sale. Sounds boring. But I can't think of anything better, and Doris has offered to make something.

I mentioned it to Jacky this evening. "Don't expect me to make anything. By the end of the day I'm sick of cooking sponges and Swiss rolls and the like. Mind you, if it was for something really important, I might change my mind."

"You're not big on church, are you?" said Dad.

"Don't start that again," said Jacky. "You know what I think and you're not changing my mind."

"What do you think?" I asked, but Jacky only glared at me, and I felt I had to say sorry.

April 1st

April Fool's Day always makes me nervous at school, even more so today as it was the end of term. Fortunately Timmy was off sick, and although Steve tried to get Mrs Percy to sit on a drawing pin, the rest of the day was quite quiet really. Cherie even offered me a sweet at one point. I sometimes sense she isn't always that comfortable following Maxine around.

I mentioned the cake sale at youth club today. Daisy was up for it, of course. She was wearing a pair of trousers that looked like they'd been made out of old curtains. It occurred to me while I was looking at them that perhaps her family has even less money than us. Never thought of it like that before. Don't even know where she goes to school. Perhaps I should make an effort someday to find out. Rather more surprisingly, Alex also offered. It seems he likes making cakes. Now seriously, that kid is weird. Still, as John keeps telling us, it takes all sorts. I thought about my Dad and I kind of saw what he meant.

April 9th

Something odd happened today. I went into Drumchester with Doris and her family. They have an old Post Office van that smells of baby sick and dog poo, but it does fit us all in somehow. Agnieszka could tell we didn't want to be trailing round with the kids all day, so she let us go off on our own until lunchtime. I wanted to look for a new coat. I've grown out of my old anorak, which is too little-girly in any case, and I asked Doris help me find a new one before Jacky decided what I was going to wear. One day I'll have a leather jacket with studs, but not for school. We found something reasonable in *Primark* and then, as we still had some time, we went into the record store next door. I tried to interest Doris in the hard rock section, she tried to interest me in the folk. Neither of us won, but we had real fun. We were just about to go out the store, when David Prout walked past. At least, I was sure it was him. He didn't see me, and I made sure he was out of sight before we emerged from the shop. The thing was, he was hand in hand with a woman. And it wasn't Janine.

"What will you do?" asked Doris.

I shrugged my shoulders. "Nothing to do with me."

This evening, Janine rang and said she was busy tomorrow. "That's fine," I said. "Saturdays are a bit difficult for me at the moment." Not true, but I couldn't think of anything else to say.

"Who was that on the phone?" asked Dad.

"No-one," I said. "At least, nothing important."

"You tell yer Dad if there's a problem."

"No, Dad, there's no problem. Everything's fine."

April 24th

Easter Sunday. It was great to see the church so full. I had been practising hard with the worship band during the week, and it was great to hear so many people joining in. What made me nervous though was the thought of giving out a notice about the cake sale at the end. As we reached the end of the last hymn, I was dreading John giving the nod to come forward to say something. But instead he invited Pete and Ally forward. They both looked at each other shyly, and then announced they wanted to get baptised. Not in church. But in the sea. May bank holiday, with a party on the beach afterwards. The applause round the church was deafening. I so, so wanted not to have to stand up after that. John kind of sensed that, and instead made a big play of it in the announcements.

Afterwards I realised Daisy had come along on a Sunday for once. I found her in the hall on her own with her Mum and Dad. Dad was in a wheelchair. Tractor accident a couple of years ago, apparently. Daisy explained she was normally too busy on the farm on Sunday mornings. Her mother and her brother were trying to keep things going, but they liked the help at weekends.

"I don't mind coming along," I said.

"Like, seriously?" said Daisy.

"Like seriously," I replied.

"Only if you're sure, love," said her mother who was called Elspeth.

"I usually have Saturday mornings free. I can come next week, if you like?"

"That'd be grand. Daisy is home-schooled so she doesn't often see children her own age."

As I went off to find Ally and his Dad, I heard Daisy telling her Mum off. I don't think she was supposed to mention that bit.

April 30th

"You're going where?" asked Jacky at breakfast.

"Tinkerman's Farm."

"Where's that to, then?" I told her. "That must be seven or eight miles away. It's too far to cycle."

"But, Jacky…"

"No, but Jacky. You should have thought about it before you offered to help. There's plenty of other things you can do round here on a Saturday morning."

"But I promised."

"Tell you what, cycle down to the station and see if you can make your way from Drummington Marsh. Keep your phone on you, and you owe me for the train fare."

"Thanks. I'll do the washing-up tonight."

"You better, I'm going out. For once."

I got to the station with a couple of minutes to spare. There wasn't a lot of room for my bike, but I only had two stops to go, first Drumley Green and then Drummington Marsh. I rode back down the river a little way, then found the lane off to the left Daisy told me about. It was a hot day, and there was little shade from the sun. I was glad to turn off about ten minutes into some woods, but by then I was starting to go uphill. I was wondering why I had agreed to come, when I saw the sign to Tinkerman's Farm. It was broken and looked like it had been painted years ago. Bit like the rest of the farm. A tall, spotty lad caught sight of me as I carefully wheeled my bike over a muddy farmyard past a rusty wreck of a *Landrover*, and through a flock of scraggly chickens that clucked excitedly, as if I was going to feed them.

"Oi, Daisy. Your friend's come," he yelled. I later learnt he was Daisy's brother, Derek.

Daisy came out of the cottage in the same pair of trousers I'd noticed back at the youth group. She gave me some home-made lemonade which was a strange colour but cold and surprisingly good. "Made it myself," she said proudly. "Now if you can fit into my old pair of wellies, I'll show you around."

Apart from the scraggly chickens, Daisy's family kept sheep, and a few goats. "Not many people want goats," explained Daisy, "but there's more money in the goats than in the sheep."

Today's job was to help Elspeth with the foot inspection. She had penned some of the ewes down behind the farmyard, and she needed help keeping them still while she trimmed their toes and dealt with any foot rot. Sounds gross, but I found it fascinating. It was hard work though, and in the end, I was glad I hadn't cycled all the way there. Perhaps Jacky was right, after all.

May 8th

The day of the cake sale! We made the grand sum of £28.61 and 13 euros. Alex's Mum, Sarah, promised to spend the 13 euros the next time she's in France. She's a French teacher somewhere, Dewglass Secondary, I think. As we were clearing up, Helen came up to congratulate me and asked if I wanted to help her and Emily choose some toys. I immediately thought of Doris and all her brothers and sisters, and asked if I could bring a friend.

"Sure, why not?" said Helen. "I'll give you a ring when I'm free."

May 18th

Stacey came back to school today. She'd had a riding accident at the weekend, and she'd badly cut her knee. As she was explaining what happened, us girls started talking about our various scars. Doris showed the scar on her finger where she trapped it in a door when she was little. A girl called Martinique said she had a scar on her stomach where her appendix was taken out. Cherie, who was on her own for once, talked about the scar where she'd put her foot through the French window at home. And then they all turned to me and asked about the scar under my left eye.

"How did you get that, KT?" they all asked.

There was a kind of embarrassed silence and then Doris said, "I don't think KT wants to talk about it."

The rest of the girls shrugged their shoulders and drifted away. I found myself crying on Doris' shoulder, and bless her, she didn't ask any questions.

I don't remember anything about the accident, only waking up in hospital. My head hurt, and I couldn't see out of my left eye. Later, I learnt I had been thrown out of the car onto a soft verge, and that had probably saved my life. I still recall slowly opening my right eye to see Dad sitting next to me, holding my hand, and behind him, John who had only recently arrived as our new vicar. My favourite teddy bear was next to me. Dad smiled at me with tears in his eyes. I wanted to know what was wrong. Then I saw the cross Mum always wore on the bedside table next to a night light. And then I knew. I didn't have to ask what happened.

After school, Doris and I met Helen and Emily in town. We couldn't find a decent toyshop anywhere, so in the end we had to go to the big supermarket that everyone goes to. While Doris was helping Emily choose some toys, I told Helen what had happened today. She put her arms around me, and held me tight for what seemed like ages, even though it was probably only a few seconds. Then Emily came running towards us with a huge stuffed crocodile she had taken off the shelves, and the moment was over.

May 31st

The day of the baptism. Yesterday it was bucketing down, and John was still having trouble getting permission from the council, and Pete wasn't feeling too good... but today it all went brilliant. The sun came out, as I went down with Jacky and Dad to the café. We had to talk Jacky into her letting us use the café, but in the end, she agreed, providing nobody was expecting her to provide any free food. The three of us cleared the chairs to one side, and church folk came in with all the stuff for the lunch. Jacky went behind the counter, and started dishing out cups of tea and coffee, half-price, at her 'concessionary rate'. Once that was all set up, Dad and I went down on the beach, and Dad helped John and the crew sort out the PA system. Finally, just before 11, Pete and Ally turned up. Ally seemed to have brought most of the Drumchester City under-14 team with him, while Pete's boss Marvin also put in an appearance.

I found myself next to an elderly, grey-haired lady who was chatting away to anyone who would listen how proud she was of her son and grandson, and who wished Ally's mum could be there. She was on the point of telling me something about her own church, when Sophie, Alex's sister, came up to the microphone, and began singing, *I am a new creation*. We didn't have the words, but somehow it didn't matter. Then Pete came forward and explained how God had helped him through his recent cancer scare, and how he came to church last Christmas and discovered Jesus loved him, and we all started cheering. Finally John, dressed in a clerical shirt and shorts, led Pete and Ally down into the sea. After asking them whether they believed, he pushed first Pete and then Ally beneath the water. At that point a seagull swooped low overhead.

"I always thought the Holy Spirit was a dove," said Ally's gran, "but maybe it's something different in the Greek. I'll have to ask my minister when I get home." She carried on chatting, but nobody was paying any attention. By this time Dad had joined Sophie on stage with his acoustic, and we were all singing *Amazing Grace*.

I would have said it was like heaven, except at that point I noticed Maxine and her gang standing on the road above the beach giggling. Well, I suppose Jesus loves them. Wish I didn't have to as well.

June 3rd

Got home to find a letter from my Mum's sister, Jenny, who said that now I'm older, would I like to stay with her over the summer holidays? Dad said it was fine by him, so he agreed to get that sorted. I've only met her a few times before; it will be funny spending time with someone who was part of Mum's family. But I think I am looking forward to it.

Youth club tonight was strangely flat. I thought Ally would still be on a high after the baptism, but instead he was asking for prayer for Harry. His Mum thinks there might be something wrong, and he's going for tests next week.

Daisy announced it was her birthday in a few weeks' time. When I asked her what she was doing, she said, "Nothing special." I decided to invite her to go into Drumchester with me and Doris. "But what about me Mum?" said Daisy.

"It's your birthday. Surely you can have one day as a special treat?"

"S'pose so," said Daisy. "I'll have a word with her and see what she says."

June 6th

I guess it was coming. Ever since the baptism, I've been finding all kinds of rude words written on my work. From the spelling, I was sure it must be Maxine and co, but I couldn't prove it. Only today, the English teacher, Mr Small, caught her at it.

"What are you writing on KT's book?"

"Nothing, sir."

"Show me."

"I can't show you nothing, can I?"

"Show me. Hmm, I see. Not only is it not nothing, it is something extremely rude and extremely offensive. I want you to apologise to KT."

"No, shan't."

"I'll give you a second chance."

"No, shan't."

"Then you are in detention for the rest of the week, and I will report you to the head of year."

"That's not fair, sir," said Cheryl and Cherie together.

"What's not fair? Would you like to join her?"

They muttered something and shut up.

That evening Dad went out to his regular AA meeting. Jacky had a private evening party at the café which she didn't want to turn down, so I was left on my own. Jacky gave me a kiss, told me to be in bed by 9, and to ring our neighbour Mrs Mooney if there was any problem. At half 9, having just finished my latest DS game, I was getting ready for bed, when I received a text message. *I know where u live, and I'm gonna kill you.* I read it, ignored it, and turned out the light. Ten minutes later another text. Same message. I rang Mrs Mooney who came round straight away.

When I told Dad later, he was furious. "Don't worry, love," he said. "We'll get it sorted."

Still couldn't sleep though. I held my Mum's cross tight that night, and prayed Jesus would keep me safe as well.

June 7th

By the time I got downstairs this morning, Dad had already arranged with work to go in late. It was already quarter to eight, and I could see he wanted to be at school already. I ate my breakfast and brushed my teeth as quickly as possible, and then we walked together to school.

"Take me to the head's office," Dad growled as we reached the gate. It was only ten past eight, but the head was already in. Dad didn't so much knock, as push the door off its hinges.

"Excuse me, can I help you?" said Mr Jenkins as Dad bore down on him.

"Show him your phone, KT," said Dad.

"You really ought to make an appointment, you know."

"You really ought to deal with girls who send messages like this."

The head put on his glasses and read the screen. He thought for a moment. "I'll get the head of year to look into it, and I'll ring you back at the end of the day."

"At the end of the day I'll be somewhere between here and Worthing. I want you to sort it now."

The head thought again. Then he pressed a button on his telephone and asked for my form tutor, Mrs Percy. Mrs Percy took one look at the phone message, and said to Dad firmly, "OK, I see the problem. KT, go and wait in the library, and I will send for you as soon as it is sorted. I promise you, Mr Lee, it will be dealt with in the hour."

"Thank you," said Mr Jenkins who seemed to have gone quite pale.
"Then I'll head off home," said Dad. "KT, let me know when it is sorted. I'll be back by ten if it isn't." Outside the head's office I gave him a kiss and went down to the library.

I was so tired, but I couldn't relax. What if the message was nothing to do with school? What if, for once in her life, Maxine turned up with her gang in the library? Every time the door opened, I jumped. The hands on the clock turned so slowly. Half past eight, quarter to nine, nine o'clock.

At ten past Martinique came in and said, "You can come now."

"OK," I said weakly. When I got to the classroom Maxine wasn't there. Cheryl and

Cherie were glaring at me. I found my place next to Doris who squeezed my hand lightly. When the rest of the class went off to Geography, Mrs Percy asked me to stay behind for a second. Turned out Maxine sent the messages on her brother's phone, and she's now been suspended for a week. The bad news, Mrs Percy wants to set up a special meeting with me and Maxine when she gets back. Won't that be fun?

I didn't want to be home alone after my drumming lesson today, so I went down to the café. Jacky was busy this afternoon, but she just let me sit behind the counter, and drink a glass of lemonade. When we got home, she cooked me a really nice tea, but I just couldn't eat it. I suddenly felt all hot and sick and dizzy and had to go straight to bed.

June 10th

Youth club was the first time I've been out since Tuesday. I told everyone what happened, and Helen gave me a special hug. "You should have let us know," she said.

"I will next time, I promise."

"There isn't going to be a next time, is there?"

"I hope not."

Then Ally shared how his Mum had gone to the hospital. Turns out Harry is a normal, healthy boy, except for the fact he is completely deaf. And his stepbrother Mark has kicked his girlfriend Kylie out 'cos she's been caught shoplifting.

"You know," said John, bringing in a huge plate of hotdogs, "some of us are dealing with some really heavy stuff at the moment. Before we get going on the food, I'm going to light a candle, and pray for each one of you by name."

I don't know what he prayed, but it was like a dam burst, and I found myself once more in floods of tears. Seem to spend a lot of time crying recently. Helen says it's OK and it shows I'm growing up. I didn't think grown-ups cried that much. Then she told me about the shortest verse in the Bible, and I think I understood.

June 13th

The day of the meeting with Maxine. I hardly slept at all the night before and skipped breakfast. Maxine was late at lunchtime, and it was awkward waiting on my own with Mrs Percy. At last she came into the classroom, chewing gum and pretending to be bored, as if this really was all too much effort for her.

"Come on," said Mrs Percy, "we haven't got all day." Maxine sat down slowly and leant back on her chair as far as she could. "You know why you're here, don't you, girls?" I nodded; Maxine remained silent. "So, who's going to start?"

Maxine carried on chewing gum, as if she hadn't heard a word. I said a short prayer to myself, and I started, "Ever since I've been in primary school, Maxine seems to have had it in for me. This isn't the first time Maxine's been in trouble for winding me up." I told Mrs Percy about the incident on the school trip last year. "Even if she doesn't want to be my friend, I want her to stop making my life a misery."

"Thank you, KT. You've made your position quite clear."

"What do you have to say to that, Maxine?" Maxine just shrugged her shoulders. "I want you to take the gum out of your mouth and say something. I haven't given up my lunch time for your entertainment, young lady."

Just as slowly, Maxine got up, walked to the corner of the room and spat her gum into the bin. Then she turned round and said, "It's obvious, innit? She don't look right, she don't wear the right clothes, she don't listen to the right kind of music. She thinks she's some ****ing rock chick, but she's nothing."

"And you have the right to decide that?" said Mrs Percy. Maxine said nothing. I wanted to say something back, but Mrs Percy firmly put her hand on my arm. "I said, what gives you the right, Maxine Jones, to pass judgement on others?"

Maxine just turned and walked out the room. "Leave this to me, KT Lee," said Mrs Percy. "She'll be sorry she ever crossed my path."

"Is that it?"

"Don't worry – I've seen girls like her before. From now on I will be marking her every move. And, KT, don't let any of her words get to you. You're a good girl and if you stay out of trouble, you'll go far."

"Thank you," I said and went off to find Doris. She hugged me and gave me a currant bun she bought specially for me from the canteen. I'm so glad I've found a friend like her.

June 19th

Sarah, Alex's Mum, has just come back from France with a trip from school. She was waiting for me at church with a stuffed rabbit that she bought at a supermarket over there. "Only 15 euros," she said. "And I won't owe you for the other 2."

I laughed and added it to the pile of new crèche toys in the hall.

June 25th

Daisy's birthday today! Doris' father had the two little ones at home today, 'cos Agnieszka was going into Drumchester with Maria and Pavel to take them swimming.

As arranged, Doris and I also went along, and we picked up Daisy on the way. I wondered how Doris and Daisy would get on, but I sensed they were soon firm friends.

I had learnt already that Daisy wanted some new clothes for her birthday, so once we had been dropped off in town Doris and I decided to take her off on a shopping spree. Daisy had ten pounds from Mum and Dad, and Doris and me said we would each give her five. OK, so she only had twenty pounds, but it was great fun going round the shops seeing what we could find her. In the end, we settled on two T-shirts, a pink hoodie (Daisy wanted purple, but there wasn't one her size) and a cheap pair of jeans Daisy said she would decorate herself once she got home.

By this time we were hungry, so with our last loose change we bought a pack of doughnuts and went down to the big playground by the river. We wanted to have a go on the swings, but there were too many screaming kids there, so we walked along by the bank, seeing who could eat a doughnut the longest without licking their lips.

As we wiped away the last of the sugar, Daisy suddenly said, "I wish I could go to your school."

"It's not all it's cracked up to be," I said and told her briefly about Maxine.

"I know what it's like to be bullied," said Daisy sadly. "That's why my Mum took me out of primary school."

"That's horrible," said Doris.

"You see that sign over there?" said Daisy. "What does it say?"

"Easy," I said. "No swimming."

"It might be easy for you," said Daisy. "Do the letters move around and get jumbled up when you try and read it?"

"No."

"It sounds kind of weird, but that's what happens when I try to read anything. I have to focus really, really hard to get them to line up in order, and it can take me hours to read a whole page."

"Is that why you wear glasses?"

"Sort of. My Mum has tried everything to try and help me. People say I'm thick and I'm stupid – at least that's what they said in primary school – but I'm not really. I have this weird condition that makes reading and writing difficult."

I didn't know what to say at that point. But Doris as usual did the right thing. She put her arm in Daisy's and whispered something in her ear that made her laugh. Then Agnieszka rang Doris to tell her to meet us back at the playground, where she met all of us with a large ice cream. With a flake.

When it came to dropping Daisy off, her Mum, Elspeth, came out to meet us and invite us all in for a slice of birthday cake. Maria didn't want to come out of the bus 'cos she was frightened of the hens, so I picked one up and let Maria stroke it. The hen squawked away noisily, and we made our way in the kitchen, where there was a huge cake and a large jug of that strange coloured, lemonade on the table. Even though we were full of doughnuts and ice-cream, they didn't last long. Towards the end, Derek came in and Elspeth asked him to take a piece of cake up to his Dad. He shrugged his shoulders and went out again, as if he couldn't really see the point of what he was doing.

I didn't have much time to think about this, as by this stage Maria and Pavel were wanting to go home. On the way back, Agniezka said, "I think you've made someone very happy today, girls. It can't be easy for Daisy growing up on that farm."

"No, it isn't," I said, as Doris and I looked at each other.

July 1st

At youth club tonight, John asked what we all wanted to do for the last meeting of the year. None of us could think of anything 'till Joe piped up. "We could do something on the beach again. Like have a barbecue, with a DJ and a volleyball net, and all that stuff."

"I'm not sure we'd be allowed to have a DJ," said John, "but I'm sure we could find a net somewhere."

"You've got your own DJ right inside your MP3, in any case," said Alex.

I'm not sure he meant it as a joke, but everyone else laughed.

"Why don't you all see if you can bring a friend along?" said Helen, who had just come in from Emily's bedtime.

"Sounds even better," said John. "Let's make a list of numbers next week."

When it came to prayer time, Daisy asked for prayer for her Dad who wasn't well. She wouldn't say what the matter was, but it sounded serious. Ally wanted prayer for his Mum, who was desperate to return to work and was having trouble finding a suitable babysitter for Harry. And Mark has kicked Kylie out again, but not before she's announced she was pregnant. Me, I just wanted prayer for next week. It's activities week, but there's hardly anyone from my class doing the outdoor adventure option with me. If that isn't bad enough, Doris has ended up going with Maxine and the gang to Disneyland in Paris. OK, so it's not as bad as having a Dad who's sick, or a Mum coping with a deaf baby, but it seems pretty scary at the moment.

July 8th

In the end activities week turned out a lot better than last year's. It didn't start out too good though. By the time we got to the middle of Cornwall, it was pouring with rain, and we couldn't go orienteering that afternoon. Then I found out I was sharing a room with Stacey who 'cos she goes horse-riding thinks she knows there is everything to know about the great outdoors. Then I found out my other roommate was a girl called Siobhan who I hardly knew at all but had hair like Maxine's. All this before our teachers discovered the hot water in the hostel had been turned off and we had to have cold showers that evening.

But things gradually got better. The sun started to come out, and by the end of the week it was really hot and baking. Stacey was still Stacey, so I couldn't do a lot about that. And Siobhan – it turned out she lived with her mother and her grandmother in a little village between Drummington-on-Sea and Dewglass called Dulling St Mary, I think, and she was used to getting her hands dirty on the allotment they had there. So we quickly worked out that whatever Stacey thought she knew, we knew quite a lot more. And over the week I found out she had a pretty similar taste in music to mine. She was starting to learn the bass guitar and had Guitar Hero on her Wii.

By the end of the week I had decided to invite her to the barbecue next week. Then when I got home, I suddenly thought about Doris and realised I should have invited her instead. Or maybe it was OK to bring two friends along? I couldn't ask at youth club tonight as Helen wasn't very well and John had to cancel it at the last minute. I tried ringing Doris at home, but the ferry was late, and she wasn't going to be in till midnight. So as I'm sat here writing my diary, I'm wondering if I've made the right choice. It's not like I know Siobhan. But I can't exactly see Doris chatting away to a bunch of strangers at a barbecue. Sometimes it's all very confusing.

July 10th

I couldn't find a time to catch John and ask him how many friends I could invite. He was there on his own today, it turns out that Helen is expecting again, sometime in February. I asked my Dad if that meant there would still be a youth group, and he said, "Yeah, I reckon so. I'm sure someone else will come and take it on." We had someone come to the service this morning and talk about a project that involves sending cows to Africa. Ally and Alex thought it was a daft idea, but it sounded really great to me.

"That's 'cos you're a girl," said Alex, "and you're crazy about animals."

That boy so gets on my nerves sometimes.

I did manage to ring Doris, though. Turns out Mrs Percy went along with the group, and she went everywhere Maxine went. So Doris was able to do lots of stuff without anyone bothering her, and it sounds like she had a great time. I asked her what she was doing next Friday evening and it turns out that her aunt and uncle are coming round with her family.

"Is that a problem?" she asked.

"No, not at all."

"I have been thinking though. Maybe one day we should meet up with Daisy after school. Invite her to have an ice cream with us. Something like that."

"Last day of term," I said.

We carried on chatting till my Dad mentioned something about a phone bill. Grown-ups can be so boring sometimes.

July 15th

I wondered if Siobhan would ever turn up for the barbecue. I got down there early to help John and Helen set up. Then Alex came with a short boy with thick glasses and freckles, called David. Joe arrived with Tex who had an earring in one ear, and wore sunglasses all evening, followed by Ally and a boy called Phil in a tracksuit. I was feeling left out as the only girl until Daisy turned up on her own. She was wearing the clothes we'd bought her for her birthday, and she'd finished decorating the jeans, with butterflies on her pockets, and a flower down one leg. She looked great, and for once she seemed really happy.

"Where's your friend?"

"I don't know," I said. In fact I'd hardly ever managed to catch up with her last week. But then this bright red sports car came along the beach road and came screeching to a halt, and out jumped Siobhan wearing a spotty sun dress and a straw hat. She seemed more interested in the boys than in us, but at the end she thanked me for a great evening and left before John could round off the evening with a few words.

July 20th

The last day of the school year. I've survived. Even despite all that upset with Maxine, I've done fine in my end of year exams, and everyone seems pleased with the progress I'm making. Well, not Mr Snow the geography teacher. But he's always like that. Especially today when he knows he has to teach the last lesson before we all charge off on our holidays. He couldn't wait for the school bell to ring. Nor could we. Doris and I dumped our school bags at my house before going off down to the beach.

We met Daisy outside Jacky's café as we agreed, and we went next door to *Digby's* which as everyone knows is the best ice cream parlour in town. Daisy said she hadn't any money, but Doris said no problem – she had minded her brothers and sisters twice last week and had double the pocket money. We crossed over the road and walked along by the beach which was heaving with tourists. Daisy said she wanted to paddle, so we showed the spot where all the locals go – across the bridge, up the hill, and then down the narrow zigzag path to Drake's point. Tourists behind you, an unspoilt, uncrowded beach in front of you.

We were just making our way down the steps when, of all people, David and Janine Prout, came up the other way.

"How lovely to see you, KT," said Janine. "Are these your friends?"

"Yes," I said, but I didn't feel like introducing them.

"You haven't been up to our smallholding recently."

"Things were difficult, you said, so I didn't go."

"Well they were," she said, as she turned and smiled at her husband, "but they're not now. You're always welcome to come up during the holidays."

"Oh yes," said David, holding her hand.

"Thanks," I said, and walked on.

"Who were they?" said Daisy.

"You don't need to know. Come on," I said, taking my shoes off, "who's coming with me in the water?"

July 24th

Dad hired a car and took me off to my aunt's today. He hires a car every year to spend a week with a friend of his called Nick he met shortly after his release. They spend the week jamming on their guitars and Dad usually comes home with a few new worship songs and riffs to practice. It turns out that Nick only lives a few stops up the motorway from my aunt, Jenny, so the plan is for me to spend a week with her family, then spend a fortnight on holiday with them, and come home on my own on the train. Sounds simple, but I'm quite nervous. I've never met Jenny's family before. I think her children are older than me, and I wonder if they'll get on with me. It doesn't help there's a big accident ahead of us, so we have to crawl past Bristol with lots of other hot, angry motorists.

By the time we turn off the motorway, it's late, and we're both hungry. Dad pulls in at a *McDonald's*, and we sit in the car with our takeaway.

"It's going to be all right, KT," he says, "I've spoken to Jenny a fair few times on the phone, and she's going to take good care of you."

"You're going to be OK without me?"

"I always miss you when you're away," says Dad, "but I guess you've got to grow up some time, and now's the time. By the way, I nearly forgot, I got you these to remember me by," and he pulls out two CDs of a band I've never heard of but he says are really good. "Saw them live in the bad old days, and they were amazing. I always wonder if I could've been in a band."

"You can make a guest appearance when I'm famous," I said.

Dad laughed, "Best be going. Jenny'll wonder where you are."

It wasn't that easy finding her though. Jenny lives in one of those new estates where all the streets and all the houses look the same. It was called something like 'Barnard's Farm' but the last sheep and the last chicken must have left years ago. In the end we found her big, square house at the end of a cul-de-sac, with two shiny new cars parked on the drive outside. I suddenly felt very small and very scruffy, but once I had taken off my shoes, Jenny made me very welcome and introduced me to the rest of the family.

I'm in the guest room over the garage. I might even be the first person ever to stay in it. There's not a speck of dust anywhere, and certainly no posters on the perfectly white walls. The bed's comfy though, and I don't think it's going to be long before I'm asleep.

July 29th

That has to have been one of the most boring weeks of my life. Apparently, Jenny was planning to take the week off but there was "an emergency at work" whatever that means, so she only managed to stay at home today. Her husband Gordon goes out early and comes back late, so I've hardly seen anything of him. The twins, Rose and Jordan, are all right, but they're seventeen, and they spend most of their lives in front of their computers. And when they go out, they don't want to take their little cousin with them. I have found my way to the local shop and discovered a small playground, but that seems to be all there is apart from rows and rows of houses. I did find a small footpath that said, 'To Barnard's Countryside Park', but it was really narrow with high fences on either side, and I didn't want to go down there on my own.

So I've been listening to the CDs Dad gave me, and the stuff on my MP3. I reckon I have worked out the drumming patterns on most of the tracks by now, but of course I don't have any kit with me. Rose did let me use the keyboard she has in her bedroom, but I can't really play it that well.

"We've been neglecting you this week, haven't we?" said Jenny at tea last night. I didn't say anything, 'cos I didn't want to seem rude. "Yes, I know. I'm going to sort out some bits and pieces tonight that I'll show you tomorrow."

These bits and pieces turned out to be things of my mother's that Jenny had managed to keep. There was a photo of my Mum at Jenny's wedding, looking very beautiful as one of the bridesmaids. She had the same wispy, white hair as me, and the same pale skin that I guess must have burnt really easily. Then another photo, this time of my grandparents on their wedding day.

"Your Gran died only a couple of years ago," said Jenny, "but she'd been in a home for a long time."

Funny there was all this family I didn't know about. Then a photo of a very tall man with his family at some seaside or other. "Who's that?" I asked.

"Haven't you ever met your Great-uncle Arthur?"

A dim memory of when I was very little came to mind. "Not really... at least, I'm not sure."

"Well, we'll be calling in and seeing him and Peggy next week. You'll probably meet my cousin Suzanne; she lives just round the corner from them."

"I'm not that good with new people," I confessed.

"You'll like them, I promise," and the way Jenny smiled at that point reminded me of my Mum and I felt if she said so, then I probably would.

We went through a few more photos, going further back in the family. I can't remember all the names and all the details, but there were at least a couple of people who served in the war. I wondered for a moment what was the secret of Dad's family, then decided I probably wouldn't want to know.

Finally, at the bottom were some other things. Photos of Mum as she was growing up; her exam certificates; a book of flowers she had pressed; her old Post Office savings book; a Blue Peter badge; a letter from the MP when she wrote about the traffic outside her school. Jenny gave me time to handle each precious object with care.

"I've probably got some more up in the loft."

"I think this is enough for now," I said quietly.

"I miss her too, you know," said Jenny, and I caught a glimpse of the cross she wore round her neck – it was the same as mine. "Your grandfather had them made for us when we were born. I'm so glad you're wearing Susan's."

"It never, ever leaves me," I said, and Jenny kissed me gently on the head.

I looked up and I said, "Tell me more about my Mum. There's so little I know, really."

"That's why we're going on holiday together," said Jenny. "To give us time to catch up, properly. I shouldn't have stayed away all those years."

We didn't say much more. In the end I helped Jenny put the stuff back in the box. As she put it back on top of the wardrobe, she said suddenly, "Wait a moment." She opened the wardrobe door, rummaged around at the back and pulled out a headdress with pink roses. "Your mother wore this at her wedding. Maybe one day when you get married, you'll be able to wear it as well."

"I'd like that," I said. And then I went to the bathroom so she wouldn't see I was upset, and after a few deep breaths, I washed my face. As I looked up into the mirror, it was as if I saw my mother in front of me, and I suddenly realised part of her was still living in me. And I felt proud to be her daughter - no longer just "Trevor's little girl," but Susan's too. I kissed the cross I was wearing round my neck and put it safely back inside my T-shirt.

August 5th

The first week of our holiday has gone by so fast. We're staying in a rather posh hotel in the Yorkshire Dales. After breakfast, Gordon goes out with Rose and Jordan as he is teaching them to drive. There've been no accidents yet – but everyone tends to come back rather hot and bothered. This leaves Jenny and me to spend the day together. Mostly we go walking, but one day when it was really wet, she took me into a town called Harrogate and bought me a couple of skirts (there aren't many girls in jeans at dinner time in the hotel). I haven't really been concentrating on what we've been doing, though. I've been listening to Jenny talking about my Mum, and what it was like growing up together. Apparently, I'm the spitting image of my mother at this age, and Jenny has all kinds of stories of the things she used to get up to. Makes me wish sometimes, I was growing up with a little sister. Then I think of Doris and the way Maria sometimes pesters her and I'm not sure.

Today we found a quiet teashop for lunch. The food wasn't quite as good as Jacky's, but the ginger beer was something to die for. Jenny had for the time being run out of stories, and there weren't many people around, so I decided to ask the question I'd been dying to ask ever since I met her. "So what did you think when Mum and Dad got married?"

"To be honest," said Jenny, gently laying her hand on mine, "we were all so upset. We did come to the wedding, but we couldn't see the marriage lasting."

"Why ever not?"

"It might be hard for you to understand but try to see it from my point of view. Here's my little sister I'd been looking after almost from the day she was born. I cared for her deeply. I would have done anything to protect her and make sure she was safe. And then she marries – after only a few months –a man who has beaten someone unconscious in a pub. It wasn't the first time he'd been inside, either."

"But Dad changed in prison."

"I think that was the bit we found hard to believe. We did meet Trevor a few times. He seemed nice enough, but, you know, he's a big man. He moves wardrobes for a living."

"Dad would never, ever do anything to hurt Mum. I never even heard them utter a cross word." I realised I was starting to my raise my voice and lowered it again quickly when I noticed folk across the room were looking at me.

"KT, grown-ups do sometimes make mistakes. I realise now I was wrong about your Dad. But sometimes it takes time to trust someone."

I was silent. I had so many questions. Did my aunt now really trust my father? Were my memories of Mum and Dad correct? How much did I really understand of my Dad's past?

"KT, I'm sorry. For so many things."

I looked at her and realised how much she didn't look like my mother at all. Two weeks ago she had been a stranger to me. It was going to take more than a single holiday to get things straight in my mind.

August 8th

My aunt, Jenny was right about one thing. I did like Arthur and Peggy. They were far younger than I imagined them to be. They lived in a little town in Cumbria, where Arthur had retired as the local postman, and Peggy still did a couple of days a week down the chemist's shop. Peggy made such a fuss of me when I was introduced – it was almost embarrassing. While everyone else was sitting round the pile of cakes making polite conversation, my attention wandered to the garden. It was a long, thin strip of land, with neat, raised vegetable beds full of runner beans, and cabbages, and other things I didn't quite recognise. And right at the end, I spotted the hen house. It was my chance to escape.

"Can I go out and look at your hens?" I said.

"You interested in chickens, lass?" asked Arthur. "They're my pride and joy. Keep me busy now I'm no longer delivering letters. Shall we leave them old folk nattering, and get you properly acquainted?"

There were a flock of about a dozen light Sussex proudly watched over by a cockerel called Sid.

"Why Sid?"

"Because he can be vicious when he wants to defend the honour of his ladies."

I didn't get the joke, but I liked the way Arthur's face lit up when he told it. I could see he had the same wispy, white hair as my Mum. "Can I get to pick one up, I asked?"

"You're used to chickens?"

"Help on a farm most Saturdays."

"Ah, it must be in your blood," he said picking up a flighty bird called Mabel. "My grandfather was a farmer. In fact this house is built on the very land he used to farm." Mabel clucked contently in my arms, while Arthur chatted on about the town and the valley, and how many of his ancestors lived in these parts. He seemed to be a lot happier now he was outside in his garden. "And to think my great-niece now lives at the other end of the country. Anyway, best be going back."

"Thank you," I said.

We arrived back just as Gordon was telling Peggy all about the driving lessons. "Make sure you don't bring muck into the house," said Peggy.

"I won't," said Arthur.

"And wash your hands."

Arthur winked at me, and I laughed. We washed our hands and went back to the boring conversation in the lounge.

At the end Peggy said, "You must keep in touch," and she gave me a proper little card with her and Arthur's name and address on it. I've never been given one of those before. Must be what Dad means about growing up.

August 13th

Something strange happened as we had our last breakfast at the hotel. "Here," said

Jordan, who had barely spoken to me all fortnight. "You're from Drummington-on-Sea, aren't you?"

"'Course I am," I said.

"Well, there's something about it in the paper," he said, passing me a copy of the *Daily Mail*. It was a photo of David and Janine Prout.

"You know them?" asked Jenny, who had picked up my stunned silence.

"Yeah, I used to help out at their smallholding."

"So what's the article all about?"

I read on: "In a dramatic raid yesterday, police swooped on a farm outside the sleepy coastal resort of Drummington-on-Sea. They'd had a tip-off that David and Janine Prout had been falsely claiming benefits for a number of years. The Prouts lied that they fostered scores of children over the past ten years. A spokesman for social services confirmed they had never acted as foster parents in the county. David Prout was already known to police. He served time in the early 1990s for handling stolen goods. Police took away a number of items from the property, including computers and bank statements. The couple will appear in court later today. Police said other charges might be forthcoming but refused to say what they might be."

"Well, at least the sleepy coastal resort of Drummington-on-Sea has woken up," said Jordan.

"That's not funny," said his mother.

"I wonder what will happen to the animals?" I said out loud.

"Is that all you think of?" asked Jordan.

"Shut up!" I said fiercely. "I need to go and make a few phone calls."

I was going to ring Doris, but realised she was still on holiday. I tried Daisy's number. I got hold of Elspeth, but she hadn't heard the news. In the end I found Ally's number on my phone and texted him.

He rang straight back. "Whole place was crawling with police officers last night. There were a crowd of us watching. Don't know about the animals – I think someone said the RSPCA were coming today to take them away. Got to go, the new season's just about to kick off."

"Thanks."

"You're welcome."

"All sorted?" asked Jordan sarcastically as I walked back in.

"Cool it," said his mother. "We've a got a long journey home, and then after lunch we need to put KT on the train."

If I'm honest, I was glad to get home. Because despite all that Jenny had shared with me, home was and could only ever be in Drummington-on-Sea. It seemed like I had been away from Dad, and Doris and Daisy, and John and Helen, forever, even though it had only been three weeks.

As Jenny helped me onto the train with all my stuff, she handed me an envelope. "They're all duplicates. You can keep them."

"Thanks," I said and kissed her.

"Please come again."

"I will," I said, though I wasn't sure it was going to be any time soon.

The duplicates were photos of my mother. One when she was a little baby, with Jenny brushing her hair. One when she was about my age, wearing ridiculously flared trousers, and a flowery top. One when she was in full make-up and eighties dancewear at her eighteenth birthday party. And one when she was slightly older with her arms around Jenny, but with a slightly embarrassed look, as if she was only doing it for the camera. I tucked them away in the special zip section of my rucksack. I would look at them some time soon. But for now I just wished the train would get me home a little faster. The journey was long, and the train was dirty, and there was a very sweaty man sitting opposite me most of the way.

"Had a nice time, love?" asked Dad as he met me at Drumchester station.

"Yes," I said, "but it's so good to be home." I gave him a kiss. "I missed you."

"I missed you too. Cor what happened to your suitcase? I swear it's twice the size."

"Jenny took me shopping."

"Ah, that explains it. Fortunately," he continued, "Pete's taxi is just over here."

And Pete Green got out of his cab and opened the door for me, and said, "Welcome back, KT. It's been dull round here without you."

"That's not what I've heard," I said as I put on my seatbelt.

"Oh yes, it has. City drew 0-0 today. Ally says it was the most boring match he's ever seen."

"Football - is that all you men ever think about?"

"Now that would be telling," said Pete, and he and my Dad laughed. That was another joke I didn't understand, but I joined in the laughter anyway.

August 19th

Had a lazy week at home. I went round to Doris today. She's just come back from visiting grandparents in Poland. "Just how big is your family?" I asked.

"Don't ask," she said. "I've lost count. But my mother says that when my grandparents get older, we will need to move back to Poland to care for them."

"But, Doris, you can't."

"I don't want to. I live in England now for ten years – sorry, I have been living in England now for ten years. This is my home. This is where I belong."

"And you've told your mother this?"

"She knows. But she won't listen. She does say it won't be for a few years yet. Maybe I will be old enough to stay here on my own."

"Let's hope so," I said, and I gave her a present from my holiday, the sort of miniature teddy bear Doris likes to collect.

"How was your holiday?" I told her about Jenny, and Arthur and Peggy. "You did say you wanted a larger family."

"True, but it's weird. I still can't think of them really as family. They live such a long way away."

"Not as far as Poland."

"I don't know. Maybe I haven't had time to get to know them."

"It takes time," said Doris, gently.

We walked up the cycle path from her house, out into the countryside and down the track to Prout's Farm. There was still a single policeman standing outside the gate, police tape across the entrance.

"It's still hard to believe all this has happened," I said. "I know David gave me the creeps, but Janine? She always seemed so nice."

At that moment, another policeman came out of the house and shouted out, "I've finished now, sarge. You can stand down now."

The sergeant opened the gate into the yard and got into the door of an unmarked car. The two men drove away, having shut the gate after them, and the farm stood in front of us, still and lifeless. Not even a chicken in sight.

"I don't like this place," said Doris. "Let's go back for lunch." I agreed, and we turned back along the way home.

August 25th

Daisy invited me over today. I met her Dad, Bill. He was working at the kitchen table with a pile of paperwork strewn all over it.

"How are you, Bill?" I asked.

"Mustn't grumble," he said, "even if I am doing the farm accounts."

Daisy and I went into the little garden round the back of the cottage where we sat on an old, worn bench among long grass, in the shade of an old apple tree. Daisy explained her Dad was happy because the lambs had fetched a good price at market last week. I asked her if she had been on holiday.

"Don't tend to get away in the summer," Daisy said. "There's too much to do on the farm. But I am going to my granny's in October. I am looking forward to that. No chores for a week. And plenty of home-made cake." I had a present from my holiday for her too, a scarf I found when I was shopping in Harrogate. "You are good to me," said Daisy and she gave me a big hug. "I don't often get treats like this."

September 5th

More news about the Prouts came out today. When they appeared in court, they were charged with "obtaining property by deception." I asked Jacky what that meant. "They lied when they got the money from the bank for the farm." She carried on doing the ironing. "Must have been a bit of a shock for you, KT?" I nodded. "You best learn to forget about them. For some people lying just becomes a habit, and they never notice until one day the truth catches up with them. Let's hope at least they might learn to kick the habit in prison."

"Let's have no more talk about prison," said Dad as he came in from his meeting. "And why aren't you in bed, KT? You've got school tomorrow."

"I think I know," I said.

"By the way," said Dad, as I kissed him goodnight, "I met someone tonight who's looking to form a band. Blues, metal, all that kind of thing."

"Your big break," said Jacky.

"Well, maybe," said Dad. "Here's hoping."

September 6th

Civil war broke out today. It turns out Cheryl and Maxine have had a major falling out. Maxine was staying with Cheryl while her Mum went on holiday with her new boyfriend. Only Maxine broke Cheryl's hairdryer and tried to pretend it wasn't her fault. And then she borrowed some of her make-up without asking. Now every girl in their gang is trying to work out who will be their new leader. Some are sticking with Maxine; some are going with Cheryl. Me and Doris are just trying to stay out of the way.

We were hiding in the library at lunch time today when Cherie came in, on her own. She didn't look happy.

"What's the matter, Cherie?" said Doris.

"Can I talk to you two on your own?"

"'Course," I said, "everyone else is outside."

"It's just that I don't know who I want to be my friend. The three of us – like we've been friends since pre-school. Every time Maxine sees me, I think I should go with her. Then I see Cheryl, and I think I should go with her."

Doris thought for a moment and said, "Cherie, let me ask you a different question. What makes you happy?"

Cherie hesitated and then she said, "Promise you won't tell anyone. I went horse riding with me Mum and Dad over the summer. Maxine and Cheryl would only laugh at me, but I really, really loved it. Hadn't done anything like it before."

"Do you know who else likes horse riding round here?" I asked.

"I dunno. I thought I was the only one."

"Talk to Stacey," I said. "She thinks she knows everything there is to know about horses. But once you get to know her, she's all right. I'm sure she'd like to take you horse riding."

"So make friends with Stacey instead?" she asked, as if she was struggling to solve a really difficult problem.

"I guess so," I said.

That afternoon while we were in lessons the sky grew darker and darker – a bit like Maxine's and Cheryl's mood. By the time the bell rang there was this enormous thunderstorm and we all got soaking wet on the way home.

September 12th

Siobhan is being really nice to me at the moment. She bought me a muffin at break today, so I helped her with her maths homework. For some reason, I've been put in the top set this year, so I keep on getting these requests for help. At lunchtime I noticed Stacey and Cherie were sitting together, chatting about something – horses, probably. Cheryl has announced she wants to set up a pop band, and her gang are going to start doing rehearsals soon. Maxine came in late today, looked like she'd had a late night. She was a lot quieter than usual. Maybe things are starting to settle down at last.

September 16th

Usually I get a lift from Pete and Ally to youth group, but tonight Dad borrowed Jacky's car. He has booked the church hall for band practice, and he needed the car for all his kit. I agreed I would walk over from the vicarage after youth group. I wondered what the neighbours would make of the noise. "Well, if we wake the dead, stay clear of the churchyard," Dad advised.

We had some new girls at youth club tonight, a couple of year 9s from Alex and Ally's school. Alex brought David along, but he didn't seem very comfortable being there. We started talking about summer holidays. Alex had been abroad, as usual, camping somewhere in France. Ally has been in training for most of the holidays, but right at the beginning he went with his Mum and family to a holiday camp. Glad to get home to some peace and quiet, he said. Daisy, as I knew, hadn't been away. And what about me? How was your holiday, KT? I said I stayed with my aunt, Jenny and met Arthur and Peggy. It didn't seem right with all those new people to talk about my Mum.

Just as we were leaving Helen invited me into the kitchen to see a picture Emily had drawn of Monsieur Rabbit, as he was now known. "Was everything all right with your aunt, KT? I know you weren't looking forward to going."

And for some silly reason I burst into tears again. "Yes, it was fine," I said, blowing my nose. "It was just well... all a bit confusing. I learnt so much about my Mum. There was so much to take in."

And Helen said nothing, but just gave me one of her special hugs. I like the way she doesn't try to explain everything, but is just there when I need her.

When I had washed my face, I walked over to the church hall. Even though it was dark, it wasn't hard to find my way there with the noise coming from the building. Actually, it sounded pretty good, and I could tell my Dad was having a whale of a time. It took some time for the band to realise I was actually there.

"Hello, love," said Dad, as the place fell quiet. "We were just about to pack up anyway."

"Like heck," I said. "You'd have gone on all night if I hadn't come along."

Dad just grinned, and I waited while amplifiers were disconnected, drum kits disassembled, and guitars put back in their cases.

"Hello, Lemmy," said Jacky as Dad walked in through the door.

"He plays the bass," said Dad.

"And he can't sing," I added.

"Neither can I," said Dad. "In fact, what we really need is a decent vocalist."

"Don't look at me," said Jacky. "I only cover Bananarama numbers."

"No wonder I've never heard you," said Dad.

"Enough of that. Now, KT did you eat enough at club or would you like the remains of today's Swiss roll before you go to bed?"

Silly question. It went down a treat with a mug of hot chocolate.

September 24th

Life's been really quiet since the summer holiday. I like it like that. Most evenings I go home with Doris. Sometimes we just chill out together, sometimes we let Maria into the bedroom. She likes to read to us, and Doris often sits and brushes her gorgeous, long brown hair. I wish I'd had hair like that when I saw seven. Yesterday she made a joke about me with her sister in Polish, and Doris wouldn't translate. I can't imagine it could ever have been anything nasty, though.

Today I was going to Daisy's, but she rang and said her Dad wasn't well, so I went into Drumchester instead. I needed to buy some picture frames for Mum's photos. I've cleared a space specially on top of the wardrobe so they can look down at me. But the one of her my age I've put on my bedside table. It's the last thing I see before I go to bed, and first thing I see when I wake up. It's like she's there beside me all through the night.

September 30th

Daisy wasn't at youth club tonight. John asked us what we had to be thankful for at the moment. Alex just shrugged his shoulders and said, "Nothing – except maybe it's quieter now Sophie's at university." Ally was grateful that Pete had been given the all-clear at his cancer check-up. One of the new girls, Claire, gave thanks that her aunt has just had a new baby. And Helen grinned and wanted to give thanks that her pregnancy was going so well. I simply said, "Family," and Helen smiled at me.

John was just about to round the session off, when my phone rang. The first time I ignored, but the second time I looked at the screen and saw it was Daisy. It turns out that her Dad has just been admitted to the Mental Health Unit at Drumchester General, and Daisy is going to her Gran's for a couple of weeks tomorrow, for a break.

"Not a lot to be thankful for there, is there?" said Alex.

"Apart from the fact, whatever we go through, God hears our prayers," said Ally.

And John and Helen just looked at Ally as if he'd said something really profound. "How right you are," said John and I could see Alex was sulking. He didn't say a lot for the rest of the evening.

October 2nd

Elspeth turned up at church this morning. She was late and she was in tears for most of the service. Afterwards, John and a lady from the prayer team called Molly took her into the side chapel and spent some time with her. I went outside and was about to text Daisy, when I realised it would be better to give her a ring. "How are you doing, Daisy?" I asked.

"I've just got up, and Gran's going to take me to the cinema this afternoon."

"Sounds great."

"Yeah, well, it's good to get away."

"You've had a rough time. You should've let me know."

"I know. It's, just like, difficult. Dad wouldn't want anyone talking about him."

"Your Mum was in church today. She seemed pretty upset."

"I'll ring her later. If you see her, give her my love."

"Is Derek OK?"

"He never says anything. Just works and works, listening to his music. I s'pose he is."

"I'm going to miss you."

"It's only going to be a couple of weeks. Gran's promised to spend lots of time with me on my reading and schoolwork. It'll be good to focus on that. And say hi to Doris for me."

"I will. Ring me any time you need to talk."

"Sure," and with that I rang off and went into the hall to chat with this new girl Claire.

In the afternoon Molly rang. John is arranging for a working party to go over to Tinkerman's Farm next Saturday. Not to help with the animals, but to do any odd jobs that need doing.

"No problem," said Dad. "That's what being a church is all about, after all."

"Can I come too?" I asked.

"I was expecting you there," said Dad. "I know how much you like Daisy and I'm sure there's something you can do."

October 8th

In the end about ten of us went over. Elspeth was so pleased to see us all there and made a wonderful lunch for us all. Trevor and Pete repaired and painted the windows of the farmhouse. I helped an older man called Len in the garden. I picked up the apples, and he cut the grass, and together we weeded the border. I got stung on the stinging nettles, and he showed me how to put a dock leaf on the sting. In the afternoon it started to drizzle, so I went inside and helped Elspeth sort out the kitchen drawers.

"Should have done it ages ago," said Elspeth, "but I just haven't had the energy. Daisy will be so pleased to see the house looking so nice when she gets home. I wish I had a better place for her to live in."

"You look after Daisy fine," I said.

Elspeth put a hand on my arm, and I could see the tears in her eyes. "Best put the kettle on, love," she said. "The workers will be wanting their tea soon."

October 16th

Elspeth and Daisy made it to church today, and they stood up and thanked everyone for all their hard work. Afterwards I asked Daisy if she liked the garden, and she just gave me a big hug, and an apple she had picked from the tree. "Any news of your Dad?" I asked.

"He'll be in a few weeks yet. Mum has been to see him, but she says it's best I don't go yet."

"Have you heard from Doris?"

"I'm going shopping with her next Saturday, after I've done the chickens. You coming?" I nodded. Daisy started to tell me what she'd been up to with her Gran, but I was needed to sort out a date for worship practice next week. "See you Friday," said Daisy, and I noticed how when she smiled like that, how pretty she looked. I wondered why I hadn't noticed that before, then realised she hadn't had much chance to smile recently.

October 18th

Did I say I wanted a larger family? After all that's happened today, I'm not quite so sure.

I went home after my drumming lesson, and had just got changed, when there was this ring on the doorbell. I don't like to answer it when I'm on my own, but when I ignored it, whoever it was, knocked on the door. Very carefully I put the door on the latch and opened it a crack. There was a spotty youth there, with a large rucksack, and even at this distance he didn't smell too good.

"Is Trevor Lee, there?"

"No. He's at work."

"Then I'll wait for him."

"You could have a long wait."

"That's OK. I'm his son."

"I beg your pardon?"

"I'm his son."

"You must have the wrong Trevor Lee. My Dad doesn't have a son."

"Trevor, what lives with Jacky O'Toole."

"I'm not sure what you're on, but I'm going to shut the door now, and I want you to walk away before I call the police."

"I don't mean to upset you."

"Then why are you telling me all this rubbish?"

"'Cos it's true that's why. But I'm happy to wait outside. I don't want to be a bother."

"Apart from the fact you say you're my Dad's son, even though he's never mentioned you and I've never seen you in my life."

"I can explain."

"Don't bother," I said and slammed the door.

By this stage I was visibly shaking. I looked at the big pad of paper by the phone and found the phone number for *Drummington Removals*. I got a telephone menu. I waited impatiently as I listened to all the options. I didn't want a quote. I didn't want to arrange a delivery date. I didn't have a complaint. I just wanted to speak to my Dad five minutes ago. In the end, I got through to a lady who said in a very false voice, "*Drummington Removals*. How may I help you?"

"This is KT Lee. I need to speak to my Dad now."

"You mean, Trevor?"

"Yes," I said through gritted teeth.

"He's on a job. May I take a message?"

"I know he's on a job. I wouldn't be calling unless it was an emergency." This youth, whoever he was, was now sitting on the kerb on the other side of the street, picking his nose.

"I'll see if I can connect with his mobile." There was a humming noise, then a crackle, and then I heard my Dad. "KT, what are you doing ringing me at work?" He sounded cross.

"Sorry, Dad, but there's a youth just turned up at my door, and he claims to be your son."

Dad uttered a word I have very rarely heard him say and then he said, "Don't whatever you do let him into the house. You need to take him down to Jacky's but don't go on your own. I dunno, maybe Mrs Mooney can go with you?"

"He is your son?"

"He's part of my old life. I've never actually ever met him. Can't explain everything now. Just wait with him at Jacky's until I come. Whatever you do, don't give him any money, and make sure the house is locked. OK, Stan, I'm just coming. Love, I've got to go. Please don't worry – I'll get it sorted."

I put the phone down slowly. I thought of all Jenny had said over the summer holidays. How much more was there Dad hadn't told me? The spotty youth was still there, looking bored and tapping his feet. I tried to ring Jacky, but there was no reply. It was a warm autumn evening, and no doubt the café was still busy. I then rang Mrs Mooney. "I need to take a visitor down to Jacky's. My Dad says I need an adult with me."

"I just need to give Fluffy her tea and then I'll be round. Is everything all right?"

"It's complicated. I don't understand what's going on, so please don't ask me any questions."

I just had time to text Helen when the doorbell rang again. I could tell this time it was Mrs Mooney. "Hello, Mrs Mooney," I said.

"Hello, KT, dear. And where is your visitor?"

"Over there." I pointed at him. "Come with us," I said.

"Where we going?" he asked.

"We're going to Jacky's and we're going to wait there until Dad comes home."

He said nothing, and Mrs Mooney, I could see, had decided it was best not to interfere.

It was the longest walk I ever had to make to Jacky's. Down our street, into Stone Street, across the town square, past the parish church, along by the shopping arcade, and onto the seafront.

"Hello, KT," said Timmy, coming in the opposite direction with his mate Steve. I didn't say anything, but I heard Steve whisper something about hormones.

As I guessed, Jacky was working flat out when I arrived. I couldn't exactly wait in the doorway, so the three of us squeezed against the hatstand as people came in and out. Jacky scowled at me as she took an order, and cleared away the trays from the table next door. She saw we weren't going anywhere, so she came over and said, "KT. This is a really bad time."

"I know. But Dad sent me here."

Someone motioned to her for the bill. "Just coming," she said.

"This lad here turned up on the doorstep," I continued. "He claims to be my Dad's son."

"Are you, Lee?" asked Jacky. Lee nodded. "Go into the kitchen at the back and sit on the stool there. Don't touch anything, don't breath on anything, don't say anything. I'll work out what to do with you later."

"If it's all right with you, I'll be off," said Mrs Mooney. As I thanked her, she slipped a pound into my hand.

Jacky went over and took the bill. "Now you're here," said Jacky, "make yourself useful. Carrie's off sick again and it's bedlam in here. Wash your hands in the special sink, and you can clear and wipe tables."

So that's what I did. It gave me something to take my mind off events. Every time I went back into the kitchen, Lee was just sitting there, with the same bored expression. Sid the chef, and Betty, the other waitress, worked around him, as if he was part of the furniture.

In the end it was six o'clock. The last customer left, and Sid and Betty got ready to go home. "Thanks for all you've done today," Jacky said. "If Carrie's off one more day, I swear I'm going to sack her." Jacky gave Sid the takings to bank in town, and Betty took the rubbish out to the skip. Then it was just the three of us.

"So what do we do now?" I asked.

"We wait," said Jacky. "There's plenty I can do here for the next couple of hours," so I helped Jacky with the stocktake, and next morning's order, and we sorted out the lost property customers had left over the past week or so. Then Jacky set to work on cleaning out the machines, but not before she had made me an extra-large hot chocolate for working so hard today. And still Lee sat and sat and sat. I could kind of sense he wasn't that bright.

In the end Dad turned up just as it was getting dark. As I saw him knocking on the glass front door, I found it hard to believe this smelly, skinny youth could really be his son. Though maybe there was something similar about the eyes… it was hard to tell really.

"Where is he?" asked Dad.

"Back here," said Jacky.

Lee stood up and came out into the café.

"Have you got any identity on you?" demanded Dad. Lee got something like a photocard out of his back pocket. "So you really are Lee Chesters?" Lee nodded. "How the hell did you find me?"

"Me Mum chucked me out and I had nowhere to go. Then I remembered you'd gone to live with Jacky, and I came down here. There weren't too many O'Tooles in the phone directory."

"Dad," I asked. "What's going on? Why have you never told me anything about this?" Dad tried to put an arm around my shoulders, but I shook him off.

"Just before I got put away, I got friendly with this barmaid. She was called Nora Chesters, but we all called her Chesty. I don't need to explain that to you. She found out she was pregnant about a month before I was sentenced. She wrote to me a couple of times when I was inside. I heard she'd had a boy and he was called Lee. But that was it. I never saw him, and Nora didn't want to keep in touch. When I came out, I thought my old life was completely behind me. I didn't tell you, 'cos frankly I didn't think he would ever turn up on my doorstep. But now here he is, and we've got to work out what to do with you."

"I just need somewhere to kip and sort my life out."

"We'll come to that in a moment. Why did yer Mum chuck you out? What were you doing? Pot? Hash? Ecstasy?"

"No, it was nothing like that. I was doing steroids. I wanted to be a body builder." If this wasn't quite so ridiculous, I think we'd have all burst out laughing. Lee was about a quarter the size of my Dad.

"And are you on the run?"

"No, the police cautioned me and told me to stay out of trouble. But I'd borrowed this money off me Mum, and I couldn't pay her back."

"Well, you won't get a penny out of me. OK, a few house rules. If you ever come into my house, number one: you lay a finger on KT, and I'll break every bone in your body. Very slowly. I'm rather out of practice, you see. Secondly, if I ever find you with drink or drugs, you're out on the street. Thirdly, you pays your own way. You learns a trade and you earns your keep. Are you still with me?"

"Yes, Dad."

"Don't you 'Dad' me," Dad suddenly roared. "I'm Trevor to you, and don't you ever forget it." "No, Dad, I mean Trevor." Lee looked for a moment like a rabbit caught in headlights.

All this time Jacky had been silent. She had been polishing the top of the counter and tidying up the magazines there. "Just one thing," said Jacky. "Where are you expecting Lee to sleep? We only have three bedrooms at home, and as far as I'm concerned, no-one's sharing with me."

"I only need a sofa," said Lee.

"Shut up," said Dad, and Lee shut up.

There was silence for a moment, and I could hear the fridge in the kitchen humming. Then suddenly I found myself saying, "What about Tinkerman's Farm?"

"What about Tinkerman's Farm?" asked Dad.

"Elspeth and Derek need all the help they can get. I'm sure they must have some room, even if it's only in the barn."

"That, KT," said Jacky, "is an inspired suggestion."

"Lee can do some work, and in return he gets a roof over his head. I like that idea."

"But I don't know nothing about farms," said Lee. "We don't have no farms in Dagenham."

"Well, it's time you learnt," said Dad. "Or do you have a better suggestion?" Lee shook his head. "I can't take you there tonight, but I'll ring Elspeth and put the proposal to her."

"I don't know about anyone else, but I need to go home," said Jacky, "it's been a long day."

We all agreed. "Just one more thing," said Dad. "If you end up at Tinkerman's Farm, then I want you to come to church with me every Sunday at Drumley End, and you'll have lunch with us. No arguments. Think of it as point number four, if you like."

"OK," said Lee weakly and we all got into Jacky's car and drove home. Jacky made Lee have a shower before dinner, and he's downstairs at the moment, on the sofa. Dad came in just now to say goodnight.

He kissed me and said, "I'm sorry about this, KT."

"Is there anything else I need to know?"

"Not that I can think of. I know I've been a bad man in my time, and I've learnt you can't sort everything out at once. But I hope I would never, ever lie to you."

"Promise?"

"I promise. God bless. Sleep tight."

I am trying to sleep. But with Lee in the house, it's easier said than done.

October 22nd

"How's it going?" I asked Daisy as Agnieszka picked us up on her weekly swimming run into Drumchester.

"I think Derek will be glad when Lee goes over to your place tomorrow. As my mother put it, he's not the sharpest pencil in the box. Derek has never had that much patience explaining anything at the best of times. And these are not the best of times."

Doris lightly squeezed Daisy's hand. I had told her during the week what had happened and my idea to send Lee over to Tinkerman's Farm. "He's only been there a few days," I said.

"Don't get me wrong, we're grateful to have him. He's actually far stronger than he looks. Derek has got him hammering fenceposts into the ground. But I don't think he will trust him with the animals just yet."

None of us had much money to spend this week, so we didn't do much in town. I helped Doris find a present for Pavel's ninth birthday, and Daisy a card for her Dad. Daisy's hoping to see him this week. If he's well enough. I don't really understand what that means, but I'm not going to ask any questions. I'm sure Daisy will tell me anything I need to know.

October 23rd

As usual, Dad drove to church early in Jacky's car with his guitars in the boot. He sorted out the amplifiers and got his electric tuned. Usually at this point he would start warming up with the rest of the band. But this week he decided to wait out the front for Lee. There was a clock at the back of church I could see from behind my drums. It was ten o'clock. I started playing. The minutes ticked by. Ten past. Twenty past. At this point we stopped and prayed for the service that was about to start. Twenty-five past. In my mind's eyes I could see Dad looking at his watch and getting restless.

John went into the vestry, and we followed. "Where's Trevor?" he asked.

"Waiting for Lee," I explained.

"Of course, you told me at youth group on Friday."

We were just about to go out the vestry door when Dad walked in hurriedly. "Sorry," he said.

John just slapped him on the back, and Dad fell into line.

"Is he here?" I whispered.

Dad didn't have time to answer as the crucifer had already started the procession. But there was Lee, sat on the front row, looking miserable, as if he had just been told off. Which he probably had. He remained sitting throughout the service, although he did start tapping his feet during some of the songs. He spent most of the sermon picking his nose, and then wiping his hand on the pew. Hard to imagine this person really was my half-brother. Then I realised the theme of the sermon was 'How many times must I forgive my brother?' and I wondered if that included someone who you had never met before in your life.

I tried to be nice to him after the service, so I showed him where the hall was, and made sure he had a cup of tea. He even said "Thanks," as I passed him the sugar. He didn't say anything else though, so I left him reading the church noticeboard.

"Who's that?" asked Alex.

"Someone we're looking after at the moment," I said. Alex was the last person I felt like explaining the situation to.

There was a moment's lull in the conversation and then he suddenly said, "I thought you played really well this morning."

"Didn't know you were musical," I said rather more sharply than I intended.

"Not sure it's your type of music. Piano. Classical, mostly. Anyway, I just thought I'd tell you."

I realised that Alex was embarrassed, and that I should have accepted his thanks. I mumbled something and we both drifted away. Something inside told me that maybe Alex was someone I ought to be more forgiving to.

Then Claire came up to me and said, "Enjoyed the music this morning."

"Thanks," I said without thinking. Then I became aware Alex was still within earshot and added hurriedly, "Not sure it was a lot to do with me, though."

Lee was still standing in front of the noticeboard when Dad and I scooped him up to take him home. Someone had taken his cup, and Len had tried to find out if he did any odd jobs, but I don't think he had spoken another word. When we got home, Jacky had as usual left us dinner in the oven. I set the table, while Trevor packed away his guitar, and Lee sat on the sofa, reading the TV times.

"Dinner's ready," I said.

Lee came and sat in Dad's seat, but Dad motioned to me not to mention it. "Are you hungry?" asked Dad, as he started carving the joint. Lee nodded. "Help yourself to the vegetables." Lee obeyed silently. "I thought you played well this morning, KT. You're starting to get more confident."

"Thanks," I said.

"Did you enjoy the music, Lee?"

"I dunno," said Lee, piling a heap of potatoes on his plate. "It was very strange this morning," he added, finally putting a whole sentence together.

"What d'ya mean?" asked Dad.

"I never thought you'd be all religious. Playing the guitar, singing about Jesus, going to church. All kind of weird."

"What did you think I'd be?"

"I dunno."

"There's an awful lot you don't know about me. But keep coming on Sundays, and I think you'll find out rather more that'll surprise you."

"OK," said Lee, and he started eating, with his mouth open.

There was a long silence. Then suddenly Dad asked, "Who told you about Jacky?"

"No-one really," said Lee. "I mean, Mum never ever talked about you. She just said my Dad was a bad man who'd been in prison. And then I asked her once, 'Where's Dad now?' and she said, 'Ran off to Drummington-on-Sea to stay with his cousin Jacky O'Toole. Leastways, that's the last I heard. 'Spect he's dead by now'. I thought that meant you married her. But when I got here, there were loads of T Lees in the directory, so I tried J O'Toole. Guess you must be living together, instead."

I looked at Dad and Dad looked at me. I wondered what Dad was going to do next. He put his knife and fork down on the plate, turned to Lee, and … he laughed. I have never heard Dad laugh quite so long and quite so loud as he did then. I thought he was never going to stop.

"Did I say something funny?" asked Lee.

"Did your Mum never tell you I was married when I came down here?"

"No, I guess she never knew."

I brought the photo down from the mantelpiece. "This is my Mum," I said quietly, trying to control myself. "She died five years ago."

"Come here," said Dad, and he gave me a huge hug. "It's all right, KT. Lee couldn't have known, could he?"

"S'pose not. But sometimes it all seems so unfair."

Dad let me leave the rest of my lunch. I went up to my room where I'm writing now. I've put my headphones on, and I'm listening to my favourite band. Very loudly. I think I've just heard Dad go out again. He must be taking Lee back to the farm. I don't want Lee to come back. Ever. And don't ever talk to me again about forgiving him. God knows I can't.

October 29th

Mrs Mooney has had the grandchildren this weekend. Yesterday I asked her if I could come round for lunch today after church and help look after them. I think she was glad I asked. Dad wasn't happy though. "Like it or not, he's family," he said.

"He may be your family. He's not mine."

"That's not totally true."

"Leave it, Trevor," said Jacky firmly. "If ever any of my family from Essex turned up, I'd be pretty upset, and I certainly wouldn't want KT to meet them."

"OK," said Dad, although I could tell it still wasn't OK with him.

I went into the kitchen to help Jacky with the vegetables for tomorrow. "Give it time, love," she said softly. "You've had so many shocks this year." I gave her a kiss. "I swear you're growing. You don't have to stand on tiptoe any more to kiss my cheek."

"I must be. That reminds me, I need some new school shoes."

"And here I was thinking I could afford to retire on my hard-won fortune. We'll go after school on my day off next week, and I'll get the money off Trevor."

"Thanks." We were just finishing the vegetables when a question came into my head. "Jacky?" I asked.

"Yes?"

"When Lee came into the café, you knew his name. Had Dad told you about him?"

"Only the once, when he first turned up here with your Mum, Susan. You think it was a shock when Lee turned up last week? I tell you, it was one hell of a shock when big bad Trevor Lee turned up in the café. It was 'cos of men like him I ran away from home just as soon as I could. I was only a waitress then, and I got into trouble for dropping the tray. But there he was, saying he needed somewhere to stay. And yet it wasn't the Trevor I knew, if you know what I mean. The old Trevor would be wearing a bicycle chain round his neck and have a snooker cue in his hand. This Trevor had a wooden cross round his neck and was holding the hand of this amazingly beautiful and clearly pregnant woman. You think you've had a shock, KT. Trust me, I know what it's like. As soon as I could, I got a lock fitted on my bedroom door. I bought a safe for anything I might have that was valuable. Every day I came home from work I expected to find the flat I was then living in trashed or empty. Took me months before I felt I could trust him. And that was after he started going to church and landed a job with *Drummington Removals*."

"You never ever told me anything about this."

"I hoped to God you would never need to know. And I wish you didn't have to know now. Here you are, not yet thirteen, learning about all the crap there is in the world. You shouldn't have to know about any of this. You really shouldn't."

"It's really upset you, hasn't it, Lee coming here?"

"KT, I've barely slept a wink since. I didn't run away 'cos I wanted to. I knew it would only be a matter of time before I was beaten up, raped, or dead in a gutter. And I wonder if they are still out there somewhere. I thought Drummington was far enough. I don't know what God you believe in, KT, but pray it is."

"I will."

Then it was Jacky's turn to kiss me, and she held me tight for such a long time. "I'm sorry. Try to forget I ever said any of this. Come on, let's find some trash on TV and open a large box of chocolates. And KT?" she added, as I went to look in the cupboard, "it's not something I say often enough. I love you."

November 4th

I'm not sure what John had planned this evening for youth club, but we spent most of the evening talking about the situation with Lee.

"Families are complicated," said Ally. "It was a big enough shock when my stepbrother, Mark, came to live with us last year to work for my Dad.

"Thing is," I said, "I can't even think of him as my brother," and I talked about how Lee thought my Dad was living with Jacky and asked whether I was supposed to forgive him.

"What do other people think?" asked John.

Alex couldn't see the problem and mentioned something about the prodigal son. Daisy thought a brother was someone you lived with, so Lee couldn't really be my brother. Ally and Claire kind of agreed. Sian – the other new girl – thought we should always try to forgive people, but sometimes it took time.

"What do you think, John?" we all asked.

"It's so difficult, and I can't give you a nice, neat answer. But when there's something like this, and you're not sure what to do, someone once gave me some wise advice, which was to look at the cross. If we think it's hard to forgive someone, think how much it cost Jesus for God to forgive us. I think Jesus knows how hard it must be for you, KT, but I do think He wants to help you."

We prayed about that, and then Ally asked for prayer about Kylie's baby, "'Cos she's split from Mark, and it looks like she might be going to prison, and that baby could be Lee in twenty years' time, trying to find his Dad."

I asked Daisy how Lee was coming on. "He's doing OK. Mum's got these forms for agricultural college. There's one near Dumpley End apparently, and she wants Lee to go there."

"Will he?"

"Dunno. Truth is, I try to stay out of his way. It sounds kind of silly but, like, when he's around, he makes me feel uncomfortable. Something about the way he looks at me. But I could just be imagining it."

I thought for a moment. "Why don't you sleep over one weekend? Come back to me after youth club, and go back with your Mum after church?"

Daisy's face lit up. "Like, I could really?"

"I'll have to have a word with Dad and Jacky."

"That would be awesome."

November 10th

Jacky finally had a day off today. Carrie was definitely back at work, but she'd left Betty running the café and Sid's wife was in as an extra pair of hands. We went and bought some new school shoes after school, and some trainers for PE. I said all my shoes were too small, but she said that was all she could afford at the moment. I tried not to sulk. On the way back home, I asked her about Daisy coming over for the weekend.

"All right," she said. "So long as you don't have a sleepover for your birthday. The last one we had was chaos."

"I was only eight then," I said.

"And teenagers are better behaved than an eight-year-old?"

"Some of us are," I said, and Jacky laughed.

"OK, so what do you want to do for your birthday?"

I thought for a moment. "A proper grown-up meal. I don't want any more parties with chicken nuggets and chips, or blue raspberry slush. I want somewhere where there's a real menu, and a choice of dishes."

"So long as you don't get bored waiting, and I have to ask for a packet of those cheap crayons."

"It's a deal," I said.

"Then," said Jacky, as we turned into our street, "it's a deal. Leave the details up to me."

November 14th

Siobhan asked me for a couple of pounds at lunch time. She'd forgotten her purse or something. "Pay you back tomorrow," she said as she disappeared off with another group of girls in the canteen.

"Did Siobhan ask you for some money?" asked Stacey, as she came to sit down at my table. "That's the last you'll see of that, then."

"How do you know?"

"She's always asking for money. Pretends to make friends with someone, gives them sweets, that sort of thing. Then she asks for money, and, like, it's gone."

At this point Doris joined us. "Are you talking about Siobhan?" she asked.

"Did you know?" I asked.

"I heard something. I'm sorry, I should have told you."

"It's a pity. She can be quite nice, sometimes."

"There's a reason I prefer horses, you know," said Stacey. "You always know where you are with them."

"Is that because you are sitting on them?" said Doris in her most Polish accent, and at that point I couldn't help cracking up with laughter. Stacey didn't get the joke.

November 18th

I was just about to come in after breaktime today when I spotted Timmy and Maxine having a furious row just by the car park. I couldn't hear what they were talking about, but Maxine stormed past me with tears in her eyes, smudging her make-up. Timmy followed rather more slowly, still red in his face, but with a more serious expression than I'd ever seen on him before.

"Dare I ask what that was all about?" I said.

"I caught that bitch," said Timmy, almost spitting out the word, "trying to bully a year 7. I thought even she might have been clever enough to learn something by now."

"You don't like her, do you?"

"Not when her Mum is living with my Dad."

"I'm sorry," I said. "Families are so complicated, aren't they?"

"You're right there," said Timmy, as we walked into the corridor. "By the way, if Maxine ever tries anything against you again, just let me know."

"Thanks." I've seen Timmy play prop forward for the school – it was a fearsome sight. It's just good to know he's on my side.

This evening we were somehow talking about forgiveness again. I mentioned the situation with Siobhan.

"That's a tricky one," said Helen, with her hands on her rapidly growing bump. "What do you think is the last thing Siobhan would expect you to do?"

"Stay friends with her, I s'pose."

"That's not going to be easy, is it? But think about it from her side, if you can. She goes around asking for money. She knows that every time she does this, she loses a friend. But for whatever reason she feels she needs the money. So she carries on with fewer and fewer friends and gets more and more unhappy. Perhaps she's decided as no-one wants to be her friend, she'll carry on borrowing in any case."

"I was going to invite her to my party before all this happened."

"Inviting someone undeserving to a party? Hmm, I think I know a parable or two about that."

"OK, you win," I said, laughing, "but don't try and make me feel guilty."

November 21st

I've sorted out with Jacky who's coming to my party. She says a posh meal in a restaurant doesn't come cheap, so I can invite four people. I've rung Doris, and Daisy, and I told Claire yesterday. Today I found Siobhan at lunchtime. I hadn't seen her for a week, and she looked guilty as I approached her. I took a deep breath: "I can't forget about the two pounds, but I'm still going to invite you to my birthday party a week on Saturday."

Siobhan definitely wasn't expecting that. "Like, seriously?"

"Like, don't you ever ask for money again, but you can still be my friend, if you want to." Then I thought of her turning up to the barbecue. "We're going to a restaurant, so wear something smart."

"I'll look forward to it. D'you want a toffee?"

November 26th

Daisy came home with me after the youth group. As we made our way over to the church hall, the noise coming from there told us Dad's band had found a vocalist.

"What is that racket?" asked Daisy, rather fearfully.

"I think it's van Halen."

"Whatever it is, I have never liked loud music," said Daisy as we entered the hall.

As usual, it took a few bars before the men realised we were there. To my surprise I recognised the new vocalist from primary school. It was Steve's Dad. "Hello, KT," he said. "Did I never tell you I was in a band?"

"No, Steve's never told me about the platinum discs on your wall."

"Hey, don't be cheeky."

"Hello, KT," said Dad, wiping the sweat off his brow. "What do you think of it so far?"

"What's the word when something isn't quite right but you know it's going to get better?"

"Potential," said the bassist, going through a few chord changes.

"You know, that would make a great name for the band."

"What?" asked Dad.

"The Potential."

"That kind of works," I said. "Sounds like electricity and power and high voltage, and all that stuff."

"Go for it," said the drummer. He beat out a rhythm, and suddenly everyone was playing that song again, only this time tons better.

I was singing along, when I realised Daisy was still standing by the door, totally confused as to what was going on. "Sorry," I whispered. "They'll be packing up in a moment. I promise."

Later that evening, as we were sorting out the room for the night, Daisy caught sight of the photo by my bed. "Is that your Mum?" she asked. I nodded. "She looks just like you."

"That's what everyone says."

"You must miss her terribly."

"It's something that's just there. You know, all that stuff to do with the music tonight, it helps me to forget. When I'm singing or playing, it's like in another world, a happier world where you're free."

"I know it's not the same," said Daisy, "but in a funny kind of way I miss my Dad. You never knew my Dad before his accident. He was a big strong man, who could work all day, and in the lambing season, all night as well. Now he just lies in bed for weeks on end, and it takes all Mum's and Derek's strength to move him, to make sure he doesn't get sore."

"Is he getting any better at the moment?"

"Not really. Home by Christmas is what they say. Not sure Mum is looking forward to it." I gave Daisy a hug, and she dissolved into a flood of tears. "Sorry, I'm not sure what came over me."

"'S all right," I said, and I meant it.

When I woke up next morning, Daisy was already up and awake. She was sitting on her sleeping bag cross-legged with her glasses on and, as far as I could tell, was drawing me. "What are you doing?"

"Hope you don't mind. This is my sketchpad, see? It's like a kind of diary, except it doesn't have any words."

She showed me some of her sketches, all done in pencil. I'm not much of an artist, but I can recognise someone who is. "They're amazing," I said. "Love the one of the lamb and its mother." "Mum says I have a gift. I don't like showing them to many people, it's personal you know. But like your music, it helps me to forget. Forget about Dad being unwell, about the difficulties I have reading and writing."

"So, d'you want to finish your drawing?"

"That would mean you'd have to lie down and pretend you're asleep, and it wouldn't be the same."

"Especially as I'm feeling hungry." Daisy laughed. "C'mon, let's go find some breakfast."

November 27th

We took Daisy to church for her to meet up with Elspeth. As we parted before the service, she kissed me and thanked me for a lovely weekend. The service went well, and John told a very funny joke at the start of his sermon. I can't remember anything else he said, but I went home in a very good mood. Even if Lee had come home as usual.

After I'd served up lunch, I tried to be nice to him. "What did you like doing at school, Lee?"

"I dunno." He thought hard for a few moments and then he added, "When I was young, I liked reading books. But we didn't have no books at home, and I found out it was only the girls in my class that read, so I stopped."

"But that's silly. Boys can read as well as girls."

"I would like to read again, but dunno what."

"I'm sure Elspeth has loads of books."

"Yeah, I've already borrowed one. I've only read a few chapters, but, yeah, it's all right."

Lee was looking embarrassed again, but Dad joined in at that point, "I didn't read nothing either at your age. Got my solicitor to do all the reading I needed." I think he was making a joke, but it passed us by. "The first book I read properly was the Bible. It changed my life."

"Didn't know there were any good bits in it."

"If you like, I'll give you one someday and show you where to start."

"Yeah, thanks," said Lee hurriedly. "What do you like doing at school, KT?" he asked changing the subject. And I realised that we were having our first proper conversation, and for once he actually seemed interested in what I was saying. But no matter how much we talk or how many Sunday lunches we have together, I still can't think of him as my brother. If anyone asks, he's my Dad's son, Lee.

So after lunch I left Dad and Lee together, talking about whatever it is they talk about, and went up to my room, where I found Daisy had left me her sketch under my pillow. I wondered for a moment what to do with it. I didn't think Daisy meant me to show it to anyone else, so I carefully folded it in two, and slipped it inside the photo frame, behind the picture of my mother.

December 3rd

Birthday today, and it's on a Saturday! That means I can open my presents in the morning, for once. As usual, it was Jacky who had bought the best present for me, a pair of knee-length boots that looked and felt fantastic. "After all," she said, "you can't go out tonight in a pair of trainers." As she was taking the day off, she said she was going into Drumchester later, and she would help me buy a couple of skirts if I tidied my room first.

"What's wrong with the old ones?" asked Dad.

"They're all getting too short, in case you hadn't noticed," I replied. Honestly, I wonder why he never notices these things.

I managed to persuade Jacky to let me have a proper haircut as well today, so by the time 5 o'clock came I was more than ready for the party. Doris came first, because Agniezka was going to let us have the van for the evening. "You look great," said Doris.

"Thanks."

"Hope you don't sit on anything sticky in the van. I had to help Dad clean it out this morning. It was disgusting. I think we've got rid of all the old sweets."

Next came Daisy in Elspeth's beaten-up old *Landrover*, followed closely by Claire. It was Siobhan, who as usual was late. She was wearing a low-cut top, and high heels, which as it turned out wasn't such a great choice.

Jacky explained she had difficulty finding anywhere suitable early in December. In the end, she had found a country pub on Dumpley Common, just above Dumpley End. The main restaurant was fully booked, but she'd done a deal that meant they put a table in the skittle alley which we could use for the whole evening.

"Have anything you like," said Dad, "and I'll finish what you don't manage."

Jacky looked at him. "I think he's joking." While we were waiting for our orders to arrive, it was time to open the presents. Daisy gave me a cloth bag she had made. Claire had produced a piece of home-made jewellery, while Doris gave me a CD she knew I wanted. There was then a moment's pause before Siobhan handed me a cheap birthday card.

"Sorry there's nothing more," she said. "Mum maxed out on the credit card again last month. I asked my Gran if she could help, but she said her pension didn't stretch that far."

I looked at Doris, and she looked at me, and we both suddenly realised why she was always asking for money. "It's the thought that counts," I said. Siobhan was quiet throughout the meal, but by the time it came to the skittles she was back to her usual, bouncy self.

But, no matter how much we tried, no-one could get the better of Claire that evening. "That's what happens," she explained, "when you have three older brothers. You're always out to show you can be as a good as them."

"I'll make sure I'm never playing football against you," I said, and we all laughed. It was turning out to be one of my best birthday parties ever.

December 9th

Dear Lord, can life get any worse?

Last night the phone rang. Dad was for once busy in the kitchen doing the washing up, while I think Jacky was mending a blouse for work tomorrow. "Can you get that, love?" she asked. "I'm a bit tied up at the moment." I wish now to God, I had never answered it.

"Hello, can I help you?"

There was a woman on the other end of the phone. From the sound of her voice, she was a heavy smoker and possibly half-drunk. "Yeah, can I speak to Trevor?"

"Who is it?"

"It's his mother. Lee gave me his phone number."

"Hang on," I said. I knew this wasn't good news.

"Who is it?" asked Jacky.

"It's some woman claiming to be Dad's mother. Says Lee gave her the number."

"I'll take that before Trevor works out what's going on." Jacky got up and took the call. I don't know what she said, but even at a distance I could hear the shouting and the swearing from the other end. As Jacky slammed the receiver down, Dad walked in and demanded to know what was going on. "That was your mother," said Jacky, looking straight at him. "Lee gave her your number."

"Like hell he did," said Dad, throwing down his tea towel and going to get his coat.

"What are you doing, Trevor?"

"Going to find Lee, that's what."

"Trevor, stop. It won't do any good."

"Like you're going to stop me?"

"Engage your brain for a moment. Think about KT, think what you're going to do."

Dad said nothing but stormed into the hallway. A moment later the front door closed behind him.

"Can't you do anything?" I asked.

Jacky shrugged her shoulders. "I don't know what god you believe in, but you better start praying right now."

I went up to my room. I tried to phone John, but I only got the answerphone. I texted Helen and asked her to ring me.

"KT," shouted Jacky up the stairs. "What's Elspeth's number?"

"Coming," I said, as I caught sight of my Mum's photo and wondered what she would have said in this situation.

"Is that Elspeth?" asked Jacky. I could see she was nervously tapping her fingers on the table. "Hello, this is Jacky. Yes, I'm fine thank you. Could I have a word with Lee? Of course, I'm happy to wait." Jacky looked at me grimly as she waited. The seconds passed. "Lee? Can I ask you a question? Are you as stupid as you make out, or did you just forget to engage your brain? Can't you guess what I'm talking about? You gave Trevor's mother his phone number, that's what. Haven't you worked out by now Trevor never, ever wants to speak to his mother again. His mother is a monster, she's pure evil. You're sorry, are you? Just wait until Trevor turns up on your doorstep. Then you'll be sorry. No, I don't know if he's coming or not. He stormed out of the house about five minutes ago though. OK. One final question: did you give her our address as well? Let's be thankful for small mercies, eh? You'll be needing all the mercy you can get." With that she put down the receiver and let out a deep sigh.

"You don't reckon Dad will go round to see Lee, do you?"

"Think about it," said Jacky. "Your Dad is upset. Your Dad is also an alcoholic. There's no knowing what he'll do. I hope to whatever god I believe in he won't go over the edge."

"So what do we do?"

"We wait," said Jacky. "There's nothing more we can do, until your Dad comes back or we get a phone call."

"I've never seen Dad act like this before."

"I have only once. You were at school, and your Dad was off work with a bad back. He got a letter to say that Susan's life insurance wouldn't pay out. He'd been counting on that money to come through for weeks. He was planning to buy a little house just for you and him. He stormed out the house at lunch time. The next time I heard of him was from the police in Dewglass. They'd picked him up for destroying a bus shelter. It was all I could do to stop him from being put away."

"I knew nothing about this."

"What could I say? You were only eight."

I curled up in Jacky's arms. We sat on the sofa watching the clock. First, we counted the minutes, then the five minute intervals, then the quarter hours. Then my phone rang. It was Helen. "Let me know if there's anything I can do. John's away all this week, but he'll be back tomorrow afternoon."

"I have to say," said Jacky, "for religious folk your John and Helen aren't bad people."

"They're not, are they?"

Jacky went into the kitchen to make us both a hot chocolate. By this time, it was half past nine, and I was getting tired. But I couldn't go to bed. Not until I knew. We tried watching TV, but we could only find some silly comedy show and we didn't feel like laughing. We sat and watched the news, but that only made us more depressed.

The phone finally rang about a quarter to eleven. I had started to nod off, but when I jumped up, Jacky said firmly, "I've got it." To our surprise it was Alex's Dad, Joe. He had come back from an evening with a client in Dewglass, and he nearly ran over this big man who was staggering along in the middle of the road. Other motorists were swerving to avoid him, but he didn't seem to care if he was going to get hit or not. Joe recognised it was Trevor, and with difficulty got him into the car. He kept mumbling something about wanting to see John. Joe explained that John was away, but he would take him home and look after him until morning.

"Well, at least he's safe," said Jacky. "I dunno about you but I'm shattered."

"Good night," I said and gave her a kiss. I was too tired to write my diary. As I lay down to sleep, I kept my hand on my Mum's cross and prayed: "Dear Jesus, keep Dad safe tonight."

Jacky and I had a row this morning. Jacky reckoned I should go to school today. I knew I wouldn't be able to concentrate on my lessons. Jacky replied she didn't want me around when Dad got in. In the end I phoned Helen and she invited me up for lunch. It was raining hard, and she was stuck in with Emily who had a cold, and she would be glad of the company. She came to collect me about half ten. I was exhausted, and Emily was miserable, so we kept each other company, watching kids' TV together, and making a house out of a cardboard box. The she got tired, and snuggled up to me, sucking her thumb, and we both pretended to be asleep, until Helen called us in for lunch.

By the time I got back home, Dad was there. I just gave him a great big hug. I didn't want to let him go. He didn't want to let me go.

"I promised your mother when you were born," he said, "I would always be there to look after you. I broke that promise last night. I am sorry."

The phone rang. "It's your counsellor from AA," said Jacky.

"OK, I'll take it," said Dad finally releasing me from his arms.

"The school rang," said Jacky. "Wanted to know where you were. I said you had a cold."

"Thanks."

"Just this once," she said.

"It better be," said Dad, coming off the phone. "I have to go out to see my counsellor for about an hour. But I promise, I'll be straight back."

When Dad returned, he had an enormous bunch of flowers for Jacky, and a necklace for me. He'd also seen his boss and agreed to work tomorrow to make up for the lost hours today. "OK," he said, "I've been engaging my brain. I think I'm going to ring Lee tonight and tell him I mean him no harm. He's still coming for lunch on Sunday."

"Is that wise, Trevor?"

"Soonest dealt with, soonest mended. And, KT – when you go out tonight, just enjoy yourself. 'Course you can speak with John and Helen but try and have a good time with your friends. Don't let your old man spoil your fun."

"I'll do my best," I said.

Everyone commented on my necklace tonight. "Late present from my Dad," I said.

John and Helen explained that next week would be the last time they'd be taking the youth club for a while, but Alex's Mum and Dad would be taking it on. I thought Alex would be really sulky about this, but he was in a surprisingly good mood. It turns out he has landed the part of Benjamin in *Joseph and the Amazing Technicolour Dreamcoat* next term in some youth theatre production. Then everyone else shared their good news. Daisy said her Dad was on some new drugs and was feeling much better. Ally had been asked to play for the regional team in the New Year. Claire's aunt was planning to get her baby christened.

"And what about you, KT?" asked Alex, smiling at me.

"Well, yeah, I had a great birthday party last week and I'm now officially a teenager." I tried to sound cheerful, but the truth be told, I was drained.

John and Helen had cooked a large bowl of spaghetti bolognaise, but I could only manage a couple of mouthfuls. Then Emily woke up and was crying.

"Do you want to help me settle her?" asked Helen, and that gave me the excuse to slip out of the room with her. The three of us had a long cuddle, and we stayed there while we heard everyone else laughing downstairs. Emily had fallen asleep in my arms and as I lay her down in her bed, I suddenly wished I could go to sleep as easily.

December 16th

The last youth club with John and Helen. They decided to make the evening a social where we all brought along something we made. Alex excelled himself and made a proper Christmas cake. It tasted very good. The other girls, it turned out, were also excellent cooks. I had managed to make a plate of sandwiches, which at least was more than Ally had done, 'cos he'd simply forgotten. As we started eating, Joe and Sarah joined us. Alex never said a word to them all evening, but they got along with the rest of us fine. They seemed keen to find out what we'd like to do, and by the end of the evening we'd sort of made a programme for next term.

As we were leaving, Helen took to me one side, "Just because I'm going to be busy with baby, it doesn't mean I'm no longer here for you. Any time you want to, get in touch, promise?" I promised and gave her a hug. "By the way," she added, "Emily drew a Christmas card for you today." She gave me a sheet of paper with red and green scribbles. My first proper Christmas card this year.

"Thanks," I said. "That's really special."

December 20th

Today was the school carol service in Drummington parish church. I've never liked going in there. It is a long, gloomy building and it never seems cheerful even when it's packed to bursting with a crowd of bored teenagers. It didn't help that the vicar led the whole service in the same, flat voice and I think we all stopped listening halfway through. As my mind wandered, I asked myself why this church seemed so different to the one at Drumley Green. I realised the answer was simple: this place was a museum. The hymnbooks were old and falling apart, and full of 'thees' and 'thous'. The music was played on an ancient organ that squeaked and groaned all through the carols. The front of church was decorated with banners that looked like they had been made in the 1950s. There was a children's corner at the back, but it was full of those Ladybird books my Mum must have read when she was young. In fact I reckoned if you came into this church forty years ago, it would have looked exactly the same as it did today.

As the service came to the end and everyone came out grumbling, I also realised that for most of my classmates this was their only experience of church. Getting cold and bored once a year in a school carol service. No wonder they thought I was strange going off to Drumley Green every Sunday. Then I wondered what Doris made of it, and she said, "It's not that different from our church. But you get the feeling the vicar is bored with God. And that makes me sad."

We went down to Jacky's café after school. It was really quiet. The only customers there were the regulars, Mavis and Pearl, having their usual arguments over the weather. So we helped Jacky decorate the café for Christmas. Jacky and Betty put the lights up, while Doris and I put Father Christmas and a jolly snowman in the window. They looked out onto a bleak winter's evening with the sea crashing across the beach.

"Your aunt doesn't have a crib?" asked Doris.

"No, that's not really her thing," I replied.

"That makes me sad as well."

At that moment the door opened, and Janine Prout walked in. She was so different from when I last saw her. She looked exhausted, with bags under her eyes, and lines across her forehead. It looked like she hadn't brushed her hair for months. I turned round to say hello, but when she caught sight of me, she turned round and left in a hurry. I later learnt that she and David were going to appear in court early in the New Year. I also learnt from Doris that the farm is up for sale. No-one seems to know where David and Janine are living, but it's likely this will be their last Christmas before they go to prison. I suppose in a way I'm sorry for them, but if I'm honest, I'm just glad they don't have any real children waiting for them at home.

December 24th

As the carol service got underway today, I couldn't help noticing the difference from Drummington parish church. The whole place was buzzing with a kind of energy, and there were even more people than last week. I looked around and realised just how much had changed in a year. There were Pete and Ally, of course, who couldn't help singing their hearts out, right there in the front row. Near the back, I think I glimpsed Daisy with Elspeth, and I thought how good a friend she had become during the year. Elsewhere there was Claire with two older boys I assume must be her brothers, and her father. And there was Sian, and her mother, whom I'd never seen before. I had invited Siobhan, but she said it was a long way to come, and of course I knew Doris would be worshipping in her own church. I also spotted Alex with his family, but when he saw me, he rapidly hid his face in his songbook. He is strange, that boy.

John spoke about families at Christmas and how important it was for the church to be a family at Christmas time, and I thought, *Yeah, this really is my family.* We had a great time in the church hall afterwards. As everyone was chatting and snacking, Ally caught up with me and shared how seeing Dad and me last year helped him realise this was the church for them.

"Well, let's hope this year someone else will make the same decision," I said, "I don't know what I'd do without this place."

"Me, neither."

Then neither of us could think what to say next, so I said, "Happy Christmas," and went to meet up with Daisy. She couldn't stop as they were on their way to pick up her Dad, but we swapped presents, and I promised to keep on praying.

December 25th

I've got some extra presents this year. Jenny sent me a scarf and a book token; Arthur and Peggy a couple of tea towels with chickens on them. "You did send them a card, didn't you?" asked Jacky.

I nodded, and then I added, "You know, one thing I've learnt this year is how complicated families are. This time last year, if you asked who my family was, I'd have said, Dad, me and you. Now I'm not so sure. I think it includes Jenny and

Gordon, and Arthur and Peggy. I'm not sure about Lee, and I don't know if there's anyone else out there I haven't yet discovered."

"I know what you mean," said Dad. "I think I must've spent my whole life working out who I belong to. But then again, I guess this is why the Christmas story is so important to me." At this point Jacky excused herself to go and check on the turkey.

"What do you mean, Dad?"

"Well, you see that there crib. Joseph, Mary, Jesus. We even call them the holy family. But I reckon Jesus' family was a lot bigger than that. There were aunts and uncles and cousins, and people they spoke to, and people they didn't speak to. I heard someone once say that's why there was no room for Joseph and Mary in Bethlehem – their family had turned their backs on them, and warned folk there not to let them in. I don't know if that's true. I can only speak as I finds it. But it seems to me, yeah, if you know what I mean, Jesus understands this whole messy business of family."

We were both silent for a moment and looked at the figures we had put on the mantelpiece. I think I knew what Dad meant. Then Jacky asked if we were expecting her to run a café on Christmas Day, and if anyone was going to lay the table. "Just coming," we said, and I gave my Dad a kiss.

THE DRUMCHESTER DIARIES: VOLUME 3
FINDING THE PAST
THE DIARY OF ALEX ANDREWS, AGED 13

January 1st

Absolutely freezing today!

I was given a weather station for Christmas, and it told me that the temperature last night was -3°C. Mitch wanted to know if that was outside or inside. We were probably the only people who thought church today felt warm. Everyone thinks that because we live in a big house we must be rolling in money. They haven't seen the size of our heating bill.

As I write, most of the family are gathered in the kitchen. Sophie is wrapped in scarves trying to finish a university assignment. Dad is on his laptop, working, because he's Dad. Mum is cooking tea at the stove. And Mitch, well, Mitch is out somewhere with friends. Mitch is always out somewhere with friends. Someone will bring him home sooner or later.

I'm up in my room watching a production of Joseph. I've landed the part of Benjamin this term and I want to be ready. Mitch reckons I can't really sing, but what does he know? He's only eleven, after all.

January 4th

First day of school today. Someone nicked my dinner money. My dinner money always seems to be going missing. People seem to think they need my money more than I do. Fortunately my last subject before lunch was with Ally, and he had just enough to buy me something. He was talking about football, as usual. I try to get him interested in music, but he just doesn't seem to want to know.

January 9th

Dad had a letter from my grandparents today. Apparently, Great-Aunt Eveline is going to be 100 at the end of the month and we are all invited to a party at her nursing home in Bournemouth. Sophie (who went back yesterday) said she would make it from university. Mitch is excused because he's going bowling with friends – what a surprise.

"And what about you?" said Mum as she came in from work. "Are you coming, or do you want to stay with a friend?"

"Who would he stay with?" asked Mitch.

I wanted to hit him at that point, but honestly, where would I go? Ally is always playing football at weekends. There's Dave, who lives in the village and is nice enough, but he's so boring. He's always making model cars and planes and things like that with his Dad. I don't want to spend a whole Saturday doing that. "No, I'll come. I'd like to see her again," I said, lying.

January 13th

Mum and Dad have taken over the church youth club on a Friday evening. Worse than that, they're holding it in our front room. I don't want a load of girls coming in and seeing all those photos of when I was a baby, with Mum and Dad hugging me.

Fortunately, I don't have to be there. Rehearsals start tonight. One of Dad's clients runs the youth theatre and he agreed to pick me up. His name is Malcolm, and he has three earrings in one ear, but not in the other. He had a funny smell; I think he must wear perfume. He came in a two-door *Mazda MX5* and drove very fast. He seemed impressed by how much I knew about sports cars.

We meet in a large church hall on the far side of Drumchester. It has the same chairs as in our church, ancient metal frame affairs with worn and sagging canvas for seats. At one end there is a large wooden stage with faded red curtain, and a tinny sounding piano in front of it. There is a strong whiff of disinfectant in the air, and the toilets are none too pleasant.

I thought we would be getting straight into our parts, but most of the evening seemed to consist of warming-up exercises. I've sung in school choirs before, but this was something different.

"Projection, volume, diction," said Malcolm over and over again, slowly drawing out every syllable as he spoke. By the end I knew all about pro-jec-tion, vo-lume, dic-tion. If I close my eyes, I can still hear those words ringing in my ears.

There was a girl there called Martinique. I don't chat with girls usually, but it turned out she was in the same form as KT Lee who comes to our church. That reminded me to find out how the youth club had gone. Everyone had left when Malcolm dropped me off, but Mum and Dad were still clearing up. Apparently there had been another couple of new members tonight. Both girls. I think I was glad to be out tonight.

January 18th

It was -5°C last night, a new low. It was cold waiting at the station with Dave, and the train was late. The previous one had broken down and this one was overcrowded. At Drummington Marsh we were delayed again, because we had to wait for a signal. While we were waiting, I saw a heron standing quite still by the river. Dave didn't seem interested.

As we arrived at the academy, late, I thought it wasn't going to be a good day. But it turned out all right. All the sports pitches were frozen, so we had to have PE indoors. That meant I had a chance to go on the new climbing wall. I've always had a head for heights, and I enjoyed the challenge. I hope I can go climbing again soon.

January 27th

We finally got into our parts today. So many lines to learn, and I was really nervous I would miss my cue. But somehow I came in on time, on the right note - mostly. Malcolm said I did well, and not to worry, we had another two months before the performance.

On the way home he asked me what I made of the whole Joseph story. "I mean, all this rags to riches stuff, the family split apart, famine and feast. I've always thought it was too much like a soap opera for my liking."

"Well, it's there in the Bible," I said.

"That doesn't mean anything, though, does it?"

"Doesn't it?"

"Don't get me wrong. The Bible's a great book. But at the end of the day it's just a book. You don't have to believe everything that's written it."

I wasn't sure about that. Mum and Dad have always read the Bible to me, and it's just part of my life. But what if Malcolm was right? I didn't say anything, and Malcolm changed the subject.

Youth club had overrun, and everyone was still there when I got back home. There was Ally talking about his brother's girlfriend who was in trouble again. And KT Lee talking about her half-brother learning to work on a farm. Those are two seriously mixed-up families. Then my Dad started reading something from the Bible about prayer. I was still thinking about what Malcolm said. Standing by the doorway, I felt like for the first time I was looking from the outside on all these people. Everyone prayed for a while, and then slowly made their way out. I remained by the door, wondering.

January 28th

We went to see Great-Aunt Eveline today. Not Mitch, of course. He was staying the whole weekend with a friend. On the way Mum was listening to some weird French music from the 1950s. I suppose that's what comes from having a language teacher as a mother. Dad was driving, as usual, and I guess he was probably thinking about work. So I ignored them both and listened to Joseph again, trying to make sure I knew my part off by heart. It was a long, wet journey with nothing much else to see or do, and I was glad when we finally arrived.

Great-Aunt Eveline lived in an enormous house with its own palatial grounds. The car park apparently used to be the tennis courts and a pair of stone eagles watched us as we made our way up to the front door. I half expected us to be greeted by a butler with a waistcoat, but instead we were met by a posh and rather large woman in a nurse's uniform. As the door opened, an unpleasant smell of chemicals mixed with something else wafted towards us. We were shown down a long corridor past several bedrooms into the lounge that apparently Great-Aunt Eveline had taken over for the day.

There was a simple buffet style lunch laid on a large oak table by the window, with my father's great-aunt sitting nearby on her favourite chair. She's completely blind now, and rather deaf, but she was as bright as a pin. She knew exactly who I was, and how old I was, and wanted to know where Mitch was. I tried to explain about the bowling, but in the end, I had to settle on telling her he was with friends.

There were loads of other people, of course, all of them old, and I didn't know any of them. So I loaded up my plate and retreated into a corner. I was just wondering whether I would be allowed to listen to my MP3, when my Granddad and Grandma walked in. "Not really your sort of thing, is it?" said Granddad coming over to me with a sandwich in his hand. I shrugged my shoulders, as I thought it would be rude to say no. "I remember when I was your age. I had a great-aunt born in Victoria's reign. No buffet, then, when we went to visit. Best shirt and tie, and the toes of your shoes scrubbed until they shone."

"The good old days," I said smiling.

"I wouldn't exactly say that," said Granddad. "There are some advantages in living in the modern world. You wouldn't believe it, but I have finally persuaded your grandmother to have a computer in the house. You'll be getting an e-mail from me shortly, if you let me have your address."

"Don't forget to send one to me." It was Sophie who had just come down on the bus. She gave Granddad a kiss and then went over to sit with Great-Aunt Eveline.

"She's not a bad girl, your sister," he said.

"I wouldn't know. I don't have much to do with girls," I said.

"You will, my boy. You will, soon enough."

I wasn't sure what to say to that, but the party was interrupted by the arrival of a large, garish bouquet of pinks and purples. "No guessing who that's from," said my grandfather, as he went over to collect it. "It's from Paul," he said in a loud, clear voice to his aunt.

"And how is that naughty boy?" she asked.

"I don't know. Probably as naughty as ever."

"That would be about right," said my Dad.

Dad and Uncle Paul have never seen eye to eye. Dad is the typical hard-working, maybe even slightly boring accountant. Uncle Paul sells cars for a living, and probably other things as well. Last time I saw him he was calling in for a brief hello, on the way to pick up a yacht and sail it to France with his leggy, blonde girlfriend. Dad reminded him of the money he lent him some time back, and Uncle Paul left in rather a hurry. As we him saw drive away, I remember Dad saying to me, "I don't care how you earn your living when you're older. Just make sure you spend your own money and not someone else's.

The bouquet made its way onto another table for gifts and cards, right at the back, until a carer finally came with a couple of vases. Soon we were all talking again, and I found I was actually enjoying the day. Mitch kept texting me to say what a great time he was having. But I didn't exactly care.

February 5th

We had a visiting minister at church today because our vicar's wife Helen had a baby last week. He was talking about the Bible as the word of God and made a joke about a bishop who preached from a book of poetry instead. I couldn't see what was so funny. I was still thinking about what Malcolm said.

The worship band had this new loud song at the beginning of the service, something about "God of the breakthrough." A rather deaf old lady sitting behind us asked in a loud whisper, "Why are they singing about grapefruit?" Now that was funny, even if everyone else was trying to be all serious and prayerful at the time.

When I got back from church, there was an e-mail from Granddad asking us to stay with them for a few days over the Easter holidays. Mum said we had nothing else planned, so that was OK.

February 10th

On the way to rehearsals I told Malcolm about the vicar's joke. "Don't you see?" he said. "They want to control what you believe in. That's why they make so much of the Bible." I had never thought of it that way before.

I'm starting to feel a lot more confident in my part as Benjamin. According to Malcolm I still need to work on my pro-jec-tion but my vo-lume and my dic-tion are coming on well. It was Martinique's birthday, so I gave her a card. She gave me a brief peck on the cheek. I don't think I have ever been so embarrassed in my life. I didn't know what to say, but she had already gone out to meet her parents who had come to collect her.

February 13th

It was half-term so for once Dad took a day off work. It was +10°C outside, and sunny, so he suggested we went birdwatching together. When you go out of our house and through the village you come to a track running down by the river. If you walk towards Drummington-on-Sea you find there is a hide just before you reach the first houses. On the other side is a hedge and behind that there used to be a farm run by a couple called by Mr and Mrs Prout. They were arrested last year for some kind of fraud, and they have just been sent to jail. You can't actually see anything through the hedge, of course, but Dad and I couldn't help noticing the bright yellow sign on the gate that said, 'Site acquired for *Morbury's* supermarkets', with the slogan underneath, 'More great buys at *Morbury's*'.

"I hadn't heard about that," said Dad. "I'll be surprised if they get planning permission." I asked him what planning permission was, and he explained the council had to approve plans to build on land. "But anyway," he said, "we've come to watch birds, not talk about supermarkets." And he took me on the little path that led up to the hide.

It was quite a low tide so there were plenty of waders to be seen. I could make out the avocets for myself with their funny head movements from side to side, and their distinctive black plumage. Some of the others I found harder to make out, so Dad patiently explained all the differences. By the end I think I had got some of them, but I still wasn't that sure.

"Could we do this again soon?" I asked as we packed up to go home.

"Sure," he said. "We haven't spent time like this in ages."

On the way back he asked me how things were going with Joseph. I told him about the rehearsals and how I was learning to sing properly. Then I told him about Malcolm and the discussions we'd had on the way to the rehearsals. Dad frowned slightly, in the way Dad always frowns when he doesn't like something. "Do you think he has a point?" asked Dad.

"To be honest, I'm not sure," I replied. "Maybe the Bible is just another book."

"It's not the Bible itself that's important," he said. "It's what it says. And if what it says is true – and the experience of millions of people tells me it probably is – then I think we need to treat it differently."

The sun was shining on the river. Somewhere a curlew was calling. We could see a train coming round a bend, ready to pull in at Drumley Green station in front of us. I really didn't feel like arguing. "OK," I said.

When we got home Helen, the vicar's wife, had come over with Emily and her new baby, Josiah, and was eating cake in the kitchen with Mum. Dad was going to join them but at that moment a builder called to look at the roof.

"This place eats money," said my Mum. "I sometimes wish I was back in our old house – no draughts, no damp patches, no massive heating bills."

"And no character," said Helen laughing.

"Well, yes, I suppose this is what this house has – character. Do you want some cake, Alex?"

I sat and took some cake – not as nice as the sort I make, but not too bad.

"We were just talking," continued Mum, "about what you wanted to do for your birthday next month."

"That's easy," I replied.

"Really? I know you were so disappointed with your film show last year."

"Yeah, well, I'm going to do something grown-up this year. I'm going to go rock-climbing." And I explained my PE teacher knew about a climbing centre in an old quarry on Dumpley Common, above Dumpley End.

"Sounds great," said Mum. "Find some friends to go with and we'll have a party."

"I'll come," said Mitch who was home for once.

"Not a chance," I replied.

I told Dad about my idea later on. "You don't fancy practising by getting up onto our roof, do you? I've just had a quote for scaffolding. You could save me an awful lot of money."

This evening I've had a phone call from Ally. He's got seriously behind with his French and his English, and is wanting some help. We've agreed he can come round after church on Sunday. I'll see if he's free round my birthday. I can but hope.

February 19th

It's been a grey, wet half-term. Not much chance to go out bird-watching again. But I haven't minded really. Our English teacher set us the task of writing a story set in Victorian England, and I've had this idea for a really great ghost tale. I suppose it's not that hard really, when you live in a large house with gloomy attics, and there are chill draughts that sweep along the corridors. Once or twice Mitch has found me writing and asked me what I was doing. But most of the time I've been left to get on with it. Dad has gone back to work; Mum has been catching up with lesson planning and she only disturbed me for a morning or so to buy me some new school shoes.

I asked Ally what his holiday had been like. "What holiday?" he asked. "If you had a house full of screaming babies, you'd be out playing football as much as me." I pointed out that the twins were nearly five, but he just gave me a funny look. I asked him how the English was coming on, but that drew a blank as well. "Not a lot of space to think recently," he replied. Still, he had a half decent plot, so we spent some of the afternoon working on that.

By this point the rain had stopped so we went out for a bit of a kick-about in the garden, until Dad pointed out we were churning up the grass. Sometimes adults don't know how to have fun. So we went into the orchard where there was a rope swing. As we were hanging about, I asked Ally what he thought about the Bible.

"Well, you've got to believe in something, haven't you?" he said.

I suppose that's the point for me – do I? What if it's all just a story, like my English homework? What should I believe then? I didn't try to explain any of this to Ally. He was wanting to get over to his Dad's, soon.

On the way indoors we bumped into my Mum who had just made a plate of biscuits. Ally very politely asked if he might have one, and answered all her enquiries about the family. I wondered what he was up to, and then I realised he was angling for some help with his French homework.

So very patiently my Mum explained about future tenses, and Ally went away, happy. He doesn't spend a lot of time worrying about things, and besides, it will be easy for him to write a few sentences on what he's going to be when he's older. After all, everyone knows he's going to be an England goalkeeper. Me, I haven't got a clue. But I can't just write *"Je ne sais pas"* so I'll have to put something else down instead.

February 24th

I realised I'd forgotten to ask Ally about my birthday party, and amazingly he's actually free for my birthday 'cos it's a weekday during the Easter holidays. I asked Dave at break, but he hasn't got a head for heights. But Barry overheard my conversation and so I invited him as well. It turns out he knows about the climbing place, as he lives in Dumpley End and has always wanted a chance to climb in the old quarry. So that's two friends, at least. Better than nothing.

After break we started moving on to probability theory in maths. Ally wanted to know the probability of Drumchester City winning all their matches until the end of the season. Mr Khan, the maths teacher, only laughed. The lesson got rather silly from then on. Barry wanted to know the probability he would be a millionaire by the time he's twenty. Dave wanted to know the probability he would win the model plane competition he's entering next Saturday.

I asked Malcolm on the way to rehearsals what he thought about chance. "If it wasn't for chance," he said, "I wouldn't have met my first wife."

"So chance is a good thing?"

"You wouldn't say that if you met her. We divorced six months after we got married. Big mistake, all round really. And all because I delivered a pizza to the wrong address."

February 26th

There are some things in life I really don't understand. After church today, KT Lee came up to me and said, "I didn't know you were rehearsing with Martinique."

"What's that got to do with me?"

"I hear you gave her a birthday card."

"What's wrong with that?"

KT then seemed to get the giggles and as she moved away, I could see her laughing with her friend, Daisy. I couldn't work out what I'd done.

Over lunch we talked about the service. One of our elderly church members had come to the front and shared how he had been healed of a painful knee through prayer.

"Quite a story, that," said Dad, as he passed round the plates of chicken.

"The knee would probably have got better anyway," I found myself saying.

"What do you think, Mitch?" asked Dad.

"I dunno," said Mitch. "Can I have another roast potato?"

I think Dad wanted to say something else, but Mum gently put her hand on his arm and said, "Alex, you're at an age when you're asking lots of questions. We have our answers to them, but you've to find the answers for yourself. But whatever answers you find, we'll always be there for you."

I wasn't quite sure what Mum was talking about. I just know since talking to Malcolm I've been thinking a lot about what I've been taught and whether I believe it, or whether it's all a matter of chance.

March 5th

I know it sounds quite weird, but I've started throwing a dice each morning to see what the coming day is going to be like. Today it came up with a six. I wasn't sure why, especially as it was pouring with rain. Still, the train was on time, and for once there was enough room for me and Dave to sit down. Dave was full of his model plane competition, and his second place, so he was in a good mood, for once.

Yet it didn't seem a six sort of day. Good marks in English and History, nothing special. No-one took my lunch money but the lunch in the cafeteria was the same old stuff (old, being the right word, according to Ally, as he attempted to dissect the contents of his pasty). I would have put the day at about a three or a four. And then in PE I found I had got my place back in the school football team. Apparently, there's been some kind of bug going around, so they're looking for a winger to play against Drummington Comp on Thursday.

I've always enjoyed football. Not because I'm particularly good at it, although I can run fast enough with the ball. But because most people think of me as a kind of nerd, always writing stories and doing history projects. At least if I'm in the school team, it makes me kind of cool. Well, I like to think so.

March 8th

7°C when I woke up. It's finally stopped raining this morning, and there's a weak sunlight coming through my bedroom window. In the orchard I can see a great tit sitting on a branch, making that piercing squeaky noise only great tits make. Beyond, the early train was making its way slowly on the great curve of track that leads from Drummington-on-Sea to the station by the river. In the sky, there was even possibly a bird of prey hovering over the distant woodlands. I felt it was going to be a good day, even if I only threw a four.

After school, we squashed with our kit into the school minibus. I've played against Drummington Comp several times in the past, but since I last played, everyone seems to have grown so much bigger. Mum tells me I'm going to have a growth spurt soon, but it hasn't happened yet. It was as much as I could do in the first ten minutes to avoid getting knocked off my feet. But gradually I got into the game. I even managed a shot on goal in the second half – but their goalkeeper, Timmy Timms, was enormous and simply spread himself to smother it. In the end it was a 2-1 defeat, not bad, but not too good either against our arch rivals.

Towards the end, I saw KT Lee come and watch us play for a few brief minutes. Apparently, she'd stayed on at school for a drumming lesson. When she saw me, she smiled and waved. So embarrassing.

By the time I got home, Dad had already been in from work, and gone out again. All very strange. Mum said he'd gone to a meeting in the cathedral. She was busy with a huge pile of marking, so I didn't ask any further questions.

March 16th

One week to go to the performance. All of us had to work really hard this evening. Malcolm wasn't in a forgiving mood if anyone of us made a mistake. "You really should have got this perfect by now, darlings," he said in his best thespian voice. We had to stay on till late, and it was hard work. But I think it was all worth it. I'm looking forward to the dress rehearsal on Thursday, and then the big night itself the next day.

Or at least I was, until Mum and Dad informed me that the Friday group were going to the show. I don't mind performing in front of strangers. If I mess up, it doesn't matter. I don't know them, and they don't know me. But in front of friends. I can almost see KT and Daisy, and Claire and Sian, giggling. The more I thought about it, the more I found myself praying that everything would be all right. Then I realised what I was doing. I haven't prayed for a couple of weeks now. It's not going to make a difference, is it?

March 22nd

I threw a five this morning. I slept really well. The sun was shining, and the blossom in the orchard is starting to open up. I did feel a kind of tickle in my throat, but I reckoned that was just because I had been practising so much. And for the first couple of periods at school I was fine. In history Mr Finlay asked everyone over Easter to do some research on a building in their locality. Then, he added, looking at me with a twinkle in his eye, "So long as it's not your own home," But by then I was feeling rather hot and thirsty. Worse than that, I seemed to have lost my voice. When Mr Khan asked me a question in maths, I opened my mouth and only this small little squeak came out.

I was really, really looking forward to the dress rehearsal tonight. But when Mum arrived home from school, she took one look at me, and went with me to the surgery in Drummington. We seemed to wait for hours. There were only some rather grubby magazines in the waiting room, and a pile of children's toys that dated from the 1980s, or earlier. So Mum tried to make conversation, but I was looking at the hands on the clock and wondering if we'd get home before Malcolm picked me up, or if indeed I would be able to go. I so wanted this part, and I hoped the doctor could do something to make me better. But he examined me and shook his head sadly, "I'm sorry, son," he said. "A bad case of laryngitis. All you can do is rest your voice for the next few days."

"Too much singing?" I croaked.

"No, just an infection that could strike at any time, I'm afraid. A simple case of bad luck."

So much for the five I threw this morning. Maybe God was punishing me for not praying and reading my Bible recently. Maybe it was just one of those things. Maybe the ceiling would fall down on the whole cast and I'd be glad not to be there. No, probably not that. Malcolm texted me to say how much I'd been missed. But, as he said, the show's got to go on. So here I am lying on my bed, angry and confused. Mitch did put his head round the door just now to see if I was all right. So I threw my slipper at him. Very hard. He retreated before I could do any real damage. Pity.

March 25th

My voice is slowly getting better, but I wasn't able to sing in church this morning. I wasn't even sure I wanted to join in, anyway. Sophie was back down from university, and John and Helen came round for lunch, so we all ate in the big front room we don't usually use. John asked me about school, and I told him about my history project.

"That's interesting," he said. "I think I've got a little job for you."

"What do you mean?" I whispered hoarsely.

"I've found this Victorian guidebook about the church. It says some of the stones for the tower came from the old church in Upper Drummington. I've never heard of Upper Drummington, and nor has anyone else I've asked. Could you shed any more light on this mystery?" That's the thing about John – he always seems to know what you're interested in. It's hard not to like him.

After lunch, John and Dad went across the corridor to what used to be the drawing-room and which Dad now uses as an enormous study. Helen and Mum and Sophie disappeared with Emily and baby into the kitchen, no doubt to talk about girly things and children. Mitch stayed behind in the front room because he has a piano exam in a few weeks, and he's decided he ought to practice for once.

So that left me alone with my computer to look up 'Upper Drummington'. I only found four hits. There was what looked like a copy of an ancient map showing various churches in the area, a copy of the guidebook John had mentioned and two references I couldn't access, from papers in Drumchester University. I told all this to Mum later. She said she knew one or two people at the university and would try to find out who wrote the papers.

That just left the map. It must have been drawn centuries ago. The churches are all represented by what look like child's drawings of towers stuck into the landscape. The one for Upper Drummington is there, but I can't relate it to any of the places I know today. There's a wonky tower next to Nether Drummington, but is that the same as Drummington-on-Sea today? And Drumley Green doesn't seem to exist at all. I'm not sure if this is the work my history teacher wanted me to do. But it would be great if I could find out where Upper Drummington was.

March 31st

The first day of the holidays. I went round to Dave's in the morning, 'cos he's invited me several times already and it seemed rude to turn him down again. He took me into the garage and showed me all the parts of his model plane, and the model boat he was in the middle of making. I tried to sound interested. We took the plane out onto the playing fields behind his house. It was quite fun actually, trying to make the plane go where you wanted it to go, and making sure it didn't crash land, or go into someone's garden.

As we were walking back, I asked Dave whether he believed in God or fate. "I dunno," said Dave. "I've never really thought about it."

"What do you think when something major happens in your life?"

"I've never had anything major happen. My hamster died when I was six. I suppose that's been about it."

I saw I wasn't going to get anywhere fast, so I asked him about hamsters instead. It turns out he gave up hamsters when he started flying model planes. I suggested he could have put the hamster in the model plane, but he didn't find that funny.

In the afternoon I went birdwatching with Dad again. He was trying to explain to me how you can tell a bar-tailed godwit from a black-tailed godwit, but I am not sure I fully got it. The tide was low, so there were plenty of waders in front of us. We spent ages putting together a list, and I reckon we must have got a good dozen species today. Then we tried to see if we could make out anything on the far side of the River Drum, but it was hard because there were a lot more reeds there.

However, as I focused my binoculars on the reeds, I became aware that behind them rose the red sandstone church tower at Peter's Cross. It was almost directly in front of us. Why did it suddenly seem so important to me? Then I remembered the map I had found on the Internet. If my memory was right, then the church at Upper Drummington lay exactly opposite on the other side of the River Drum. In other words, somewhere directly behind us.

I explained all this to Dad. He suggested I went back home and printed off the map. So I sprinted back up the path, through the village and in round the back. My mother was in the kitchen and asked me what the rush was. When I explained, she turned off the iron and came with me.

That's how Dad, Mum and me found ourselves peering over the gate towards Prout's Farm. There was a slightly sunken track that ran across a couple of fields towards the farmyard. Beyond the house there was a slight rise in the ground. I had noticed it before from the train, because the line to Drummington-on-Sea ran behind it. There was no scale on the map, of course, and we couldn't be certain. But we all agreed it was most likely that the church stood on top of this small hill.

"So what do we do now?" I asked.

"I'll get in touch with the university," promised Mum.

"I'll see what *Morbury's* intend to do with the site," said Dad.

Of course we could be wrong. Of course there could be nothing there. But it would be exciting to think we had discovered something. Far more exciting than model planes and model boats, anyway. At least I think so.

April 4th

I had an argument with Mum this evening. "Are you looking forward to going climbing tomorrow?" she asked.

"You mean Friday, don't you? That's when my birthday is, right?"

"But we've arranged it for tomorrow – I told you last week."

"I don't remember."

"You should've realised you couldn't go climbing on Good Friday – we're going to be busy at church."

"You might be."

"What does that mean?"

"You don't expect me to join in on my birthday?"

"You always have in the past."

"Well, not this year. I want to celebrate my birthday on my birthday."

"Well, I've arranged it with Ally's Mum and Barry's."

"Just because you're going to be busy on Friday?"

"It's not any old Friday."

I then asked why my family had to be different from other families.

"Do you really want to know the answer?" asked Mum.

I shrugged my shoulders and went out into the garden. I guess I don't care what my family believe in. But they shouldn't expect me to automatically join in. I'm going to be thirteen in two days' time and I have the right to make my own decisions.

April 6th

The climbing was really, really good. There was this old quarry and a sheer stone wall, about eighty foot high. The instructor showed us all the equipment needed and made sure we did all the safety checks. Then one by one Ally, Barry and myself carefully made our way up to the top. Ally and Barry are both a lot taller than me, so they found it easier to get from one handhold to the next. But we all got there in the end.

From the edge of the quarry we had a great view all the way over to the sea from

Dewglass to Drummington-on-Sea. Barry pointed out his house below us in Dumpley End. Apparently, you can tell which one is his, because his Dad started painting it years ago and never finished. So one side of the house is white and the other yellow.

I asked when his Dad would complete the job and he said, "When he next finds a job. Not everyone has money, you know."

I didn't think he should have said that but being perched on top of the cliff wasn't the best place to start an argument. I was quite glad when Barry said he couldn't stay for tea afterwards. He reckoned he was going to see his girlfriend. I didn't believe him.

So in the end it was only Ally who came home with us. But that was all right. At the moment he is trying for a place in the Drumchester City under-15s next season. There's a big cup game at the weekend, and he's been training hard for it all week. I can't imagine working that hard for something. It turns out he had already been for a run that day and was going to do some weight training tomorrow. It must be why he seems to grow every time I see him, and why he puts so much food away.

As he tucked into his third slice of cake, Mum asked Ally about his family.

"Yeah, fine," he said, through a mouthful of crumbs.

Later on I learnt his half-brother's ex-girlfriend has had a boy, but Mark hasn't had a chance to see him yet. Ally reckons Kylie might be going to prison, but she's given the baby to her Mum to look after. Ally asked me to pray for the situation. "Yeah, certainly, it all sounds complicated," I replied, not committing myself.

When Mum dropped him back at his Dad's place his final words were, "See you tomorrow."

"Yes," said Mum.

"Perhaps," I said. But I won't be going anywhere.

April 11th

We came up to Granddad's and Grandma's on Sunday. We were all planning to go home today. Dad has a meeting with John – I'm not sure about what. Mum has work to do, and there's a lady who wants to put her chickens in our orchard. And Mitch seems to want to go back and practice for his piano exam on Saturday. But I had an e-mail from Granddad last week asking me if I wanted to stay for an extra few days, and as I've got nothing better to do, I said, "Yes."

I've always loved staying with Dad's parents. Granddad once owned a chain of bookshops, and they live in a big rambling house on the edge of London stuffed full of old, interesting books. I learnt long ago that if you wanted quality time with Granddad, the best way was to ask him to show you something from his collection. And he would go to the bookshelves and bring down a book of boys' adventures from the 1930s, or some tale of Victorian adventurers, or a book about the lost wonders of the world. If you then sat patiently and were good, he would then let you carefully take the book and read it yourself. Mitch of course could never sit still long enough, so he would go out and play in the garden. But I loved just curling up in a corner with this old book, while Granddad was reading something else, and Grandma knitting in front of the fire, or setting up tea with her delicious home-made scones.

Actually, Grandma hasn't been too well recently so before he left, Dad asked me to be helpful. Grandma wouldn't let me anywhere near her kitchen, so instead I've been vacuuming through the house. I could tell it hadn't been done for a long time. Granddad wants to get in a cleaner, but Grandma won't hear of it.

Over tea Granddad asked me how the old place was. I talked about the problems Dad was having with the roof, and the fact the stables urgently needed work doing on them. "It's always eaten money, that place," said Granddad.

"Tell me more," I said.

So Granddad told the story of Drumley Hall.

"It all began," he said, "with your great-great-grandfather. He made a fortune out of making locks and ironware and he bought the hall once he sold up his business. He had four children, George, Henry, William and Eveline. He always intended George to have the hall when he died, but George died in the Great War. So the hall came to Henry, and when he died to his son, Edward.

"Now Edward loved Drumley Hall, and he and his wife Phyllis spent all they had keeping the old place up. But they never had any children. After many years it became clear they could no longer look after it on their own. So Phyllis' niece and her family moved in. But soon afterwards Phyllis died. Everyone thought that once Edward went as well, Drumley Hall would go to this niece. After all, they looked after Edward so well, and he enjoyed having young people around, 'Makes the place lived in,' he used to say to me, 'Even if we have to sometimes tidy up after them.'

"Of course, Edward grew more and more frail, and he had to go into a home. But his niece, Annie, still lived in the hall and kept it looking tidy. And three or four times a week she would still go over and see Edward in the home. Eventually it became clear Edward was dying. When Annie heard the news, she raced over to see him. But she must have been going too fast, because she skidded on a patch of ice and was killed. We were all shocked by these events. I am only glad that Edward never knew what happened.

"It was, as you can imagine, a terrible time for Annie's family. It became even worse when a few days later Edward died, and they discovered the terms of his will. 'I leave Drumley Hall to my wife's niece, Annie, or if she should die before me to such children of my brother William as survive'."

"And that was you, Granddad?"

"Yes, it was," he said sadly. "What could I do? Of course I immediately offered it to Annie's family. They had far more right to the place than I had. But they were too angry to accept. They moved out almost as soon as they heard the news."

"So you became the owner of Drumley Hall?"

"But what could I do? I was too old to take on the challenge. Besides, I wanted to make sure there was no way it would ever fall into Paul's hands. There's no knowing what he would do with it. Flog it to a scrap-dealer, I shouldn't wonder. So I had a long chat with your Dad. He wasn't that willing to take it on, but there wasn't much else I could do. So in the end I gifted it to him. And as I expected, Paul kicked up a fuss and threatened to sue me. But he hadn't got a case against me, and he couldn't afford a proper lawyer."

Grandma put her hand gently on Granddad's. "That hall's caused nothing but trouble ever since it came into the family. Now I was born in a tenement with an outside loo. It was pulled down donkey's years ago. Good thing too. Now does anyone want another cup of tea?"

There's a picture of great-great grandfather Charles hanging in my bedroom here. When I was young, the picture used to scare me. He seemed to be so stern, with eyes that seemed to follow you around the room. I wonder what he would think of his family today. Probably he would think we were all just making a fuss.

April 14th

I had a wonderful day yesterday. Sophie's studying on the other side of London, and she had invited the three of us to a concert at her university. There was some visiting French pianist giving a classical concert and she reckoned we would like to hear him. It was a long journey, especially for Grandma, on the underground, but it was an absolutely amazing experience. I've always enjoyed listening to piano music, but this was something else. There was so much feeling in what he played, and there wasn't a note wrong throughout, even in the parts that seemed so complicated and difficult. I could have gone on listening to him all afternoon. When the recital came to an end, I actually stood up and cheered.

"You enjoyed that, didn't you?" said Sophie as she took us all to the cafeteria for tea afterwards.

"Better than any of the stuff my friends are into," I replied.

But now I am back home in Drumley Green. It has been a cold, grey day. I had to walk home from the station because Mum was with the chicken lady and Dad had to see a client. It struck me as I got off the station what a small, dreary, dull place I live in. Nothing ever really happened here. Dave was probably busy with his model planes. Ally would be out somewhere playing football. Barry was with his girlfriend – yeah, right. And that counted as news in these parts.

I went past the church hall. There was a sound like a cat being tortured coming out of it. Mitch later explained that KT Lee's Dad, Trevor, and his band were practising for their first charity gig. I guess that's what people think music is round here. As I lugged my rucksack into the hallway, Mum told me not to get mud on the carpets as they'd just been cleaned. I pretended to care. But I know that when I grow up, I want to live in a big city where things really happen and there's real music.

April 28th

It's been hard to think of anything to write. Everything round here seems just so boring. Mum reckons it's a phase I'm going through. I reckon it's where I live.

At least something exciting happened today. We had a visit from Professor Smith at the university. I was imagining an old fogey in a suit and tie. But the professor turned out to be this pretty lady only just a little taller than me (and I'm five foot high exactly). She was doing some research into medieval wills and had found a reference to a William de Drumville who left his son "his boate at Upper Drumchester." She had always meant to find out more, but hadn't actually done anything about it, until she received an e-mail from Mum.

So Mum and I took her down through the village along past the station and down the river towards the hide. As we did so a flock of godwit rose up in a cloud and moved on downstream. But we weren't looking at the birdlife today.

We came to the gate of Prout's Farm, and we showed her the map we had printed off the Internet. She looked over to Peter's Cross then she turned round and looked over towards the small rise of ground where we thought the church could be.

"I've got something to show you," she said, and she pulled out a picture of an old farmhouse taken about 150 years ago. It showed a crumbling black and white building covered in ivy. She explained it was the original house on the farm and would have stood for hundreds of years before the Victorian building that the Prouts tried to do up. Back then it was known apparently as Drumwick Manor. "And where there was a manor," she said, "there usually was a village."

"So what do we do know?" said Dad.

"We talk to *Morbury's* and see if we can get access to the site," she said. "You see that track leading to the farm? It wouldn't surprise me if it was the main street of the village, going on up to the church." Then she wanted to see where the hide was. She reckoned the spit of land the hide was on could have been a good place to land cargo for the village.

When we got back home, Mitch rushed out to meet us. Apparently, he had just heard he passed his piano exam with distinction. Even Professor Smith, who stayed on for a cup of tea, congratulated him.

"Didn't he do well, Alex?" said my Mum.

"Yeah, well done," I said. But I couldn't help thinking how ever since I raved about that concert Mitch has been doing so much more piano practice. I think he's trying to remind me he's the one round here who can play. Or maybe I'm just being jealous.

May 8th

Dad went out for a long meeting last night and didn't come home until ten. Today he was back home by five, which was really unusual for him. He even cooked the tea because Mum had a whole heap of marking to get through, and got Mitch to lay the table.

Then it all came out. "I've got something to tell you boys," he said, almost excitedly. "You know John has been looking for someone to give him a hand around the place?"

"You mean, like another vicar?" I said.

"Over the past few months I've been seeing various people to find out if that was what I was called to do."

"So you won't go to work any more?" asked Mitch.

"No, I still have to earn a living," laughed Dad. "But the plan is that from September I work from home, and study in my spare time to become an unpaid vicar."

"That's why Dad's going away for a few days next week," explained Mum, "to find out if the Church want him. Although, as far as I'm concerned, they'd be mad to turn him down." She looked at Dad with a big, broad smile as though she was really pleased for him.

There was a pause in the conversation. I think Mum and Dad were expecting us to say something.

"Cool," said Mitch, as he cut up his sausage.

"And what about you, Alex?"

"What about me?"

"What do you think, son?"

"If that's what you want to do." I shrugged my shoulders but inside I was furious. I still don't know if I believe in any of this. Yet here's my Dad going off to become a vicar.

Later on I had a text from Malcolm. There's some big American musical coming up and he wanted to know if I wanted a part. I thanked him but explained my voice was breaking at the moment. At least that was my excuse. I don't feel like performing at the moment.

Then I let him know about my Dad and he offered his sympathy. At least there's one person who understands.

May 18th

Dad came home today. Apparently 'it' went very well, whatever exactly 'it' was. "So the Church wants you?" I asked.

"Apparently so." And then he added, "But you can put any questions you may have to the bishop next week."

"You mean he's coming here?" I couldn't imagine anything worse than meeting a bishop at this precise time. I mean, what could we possibly find to talk about? He's got his beliefs, and I've got mine. But that's the last thing I want to discuss right now.

The day got worse. Over the past few weeks I've been hiding when the Friday group comes round. It's not just that they are talking about Christian stuff. On the rare occasions he's not out with his friends, Mitch has started going along as well. I did point out that it was only for secondary school children, but Mum pointed out he would be starting at my school in September. As if I needed reminding.

But this evening was the official debut of *The Potential*, raising money for some school or other in Africa. I thought I'd better show willing, so I tagged along with the Friday group to the church hall. I found myself next to KT Lee who turned and smiled at me as I took my place.

"I haven't seen you recently."

"Yeah, well I've been busy," I muttered.

At that moment her Dad, Trevor, appeared on stage and she stood up and cheered. I was so embarrassed. He introduced each band member, and then they started playing.

The thing I remember most was that it was really loud. Everyone else around me seemed to be having a great time. KT was in her element, and even Ally was tapping his feet. Halfway through I slipped out to the loo, and I saw my Dad at the back silently singing along.

What's the matter with all these people? I thought. But I guess this is what counts as music round here. I suppose it was in a good cause, but I can't imagine what the neighbours must think.

May 24th

I knew the bishop was coming this evening, so I made sure I threw my dice this morning. It came up with a 1. Perhaps God was having a joke with me. Or perhaps not. Someone stole my dinner money again today. That's the third time in two weeks. Mr Finlay the history teacher made me stay behind for a "wee word." He's as excited as anyone else by my original research into Upper Drummington, but he pointed out I did need to have something on paper for my assignment. And I was bowled out for a duck this afternoon. Still, I think I am starting to get the hang of bowling leg-spin and Mr Khan invited me to nets after school next week.

The bishop came just after six. He was on his way to a big service in Dewglass. He was dressed all in black. Mitch wondered if that meant he was going to take a funeral.

"No, that's just the way bishops dress," whispered Mum.

"They sometimes wear purple," I added.

"Gross," said Mitch.

Dad glared at us to stop talking. We were all perched on the sofa with Dad in one armchair and the bishop in another opposite us in Dad's big study.

The bishop, it turned out, had come to break the good news that Dad had been accepted for ordination training and wanted to find out how the family felt about it. He looked at us through his thick-rimmed glasses, waiting for one of us to answer.

"Of course, I'm tremendously proud of Joe," said my Mum. "I guess it will take some getting used to being a vicar's wife but I'm with him every step of the way." Dad grinned at Mum, and she smiled back.

"And what about you, boys?"

"Fine by me," said Mitch. "I mean I'm happy with Church and all that stuff."

"You think he'll do a good job?"

"S'pose so."

"Excellent. Excellent," said the bishop and he took a long slurp of his tea.

Dad looked at me. "Your turn," whispered Mitch. The bishop looked at me. I felt my ears go red. "You're not sure, are you?"

"I dunno," I said. "Church isn't quite my thing at the moment."

"So you're not that comfortable with your Dad being a vicar?"

"He could be doing worse things, I guess."

"Like what?" asked Mitch. I felt I'd said too much already so I didn't answer.

"You must be at that stage when you have all kinds of questions," said the bishop.

I remained silent. I couldn't tell him he sounded just like my mother.

Dad and Mum and the bishop carried on talking. I went up to my room where I turned on my piano music and finished off my history assignment. Mitch went out into the orchard and helped the chicken lady feed the hens. In the end Mum came up and asked if I was all right.

"Why shouldn't I be?" I asked.

"I wish sometimes you'd just talk," she said. "Still, I guess you're now a proper teenager." As if my age had anything to do with it.

I stayed up late tonight and watched the sky above the great wood slowly turn pink, and then orange, and then fade to grey. A cloud of rooks came to roost, cawing noisily. The last train to Drumchester came into view from behind the little hill beyond Prout's Farm. I was suddenly struck by how big and how beautiful the whole world was, and how small I felt, looking onto my own little corner of the universe. Suddenly I sensed this need to pray. But I told myself I was being silly, and I got ready for bed.

June 8th

Morbury's took over the church hall tonight for a big public meeting about the new supermarket. There were two older men in suits who showed a fancy PowerPoint presentation about how wonderful the store was going to be, and used long words like sustainability, diversity and inclusion. They clearly thought we were going to be impressed. Then they asked for questions.

John the vicar had a roving microphone and soon the questions came in thick and fast. Were they going to build a new road to the site? What about the birds on the river?

Had they thought about flooding? Why did we need another supermarket when we already had *Asco's* at the other end of town? But the suits were prepared. They had obviously prepared all their answers well in advance, and as Dad said, they were clearly an experienced double-act. The tall one called George spoke first. And then the shorter one would begin, "That's right, George," and back up what George had just said.

After about an hour there was a pause. The two suits looked very pleased with themselves. Some people were muttering to each other, and one or two decided to leave.

"I think it's time we all broke for a cup of tea," said John.

"Good idea," said George in an enthusiastic voice.

Then suddenly a voice from the back said, "Just one thing." We all turned round. It was Professor Smith; she must have come in late.

"Yes?" said George.

"What about the archaeology on the site?"

"I'm sorry, I don't quite follow."

"There is possibly a lost medieval village on the site of the farm, and I have been trying to get hold of your head office for the past month to gain access."

"And who are you, young woman?" George asked smoothly.

"Professor Wendy Smith, Head of Archaeology at Drumchester University."

"Oh, I see," said George. He mopped his head with his handkerchief. "We'll need to talk about this over a cup of tea."

"I am sure the whole meeting would like to hear what you have to say." There was a general murmur of approval at this point.

"I'm afraid I'll have to get back to you on that one."

A couple of folk started to boo, but John motioned to them to be quiet.

"You did that very well," said Dad as Professor Smith finished grilling the men from the supermarket over tea.

"I told them they had missed something so obvious that even a teenage boy could spot it." Then she winked at me, and I suddenly felt very embarrassed. Fortunately at that point a reporter came up to Professor Smith to ask some questions.

"Some woman," said Dad. I said nothing.

June 20th

I've solved the mystery of the missing dinner money. I brought my cricket kit in today because I've been chosen for the school team. I just about got everything into my locker. But as I reached the form room, I realised I'd left my purse in the bag. I apologised to Mr Khan and shot back to get it. As I went into the locker-room, I found Barry just coming out.

"What are you doing?" I said. "The bell's already gone."

He said nothing, but I found my locker door had been forced open and my purse gone. I shut it again and ran after Barry.

I rarely shout at anyone, but I knew it was him. In the end he chucked my purse back at me. "Don't see why you're so upset," he said. "It's not as if you need the money." That's the last time I invite Barry to anything.

Barry was due to play in the match at Dewglass Comp this afternoon, but Mr Khan gave him a detention instead. So Ally stepped in - not that he had been to any extra nets or anything. But he still opened the batting and scored a rapid fifty. That guy is so talented, sometimes it gets on your nerves. I got hit all over the field, but I did take three wickets, and in the end we managed to win by 25 runs. Even better, we got to go home with Mum. A hot school bus smelling of sweat is not much fun no matter how great your victory.

July 1st

It was a beautiful, warm summer's morning. The whole family was heading off to church today, including Sophie who got back from university last night. I decided to ask if I could go for a walk instead. I don't want to be cooped up in a strange building on a day like this feeling I'm the odd one out, while everyone else worships and praises God, whoever he may be.

"I'm not sure about that," said Dad.

"Well, you are thirteen, now," said Mum. "Just make sure you're back for lunch."

So I slipped out after breakfast, with some binoculars in my rucksack, just in case I saw any interesting birdlife, and a notebook, just in case I felt like doing any writing. I've been writing some poetry recently and my English teacher says it's really good. I didn't have any plans where I wanted to go – except I wanted to be out.

In the end I found myself walking up the river towards Drummington Marsh. The tide was high, so there weren't many birds on the river, except for a flock of loud, squawking seagulls, and I didn't need to watch them. So instead I turned right up an old winding lane that started to climb away from the estuary. After a little while I passed a rundown old farm where one of the girls from the youth group called Daisy lives. I've always wondered how someone can live in such a shabby, broken-down kind of place. There was no-one about – I guess everyone there had gone to church. I stopped briefly to look at the chickens over the gate, but they weren't interested in me.

A little further on, there was a path off to the right into the big woods I can see from my bedroom window. They're apparently part of an ancient forest or something like that. I could hear a woodpecker drumming away high up in the canopy, but I couldn't see him. I could just make out the first train of the day in the distance, but apart from that there was a kind of silence. The words "a drowsy peace" came into my mind, and I began to see if I could fit them into a verse. It all seemed a world away from a noisy service with the band playing, and John making the congregation laugh in one of his sermons, and the chatter in the church hall afterwards. I knew where I'd rather be. Mitch asked me the other day why I always wanted to be on my own. I couldn't tell him why – I just do.

I reached a clearing where the path joined several other tracks that wound through the trees. By now I had reached the top of the rise and I wanted to see if I could look back at my house. But there were too many bushes in the way, and the view was getting hazy.

I wasn't really paying that much attention to the noise behind me, when I suddenly heard a voice I recognised, behind me. "Well, if it isn't that rich kid from the manor house."

I knew it was Barry. I turned round and saw he was there with his older brother. "Well, if it isn't my old mate, Barry."

"Shall we see what the rich kid has got for us today, Wayne?" he asked, turning to his older brother.

Wayne nodded. "Give us yer rucksack," he said.

I hesitated. "Come on," said Barry. "Let's not be having any trouble."

I handed over my rucksack. "Not much here," said Barry. "I've got a phone better than that," he said and threw it into the bushes. "Pair of binoculars… haven't got much use for them," and he chucked them into the bushes. "Bottle of water, a cereal bar," he continued, then he turned the rucksack upside down. My notebook fell out from a side pocket. He simply trod on it and broke my pen. "OK, now for your pockets." I turned my pockets inside out. There wasn't a lot in them.

"You'll have to do better than that if you ever come back here again," said Barry.

"That's right," said Wayne. They stepped closer. I guess they wanted to scare me, but I could only think how bad they both smelt. Then they pushed me into the bushes and ran off.

When I got back, I was slightly late for lunch.

"Did you have a good walk?" asked Mum.

"Yeah, it was fine," I said. The last thing I wanted was her kicking up a fuss. She noticed the scratches on my arms, but I said I wasn't looking where I was going and stumbled into some gorse. "It's nothing, Mum, honest," I said. And then Sophie started to talk about last term, and the friends she'd made and her plans to travel round Europe, and my walk was soon forgotten.

I spent the rest of the day up in my bedroom. I could go out if I wanted to – I'm not scared of Barry or anyone else. Only this is my place where I can be what I want to be. No younger brother asking what I'm doing. No older sister talking about what she's going to do for the Lord when she's older. No old hippies with guitars playing worship songs. Just me, my music, and my stuff. Suits me fine.

July 5th

Dad had an e-mail from Professor Smith yesterday. Apparently *Morbury's* have agreed to a trial dig on the site of Prout's Farm over the summer holidays, and would we be interested in getting involved? Mum pointed out that we were still going camping as usual in France. I protested, but she said I could always join when I got back. Mitch asked me why I was interested in a load of dead people.

"'Cos they're history, that's why."

"Shame you don't seem that interested in the living," he replied.

"That's enough," said Mum. But maybe Mitch has got a point. Historical people are less complicated, somehow. They can be what you want them to be.

July 10th

Each year we have an inter-house cricket competition, twenty overs a side. My house always comes last, so this year they decided to bring in their secret weapon – me. I didn't bowl badly in the first game, but we still got thrashed. Then in the second game I actually took a wicket. OK, the batsman simply hit the ball up in the air, rather than out of the ground, but I didn't mind. What I didn't realise was that the next batsman was Wayne, Barry's older brother. He took his guard and he grinned at me. I bowled the first ball. He went to swipe it, and it just went past the stumps.

"Well bowled," someone cried. Wayne glared at me. The next ball he tried to hit even harder. Again he missed. He finally hit the third ball, but with the top edge of the bat. It came sailing back towards me at about shoulder height. I didn't think what I was doing. I just stuck out a hand. The ball whacked into my palm, bobbled up and before it dribbled onto the ground I managed somehow to dive sideways and catch it. Everyone cheered – except Wayne who trudged off very slowly.

Later, when I got back to the locker-room, I discovered someone had thoughtfully poured a bottle of tomato ketchup into my kitbag. I told Mr Khan and explained the situation with Barry.

"Leave it to me," he said.

As for my hand, it feels about twice the normal size. But I don't care. I don't even mind that my house came last again. I took on Wayne and I won, and that feels good.

July 17th

Mum finally found out about my kitbag just before I left for school today. I had tried to clean it up myself, but you didn't need to be an expert to see I hadn't done a very good job.

"It's just someone who doesn't like me," I said.

"Is that all?" she asked in a way which reminded me she was a teacher.

"Yeah," I said and shrugged my shoulders.

"So they're going to pay for a new kitbag?" she asked.

"I dunno," I said. "They don't have any money."

"All right," said Mum.

"Mr Khan knows about it already," I added.

"Then I shall have a word with Mr Khan," she went on. Poor Mr Khan. I'd better warn him.

July 23rd

The first day of the holiday. Everyone else seems to be really busy. We're going away next week so Mum is doing her annual sort-out and completing all her work at school. Dad is finishing work at his office and rearranging his study. Sophie has found work at a local solicitor's, and Mitch is actually practising for some music festival he's playing at over the weekend.

It's been raining hard so I can't go out for a walk. I'm sure there are things I can do, but at the moment I just feel bored. In the end I walked over to the stables. They're at the far end of the orchard, up a track that runs past the side of the house. They were turned into garages long ago, but they're now full of cobwebs and dust. Dad says he will do something with them when he's got the money. But I like the atmosphere in there. I spend ages watching the drops beat against the dirty window pane and try to imagine the lost world of horses, and country houses, and servants.

I know I'm not supposed to, but after a while I go up into the old hayloft. There's just a few items of old, rickety furniture in there. Since anyone was last in there, some of the plaster has come down from the ceiling in the corner. I notice there's a piece of old newspaper showing, but I can't reach it. I drag across the table and stand on it. As I work at the newspaper, some more plaster comes down, showering me in dust. Eventually it comes loose, and I find it's a piece about a Royal Garden Party to celebrate Queen Victoria's diamond jubilee. What was it doing up in the ceiling? Was I meant to find it and if so, why?

I made my way back to the house still rather dusty, but with the newspaper article tucked inside my cagoule so it doesn't get wet. I've got this idea for a story but the words don't seem to come out right. Still, I've got the whole of the summer holiday ahead of me.

July 27th

The scaffolders came today. The plan is for the builder to start work on the roof on Monday while we are away. Dad should have been there to supervise but he had to go off to Bournemouth today. Apparently, Great-Aunt Eveline has had a fall and is in hospital. We're not sure if she will pull through or not. So Mum has been keeping an eye on things. She's also noticed I haven't been doing a lot recently – so she's got me vacuuming the whole house. All except the front room where Mitch is still practising. He seems to have been there all week – I didn't know he had it in him to concentrate on one thing for so long.

July 28th-29th

The day of Mitch's festival. As he came on stage, I noticed how small he seemed compared to the other performers. But I have to say he played really well. And I liked his choice of music. At the end he won second prize in his category. His music teacher came up to us and congratulated us. We would have stayed on for the tea and cakes, but we had a ferry to catch. All except Sophie who was apparently going on to friends for the weekend and then back to work.

We've been camping in France for as long as I can remember. Always the same routine – the late-night ferry, the car journey across France, with Dad driving and Mum giving directions, and lunch at some small-town café, with Mitch asking for chips, and Mum giving him a baguette instead. Mitch has never won the argument yet. I've never understood what the fuss is all about. French bread has always tasted far better than English bread, as far as I'm concerned.

This year we're in some remote corner of Brittany above a deserted beach. I'm sure that when the sun comes out, it's going to be a lovely spot. Only at the moment *il pleut* and there's little sign of it stopping. But as always Mum has brought something educational along with her. So here we are, playing French monopoly under canvas. And as she has the most expensive properties – the *Rue de la Paix* and the *Avenue des Champs-Elysees* – I think I know who's going to win.

July 30th

We had a phone call from Sophie first thing this morning. It seems someone has been up the scaffolding and helped themselves to the lead on our roof. Not only that, but the same heavy rain has been pouring in through the gaps left behind. According to the builder who's just turned up, the damage so far is only to the attic rooms, but apparently he's muttering something about a "large insurance job."

"I'll have to go back," said Dad with a sigh. "No doubt the police will have to get involved."

"But what about our holiday?" asked Mum.

"I don't have any of the paperwork I need over here."

"Do we all have to go back?"

"You could stay here with the boys if you want."

"No," said Mum. "I suppose we better come. But when this is sorted, let's see if we can grab a last-minute holiday somewhere."

So here we are waiting around at the ferry terminal for the next crossing. Mum, Dad and Mitch are wandering around the shop, complaining how expensive everything is. I sense they're all really fed up. As for me, well, I can manage a year without camping in France. I might even be able to get involved with the dig at Prout's Farm. If only it stops raining.

August 3rd

Finally the weather shows signs of clearing up. I've been in touch with Professor Smith and the dig's had to be delayed for a few of weeks. But she says I can come and join in, if I want. In the meanwhile all kinds of people have been coming backwards and forwards. There's this detective, PC Jones, who is apparently our 'liaison officer', whatever that means. There's the man from the insurance company who has given Dad lots of forms. There's the surveyor sent by the insurance company who is looking at the damage in the attic rooms and having long talks with the builder and with Dad.

All we know so far is that if Sophie hadn't come back early on Monday morning the damage could have been a lot worse. A couple of collapsed ceilings, and some damaged carpets, and that seems to be about it. As to "whodunit?", the police will only say they're very interested in a white van seen crossing the bridge over the railway line to the main Drumchester road about midnight on Saturday. It had been seen in the village about ten o'clock, and they are trying to work out where it went for the missing two hours.

Mum has had enough and is going off to see some old university friends for the weekend. Dad has said he will make the lost holiday up to her, but I don't think she is convinced.

August 7th

This is embarrassing. It seems some journalist has got hold of the story of the teenage boy who found a lost medieval village. So here I am today outside Prout's Farm being interviewed about my amazing discovery, and worse still, they want to take a photo of me. Apparently, this is Professor Smith's idea of generating publicity and stopping *Morbury's*. I can imagine what Barry and his brothers will think when they read about me in the newspaper. If, of course, they read newspapers.

But at least the sun is shining, so it looks like we're going to make a start next week. Professor Smith came and introduced me to a colleague who explained how they were going to survey the site, and what all their hi-tech machines did. I have to confess, I was rather distracted by Professor Smith herself. I think at one point she noticed I was looking at her, and she gave me rather a stern look. That's when I began to feel even more embarrassed. I turned back to her colleague and nodded wisely as if I'd understood every word he was saying.

August 17th

I thought a week digging on an archaeological site would be fun. Actually most of the time I have been bending over the ground with my little trowel with the sun scorching my back, and midges helping themselves to a free meal. I was told right at the outset we probably wouldn't find any buried treasure, but even so I can't work out why everyone is so excited by what they've found. They've found some little round patches of darker earth which they reckon are post holes, a couple of tiny fragments of pottery, which they date from the 13th century, and a battered lump of metal which is apparently a rather rare kind of coin. It doesn't seem that much from working for all those hours in the heat of the day. Yet Professor Smith and her colleagues are talking about "making a significant discovery." The best guess appears to be that Upper Drummington was simply wiped out by the plague.

I've been asked if I want to join in next week when they start digging the church mound. I'm not that wild about the idea, but I can't think of anything better to do.

August 21st

We found our first skeleton today. Or at least our first bones. On the side of the track leading to the top of the mound we came across what looked like a pit filled with a jumbled mass of human remains. We've only just started digging it. But I have been surprised at how small some of the bones are. Professor Smith reckons they might have been children killed by the plague, buried hastily as the disease swept through the community.

I talked over what we found with Dad tonight. "Sometimes it's hard to make sense of so much suffering," he said as he saved his work on his computer. "Do you want to go on with the dig?"

"I guess so."

"You know what," he said, unwrapping a toffee. "I thought of being an archaeologist once." The thought of my father doing anything that didn't involve a suit and tie rather surprised me. He must have read my thoughts though because he carried on, "Then I realised I was trying to escape into the past, and not dealing with the present."

"And you think that's what I'm doing?"

"All I am saying," he said, putting the toffee in his mouth, "is don't get lost in your imagination. There are enough interesting stories in the people you meet day by day."

"You mean, in a place like Drumley Green?"

"Even Drumley Green." He smiled. I wasn't quite sure where our conversation was going, so I changed the subject. But I have been thinking ever since – what could possibly be interesting about Drumley Green?

August 25th

We found about a dozen people – mostly children – in the pit in the end. We couldn't find much trace of the church, although as Professor Smith said, it wasn't that surprising if the stone was taken away and used to build the church at Drumley Green. Next week there are apparently going to be lots of site meetings with the people from *Morbury's*. I'd love to know what they decide, but I've been told it's no place for a thirteen-year-old boy. Still, at the end Professor Smith shook me by the hand and gave me a smile as she thanked me for my contribution, so that made it all worthwhile.

When I got home, I found Dad and Mum having an argument, for once. It's good to know they can occasionally behave like normal parents. Mum pointed out Dad had promised to make up for the lost holiday. Dad said he didn't want to leave the house again with the scaffolding up. In the end they decided that as the builders were finishing on Friday, they would have a long weekend away.

"What about me?" I asked.

"Don't you have anyone to stay with?" asked Mum exasperatedly. "I'm sure you could go on the youth camp Mitch is going on."

"No thank you," I said. The idea of sharing a tent with a load of years six and seven, and learning new songs about Jesus really didn't appeal to me.

"Well, you can't stay here," said Dad, firmly. "Sophie's going off on Thursday, and you can't be left alone."

"Can't I?"

"You're too young."

"I am a teenager, you know."

"Only just," interrupted Mum. "See who you can stay with - please."

"OK," I said.

I couldn't get hold of Dave. I think he said he would be away. Ally of course was out playing somewhere as it was Saturday afternoon, and even if I asked there would be no room at either his Mum's or his Dad's. And I didn't really know anyone else that well. I lay down on my bed and listened to my music for an hour, then I came down and said, "I've tried everyone I can think of, but I haven't had any luck."

"That's all right," said Mum. "I've had a word with John and Helen."

"You mean, stay at the vicarage?"

"Well, why not? It's a huge old place, and Helen said all you need to do is share meals with them. They won't even make you go to church."

I learnt long ago that when Mum has a plan, there's no point arguing.

September 3rd

I've been staying at the vicarage for two days now. Mum and Dad have found a caravan in Wales, apparently. They'll be coming home tomorrow as the new term's starting on Wednesday. It hasn't been too bad, actually. John and Helen have been true to their word. Apart from meals they have left me alone. I'm at the other end of the house from the children so they haven't disturbed me too much.

Yesterday I went on a long walk up along the river to Drumchester. The last few days have been cooler and cloudier, so as Dad would say, it's ideal walking weather. I stop to some bird-watching on the way back but there were only gulls and ducks and swans.

I found some tide tables in my bedroom, and today was going to be an extra low tide. So I set out in the opposite direction, following the main road down into Drummington-on-Sea. At the roundabout by *Asco's* I crossed over onto the beach at Drake's point. This is normally a quiet spot where the only locals go, but being a Bank Holiday, and with the sun out, it was heaving. However, as I set off along the beach the crowds soon thinned out. I had heard it was possible at low tide to walk all the way along to Dewglass and I wanted to see if this true.

As I rounded the first headland, it began to cloud over. I imagined all the tourists behind me looking anxiously at the sky, maybe some of them packing up their picnics, or perhaps the more hardy ones defiantly getting out their cagoules. In fact the shower didn't last too long, just enough to cool me as I trudged onwards over the large, smooth pebbles.

There were a couple of fishermen by the shoreline but otherwise the second beach was deserted. A narrow stream of water cascaded down the cliff to my left and disappeared into a pool above the shoreline. I washed my face in it. It felt cool and smelt clean.

It took longer than I anticipated to round the second headland. The beach was narrower here, and I could see that the furthest rockpools were starting to disappear beneath the incoming waves. It was then I realised that my timing might have gone slightly wrong. But I had looked at a map before I set off and realised that if I could get beyond the next outcrop there would be a path up to the coastal route.

The only problem, as I got closer, was that there had been a small rockfall and my route was actually blocked. It didn't seem much of a fall, and I guess it might have been possible to climb over it. But I remember Dad saying never to go under a cliff which was crumbling. As I looked at some of the boulders overhanging that part of the beach, I reckoned he was probably right.

Maybe I should have gone back. But the cliffs here weren't that high, and there seemed to be a narrow gully offering an opening through the rocks. I thought of my climbing experience, and I reckoned I just had to give it a go. Looking back, it was probably the worst decision I could have made.

The bottom of the gully was narrow and rocky. Several times I almost slipped on the loose scree that moved when I put my foot on it. Once I reached out for a small rock to get a better grip, but it just fell away onto my right ankle. I winced with pain, but realised I had to go on. I was about halfway up by now and looking back I could see that more of the rockpools were under water. I don't think I could have gone back round the headland if I'd tried. Slowly I carried on forwards. The only problem was that right at the top, a thick, thorny bush blocked my path. I had little option but to try and scramble through it. I put on my cagoule to try and stop myself being scratched but the bush still managed to attack me. By the time I got through I had long scratches down both legs, and a cut on my left ear.

I was now at the top of the cliff. But where was I and how would I get home? I had left the map at the vicarage, although it was pretty clear Drummington lay somewhere to my left at the bottom of the valley. But walking was by now quite difficult with my ankle. I could hobble but I wasn't going to make much progress.

As I was still thinking what to do, I suddenly heard a familiar voice saying, "Is that you, Alex? Are you all right?"

It was KT Lee. She was cycling along a track above me behind an old stone wall and must have spotted me sitting down by the cliff edge. "Never better," I said smiling falsely, but as I stood up to walk towards her, I realised my limp was going to give the game away.

"Yeah, right. Like you just climbed up a cliff like Superman and you're ready to take on the world."

"Maybe I have been better," I admitted, as I wondered how I was going to get over the wall. KT Lee got off her bike and offered me her hand. It was so embarrassing. Gingerly I scrambled over the dry-stone wall. I might have cut my foot in the process, but I didn't care by now. As I put my weight back down on the ground, she must have seen I was in agony.

"Come with me," she said. She put her arm around my shoulder, and we made our way back along the track to a little village called Dulling St Mary where her friend Siobhan lived.

Siobhan was standing in the front garden of her house when we came into view.

"You picked up a boy?" she asked in a not very friendly fashion.

"Cut that out," said KT Lee. "This boy is Alex and he's hurt his ankle."

An old woman called Kathleen who turned out to be Siobhan's grandmother came out with a chair. "You sit down, here," she said to me, and then turning to the girls, "I don't care what you were arguing about. Just make yourself useful."

Kathleen sat me down and examined my ankle. "Well, at least, it's not broken," she said, feeling my bones. "Siobhan, fetch the frozen peas. I'll go and get something for those scratches."

In the brief moment they were gone KT Lee asked me, "What were you doing climbing up that cliff?"

"Nothing… you tell me what's going on between you and Siobhan."

"Mind your own business. It's a good job for you I left here when I did. Otherwise how long do you think it would have been before you'd been found?"

"I'd have managed."

"Pull the other one. Do you want me to ring your Mum and Dad?"

"Oh hell," I said. "They're away having a much-needed break at the moment. Mum's arranged for me to stay at John and Helen's."

"No problem, I'll give them a ring."

"Please don't."

"Alex Andrews, you are the most stubborn and impossible boy I've ever met. Assuming you get home by some miracle on your own, how are you going to explain what happened?"

"It was fate," I said.

"Bally nonsense," said Kathleen. "No such thing as fate." Then she tipped out some stuff from a bottle and started treating my cuts and scratches. Siobhan appeared with the frozen peas. As she put them under my foot, she looked up at me and smiled. I felt all hot all of a sudden and it wasn't just that the sun had decided to come out again. I looked away and saw KT Lee had her phone out and was talking to Helen.

"She'll be over in about twenty minutes," she said at the end of it.

"You better rest up here until then," said Kathleen. "Right then, girls, go off and play nicely, and let's not have any more silly rows." Siobhan looked at KT, and KT looked at Siobhan, and suddenly they both burst out laughing and ran indoors. Kathleen brought me a drink of lemonade and I sat and waited, while she carried on weeding the garden. From time to time I could hear the girls in the house, doing whatever girls like to do together. I sat and thought about what Kathleen said. "No such thing as fate." Whoever had rolled the dice that morning, it was surely a chance in a million KT Lee was cycling past when she did.

I was still trying to work out the probability when Helen arrived. I could see she wasn't happy. Josiah was in the back of the car, crying. Kathleen and Helen helped me in. Just as I was manoeuvring onto the front seat Siobhan and KT came out of the house, and waved goodbye at me, as if I was a strange alien intrusion that had landed for a brief while. I probably was.

Helen made me ring Mum and Dad when I got back.

"And this," said Dad sternly, "is why you're too young to be left."

"As if I planned the whole accident?" I said sarcastically.

"Just get it checked out by Dr Maxwell tomorrow morning," he replied. "We'll be home by five."

September 5th

The first day of school. Mitch came down in his new school uniform, eager to be off. He'd had a great time at camp, and as usual, had made many more new friends. The plan was for me to be the big brother, and we'd walk together down to the station. But I'm not going anywhere. Dr Maxwell took one look at me yesterday and sent me off to get an X-ray at Drumchester General. John and Helen paid for me to have a taxi there as they were both busy, so I spent most of the day hanging out in hospital corridors reading a book of poetry I had brought with me. There was indeed nothing broken, but I was told I needed at least a week off school.

"I expect you'll be pleased about that," said the young doctor, in the same kind of voice you use to pat a small child.

I said nothing but waited till Mum and Dad came to fetch me home.

So instead Dave called in, and Mitch already with jam on his new trousers, bounced after him. Mum had already gone off to Dewglass, and Dad firmly shut the study door behind him. And here I am stuck again at home, feeling bored.

At lunch time I had a text from Ally. *Sorry to hear about accident. Will call round soon. Am praying for you.*

Is there, I wonder, a prayer against boredom?

September 15th

Ally invited me to watch him play for Drumchester City under 15s today. My ankle had been steadily getting better, but I still find it hard to walk long distances.

"Better not," I said. "But next time… and good luck!" I don't know why Ally is such a good friend to me and I suspect he doesn't fully understand me. He certainly looked surprised when I thanked him for the homework he brought over for me from school this week.

Dad was out all day for the first 'learning experience' of his vicar training. To my surprise, he was rather hot and bothered when he came home. "We were all supposed to be sharing stories of our faith journey," he explained to Mum over tea. "Mostly it was a chance for people to say how much they didn't believe. I'm not sure I'm looking forward to the next three years."

I wanted to say that sounded really interesting, but Mum had already begun to speak. "Never mind, Joe. John will keep you on the straight and narrow."

"What's the straight and narrow?" asked Mitch as he helped himself to pudding.

"The one truth path of enlightenment," I said.

"That's enough," said Dad, and I felt I had to say sorry.

September 23rd

I don't know why, but I felt I had to go to the Harvest Festival this morning. It's always been a big occasion in our church, and today was no exception. Some woman from an organisation I never heard of talked about World Toilet Day and explained how many people in the world didn't have access to sanitation. For some reason, Mitch kept giggling, but I found it really interesting. Then Sophie, who was going back later today, explained how she had managed to save enough to go on a team digging latrines in South America next summer. And John for once preached a good sermon on how if Jesus was on earth today, this would be exactly the sort of thing he would be interested in. I wish we had more services like that.

Afterwards we had our traditional harvest lunch based on 'foods around the world'. Mum brought along some traditional French baking that she had done with her class that week. Ally brought along a pizza because that's the only thing he knows how to cook. Others brought along dishes from places like Morocco and Thailand. But we all agreed the best came from Daisy's mum, Elspeth, who had cooked up a genuine goat curry from an animal on the farm. As we all chatted, I wondered why exactly I had stayed away all these months.

Everyone seemed really pleased to see me again. It was the first time KT Lee had seen me since my scrape on the cliff, and she seemed genuinely concerned to know if my ankle was feeling better.

"A couple more weeks, and I will be scorching down the wing again," I said. Then I realised I was sitting next to Ally who was playing in a county match next weekend. Why do I say such embarrassing things when girls are around?

October 2nd

I went to the hospital yesterday, just to check everything was OK. "Yes," said the doctor, "it's all healed up beautifully. There's no reason why you can't take part in sport again."

So here I am out today on the school playing fields. It's been raining hard for the past few days, so the ground underneath is soft and boggy. It turns out this term the sport for the boys is rugby. As we get changed, I think I realise just how much everyone else seems to have grown bigger and stronger over the last few months. We jog out onto the playing fields just as a soft drizzle begins to set in and we learn that the task today is scrummaging practice. What fun!

Now I'm not a wimp – at least I don't think I am. I like to give as good as I get. But there's no way I can compete with all these other guys. Soon I am slipping and sliding all over the place and getting covered in mud. Even worse, every time I get up, I have to lock my head next to someone's sweaty armpit. I decide halfway through I need to rest my ankle and I am sent for an early shower. Suits me fine. By the time everyone gets in, the soft drizzle has turned into a grey, persistent rain that cloaks everything in a fine mist. I feign a slight limp as I leave the changing rooms.

October 10th

Dad had a phone call first thing yesterday. Apparently, Great-Aunt Eveline had taken a turn for the worse, so he cancelled all his appointments for the day and went up to Bournemouth. When he came back, he told us it's only a matter of time.

This evening we had another phone call to say she had passed away. I don't know why but that news has hit me quite hard. I guess for me she was the kind of link between the present and the past. When she was born, the First World War hadn't yet started. This house, her home, would still be full of servants living up in the attic, with horses out in the stables, and steam trains puffing their way down to Drummington-on-Sea where bathing carriages would await the lords and ladies who had come for the sea air. Indeed, the top end of Drummington-on-Sea would still be fields, with stacks of hay, and grain taken down to the old mill for grinding. Hard to believe someone in that era would grow up to witness space flight, and the Internet, and nuclear power.

I said something of all that to Dad. "Yes, that's true," he said. "But she was also a very special person as well."

"Show the boys your photos," said Mum. So Dad disappeared into his study and produced an enormous photo album full of a young Eveline between the wars. "Quite a beauty, wasn't she?" said Mum. I nodded, but I found it hard to connect all these pictures with the very elderly lady I had been used to visiting.

October 23rd

We all went up to the funeral today. It was held in the parish church of the small Dorset village where Eveline had lived for most of her life. I was surprised just how many people turned up. Many of themselves seemed quite frail and elderly, some were in wheelchairs but nearly all the senior residents of the village were determined to be there.

After a solemn and rather dreary hymn, Granddad got up and told the story of his aunt's life. He had written all of it down in his neat, precise handwriting, and put on the gold-rimmed reading glasses he hated wearing, but actually he hardly looked at his notes at all. I began to realise just where I had inherited my love of storytelling from. He talked about Eveline entering the Civil Service, and how she did some job during the war that was some great secret; her brief marriage to a flying officer who was killed only a few weeks before it was all over – something I never knew; how she helped him set up his first bookshop; her long years of service to the local church; and how she never quite mastered the mysteries of her first video recorder. He could have talked for hours but after about fifteen minutes the vicar gave him a little nod, and he suddenly remembered himself, and came to a conclusion.

I wondered how the vicar – a tall, white-haired man with a thin, narrow face - could possibly follow that. We sang another hymn, and then he began to talk about Eveline's favourite Psalm, Psalm 121 - *I will lift up mine eyes unto the hills, from whence cometh my help.* I can't remember exactly what he said, but it was something about how through all the changes in her life Eveline kept looking up to God, that she knew all things were in his hands, and how we could all learn from this example of faith and trust. I realised at that point I still had my special dice in my pocket, even though I haven't thrown it for a couple of months now, and I felt rather foolish.

I didn't have much time to think for the rest of the day, however. After another brief service at a cold and bleak crematorium in the middle of nowhere, we all went back to this rather posh hotel and what Mum and Dad explained to me was traditionally called the wake. Mitch and I were starving 'cos we'd had to leave really early to get to the service, and there seemed to be a whole banquet of quiches and canapés and pork pies in front us. But we kept getting interrupted by cousins and second cousins and second cousins once removed, and other relatives even more removed, who came up to us and said how much we had grown. And we looked at each other and gave the usual answers about school and what we liked doing and what we wanted to be when we're older. In the end we decided to take questions in turn, so one could do the talking, while the other could carry on eating. Otherwise we reckoned we'd still be starving.

Uncle Paul wasn't at the service. He came straight to the wake, in an old, white *Rolls-Royce* that seemed to produce a lot of smoke. He has a line in wedding cars now, apparently. The general buzz died down when he came into the room. He still had the same leggy girlfriend by his side, but she seemed a lot more careworn and less carefully made-up than when I last saw her.

"Hello, Paul," said Dad. "Glad you could join us." I wasn't sure if he was being sarcastic or not.

"See you've still got your collar the right way round – at least for now," said Paul. "You remember Chantelle, don't you?"

Chantelle came forward. I think she was expecting an air-kiss, but Dad doesn't do air-kisses, at least as far as I know. He took her hand. "Glad to see you again. Are you well?"

"Fine." She cast a sideways look at Paul. I could tell she was really uncomfortable with the surroundings. But Paul had already made his way over to Sophie and kissed her on the cheek. Sophie grimaced at me. I winked back.

Paul and Chantelle didn't stay long. As Paul was able to leave, he asked Dad if he could have a quiet word. "Not if it's about money," said Dad.

"No, Joe," said Paul, "nothing like that." As they went out, I could see that they were brothers. Both with the same bald spot, both with the same small, slightly piggy nose. Dad came back a little later. He wouldn't say what they had spoken about, but I could tell he was quieter for the rest of the day.

For once Mum drove home. Dad explained that Chantelle had just been diagnosed with breast cancer, for the second time. "I may not get on with my brother," he said to us, "but I would never, ever wish that on anyone."

There had been some accident on the way home, so we had to take a long, twisty diversion along narrow lanes. It was starting to get dark, and no-one felt like saying anything. I was still thinking about those words the vicar had said. Had it been just a random accident that KT Lee had been there at the top of the cliff? It certainly hadn't felt like chance at the time, and now I was convinced more than ever my help had come from the Lord – whatever that meant. Of course, I couldn't prove that, but then you couldn't spend your whole life waiting for proof. Somebody in church had once said something about taking a chance on God. Maybe now was the right time to take that chance.

By the time we arrived home, it was pitch-black outside, and bitterly cold. The weather station in the hallway said the temperature was already only +4°C outside. I went up to my bedroom but before I drew the curtains, I looked at all the stars spread out across the sky. I thought of that time when I told myself it was silly to pray and realised that perhaps I had been wrong. I began to pray for Great-Aunt Eveline, and for Paul and Chantelle, and all the other people I had met today, and trusted that somehow my prayers would make a difference.

October 29th

We don't usually go away at half-term but as we never had a holiday in the summer, Mum and Dad have booked a cottage in the Forest of Dean. They've explained how they've both had to take a lot of work with them, but that's OK. The cottage is on the edge of a huge forest, so it looks like Mitch and I will be spending the week exploring that.

Sophie's come down for the first weekend. She's brought her boyfriend, Eddie, with her. Apparently, they met about a month ago, and I can see that Sophie is soppy about him. She's happy and smiley most of the time, but when he's around she has this kind of dreamy look and laughs a lot.

We wanted to go to church this morning, but Sophie and Eddie decided they would stay at home and read the papers. When I said I would come too, Mum couldn't help saying, "Well, this is a turn up for the books."

I haven't told anyone what happened at Great-Aunt Eveline's funeral. I think it's kind of private, between me and God.

The church was an old Methodist chapel, and the congregation only slightly younger than the building, although there were a couple of young families sitting at the back, next to a kind of play area for the kids. They were going to sing unaccompanied because the organist was in hospital, but Mitch spotted an electric keyboard, and volunteered to try and play a few of the hymns. He actually did really well, and I told him so at the end.

"Good to see you two get on so well," said Mum. I wish she didn't have to keep commenting, but I suppose that's mothers for you.

When we got back, we found Sophie and Eddie had cooked us lunch. There was this wonderful smell of roasting coming out from the front door. They had been down the local *Spar* shop and got chicken, vegetables, stuffing, even a bottle of wine. Eddie was great company. Dad and I got him talking about cricket. There was nothing Eddie didn't seem to know about the West Indies, and it turned out his father had once been a club professional up in Lancashire.

"He's over 50 now," said Eddie, "but I still don't let him bowl at me. He's too fast, way too fast, for me." And Sophie laughed, and squeezed his hand, and Eddie gave her a peck on the cheek.

"I guess this is what it's like, being in love," said Mitch, whispering to me.

November 5th

Usually the youth club meets on a Friday, but Dad has an arrangement with a local fireman he knows to hold a display in the back garden. As it's well over an acre, there's plenty of space. Mum had had a long day at work – something to do with a pupil being excluded – so I helped out with cooking the sausages and burgers.

Ally ate most of them. He was in some big tournament over half-term, and he may be getting a place to play in some tournament in Holland next year. I told him about our holiday, and about Sophie and Eddie.

"First love's like that," he said. "When my brother, Mark, first started going out with Kylie, they only had eyes for each other."

"All fairly gross isn't it?"

"Probably happen to you sooner than you think," said Ally, mischievously. The he added, "Anyway, Kylie's now got three years. Acting as lookout for an armed robbery. Mark reckons she's got everything she deserved."

We carried on chatting for most of the evening. We were, after all, the only two boys there, apart from Mitch. There were Claire and Sian, and KT and Daisy, and another couple of younger girls I didn't know, and they were busy talking about girly things as usual. But they all seemed very glad to see me again. I promised I would come again on Friday, and I know I will. They're not a bad bunch, really.

November 9th

Dad took us through the story of the Prodigal Son tonight. He got us all to role-play and imagine what it must have been like for the father watching the younger son go off with half the family fortune. Sian wanted to know where the mother was. Claire suggested that if she had been around, she would have told him not to be such a silly boy. Everyone laughed at that point.

Then we thought about the younger brother, and Dad asked us to think what the elder brother thought of him squandering all that money. Then he got us to focus on the older brother and asked him to imagine his reaction to the younger brother turning up. I could see Dad was really getting into the part. And then I wondered if he was actually thinking about him and Uncle Paul – except Paul's the older son, of course.

At the end we all had to pray for each other's brothers and sisters. It was a bit awkward, really, with Mitch there. Daisy talked about her brother, Derek, and how hard he found it to keep the farm going. I remembered walking past there last summer, before my encounter with Barry, and for some reason I actually found myself praying out loud for him. I've never done anything like that before in my life, and I was really shy when Daisy thanked me afterwards. And then she had a little cry, and KT Lee put her arms round her, and I wondered what I'd done wrong.

"She's OK," said Mum later, "she just sometimes finds it hard to believe there are people who care for her."

November 17th

Mum had an e-mail from Professor Smith on Wednesday. Apparently dealing with *Morbury's* has been "like getting blood out of a stone." But they have agreed to call the site their Upper Drummington store. They were going to flatten the hill to make a new access road, but now they're going to leave it intact and erect a small memorial to the lost village. And they're going to draw up a new plan to the council once they've had a public meeting next month. So at least that's progress.

I went down to the bird hide today, and on the way, I looked over the fence at Prout's Farm. It had been raining hard recently, and there were large puddles in the fields. At first, I thought there was nothing there, then I saw some movement, and realised a large flock of teal and widgeon had arrived. I guess without anyone to work the land, it's an ideal habitat for wildlife.

There was another bird-watcher in the hide I knew slightly, I think he's called Mr Small. I told him about the teal and the widgeon, and he said he'd mention it at the next public meeting with *Morbury's*. Then I had an idea for a poem and tried to imagine the first people who moved into the area, and their battle against nature to work the land. I didn't spot too many birds after that; I was too busy concentrating on getting the words right.

November 22nd

We all had a bit of a disturbed night last night. Dad had come downstairs about two in the morning because he'd had an idea about an essay he was writing for his vicar training, and he heard this ruckus coming from the orchard. He guessed at once what was going on and got to the chickens just in time before the fox could do any real damage.

The chicken lady came very early this morning to see what had happened. A couple of chickens had died of shock, but as she pointed out, the real issue would be that the fox would start coming back. She and Dad eventually agreed to go half and half on an electric fence, although Mum's not happy about us paying anything towards it.

So I was rather bleary eyed today at school and didn't pay much attention to anything that was going on. Only in English, my teacher read the poem I had written at the weekend and said that she'd very much like to get it published. She even suggested putting it into the local paper to generate some publicity against the development of Upper Drummington. But I wasn't too sure about that. I remember the last time I was interviewed, and the last thing I wanted was for my photo to appear in the paper again. Barry keeps his distance nowadays, but he still makes comments about the "rich writer boy" when he gets the chance.

December 3rd

Apparently, the electric fencing has some kind of alarm on it which wakes up Miss Watson, the chicken lady, when it's been activated. She's been up at midnight twice already, but they've turned out to be false alarms. But last night was different. She was driving from Drummington Marsh when she nearly collided with a white van being driven fast in the opposite direction. She went into a ditch, and the van hit a small tree. The man driving the van got out to check the damage, and then drove on. Miss Watson was so annoyed she took down the registration number of the van and phoned the police.

The upshot was that thirty minutes later the police swooped on the van outside the church in Drummington Marsh and arrested a gang of lead thieves, caught in the act.

(The chickens, by the way, were fine.) So today PC Jones has been back round to tell Dad proudly they've worked out who stole our lead. Not that we will get any money back for it. But as Dad says, it will improve their statistics. So at least somebody's happy, then.

December 12th

Morbury's came back for their public meeting tonight. Maybe they thought a meeting on a dark, dreary night, with sleet in the wind, and frost in the fields, might put a lot of people off. If so, they were sadly mistaken. The church hall was again absolutely packed. I spotted Professor Smith at the back, and she waved at me. I shyly smiled back.

Tall George and his faithful assistant had rigged up an elaborate PowerPoint presentation to show how *Morbury's* had been listening to everyone's concerns. At the end they beamed proudly and invited anyone to ask any questions.

Mr Small stood up at once and asked about the teal and the widgeon. George turned to his assistant and his assistant turned to George. Then George turned back to him and promised they would carry out an "environmental sustainability assessment."

"Meaning what?" asked Mr Small gruffly.

"Meaning," said George, hesitantly, "we might build you a bigger bird hide, with better access."

"Not that we can make promises," said his assistant quickly.

"Not that you are trying to buy anyone off, you mean," said Mr Small. Everyone laughed, except the two men at the front. It was going to be a long, difficult evening.

At the end they left still trying to smile bravely. "Does that mean we've won?" I asked Dad.

"Not a bit of it," he replied. "If they want to build, they'll build. We're only the little people. We don't really count."

December 21st

The last day of term. As we were eating our lunch today, Ally asked me if I was looking forward to Christmas this year. I thought for a moment and said, "Yeah, I think I am."

"You don't sound too sure."

"No, it's not that. Only last year, I went along with all the Christmas stuff just because that's what I was always did. Now I want to celebrate it for myself. Does that make sense?"

"I think I know what you mean."

"You coming to the carol service again?"

"You bet. Even my Gran enjoys it."

"Well, that's what carol services are for," said a girl sitting next to us called Erin.

"Why do you say that?" I asked.

"'Cos that's who they're aimed for – good little boys and their grandmothers," she replied.

"That's why ours has the electric guitars and the drum kits," said Ally.

"And the drama," I added.

"That's just plain weird," she said, and got up.

Ally looked at me and we burst into laughter. "Some folk," he said. "They just don't get it."

When I got home, Sophie was there with Eddie. They're spending Christmas with us, and then going on to Eddie's folks. And they're still madly in love with each other. They went to Sophie's room after tea to do some studying, but all I heard across the landing was a load of giggles.

December 25th

As usual the carol service last night was brilliant, and absolutely packed. We all went to the morning service today as well, except for Sophie and Eddie who promised to cook the dinner. After the service I volunteered to go home and lay the table, 'cos I didn't want to be washing up later.

What struck me when I got in was the fact I couldn't smell any dinner. Worse still, I could hear Sophie and Eddie having an argument. I've never heard Sophie shout like that before. I wasn't sure what to do, but after a couple of minutes Eddie stormed past me, and drove off.

"Sophie?" I said.

"Go away," came a voice from the kitchen.

"OK, I'll go and tell Mum and Dad what happened."

"No, don't do that. Come here."

Sophie was in floods of tears on the kitchen stool. When she saw me, she blew her nose and tried to stop crying.

"Actually," she said, "it's far better facing you than Mum and Dad. They'd only try to make things better."

"So what happened?"

"Eddie wanted me to go to Jamaica next summer to meet his folks. I said I couldn't. He asked why and when I told him, he said that was a stupid reason. If I really loved him, I wouldn't go to South America."

"And dig latrines."

"And dig latrines. You know, for a minute I thought he was right. But then I thought of all the people who were supporting me, and all the people I'd told, and I couldn't back out, I couldn't." And Sophie began to cry again.

I didn't know what to say, so I changed the subject. "Can I help with the dinner?"

"Oh hell, is that the time? Mum and Dad will be so cross, I've only just got the turkey in. Do you know how to use a vegetable peeler?"

So Sophie and I set to work, in total silence. When Mum and Dad came back, I explained everything. Mum didn't try to make everything all right, she just gave Sophie a big hug and Sophie started crying again. Dad looked at Mum and took over helping me with the vegetables.

"What shall we do with Eddie's presents?" asked Mitch as we finally sat down for Christmas dinner.

"I'm sure there are a few charities who could use them at this time of year," replied Dad.

"Oh, Dad, you are so holy!" said Sophie, and for the first time that day she laughed.

December 31st

Ally came round to celebrate his birthday today. It's become a kind of family tradition here. I told him what had happened to Sophie.

"First love," he said. "Always ends this way."

"Suppose we'd best enjoy ourselves while we're still teenagers," I said.

"You? Enjoy yourself?" said Ally and he laughed out loud. "Sorry... it's just you've been so miserable recently." And then he thought for a moment and added, "But, I dunno, I reckon something about you's changed recently."

"I took a chance on God," I replied.

"You what?"

I was going to answer something clever, but Mum was calling us to tea. Maybe one day I'll tell him what happened. But as we all sang 'Happy Birthday' I reckoned that could wait for another time.

THE DRUMCHESTER DIARIES: VOLUME 4
KEEPING ON WITH THE GOAL
THE DIARY OF ALLY GREEN, AGED 14

January 1st

"You are coming to Harry's birthday party on Saturday, aren't you?"

"But I'm going to Dad's, and you know I have a match in the afternoon."

"You and your football. There are more important things in life than that – like your brother."

I could sense I was about to have another argument with Mum, and I knew who was going to win. I do like Harry, I do. But he's two years old, and he cries a lot, and often gets frustrated. And it's even worse for him because he can't hear a word we are saying. Carrie and Nina have this weird way of communicating with him with all kinds of secret signs, but I haven't been able to spend much time with him recently.

"OK, so when is this party?"

"It's the morning so Harry won't get too tired. And that gives you time to go to your precious football after lunch."

I rang Dad. "Happy New Year," he said laughing.

Mark came round in the evening. I could tell he wasn't happy.

"Did you get to see Kai?" asked Mum.

"What do you think?" he snapped back. "Wasn't even allowed to hand in my Christmas presents to my own son."

"Sounds like you need a beer," said George, handing him a lager.

"Think I need a solicitor," Mark replied. "Kylie's Mum is one tough bitch," at which point Mum nodded to me and I made an exit. The three of them had decided this was clearly grown-up business. I think they forget I am now fourteen. But, hey-ho, I get to go to my kid brother's birthday party. What fun that will be.

January 5th

It was only last night Mum and George remembered to tell me that George's brother, Bill, was coming down to the party. I think they know I don't get on with Bill. He's a children's entertainer and I've suffered too many Christmases being entertained at his hands. But I could see that even at this late stage there was no escape. Harry was having a party and I had to be there. I stayed up late playing Fantasy Football Manager to try and blot out the thought.

But this morning reality struck. I had to keep Carrie and Nina occupied while the lounge and dining room were being cleared. As I helped them dress Barbie for goodness knows how many times, I wondered how many others in the squad were preparing for the match like this. In the end Mum came in to get the terrible twins dressed. As I headed downstairs, I could hear George and Bill laughing about something. I hoped this was some kind of nightmare but no, this was really happening.

Then the doorbell rang. A few children from Harry's special nursery came with their parents, and they were ushered into the lounge. I wondered what they would make of Bill's performance. Eventually he entered in a bright yellow waistcoat and red shirt, and my heart sank as he pretended to slide on an invisible banana skin. But I have to say he was really, really good with the little ones. He made eye contact with every single one of them. Even Harry laughed when he did his special balloon trick. I hadn't heard Harry laugh like that before.

Mum was merciful and let me escape before the hordes attacked the party food. Just as well, because I wanted to get to the training ground in good time and make sure I was properly prepared for the match. I really wanted to get into the team for Bristol in a couple of weeks' time. If I make that team, who knows? I could make the under-15s in September, and possibly even an apprenticeship. That would show Mum just how serious I am about this football business.

When I arrived the weather wasn't too bad. But I could kind of sense it was going to take a turn for the worse. When you spend most Saturdays out on a football pitch you start to learn about what the weather's going to do. I know Alex has got this fancy weather forecasting kit, but all you need to do is to see how the clouds are moving.

Sure enough, by the time kick-off took place the wind was really getting up. In the first half it was all I could do to get the ball up to the halfway line. In the second I struggled to make sure my goal kicks stayed in play. And of course nobody plays well in this kind of weather. We ground out a scrappy 1-1 draw. I don't think I was at fault for the goal. You can't save a deflected free-kick that is suddenly blown towards the far corner. But had I done enough to get to Bristol? I think so, but I will only know in a couple of days' time.

January 11th

I needn't have worried. I am in the team.

At youth club tonight, Alex's Dad, Joe, asked us all what our hopes and ambitions were for the coming year. It's not my fault I was the first to answer. Everyone else had fallen silent and I felt I just had to say something. But when I spoke, Claire whispered something in Sian's ear and they both giggled, in the way girls always do.

"Did I say something funny?" I asked crossly.

"No… it's just you and your football," she replied. "Don't you think of anything else?"

I shrugged my shoulders. I didn't like being put on the spot like that. I was trying to think what to reply when Joe turned to her and asked, "So what are your hopes for the coming year?" Then she started talking about exams, and college, and stuff like that, and no-one giggled when she spoke. Yeah, I know school is important. But you've got to think beyond that. At least that's my opinion.

After that, the group carried on chatting for a bit, and then Joe challenged us to pray about our plans for the coming year. Funny that. I'd never really connected praying with my football career. I guess I reckoned it would just happen. But perhaps Joe's right. Perhaps I do need to pray a bit more about it.

I was still thinking about all this when Dad came to pick up me. On the way home I asked him what he hoped for in the coming year. "To find another job," he said grimly. It turns out Marvin came into the store today and told him his job was going down to three days a week. But as Dad said, you can't really blame him. Very few people in Drummington-on-Sea seem to want discount furniture any more, and he knows what it's like having a shop going bust.

January 19th

The big game today – up in Bristol. We had to arrive at the *Octopus and Trumpet* by nine for the long coach trip up the motorway. Fortunately George had to pick up a car from a customer nearby, so he was able to drop me off. As usual, someone else was late, and as he was the captain, we couldn't really go without him. So at about quarter past, after we'd loaded all the kit into the bus, we began to set off in the rain.

The ground in Bristol seemed to be tucked somewhere behind an industrial estate. There were stray bits of plastic blowing across the pitch, and on the far side, an ugly bunch of brambles were sprouting over the top of the terraces. Even before we reached the changing rooms, we knew they weren't going to be that pleasant.

Fortunately we had arrived early which meant we had time to warm up properly for the game. Mum says I'm going to be six foot by the end of the year, and after sitting on that coach for all that time I needed time to stretch and bend properly. Lee had come along to do some work with me before the game, and as we caught the first glimpse of our opponents, I could see why. They looked really up for it, and they all appeared to be a couple of inches taller than us.

But I know I've been playing well recently, and I was determined to show just how good I can be. Within the first quarter of an hour I made a couple of decent saves. We weren't getting much of the ball, but the defenders were playing a blinder. We might be in for a long hard afternoon, but we were prepared to stand our ground.

Then disaster struck. Their centre-forward unleashed a stinging shot almost straight at me. I thought I had got my body behind it, but somehow the ball squirmed out of my grasp. It spun and trickled away slowly along the muddy surface, and towards the post. Instantly a great scrum of players converged on the ball. I wanted to throw myself on it, but I couldn't get through the sea of legs. In the end someone managed to squeeze it over the line. We were 1-0 down. I was gutted.

It took a few minutes to calm down after that, but once I had cut out a couple of dangerous crosses, I began to regain my confidence. By the end of the first half I reckoned I was the one keeping us still in the game.

At half-time Lee told me to stay focused, and not to dwell on my mistakes. We began to play with more belief after the break, but we didn't create too many clear chances, and the other team took less risks. When the final whistle blew, the score was still "1-0 – goalkeeping mistake by Ally Green." Fortunately there weren't any reporters there to record my blunder.

Alex asked me at my birthday party a few weeks back why I was so keen to become a goalkeeper. It used to be because no-one else wanted to play in that position and I enjoyed it. But recently, I've realised it's probably the one thing I'm good at. I can't write like Alex or do maths like Dave, but put me between the sticks, and I can (usually) do a decent job. That's why I'm hoping I can make it into the academy next year. I'm not sure what I'd do if I didn't make it. Failure, though, isn't part of my plan.

On the way home, I had a text from Mark who'd gone up to London to see his mother. Or perhaps more accurately, watch his beloved Charlton Athletic and possibly fit in a visit home.

Great result for us today! Drumchester City – ha, ha, ha! Actually I already knew the result. We'd lost 5-0 away, but as Lee pointed out, what did you expect when you'd just sold your two best defenders? There are all kinds of rumours going round that the club is in trouble. Our left-back, Anthony, has a brother who's a first-year professional, and he reckons his wages were only paid yesterday.

But I'm sure there will still be an academy in September and I'm definitely going to be part of it. Or at least I am praying I will be.

January 26th

Mark rang me this morning and asked if I would like to go and see Drumchester City today. He sounded unusually cheerful. When I met him outside the ground, I found out why, as he introduced me to his new girlfriend, Olivia. She certainly is a lot prettier and a lot less made-up than Kylie. And she's as mad about football as he is. She was actually wearing a Drumchester City shirt. OK, it was last season's strip, but anyone who wears the shirt is fine by me.

Usually by kick-off the ground would be heaving and there would be chants going all round the ground. But the atmosphere today was oddly quiet and there was a whole row of empty seats in the Shed End. Apparently, the board have put out a statement that they are looking for new owners, and someone reckons the manager's said he'd resign if he didn't get any more players. Someone else though reckons the manager's going to be sacked soon anyway because the club can't afford him.

Whatever the rumours, you could see the players were nervous. There was a new player at the back, who I'd never heard of. He didn't look a lot older than me, but apparently was the star of some Championship academy side. He didn't do badly but he clearly had only just met up with his team-mates. It was no surprise that we went in 1-0 down. We weren't able to string more than two or three passes together.

At half-time Olivia bought me a pasty, and we chatted a bit. It turns out her Dad works in the club shop, and he got paid late last month. So what Anthony said about the club was true, then. We really are in a mess. At least on the pitch we improved second half, and when the opposition defender stupidly decided to push the referee over, we even had an extra man. In the end two late goals sealed it, and somehow City lurched away from the relegation zone, with a 2-1 win. As Mark says, it's not how you get the three points that matters.

I would usually have gone back to Dad's after the match, but he is driving his taxi all weekend, to try and make ends meet. Still, I was hoping to escape the little terrors by going over to Phil's later on. But Mum spoiled all that by asking if I was planning to do any work for the exams next week. The exams! I'd completely forgotten. So instead I have spent a wonderful Saturday evening revising. Or truth be told, learning some of the stuff I should have picked up ages ago. I do try my best at school. Only I find it hard to get excited about it sometimes.

January 28th

Last exam today! I don't think actually I've done too badly, apart from in RE which I hate, and in science where I've always struggled.

George was home when I arrived which surprised me. Usually I have an hour or so to chill out before Mum comes back with Harry, and Carrie and Nina are dropped off by the childminder. And then it's all systems go as we deal with three, tired, tantrumming children who have to be fed, washed and put to bed. George often doesn't come back until half six or later, depending on just how much needs to be done at the garage. He claims it's because he has so much paperwork to do. I wonder if he's just making excuses.

But today George is home early. "Got a surprise for you," he said. "Heard of a gym that was going bust. So I got myself busy over the weekend."

"What do you mean?" I knew that whenever George smiled like that, he had something up his sleeve. It was the time he most looked like his brother Bill.

George led me out to the garage. "I've had to do a bit of negotiating with your Mum," he said. "I'm going to have to pave over the front garden to get all the cars in, now. But I think you'll agree it'll be worth it."

And he lifted up the garage door. Usually the garage is a mess of toys, gardening stuff and bicycles. But all that had miraculously been tidied to one corner. And in the middle hanging from the main beam was a punchbag, with two sets of gloves on an old workbench. "A kind of late Christmas present, so to speak. I know they're always going on at you about having more upper body strength."

George isn't my Dad, and I don't even think of him really as Mum's husband. But he can be a good friend at times. "Thanks," I said.

"OK, let's show you how to use this thing," he said, putting on a pair of gloves. "Wouldn't do you much good breaking a knuckle, would it?"

I never knew there was a proper way to punch before. I didn't even know George knew anything about boxing. Turns out his Dad used to run a boys' club in Peckham, and the lads there certainly weren't into stamp collecting.

We spent a happy half an hour in the garage and just as my arms were beginning to ache, we heard Mum's car pull up. As she got Harry out of the car seat, he saw George with his gloves on and began to cry.

I won't say what happened in the next couple of hours, except that the more George tried to help, the more he seemed to get in the way. I reckon he won't be coming home early again anytime soon.

February 1st

It seems that somehow or other I have managed to scrape a pass mark in all my exams, except RE. I even somehow managed to get an A in French, not that I've ever been to France, or taken that much interest in the subject. Of course, Alex came top of the year in that subject, but it's not that surprising considering his mother is a French teacher.

Alex told me at lunch that my Dad had been round to see his father last night. I guess that means Dad is getting really worried about money again. Last weekend his taxi broke down and I know he really needs a new vehicle. For a moment I thought about telling George 'cos he knows everything there is to know about cars. But there's no way George and Dad would ever do business with each other.

I asked for prayer for Dad at youth group tonight. It turns out I'm not only the one worried about their father. There's a girl there called Daisy, pretty but a bit wet. Her father keeps going in and out of hospital, not quite sure what the matter is, and her brother is struggling to keep the farm going. As so often happens, she was quite tearful, and KT Lee was mopping her up. I could also tell Mitch and Alex had just had a blazing row, so it wasn't a happy evening all round.

February 7th

Last year we heard about a big football tournament in Holland this Easter. But with all the uncertainty at the club it had gone a bit quiet recently. The players were paid late again this month, apparently. At training tonight, though, we were told someone has come forward to sponsor our trip so it's definitely on. That might explain why we trained quite as hard and as long tonight. Everyone wanted to show just how fit and keen they were. By the end I was exhausted.

By the time I got home, it was nearly ten o'clock. It turned out I had just missed

Mark who had come round for the evening with Olivia. As far as I know, Mum and George never met Kylie. But it's clear Olivia's something different. They were still talking about her when I got in.

"He could finally have found the right one," said George, and Mum seemed to agree.

"Even if she is daft on football."

"Well, you can't have everything," said George, and they both began to laugh.

February 11th

We're supposed to be coming in for training all half-term, but yesterday it began to rain. A little drizzle, at first, just as I was coming out of church with Dad. Then slightly harder as we went round to lunch with Trevor Lee, KT's Dad. Then harder still as Dad started on his evening taxi round. By the time I got to bed, it was the proverbial cats and dogs. And according to the weather forecast this weather was going to go on all week.

I was woken up this morning by a loud knocking on the door. Dad, still bleary-eyed from his night shift got up to answer it. It was the landlord with a couple of sand bags. Apparently, the drains further up the road were filling up fast, and he wanted to make sure we were ready for any events.

"That's grand," said Dad, after the landlord left. "I notice he didn't offer to help us move any of our stuff upstairs."

"So what do we do now?"

"Turn on the local news and see what's happening."

I didn't really think it was that dramatic, but it turned out the railway line was flooded at Drummington Marsh and the main road up to Drumchester was blocked by a falling tree. "I'm not going to get to my training, am I?" I said.

"Doubt there'd be anything on in this weather, in any event," said Dad.

We were about to get dressed, when we suddenly saw a small trickle of water run down the wall into the small courtyard that fronted the basement. Within about a minute, this trickle had turned into a torrent.

"Oh hell," said Dad, as this wave of water burst through under the front door and rushed through the apartment. I say water but it was this funny brown colour, and it didn't smell too good. Soon we were wading in the stuff.

"Put some clothes on and get out onto the street," yelled Dad.

I did as I was told, even though my bedroom too was starting to fill up.

Out on the street, we found a whole knot of neighbours huddling together under umbrellas. There was only about a foot or so of water on the main road, but that wasn't too surprising, as the basements along the side of the street had become the main drain. Someone had called the fire brigade, and soon three engines came screeching to a halt in the road. It was amazing how quickly they got their pumps working. But it was little consolation for Dad who was busy talking to the insurance company. I noticed how strained and worried he was looking, and I thought about how ill he had been a few years back.

Trevor Lee turned up a bit later, in the most enormous pair of waders I'd ever seen. Although his house was only a couple of streets away, they didn't have basements, and the drains there were clear. Trevor put a friendly arm round Dad and said, "You better stay with me for the time being. I might even find you some clothes that fit." Then he said to me, "You better go home to your mother."

"What about my stuff?" I said.

"Sorry, son, that's all gone."

"But it's my football kit, and my clothes, and everything."

"That's why you have insurance companies."

I couldn't really take it in. One moment it was an ordinary Monday morning, and I was looking forward to football training. The next our flat was full of water, and everything was ruined. At least I had another home to go to. Or at least if only I could find a way of getting there. I rang Mum who was at work.

"It does happen to your Dad, doesn't it?" She told me to wait with Trevor until the main road or railway line was clear, and then to make my way back. I wanted to tell her about all the stuff I'd lost but another customer had just come into the shop, and she said she had to hang up. As if selling a mobile phone was more important than helping out her son.

So no matter what Trevor said, I decided to stay with Dad that day. We huddled under Trevor's enormous umbrella as some of the firemen began to pump the water out of the basement. Further up the road the rest of the team were unblocking the storm drain, which was just as well, as the rain was still sheeting down. A neighbour Dad knew slightly brought us a flask of hot tea, and invited us in. We decided to stay put, as we were already soaking wet. But the tea was good – I think she might even have put some whisky in it.

In a while the landlord turned up. "Best get your stuff shifted," he said, "so we can see what damage there's been."

"Not of course that you want Pete out of the way or anything like that," growled Trevor.

"No, of course not," said the landlord and he scuttled away again.

Eventually one of the firemen came over to us and said it was OK to enter the flat, so long as we didn't touch the electrics, and did we have any boots? Trevor told us to hang on a moment, and he made some phone calls. "Right, all sorted," he said. "Two lads coming from the depot with a van in about an hour, with some wellies. Not much you can do now. Best come to my place and wait in the dry."

Truth be told, by now we were both shivering and starving. Mum texted me to find out where I was. I ignored her. Trevor asked KT to fry us both some eggs and bacon, and we sat in the lounge eating a huge pile of butties and warming up in front of the fire. We were just about dry when Trevor's workmates turned up, not just with wellies, but with overalls and gloves as well.

And we needed them. Up to about a couple of feet inside the flat there was a foul smell sludge covering everything. And I mean everything. The football kit I had left under the bed. The mattress on the bed. The pile of DVDs in the cupboard. Dad and I were both completely stunned, and in the end Trevor and the crew just worked round us.

"Right, lads, anything above waist high get into the van. Anything below waist high will go into the skip."

"What skip?" asked Dad.

"The one that's arriving this afternoon," said Trevor grinning. "All part of the service."

Actually, there wasn't much that could go into the van. Some pots and pans from the kitchen, a few clothes, one bathroom cabinet and some odd ornaments. Dad didn't really have that much in the first place. The only good thing was that he was able to salvage all his family albums and coin collection which he kept high up in the wardrobe.

"At least I'll be able to tell Gran that's safe," he said smiling weakly.

"So where are you going to stay?" I asked as we left the flat.

"The insurance company said they'd put me up in a hotel for a couple of weeks."

"Looks like this'll take more than a couple of weeks."

"I know, son," he said, "But let's take it one step at a time."

The next step was to get back to Trevor's to get showered and changed. I felt awkward being there with KT around, so I turned on the local news to see if I could get home. Actually, if anything, the situation was only getting worse. The railway line was fast disappearing under the flood water, and the fallen tree on the main road now looked as if it was floating in a lake. Somewhere between the two the little village of Drummington Marsh looked more like an island than part of the mainland.

This time Mum rang and demanded to know where I was. I told her to look at the local news. She said if I had come home when she said there wouldn't be this problem. I said that wasn't fair. Actually I shouted, and then I realised KT was looking at me, and I felt all embarrassed. Mum hung up at that point, and I suddenly wished I didn't have to go home to her. But I did.

In the end Trevor said, "There's always the back road up to Dumpley Common. You might be able to get back that way."

And Dad said, "Well, at least I've still got my taxi stored up in Steve's garage. Come on, son, let's see how far we get. After all, I can't sit around waiting. I have to do something."

So now I am home, after a long, slow journey with all the other traffic using the back road, splashing through enormous puddles and reversing every time we met someone coming the other way. Mum was still at work when I got in through the front door, so why did it matter to her quite so much where I was?

February 17th

I haven't been speaking much to Mum this week, except when dealing with the kids. But we had another argument. I really wanted to get to church this morning. But George was helping a friend because his van had broken down, and Mum said she couldn't possibly spare the time to take me. Then she said she couldn't see why church wasn't that important anyway. I bit my tongue at that point, and went over to the garage. After about half an hour with the punchbag I felt calm enough to phone John and explain the problem. It turns out he knows a family in Drumchester who come to church, and soon it was arranged they could pick me up.

The road down to Drumley Green was very different from when I last went down it. There were huge piles of mud in the fields on either side of the road, and the road surface was still muddy red-brown. Near Drummington Marsh one half of the road was still cordoned off where the tree had fallen down, and a bit further on a tumbled down wall was all coned off. Just outside Drumley Green there was a car stuck in the ditch, all covered in police tape. The children in the car found it all very exciting.

Dad stood up in the service that morning and thanked everyone for their help. He said he was a bit embarrassed everyone in the church now knew his measurements, but was so grateful for all the clothes that fitted. He also added that the meals he had been given were a considerable improvement on the dishes at the *Swan Hotel*. Everyone laughed at this point, and then John and one of the elders prayed with him.

I must confess I hadn't really been that bothered recently about coming to church, but that day I kind of realised just how important it was. At the end of the service KT and Daisy came up to me and asked how I was doing. I told them how the club had found some spare kit for me, and I'd only missed a couple of days' training. Alex came over and asked how things were with the insurance company. Well, I guess that comes from having an accountant for a father. I knew he meant well.

We were about to go off to Joe and Sarah's for lunch when an older member of the congregation called Len came up to Dad and said, "You know, what you said got me thinking. I don't really use the upstairs now that Marjorie has died. My son uses the box room when he visits, but that still leaves two bedrooms and a bathroom free. You'd have to share the kitchen, though, but that would be all right, wouldn't it? I could certainly use the odd bit of company, and if you know anything about gardening, well, I dare say, a helping hand wouldn't come amiss."

I could see at that point Dad was struggling not to cry. As he said later, the shock of the week was finally coming home to him. "That would be grand," he said. "So long as Ally can come to stay sometimes?"

"The more the merrier," said Len, and then turning to me with a stern expression that turned into a grin, "but no wild parties mind."

February 21st
It's not been a good couple of weeks. I got a detention in RE for failing to do my homework. I pointed out I couldn't as I didn't believe all paths led to God. My RE teacher said that I should have written something to that effect and praised Alex for his erudite and worthy exposition of the same argument. I merely shrugged my shoulders. I'm giving up the subject in a few months, so why should I care? Unfortunately the RE teacher didn't share my point of view.

So a tedious, wasted hour before a mad rush to help Mum get the kids' teas and then out to football training. Only, when I arrived, I discovered I wasn't the only goalkeeper there. This huge Nigerian lad called Ade was there, and it soon turned out he was good, really good. Apparently, he had turned up on the Monday I couldn't be there. His father has just become the pastor of some Pentecostal church or other that's recently opened in

Drumchester. So on the one hand, I now know there's another committed Christian in the team. On the other, he's aiming to take my place. I remembered what Joe said about praying about your hopes and ambitions. But it didn't seem to make it any easier.

March 2nd

The final game before the Holland squad was announced. I found myself in the first half on the bench. I don't like being a substitute at the best of times and as I watched Ade making save after save, I was getting more and more uncomfortable. His kicking wasn't as good as mine though, and the opposition nearly scored when one of his clearances landed straight at the forward's feet. But he soon made up for that with a flying save to tip the shot over the bar.

I spent half-time trying to warm up and make myself comfortable and relaxed for the second half. But it wasn't easy coming on especially as almost immediately Anthony conceded a penalty. I went the right way, but the ball went straight in the corner, and we were 1-0 down. Soon after that, it got even worse when I came out to collect a cross and was bundled out of the way by a flying forward. I was sure it was a foul, but the ref gave the goal.

From that point on I reckoned I had nothing to lose. And for the next forty minutes I know I played a blinder. We got it back to 2-1 and hit the post with almost the last kick of the match. But we lost. And I think I know who's going to Holland.

I told all this to Dad as he came to pick me up from the match. (The railway line is still out of action and will be for a couple of weeks, apparently.) "They'd still be daft to leave you at home," he said. That's what I like about Dad. He still believes in you even when everything is going pear-shaped. I know I shouldn't but it's hard not to see the difference in his attitude from Mum's.

Trevor, it turned out, had helped Dad move in today. With Len's permission they had cleared the second bedroom and kitted it out with furniture Marvin had donated. "Not that anyone is buying it anyway," said Dad grimly. "So with both our futures up in the air, and the rain still falling, let's celebrate."

At this point Len knocked on the door and we came downstairs to this most amazing Lancashire hotpot. Apparently, Len learnt to cook when on National Service, and spent most of his life running a *Little Chef*. Not that anything I've ever eaten at *Little Chef* ever tasted that good. Len and Dad watched in amazement as I ate plate after plate of it. I reckon they've never realised just how many calories a professional sportsman needs. If I am going to be a professional sportsman, that is.

March 7th

Lee had a private word with me before training started tonight. But I didn't need him to tell me. I wasn't going to be in the team. He said I could still possibly make it into the under-15s, but that would depend on finances. He also said he had a mate at Bristol Rovers on the look-out for another young keeper. I thanked him. But seriously, Bristol Rovers!?

I told Anthony what had happened, and he just said, "That's really tough, bro. Cos I reckon you're the best, no s***."

"But you can't get me on the ferry to Holland."

"Still think they made a big mistake. I mean, if Ade's so great, how come he's at little old Drumchester City?" A fair point, but it didn't exactly help me.

So I've been praying a lot tonight. Maybe God doesn't want me to be a footballer. Or maybe he does but not at Drumchester City. So what do I do now? One thing I wasn't going to do was tell Mum the whole story. It wasn't a lie, after all, to say I hadn't been selected for Holland. And as I suspected her only reaction was relief as she didn't have to pay out anything for the ferry.

March 15th

I did tell the whole story at youth club, tonight. I would have done last week, but Daisy's Dad had been admitted to a hospital somewhere up the line, and for once even I could see there were some things more important than football. But this evening Joe was teaching us about prayer. We were looking at the story of the persistent widow, and he was asking us what we could learn from the story. Alex said something he thought was clever about judges and even from the other side of the room I could see Mitch squirming with embarrassment.

Daisy talked about praying for her Dad, and Sian mentioned something about her grandmother who was poorly. As the circle came round to me, I hesitated to know quite what to say. Then somehow it all came out. How I really, really wanted to be a goalkeeper. How I thought it was going to happen. And now it might not possibly or probably happen.

Joe unwrapped a mint at this point as he always did when he was thinking. Then he said, "Well, one way or another God has given you a gift. You might end up playing professionally. You might end up teaching. But one way or another you'll find out how to use it in the end. You've just got to hang on in there. Just like I had to wait years until I finally discovered God wanted me to train as a vicar. Yes, I know when you're fourteen two weeks seems like an eternity. But it isn't. Not really."

I know he was trying to be helpful, but at the precise moment I felt like he was patting me on the head. I don't want to wait. I want to find out now. And I don't think the answer to my prayers is Bristol Rovers. At least I hope it isn't.

March 21st

Lee's mate from Bristol Rovers turned up tonight. Apparently, he was really impressed by what he saw. Who needs to go to Holland, when you're offered an all-expenses paid trip to Bristol after Easter? I do, actually. But if this is an answer to prayer, I'm going to take it. Even if Mum was planning for us to do something altogether as a family that week.

At least my end of term report has made her happy. Everyone seems to have noticed my improved attitude to work over the past couple of weeks. She thinks I've started to realise that football's not everything. Me, I'm just trying to find a plan B.

March 27th

Mark and Olivia came round again this evening. Apparently, there's a big court hearing coming up about Kai. They've seen the solicitor who asked who was going to look after Kai during the day. At this point Mark explained that as Olivia worked in a nursery that wasn't going to be problem. Olivia could look after Kai during the day, and Mark could look after him after work.

"So," said Mark, "according to the solicitor it looks like we could have a good chance of winning, after all." And at that point he beamed at Olivia and she gave him a kiss. Terribly soppy, but you could understand it.

"They really are a couple, aren't they?" said George as we did the washing up later. And I could sort of see what he meant. During supper Mark seemed to know what Olivia was about to say, and Olivia could guess what Mark was thinking. It was never like that with Mark and Kylie. Kylie was Mark's girlfriend, that's all.

"They'd be great parents for Kai," I replied.

"And that'd make you his uncle," said George. "Well, sort of."

An uncle at fourteen!? I knew some of my schoolfriends were uncles and aunts, but me?

At this point we heard Carrie and Nina out of bed, and it was time to put my uncling skills to the test. By the time we got downstairs again, Mark and Olivia were about to go, but not before Olivia said with a smile, "Good luck with Bristol. Traitor!" It really is hard not to like her. And when she smiles like that, she is drop-dead gorgeous. Not, of course, that I'd tell that to Mark. I think he knows already.

April 5th

It's been an exhausting but brilliant week. It all started on Saturday night when John decked out the church in all these candles and we had some kind of vigil for Easter Sunday. That basically meant the youth group got locked in with him and we spent half the night singing and praying. It was a very special experience. Then a fabulous Easter service, and a quick bite of lunch at Len's before Dad drove me up to Bristol (the club paid the taxi fare apparently). I must confess I nodded off somewhere on the way.

Since then it's been a week of hard, gruelling training. Bristol Rovers under-15s already have a goalkeeper, called Ben. He's about three inches shorter than me, spotty and has a fearsome crew-cut. Just as soon as he's able he's going to have a full tattoo body suit, or so he claims. He may be hard, but he has this habit of dropping the ball at the wrong moments. Of course, the rest of the team are all on Ben's side, and I haven't tried to make too many friends with them. I know what it must have been like when Ade came into our team. I've just kept my head down, done what I've been told, avoided getting into any arguments, even if it's taken one or two prayers to keep my mouth shut.

And today we had our big training match, Ben on one side, and me on the other. My team won 4-0, and at the end of the match even some of my team-mates came and gave me high fives. Ben just marched up to me and said, "You better watch out if you ever come here."

I looked down at him and said, "So had you," and I marched off to the changing rooms, where I was pushed into a celebratory cold shower. I think I could like this crowd.

Dad came to pick me up at five as arranged. "Did you have a good time?" he asked.

I nodded and was about to say something else when I kind of realised there was something wrong. "What's up?"

"Marvin's shutting up shop at the end of the month. He said he tried to keep it going as long as he could after I was flooded out. But he's got to keep his own roof over his head. Believe me, I know all about that."

"So what will you do?" I asked as we turned onto the motorway.

"Marvin asked if I would work in the restaurant he's opening up with his sister in Drumchester. He said there were always dishes to clean, and floors to scrub. But I'm not ready to be a cleaner. Not yet."

We were silent for a long time as we passed through the Somerset levels. It was only as we were nearly home, I suddenly remembered it was Alex's birthday tomorrow and I hadn't got him anything. Worse than that, I think he'd invited me out for a meal, or something like that, and I hadn't replied. Well, all that would have to wait for tomorrow. I was shattered and Dad needed cheering up. There was only one thing for it – a big *KFC* bucket in front of his favourite spy film. By the end, he was happy, and I was ready for bed.

April 7th

What was it John said a few weeks back? Something like "God moves in mysterious ways?" Well, I think somehow or other prayers have been answered. Lee rang me this afternoon which was strange in itself. I was expecting a phone call from Bristol Rovers, not Drumchester City. But it turned out Ade hadn't been let back into the country. Something about a forged visa or a dodgy passport – Lee wasn't quite sure. But one way or another Ade is not coming back. And then the question I'd been waiting for: "So would you like to join up with Drumchester City next year?"

I was very tempted to ask, "So you think I'm good enough, then?" but I managed to bite my tongue just in time. I'm going to join up with Drumchester City next year and I'm going to show them I'm good enough.

"Bro, you haven't got nothing to prove," said Anthony when I rang him and a few of the other lads. But I want to make sure there's no doubt. None whatsoever.

April 19th

Trevor Lee's band, *The Potential*, had fixed up a gig in Drumchester tonight. Something to do with raising money for Sophie's trip to South America this summer. Sophie's brother, Alex, couldn't be persuaded to come along. But then he's always been funny about music. So I invited along Phil and a few other mates from school.

I'm not sure it was a good idea. I think they came thinking they could down a few bevies, and they were disappointed there was no booze on offer. I told them to argue with Trevor if they had problems with that. Then they turned their attention to KT and the other girls from church. When they persisted in making a nuisance of themselves,

KT told them Trevor was her Dad. From that point on they sulked in a corner, drinking lemonade and *Coke*, trying to look cool. I think one or two of them were about to go home, when the band began to play.

Despite the fact they were still trying to look cool, one by one they began to join in. Then when the music stopped, they went back to sulking in a corner, as if they weren't enjoying themselves. I went over and asked if they had a good time.

"Was all right, I s'pose," mumbled one.

"Yeah, it was OK," said another.

Then an awkward silence until Phil said, "I know how to get hold of a crate of lager." Then they all cheered and rushed out of the door.

April 27th

The last match in Drumchester City's unbelievably average season. I see I haven't written much about them recently, but there's been little to say. They crawled to mid-table mediocrity about a couple of matches ago, mostly because the teams below them are even worse and have even greater money problems.

I met up with Anthony and Darren, our very own pocket-sized midfield dynamo, as the pundits would call him. Anthony reckons there's some big foreign guy coming to take charge in the summer. Darren's heard the chairman is going to stump up some more money. But one way or another, it's clear the team needs some investment.

On the plus side there's this young second-year apprentice who's recently broken into the team. He scored a hat-trick today as against all expectations we won 3-1.

"That's another one off in the summer," said Darren gloomily as the final whistle went.

We milled out of the ground deep in discussion about the club's future, when I quite literally bumped into Olivia. "Hearing's on Wednesday," she whispered to me.

"Will be praying," I whispered back.

As she disappeared back into the crowd Anthony leant over and asked, "Who is that hot chick?"

"My brother's girlfriend," I replied quickly.

"Oh," he said. "You getting some pizza?"

April 24th

Mark and Olivia were at home when I got back from school. I didn't need to ask them how the hearing had gone. They were both beaming from ear to ear.

"Mind you," said Mark, "I'm glad above all for Kai. The first thing that happened today was Kylie's Mum standing up in court and swearing at me. Her solicitor was so embarrassed."

We chatted for a bit longer and then Mum came in with Harry. Harry hadn't seen Olivia before and went all shy. But within five minutes Olivia had him rolling around on the floor and giggling, and she made some funny signs which made him laugh. Then Carrie and Nina were dropped off, and while Mum went to sort Harry out, Olivia got them both reading books.

"You don't fancy a job here?" said Mum as she went into the kitchen to sort out the kids' teas.

"She's already spoken for," replied Mark.

Later on after the mayhem of tea, and when George had decided it was safe to come home, the five of us talked over dinner about the next stage. Kai was coming to Mark's on Saturday, but according to the social worker he had nothing, really, only the clothes he was dressed in. I couldn't imagine a kid growing up like that. It was the sort of thing you heard about on the news, but I never knew it happened here.

So Mum went off with Olivia to sort out Harry's hand me downs, and any spare toys they could find. George talked over with Mark how many hours he could get off work in the next few weeks. And I sat there, praying, wondering what I could do to help. After all, if I was a sort of uncle, I ought to do something, shouldn't I?

April 28th

I rang Mark just before going to church this morning. Kai had arrived about ten o'clock yesterday. He spent the first couple of hours just holding on to the tiny teddy that had come with him. Olivia had to show him how to play with the toys, but he was still very nervous about reaching out and touching any of them.

"I don't know a lot about nine-month-old boys," said Mark, "but something seems very, very wrong."

"We'll be praying for you this morning," I said.

"Thanks," said Mark. "I'm not a believer, myself, but we're going to need all the help we can get at the moment," and at that point I could hear Kai starting to wail. "Got to go," said Mark. "None of us got a lot of sleep last night."

"The poor mite," said KT as I told her and the rest of the group after the service. "I can't imagine what it must be like growing up like that."

"I can," said her usually silent half-brother Lee, who nearly always spent coffee time on his own reading and re-reading the noticeboard, but for some reason was standing nearby.

It may not have been the best thing to do, but at that point everyone turned to him. After all, for most of us it was the first time we'd ever heard him actually speak, except when someone asked him a question or Trevor was telling him off.

"Yes, I can," said Lee, looking at the floorboards and nervously fiddling with a piece of loose skin on his finger. "Put in front of the TV all day, told to shut up, keep still, eat your tea, or else." He might have said something else but none of us could make it out and he went back over to the noticeboards to read whatever he reads each Sunday.

KT wondered if she ought to go over and say something to him, but in the way girls do, Daisy gave her a hug, and they went over to a corner together, probably to have a little cry. I was waiting for Alex to say something crashingly inappropriate, but for once he just shook his head, and went off to find his Dad.

May 11th

The end of Dad's first full week looking for work. It hasn't gone well. He reckons the only jobs going in Drummington-on-Sea are at *Asco's* and as he said himself, he's hardly likely to start working for the company that made him go bust in the first place. Of course, he's still got his taxi, but he reckons it's not going to pass its MOT at the end of the month. Len says he's perfectly happy for Dad to stay as long as he wants but his son keeps mentioning something about the rent.

"All in all, Ally," Dad said, "I'm not sure where I'm going from here."

I didn't know what to say. I finished my pasty as soon as I could because I'd promised to meet with Anthony and Darren, and a few of the others in town, to celebrate the end of the season. But as I was going out the door, I wondered perhaps if I should stay with Dad, and do something with him.

"No, it's fine, son," he said in the sort of way adults do when it isn't really. "Honestly," when I hesitated, "now clear off."

So I cleared off and went on down to the station to catch a train on the newly reopened line. Only the afternoon wasn't as much of a laugh as I thought it would be. Anthony got stopped in one shop because they thought he was nicking a deodorant; Darren was caught out trying to buy a can of cider in another. Then they wanted to look for a new mobile phone and I realised they were heading straight for the shop where my Mum worked. They couldn't see the problem with the manager's son steaming in with his gang of mates. In the end I left them hanging around outside *KFC* chatting up the girls.

"Had a good time?" asked Dad when I got in.

"Yeah," and then I realised I was saying it in the sort of way adults do when it isn't really.

May 22nd

Big story on the evening news tonight. Drumchester City has been taken over by some local businessman no-one's ever heard of who's apparently made a fortune from computer software. He was interviewed wearing a supporter's scarf over his business suit and was talking about "equity partners" and "debt consolidation" and "injection of capital," none of which I really understood. Then they began to interview the manager, but I never found out what he was going to say. Because at that moment Nina came in to show me a picture she'd drawn, and Harry, who should have been in bed, appeared with his favourite book of stories. When I tried to explain I was watching television, Mum just shouted from the kitchen for me to turn it off. She was busy helping Carrie decorate some biscuits, apparently. While I was arguing with Mum, Nina turned the television off herself, and then made some signs to Harry and they both started laughing at me.

I shouldn't have lost my temper. I shouldn't. But I couldn't help it. I screwed up Nina's picture, threw Harry's book to the floor and stormed up to my bedroom. At that moment I couldn't care less about the riot that was taking place downstairs. I put on my headphones and started playing Fantasy Football Manager, where the only problem was how to win the next match.

It was exactly eight minutes and forty seconds later that Mum came in to see me. She told me to go and apologise at once. I said it wasn't fair I had to look after the children every night. She told me that's just what it's like being the older brother.

"There's always George," I said. "He could help."

"In case you hadn't noticed, he's working every hour he can to help pay for you."

"Maybe he's just trying to escape the noise round here."

At that point Mum really lost it and told me either to put up with the rules of the house or get out.

So I got out. I rang my Dad, packed my bag and found my way down to the station. While I was waiting for the train, the phone rang. It was George. I ignored it. The phone rang again. At that point the train arrived.

"This isn't a good moment," I said, as I got on board.

"We need to talk," George said. "But let's give it a couple of days till you and your Mum have calmed down."

May 25th

Last night Dad dropped me off early at the youth club, and I had a long chat with Joe beforehand. As Dad pointed out, Joe's training to be a vicar so it will be good experience for him listening to my problems.

"So you're going to see your Mum tomorrow?" he asked, as he handed me a can of *Coke*.

I nodded. "I expect you want me to say sorry?"

"What I want you to do is beside the point," he replied, as he poured himself a beer.

"I haven't met your Mum, Nicky, have I?"

"You're not going to either."

"What do you mean by that?"

So I told him about Mum, how she didn't think I was being serious about becoming a professional and didn't understand why I would want to pray and all that stuff. Then I told him a bit about George and the children.

I was kind of used to Joe speaking a lot, 'cos that's what he does mostly at youth club, but all the time he just seemed to be listening, without making me uncomfortable. In the end, he said, "I think we better pray." But at that point Mitch interrupted us because he'd left a music book in there. When he saw me, he mumbled something and retreated. But it was too late, because Daisy arrived early, and she seemed upset, as usual, and then Claire came with a boy I hadn't seen before called Tom, and the moment passed.

Mum told me to come home by twelve. I was there just afterwards because the train was late. The children were nowhere to be seen. I expect George had taken them off for lunch somewhere. If he thought Mum would have calmed down, then he obviously didn't know Mum as well as he thought he did. It was clear right from the beginning Mum was expecting a full and total apology. I told her I would apologise to Nina and Harry. She said that wasn't good enough.

"What do you want from me?" I asked.

"To remember family comes first. Before football, before church, before anything else."

"You're being so unfair," I said. We both paused and stared at each other. "By the way," I added, "you better read this." It was a letter telling me when training for the under-15s would start. I knew that Mum always wanted us to have a family holiday in August.

"I see," she said. "And when exactly are you planning to spend some time with your nearest and dearest?" I shrugged my shoulders. I knew Mum wasn't the type to back down. "Well, when you can answer that question, you can come back home. I'm sure you're quite happy staying with your father, in any case."

"Well, yeah, I am," I said. I was going to saying something else, but I checked myself. "Just give me a moment to grab a suitcase and some more clothes."

"Fine," she said. "You've got ten minutes."

June 1st

As expected, Dad's taxi failed its MOT yesterday and it's not really worth repairing. Still, he's heard about a possible business opportunity, so he isn't completely downbeat. The only trouble is, Dad has chased possibilities before. They've usually cost him a lot of time and money.

To celebrate the end of half-term the youth group were holding a praise party in the church hall. KT Lee brought along her drums, Mitch played the rather ropey old piano, Claire had her flute and her new boyfriend Tom turned out to be a rather handy bass guitarist. I didn't feel much like praising at first, but gradually I began to see that actually there was plenty to give thanks for.

Halfway through the evening, John the vicar turned up. I didn't get much chance to speak to him, but apparently Joe had told him all about my situation. In a quiet moment, as we were about to tackle the mountain of pizza Sarah had prepared, he simply went up to me and said, "Speak to George." That's the thing about John. He has the most amazing gift of knowing the right thing to do.

So I rang George when I got in. As I expected he was working out in the garage. He was out of breath, so it gave me a chance to speak first. Eventually he stopped panting long enough to say, "You know, I've been talking things over with Nicky. She's been offered a job as area manager. Would mean slightly longer hours and more travelling, but I told her with the extra money we could afford someone to look after the kids."

"A nanny?"

"Something like that. The only question, then, is where you would stay."

"Well, I shouldn't worry about that."

"Let me finish," said George impatiently. "I've got a mate who specialises in converting garages. We could turn that into a studio flat, so you could keep your bedroom."

"And I'll need that because?"

"Because," said George, "anyone can see you're not a complete hooligan or dropout. I told Nicky I wouldn't have wanted to look after Bill every night when I was fourteen. Just bear with it for the next few months, and hopefully we'll have everything sorted."

"Right," I said. "I mean, thank you."

"Well, it's my job to fix things. See you on Monday?"

"S'pose so."

Actually that was a real answer to prayer. Len's son is coming next week and for once he has his daughter with him, so I needed to get out of the spare room. He's still talking about Dad paying the rent, so I really hope this business opportunity works out. For once.

June 10th

Exams week began today. I've been dreading this date for a long time. At least Alex helped me do some decent revision last week. It seemed ages since I last went round his place. I guess we have such different interests. He's trying to get some poetry published and he spent last Thursday at a council meeting which was all about *Morbury's* getting permission for their new supermarket. He seemed surprised he was the youngest there by about thirty years. But there's no denying he is a good friend. He patiently went through almost every subject with me while we chatted about family stuff and church and loads more besides.

It turned out his Dad, Joe, was one of the few people who actually knew the new owner of Drumchester City and where his money had come from. That was a relief because the fans' forum had been circulating with rumours for weeks. Anthony reckoned there was some dodgy Irish businessman behind it all, while Darren suspected it was some kind of Arab investor. Actually, our new chairman lives in London but, so the story goes, he had been at one time a sixth former at our school, when it was plain old Drumchester Comp.

"I guess we know who's coming to school speech day this year," said Alex.

"Guess so," I replied.

June 15th

The terrible twins' birthday today. As part of my truce with Mum, I agreed to help out before going on to Dad's this weekend. Basically this meant looking after Harry while Mum helped Nina and Carrie get dressed and look respectable, even if they were hyper about their sixth birthday. I did my best, but I've always struggled with the signing, and we both ended up quite frustrated. Fortunately, just when it was getting really tricky, Mark and Olivia and Kai turned up, and Harry instantly ran up to Kai like a long-lost friend and gave him a big hug.

While they were playing with a huge bag of bricks Olivia had brought with her, I asked them how it was going. Turns out they had their first full night's sleep last week. Then the conversation turned to me, and I explained how George had sorted everything out between me and Mum.

"Aye, he's not bad for a Dad," said Mark. "Just got a terrible taste in shirts and music. But you can't have everything."

Then Olivia whispered something in Mark's ear and they both collapsed laughing. I couldn't see what has so funny, but it was good to see Mark so happy after all that had happened.

And the twins' party wasn't that bad either. Mum had only invited four other girls over and once they had all given their presents and everyone had eaten, they all bundled into the people-carrier so Mum and George could take them off to the aquarium. That left Mark and Olivia looking after Harry, and me to clear up. But there wasn't that much to do really, and I still could get to the cinema in time to watch a film with Dad. If only life at home could be that straightforward all the time.

June 28th

Pre-season starts in a couple of weeks' time, so I've been working out in the gym at school most lunch times this week. It's amazing how out of condition you can get so quickly. Mum's funny about me going out for a run on my own, but I reckon Dad will let me in the morning.

Daisy was more upset than usual at youth club tonight, and with good reason. Her brother Derek announced on her birthday this week he couldn't stand running the farm on his own any more and he was going to join the army at the end of the year. It seems that means Daisy's farm is going to be sold to pay off the debts, and the livestock with it. I guess I've been blessed over the past few months with always having some place to go to and it doesn't really matter to me that much where I live. But Daisy's family has had the place for four generations and even I can see it's going to be a big upheaval. Sarah spent most of the evening alone with Daisy and KT Lee after that.

"This is quite a special group," Tom said to me at the end of the evening.

"Yeah, you could say, that."

"I mean, you're not half as weird as I thought you'd be." At that point we heard Alex explaining the plot of his latest novel to Sian. "Well, not all of you, anyway."

July 8th

Something strange happened at school. There's this troublemaker called Barry who's given both me and Alex grief in the past. He's been a bit quieter recently, they say because his older brother Wayne isn't around any more. But today I spotted him with something that makes me think he might be on the take again. He was fiddling around in his pencil case for something in English, and I saw this chain with all these charms on it. I couldn't remember where I'd see it before.

Then as I was halfway through PE it suddenly dawned on me I'd seen Marvin wearing it in his shop. Either Barry had nicked it from Marvin which was unlikely, or Barry had broken into the shop which was now closed and had all that white stuff all over the windows. So what to do? Do I have a blazing row with Barry? Do I leave it till tomorrow when the chances are, he's already got rid of it? Do I grass and tell the teacher?

I was at the time batting in the nets with Phil. As he was about to run up, I held my hand up and asked if I could have a quiet word. Phil nodded, then he went and found Mr Khan and told him some story about needing to get a plaster out of his bag. When he emerged from the changing rooms, he came over to me and slipped something shiny in my hand. "You owe me," he whispered.

"You can take my report home tonight, if that helps?" I replied, and Phil laughed. At which point Mr Khan told us to stop messing around and get on with it.

Barry seemed quite distracted throughout Geography. But I don't think he guessed what happened. At least I don't think he did. And he didn't get a chance to talk to me as we all had to collect our reports at the end of the day.

I've always dreaded giving my report to Mum. But it wasn't too bad. My marks in RE were awful as expected, but I'm giving that up. No-one gets a high grade from Mr Finlay the history teacher but everyone knows that. As for the rest my English and

French results were better than average and even the science teachers praised my positive attitude.

"That's better than I got at your age," said Mum. But just in case I thought she was praising me, she added, "Make sure you keep it up." It was hard not to remember she was just about to become an area manager.

July 13th

Pre-season started today! I thought I'd been keeping fit, but this was on another level. Two hours of stretching, running, jumping and ball control. Then after a short break more work with Lee, getting me back into shape, working on my kicking and handling. At lunch afterwards it was time to get to meet some of the new members of the squad. There was a massive centre-half called Byron who was even taller than me and had come up from somewhere in the depths of Cornwall. And a spotty forward with ginger hair who was unmistakeably Welsh that we all called Taff. All the talk was about the squad for the new season. There'd been a massive clear-out over the summer, and we were still waiting to see who would be signed up. We all shared rumours about possible trialists. Our second-year apprentice at least had signed up a professional contract and someone reckoned he'd met personally with the new owner.

After lunch we had a kind of friendly match against the under 16s. I guess they expected to win easily. But despite me making one mistake we only lost 3-2, and Taff had a hand in both goals. The gaffer turned up towards the end and told us how well we'd played. I've got a feeling it's going to be a good season.

July 21st

Alex's sister, Sophie, was at church today as she was about to go off on some missionary work in South America. She said how much it had cost her to do this. Everyone else was thinking about the money, but Alex and I exchanged glances and we thought about the incident last Christmas when she broke up from her boyfriend. Then John came forward and prayed for her and told us how we could follow her progress online.

I'm not going to be in church for the next couple of weeks, either. There's a big under-15 tournament in South Wales, precisely when Mum and George are going away to some Spanish resort or other with the kids. I know where I'd rather be.

I had a text from Marvin today thanking me for the chain. It was a bit tricky explaining to Dad how I got hold of it. But I think he trusted me enough to know I was doing the right thing.

August 8th

Came home today from the football tournament. We hadn't had a bad time really. We'd played five matches, won three, drawn one and lost one, and the loss was nothing to do with me. We were playing a team from a big club up north, and they were quick, really quick. Anthony and Byron and the rest of the defence struggled to contain them and towards the end they got really tired. I made a couple of decent saves, but when they broke through there was little I could do to stop their two goals.

"Why do you always worry about the defeats?" asked Dad as he picked me up from the station.

"'Cos I want to be the best, that's why," I said.

"But you won three matches and you said you reached the quarter-finals. You should be pleased with yourself." And Dad remained cheerful and upbeat all the way home. But that wasn't a surprise. For once it looks as if his new business really might be a success. He's taken over some airport transfer business and is leasing a smart, if secondhand, 7-seater. It means funny hours and starting in the small hours of the morning. But the work is there, and he'll be setting off just after midnight tonight.

I missed Kai's first birthday while I was away, so I dropped in on Mark and Olivia this evening. Such a contrast from the last time I was there. This time I could actually get in through the door, and everything was neat and tidy. When Kai saw me, he beamed and stood up uncertainly as if trying to make a few steps towards me. Then he fell down with a thud on his nappy and started laughing.

"That's his party trick," said Olivia, "he's just learnt it."

I only meant to stay a few minutes, but ended up there for a couple of hours, and at the end Mark even drove me home.

August 17th

Mum and the family flew home today. While they've been away George has had permission from the council to get the garage done. So this week his mate is going to start work. Apparently, he'll take the gym stuff as part of the payment, and Mum is going to start looking for what she calls an 'au pair' to help look after the children. Apparently, it's a foreign student who's looking for a place to stay while they're in this country, or something like that.

Drumchester City played their first home match of the season. The under-15s were due to put in an appearance at half-time. As the team had just gone 0-1 down, it wasn't the best time to be out on the pitch, and it seemed that half the crowd had either left already or gone off to get their pasty. The idea was the announcer would read out some of our names, but the PA was so crackly it was difficult to make out what he was saying. Still, it was good to get out on the pitch and dream. Maybe, just maybe I might be playing here.

At least the senior players put in a better second half performance and came back to win 2-1. At the end I found Mark and Olivia who'd left Kai with Mum. "What did you think?" I asked.

"What did I think of what?" asked Mark teasing me.

"Game of two halves," said Olivia. "And I think there was some kind of presentation at half-time, but I can't remember what that was all about." Then they burst out laughing and bought me a hotdog from Kev's burger van.

August 25th

Joe and Sarah invited me and Dad to lunch after the morning service. But Dad was still on his airport run, so it was just me. But that was fine. Sophie was back from South America full of stories about her travels and with a dark tan and hair that had grown all long and curly while she'd been away. Mitch had been at some summer camp for young musicians and left the table early to do some practice. Alex had been with his Mum and Dad in France and they were talking about the museums they had visited.

At one point Joe said, "This must all be terribly boring for you."

"No, not all," I said. As I said to Alex afterwards, it was all so very different from the sort of things my family did.

"Well, I guess we're quite an unusual family," he replied. He wanted me to stay on for tea, but I realised I hadn't been for a run for the past few days and, besides, I think he was wanting to read me his latest poems.

There was a breeze starting to pick up when I got back to Len's to quickly get changed. But I wasn't going to a let a few raindrops put me off. I'd spent enough Saturday afternoons getting soaked to the skin, after all. So I set off down the track by the river, past the site of the new supermarket (Alex had told me all the latest news) and down into Drummington-on-Sea. By the time I cleared the first houses, a few heavy drops began to fall. Then it stopped for a little while and I carried on into the town square, heading for my old primary school. I noticed the few shopkeepers still trading there were putting all their stock back inside, but I thought nothing of it. Past the school, where I saw someone had lovingly smashed a couple of windows during the holidays, and down onto the seafront.

As I turned the corner past *Digby's* ice cream parlour, the heavens opened – as my Gran would say. One minute I was slightly damp, the next I was soaking wet. Hordes of tourists scuttled up from the beach, carrying toddlers, deckchairs, rushing for their cars or the shelter of a doorway. I struggled on along the front, just as the loud thunder overhead announced the arrival of the storm. I reached the end of the promenade and decided it was time to seek shelter in *Asco's*. But by now it was just past four o'clock and the store manager decided that come what may, it was time to turf everyone out of the shop. Soon there was a scrum of people in the porch area, some coming out of the shop, others trying to get in, and a security guard standing across the entrance. We all huddled together as best we could while the thunder and lightning rolled around us, and the rain lashed down. I couldn't help noticing the store manager was sitting tight inside the shop. There was no way he was going to get wet.

Dad was just heading off for a kip when I finally turned up, cold and bedraggled. "Enjoy your run?" he asked, with a grin. Then I told him what had happened at *Asco's*. "Well, you're just the son of the newsagent they forced out of business," he said, bitterly. "Promise me you'll never end up working for them."

"Not unless they take over Drumchester City."

"Perish the thought," said Dad. "Anyway," he yawned, "I need a kip and you need a hot shower."

August 31st

Mum measured me last night. I'm not quite six foot, but I've only got half an inch to go. "Better get you some new trousers tomorrow," she said as she marked the door frame. "Lucky for you, I've the weekend off."

So instead of going down to Dad's this morning, I find myself trailing round the shops with Mum and all the children. New trousers for me, new dresses for the girls, and new T-shirts for Harry. It should have all been so straightforward, but Harry wasn't in the mood to stay in his buggy.

"When's that au pair coming?" I asked as I dragged Harry out of yet another rail of clothes.

"Next week, all being well," said Mum as she tried to stop Carrie and Nina squabbling yet again.

"I wondered why I hadn't done this before."

Eventually we got everyone moving in the same direction, and we reached the checkouts...only for Mum to realise she had left her purse in the car. So I gave Mum whatever cash I had so they could all buy a drink, while I sprinted back to the people carrier and ferreted for the purse amid the crisp packets and the nappy sacks.

By the time I got back, it wasn't too difficult to find my family. Harry was back in the buggy, but not by choice. He had thrown away whatever food had been offered him and was wailing loudly. Carrie and Nina were doing their best to cheer him up, but he was in no mood to be pacified.

"Ten minutes five seconds," said Mum. "I never knew it would take such little time for my hair to go grey. Just hold the fort while I go and pay for this lot. Please."

While I was waiting for her, I had a text from Anthony. Apparently, Darren had been nicked this morning for lifting a can of lager. I showed the text to Harry, "That's what happens when you take stuff you haven't paid for." Harry grabbed my phone and stopped crying. I wasn't sure he'd got the message but soon he was nodding off, still clutching my phone.

Mind you, as I told Mum later, if Harry had kicked off at the match a few hours later, no-one would even have noticed. Drumchester City were quite simply dreadful. For all the talk of new investment, we only had one new player on the pitch, and by half-time we were 0-3 down. An hour after the full-time whistle the club website announced our manager had been sacked. I rang round a few mates, but no-one really knew what was going on. Anthony reckoned the board hadn't got as much money as they claimed. Taff reckoned they had already lined up a replacement. Dad reckoned we'd all find out the truth later. I guess he's probably right, but I still would like someone to tell the whole story.

September 4th

First day of the new school year. Woo-hoo. Unlike Alex, I don't really think about school work over the holidays, and I spent most of the day trying to remember what I had learnt last year. Lots more homework too. And there's football training tomorrow evening.

Fortunately, all the children were at the childminder's after school. So for the first time ever, when I got in, I actually sat down and started to tackle my first assignment. Mum would have been so proud of me if she had been there. But she's doing some training course all week to do with her new job and would be out too late. So, as I suspected, George had to collect the children and get them to bed. And inevitably it was chaos. Eventually we decided to divide and rule. George concentrated on getting Harry settled, while I made sure Carrie and Nina brushed their teeth, read them a story and tucked them in.

The good news according to George is that the garage conversion should be finished by the weekend. Even better, as Mum told us when she finally came in, the au pair will be arriving some time on Sunday. So all they need to do this Saturday is get a carpet laid, a load of furniture delivered, and curtains put up. And Mark and Olivia can't have the children because they're going to some wedding somewhere.

"Don't look at me," I said. "I have a big match on, and then I'm going on to Dad's."

"It's OK, we'll manage," said George. But I'm not sure Mum was that confident.

September 7th

First game of the season. We were playing at home, but because there was a fixture clash with the under-18s we were playing on some club pitch on the far side of Drumchester. The facilities weren't bad, but the pitch obviously hadn't been watered all week and the sun was beating down, turning the ground into something resembling concrete. So with the ball bouncing all over the place, and with our rivals playing fast, free-flowing football, I knew it was going to be a difficult afternoon. It didn't help when Byron hacked down their forward and was sent off. In the end we lost 2-0, and I came off feeling black and blue.

Still, at least it was quiet and peaceful when I got back to Dad's. "You better get used to it while you can," said Len, as he served up the most enormous plate of chips.

"What do you mean?" asked Dad.

"Had a letter from *Morbury's* this morning," said Len, as he sat down. "They're going to start building that new access road in a couple of weeks' time. Soon there will be a line of excavators working about 200 yards from here."

"And there's nothing you can do about it?" I asked.

"Apparently not," said Len. "Apparently, they've offered me some money, but I'm not taking it. I'm just glad Marjorie didn't live to see it."

Later that evening Dad and I had a chat. We both think it's time we thought about getting a place of our own. Then at least Len can be free to move out. At least, if anyone wants to buy.

September 12th

Irina, our au pair, has been with us nearly a week. Until this evening I don't think she's said a single sentence to me. Which is just as well because I struggle to understand her accent. She comes from somewhere in Eastern Europe, I'm not sure where. Still, she seems to get on well with the children and as Harry can't hear her anyway, it doesn't matter that much what she sounds like.

And she can cook. Which is just as well, with George and Mum working late. She hasn't quite worked out how much a growing lad can eat, but she makes some fantastic soups with thick, home-made bread. Tonight was beetroot apparently. As we sat round the table after bedtime, she wasn't saying much, as usual. Until I happened to mention that I was going to church on Sunday.

"You go to church?" she asked.

"Not us," said George.

"Just him," said Mum.

"Can I come too?" she asked. "I'm Baptist."

"I'll see what I can do," I said, and then realised I needed to get a move on if I was to get a train to the youth club.

John and Joe had split the youth club in two, so us older ones were meeting in the vicarage. Claire was there, but not Tom. Claire's Mum had banned her from seeing Tom for some reason, I don't know why. KT had a sparkly diamond nose stud put in over the holidays which really suited her. Sian had dyed her hair black and was wearing heavy eye make-up which really didn't suit her. There were a couple of sixth formers and there was Alex, who seemed to be growing a moustache. We spent the evening planning the term, and then I told John about Irina.

"No problem," he said. "I'll ask that family who gave you a lift earlier in the year."

September 15th

Irina couldn't come to church last week because she caught a bug off the children. I was already waiting for the service to start when she came in. As soon as she saw me, she beamed a huge smile. I think this was the first time I'd seen her smile. Then to my embarrassment she sat down next to me. I had to explain to Mitch later she was not my girlfriend, even though she spent the service chatting with me and asking questions. She seemed to genuinely enjoy what was going on, even though some of the songs left her puzzled.

I introduced her to some of the church folk after the service, and she seemed quite at ease making conversation over a cup of coffee. As I left her talking, I spotted Daisy in the corner, with her mother Elspeth. I hadn't seen them for weeks and loads of people seemed to be going up to them and comforting them. According to KT they'd been busy selling off the livestock and were getting the farm ready to sell.

Meanwhile, Len was going round getting a petition up against *Morbury's*. I'd seen the bright red tracks of earth which had suddenly appeared just beyond the garages at the end of his garden. And even last night there was a security vehicle patrolling the site, its lights occasionally catching my bedroom window. Alex said something about manning the barricades, whatever that meant.

September 19th

After weeks of delay and speculation, the new Drumchester City manager was unveiled today. He's been around a few clubs, with not that much success, and I strongly suspect he wasn't our first choice. Still, the board tried to sound upbeat as they unveiled three new loan signings to strengthen our squad, although as Anthony pointed out, if they'd been that good, someone would have taken them before the end of August.

And the goalkeeping coach has left the club. No-one really knows why, but we reckon he's looking for a better job. So with Lee taking over his duties – at least for now – tonight's session with me was his last for some time. I really have grown to like Lee, and he's taught me so much. He would have been a league goalie for many years, if he hadn't hurt his knee when he was twenty-two.

"I've taught you the basics," he said at the end of the session. "Now you go on and put them into practice, and maybe one day I'll coach you in the first team."

"Here's hoping," I said.

"Hope all you want, but make sure you put in the work. And that includes the gym work." He smiled as he said this. But he knows how much I hate gym work, even though I know I need to build up my upper strength.

OK, second resolution for this new school year. One, try to keep up with my assignments. Two, go to the gym more. Not having that much success with number one at the moment, but maybe number two will be easier.

September 30th

Something happened between Mum and Irina today. I'm not sure what but when they went into the kitchen tonight, I could hear Mum giving Irina a right telling off.

Moments later, Irina marched out of the kitchen, in floods of tears. George went into Mum, and I could hear him telling her she was being a bit hard on the girl.

I hesitated for a moment what to do. Then I went round the back of the house and knocked on the garage door. "Go away," said Irina.

"It's me, Ally," I said.

"OK," she said, and let me in.

"I just wanted to apologise for my Mum. She can be hard on everyone from time to time."

Irina blew her nose. "Can I say something to you? I don't like being au pair. I am au pair because I need money for my studies. You understand?"

I nodded. "But you are a good au pair. Carrie and Nina love talking about you."

"Is that true? You are a good boy, Ally, and you have a good heart." Just then I heard George calling me but as I left to go, she gently squeezed my hand. I didn't quite know what to do next, so I turned round quickly and went inside.

"I've had a word," said George. "We can't afford to lose her, can we?"

"No," I said, still thinking about her squeezing my hand.

October 12th

George took Mum away for the weekend, which was probably for the best. Mum had taken a couple of days off sick and that's something she's never done before. Mark and Olivia came over with Kai to help with the children and I introduced Irina to Olivia. Soon they were talking away about children and girly stuff, while Mark and I got to grips with the really important matters in life, like the fact Drumchester City were still fourth from bottom. Carrie and Nina were happily drawing, and Harry was happily playing with Kai – at least until Kai decided he wanted to play his way. I don't know what they're feeding Kai but at this rate he might even grow up to be as tall as me.

Usually I would have gone down to Dad's, but he was coming into Drumchester to look at places to rent. I met up at lunchtime. He had a couple of options, and asked if I wanted to come with him. It's been ages since we've actually done stuff at weekends. I've either been busy, or he's been out driving. So I skipped Drumchester City for once in my life, and we went round looking at anywhere suitable. In the end we found this old house by the back road to Dumpley Common. The bathroom and the kitchen were ancient, and the garden was full of nettles, but the whole property was clean and freshly painted, and there was space on the drive for Dad's 7-seater. The landlord said we could do the garden ourselves, if we wanted, and he wasn't going to charge the full amount as he knew it needed work doing. It was on the way to the airport, and Drumley Green was just down the road, so it suited us perfectly.

"To be honest," said Dad as we drove back to his place, "I'm a bit worried about Len. He's taken this road building to heart, and he doesn't look at all well."

Len was outside in the garden when we arrived, and I could see what Dad meant. Len somehow looked greyer and older, and he had to straighten up slowly when he greeted us.

"Look at this," he said as he pointed to a rose bush. He wiped his finger on a leaf and removed a thin film of dust. "And that's in the front garden. Disgusting, that's what I call it. Disgusting."

October 17th

Mum has been a different person since she got back. She even drove me to football training tonight. On the way over she said, "I've been a bit of a bitch recently, haven't I?" I didn't know what to say. "Yeah, I know. That's 'cos I've got to be like that at work, and I don't switch off when I get home." I didn't understand what she was saying but thought it best to keep silent.

We don't really have a youth goalkeeping coach any more, but Stan, the under-15's manager did his best with me. We're having another big game this weekend, and we know we haven't performed well so far this year – just like the grown-ups. Stan reminded us we were playing for our futures, and it didn't matter how well we'd done last year. That was last year, and no-one remembers last year.

"So, no pressure, then?" said Anthony, as we got changed afterwards.

"Is Darren coming back?" I asked, changing the subject.

"I don't think so, bro'. Once he was nicked, his Dad came down hard on him. So no steaming round town, no football, no nuffin'. I reckon his Dad wants him in the army, or summat."

"Darren in the army?"

"S***, that's scary," laughed Anthony, "Army or football, I know what I'd chose."

"Better win on Saturday, then."

October 20th

To be fair, we haven't been playing that badly. Last match we hit the post twice, time before I was beaten in the last minute by a huge deflection. But today Stan's talk seemed to have us fired up. At least Taff was fired up, and within five minutes had received a yellow card for gobbing.

"Let the ball do the talking," yelled our captain, Blake. And within a few minutes, the ball was doing the talking. Unfortunately, at the wrong end. I came out for a cross, punched it off the head of the opponent, but sadly straight into the path of the striker behind him, who volleyed it straight into the top left corner. Not a lot I could do about that, although as Stan said, if I had more upper body strength, I could have punched it further.

Our opponents then sat back for a while hoping to hit us on the break. For the next half an hour we mounted attack after attack. But nothing. Their central defenders were heading away everything that came near them. We tried playing to feet, but we kept getting tackled and losing the ball. In the end Taff was so frustrated, he decided to have a go himself. He picked up the ball wide right, beat the full back and just kept going. While everyone else got ready for the cross, Taff steamed into the penalty area, skipped round another challenge, and another and slipped the ball under the keeper.

It was nearly half-time, but that goal really got us going. And just as the referee was about to blow his whistle, Blake picked up the ball about 25 yards out and simply belted it. It hit the underside of the crossbar and trickled over the line. Even as the goalkeeper was picking the ball out of the net, the bar was still shaking.

In the second half, our opponents had to come out fighting, but they were by now leaving gaps at the back. Taff grabbed a second, and then won a penalty as a frustrated defender pushed him over. He picked himself up and made sure of his hat-trick, low into the bottom right corner.

"That's one result," said Stan. "Great result, but it doesn't make a season. Don't forget – half-term training camp and we'll play the under-16s at the end. Winner takes on the under-18s. That sorts out the men from the boys."

November 1st

I used to think half-term was a holiday. I'm not so sure now. I've been working out hard in the gym and learning from the physio how to exercise properly. When I've got home, I've been trying to get on with my homework, though it's not that easy in a house full of kids. Alex invited me over one day, but there was no way I could fit him in. At least he was able to send me some useful stuff about my French homework.

And today was the big match against the under-16s. I think they thought we'd be quite an easy touch. They weren't trying too hard until Byron went up for a corner and powered the ball home. Then they upped the tempo, but I was feeling big and strong. Besides, the manager was watching, and I wanted to impress. So a low shot into the bottom corner, tipped round the post. A point-blank header, straight into my chest. A curling free-kick, pushed against the crossbar. I just knew nothing was going to get past me.

So tomorrow we play the under-18s and I help Dad move house.

November 2nd

As I guessed, we lost – 3-0. But none of the goals were my fault and I was still playing well. "Keep up the gym work," said Stan. "It's really having an effect."

On the other hand, I could just learn to move furniture like Trevor Lee. He came round with a van just after I got in, and I helped him load up all the bits and pieces.

It was dark when we got to our new address. Someone from church had been in and put up some curtains, and Dad had already done the shopping. So within a couple of hours we were unpacked really, and then Dad cooked us both tea.

Halfway through the meal, Trevor had a call from KT. She's staying the weekend at Daisy's apparently, helping her to sort stuff out. Someone came round the farm today, and it looks like they've got a buyer.

"So that will be another removal job," said Trevor, as he demolished his meat pie. "If this football business doesn't work out, I could set you up easily." Then he squeezed my biceps, "Still got a bit of a way to go, mind you. I was moving safes at your age, best work-out there is."

I could only guess why Trevor was moving safes when he was fourteen, but at least that might explain his size.

November 5th

Mum gave me a new phone yesterday. It was her old one from work, of course, but it was miles better than anything I had ever seen before. She said she'd seen how hard I'd been working recently and wanted to reward me. So here I am with this top of the range, 4G model. It's all a bit difficult really. Of course, I can't carry it round school, but I am slightly worried I am going to be mugged on the way home. At the moment, though, everyone seems to want to have their selfie taken. So I've taken a selfie with a few of the girls like Poppy and Erin, and Mum's let me set up a *Facebook* account.

Tonight was the firework display in Alex's garden. I've never been able to take a decent photo of the display before, but this phone took some great pictures.

"Nice bit of kit," said Alex as he looked at the results. And then, of course, the rest of the youth club wanted to have a look. So I showed it to Claire and Sian and KT. KT tried to interest Daisy, but I sensed her mind was elsewhere.

We were just about to tuck into a pile of burnt sausages, when my phone rang. I hadn't sorted out the ringtone yet, and the one my Mum had chosen was just embarrassing. But everyone's laughter died down when they realised the call was quite serious. It was from Dad. Len had been taken into hospital with breathing difficulties. It could be his heart. It could be a chest infection. They weren't quite sure at the moment, but his son was with him. We had noticed John had slipped out earlier and now we knew why.

We were eating our sausages rather quietly, and I was praying silently, when suddenly the doorbell rang. It was Irina. For a moment, I thought something else had gone wrong, but no, Irina had heard about this event happening, and had caught a taxi over. She would have come sooner, but she went to the church and had spent ages looking for the right place.

"No problem," said Joe. "Glad you could make it. You're always welcome here." And then he ushered her into a seat right next to mine. She didn't seem to mind she was in a group of mostly teenagers, and she soon got us chatting again.

At ten o'clock George came to pick us up. "That was fun," said Irina on the way home. "I hope you didn't mind me coming?"

"No, not at all," I said. But I wondered precisely what she was doing there.

November 15th

My hand is still shaking as I write this. I really can't believe what's happened today.

It all kicked off after school. As usual, I went to the school office to collect my phone. I've been really careful to hide it over the past week and make sure nobody sees me using it. Usually I would head straight out home, but today I realised I had left my pencil case in Mr Findlay's classroom. So back up the stairs, along the corridor, turn right, and into the second room on the left. There was no-one else around, or so I thought. But as I came out again, I had the misfortune to run into Barry.

"I hear you got a nice phone," he said.

"What's that to you?"

"Let me have a look at it."

"No," I said, starting to walk down the corridor.

"I said, let me look at your phone," he said, grabbing hold of my arm.

I spun round and Barry just smiled at me. "Give me your phone," he said, producing a knife from his jacket.

"Seriously, Barry, just grow up."

"Give me your phone."

"No."

At that point Barry lunged for me, but he was too slow, and I could easily dodge him.

"I think you better stop right there," I said calmly.

Barry didn't say anything but went for me again. As I dodged out of the way a second time, I decided I had had quite enough of Barry's threats, so I hit him. I didn't mean to hit him quite so hard, but my fist landed square on the side of his face, and he crumpled on the floor like an empty bag of crisps. The knife dropped from his hand and clattered under a radiator.

I wasn't sure what to do next. Barry was groaning, and there was still a knife loose on the floor. Without thinking really, I just hit the fire alarm button.

Within a few moments a whole scrum of teachers turned up, including Mr Khan. They stopped in their tracks when they saw what happened. "What the hell is going on here?" shouted Mr Khan.

So I told him. Barry went for me with a knife and wouldn't stop, so I had to defend myself. At this point Barry tried to get up and was violently sick.

"OK," said Mr Khan. "Let's phone the police, get an ambulance for Barry, and Ally, you better go to the head's office."

The head was on the phone when I walked in. "I've been speaking to your mother. She will be here in half an hour. The police are already on their way. Now if you would just like to tell me in your own words what happened."

So I told the same story to the head. Barry went for me with a knife and wouldn't stop, so I had to defend myself. I told the same story to the police when they turned up ten minutes later. I told the same story again to Mum when she turned up, cross that her day had been ruined.

I was told to wait out in the corridor while the head, Mum and the police all had a big discussion. In the end I was ushered back in and was told I had been suspended for a week. I had to stay at Mum's house and not try to contact Barry or any of his family. At that exact point the ambulance put on its siren as it left the school grounds. The head looked at me and asked if I had anything to say.

"If I could have stopped Barry any other way, I would have done," and then, handing the phone back to Mum I said, "I think you better take this back. I don't want it any more."

When we got home, George was already there. "You all right, son?" he asked.

"Yeah, I guess so." I didn't really know how I was feeling, but I went to my room to ring Dad. He was at an airport waiting for his customers, so we didn't have a lot of time to talk.

"Well done for standing up for yourself," he said.

"Even though I put him in hospital?"

"Well, what's he doing with a knife in the first place? I know I shouldn't say this, but a clip round the ear when he was younger would have sorted him out."

I wasn't sure about this, but Dad had to go, and it sounded like Mum and George were having a row downstairs.

"See what happens when you teach my son to box."

"So you tell me what he should have done. A gentle slap? A stroke of the cheek?"

They carried on like this for some time until I came downstairs, and they both fell silent. Then Mum suddenly burst into tears and gave me a hug. I wasn't sure why she was crying, but I was glad she wasn't shouting any more.

At that point Irina came in to cook the tea. George gently ushered her away again, while Mum just held me for probably longer than she's ever done before.

November 22nd

The school have decided to admit me again on Monday. Which is just as well, because I am starting to go crazy hanging around at home. Drumchester City have decided I can go back to training, but as I haven't trained this week, I won't be able to play in the match tomorrow.

There have been visitors, of course, Alex, bless him, has kept me up to speed with work, and I've done nearly a whole week's schoolwork. Phil rang to tell me Barry is on the mend and is going to be sent to a special unit, whatever that means. The police dropped by a few days ago to take a formal statement, but they don't think anyone is going to press charges. And today, two of the girls from school, Poppy and Erin, rang on my door. I've never had a visit from any girls before, but they wanted to invite me to a party next week at Poppy's.

"We think you're a real hero," said Poppy.

"We told the police we saw Barry with a knife that morning," added Erin. As they turned to go, Erin hung back for a moment and when Poppy wasn't looking, leant up and gave me a kiss on the cheek. "Do come," she whispered, "it'll be fun to see you."

The one person I've really wanted to see this week is Dad, but Mum's got this weird idea somehow he's to blame, letting me go to gym, and encouraging my ideas of being a footballer. Still, we've talked a lot on the phone (my old phone, that is), and chatted probably more than we've ever done, about the new house, about Len coming out of hospital, about Gran coming down at Christmas. And despite Mum's protests, he's going to pick me up at lunchtime tomorrow.

November 23rd

It was a cold, but sunny day today, so Dad and I wrapped up well and began tackling the garden. Since his illness, Dad isn't as strong as he used to be, so I did the heavy lifting and lugging. It was good to use my muscles again. After a couple of hours it was starting to get dark, but we had done about half the garden. Dad made me a strong pot of tea while I turned on the football results. Drumchester City had been leading 3-1 at half-time but ended up drawing 3-3 at home to the bottom side.

"Reckon they could do with a new keeper," said Dad.

"Don't say that," I said.

"Why not?"

"I dunno. What if Mum's right? What if I hadn't done all that gym work and I hadn't knocked Barry out?"

"Then you probably would have got a knife stuck in you. You were only defending yourself."

"That's what I keep telling myself, but I'm not sure. What about turning the other cheek, and all that?"

"Tell you what," said Dad, "let's talk to someone who knows a lot more about this than me."

Usually when we go round to Trevor's, KT tries to keep out of the way, but when she saw me, she gave me a hug and said, "You all right? We've been so worried about you."

"Yeah, I'm fine. But thanks for praying and all that."

And then KT slipped away into the kitchen to help Jacky get dinner ready.

"You're lucky," said Trevor. "If the police had heard my name when I was fourteen, I would have been in the nick, no matter what the story. I just hope Barry don't end up the same way. But sadly, I can see it happening. Would love to talk to that boy, but I dunno that he'd listen."

"And what about me?" I asked.

"What about you?" asked Trevor. "You did what you could. I don't think you could've done anything different. Just don't make a habit of it, or people will get suspicious." And somehow hearing that from Trevor made all the difference. I had been worried all week, that maybe I'd been wrong, that I'd upset God or something. But if anyone knew the right thing to do in that situation, it was Trevor.

Over tea KT told me about next Friday evening, and the trip the youth club was making to see this band. "Should be really good," said Trevor. "I've heard them a few times. Not quite my music, but they're half-decent."

"Sounds great," I said, and then I remembered I was going to Poppy's party. "Oh, I think I've got something else on."

"Busy social calendar?" asked Jacky.

"Yeah, something like that," I replied, all embarrassed.

November 25th

First day back. I got a police escort home.

I had to have a long meeting with Mr Khan and the school counsellor at lunch time. Something about anger management issues, and restorative justice. I didn't make a lot of effort to understand what they were saying, just said, "Yes" at the right moments.

Usually I would walk home from school. It's about half an hour to Mum's through Drumchester, past the station and up the hill the other side. I was just coming to the station, when I suddenly heard this voice saying, "That's him!" I could instantly tell that was Wayne, Barry's older brother, and he had two mates with him. They started running towards me and I thought for one moment they were going to catch me up. But they weren't as fit as me, and I soon was able to get away, up round the corner and back towards school. What I hadn't reckoned on was a shortcut through the back alleys. So the moment I paused for breath, there they were again, coming straight at me. So this time I ran all the way back to school, and made my way up to the head's office.

She wasn't pleased to see me, but she was even less pleased when I told her the story. Within a few minutes the local PCSO turned up in an unmarked car and drove me home. "See if someone can give you a lift next time," she said, as I got out. Which was all very well, but who? Mum and George are at work, Alex catches the train, and Phil goes round to his Nan.

I was still thinking this over when Erin rang about the party this Friday. "You are coming this week?" she said.

"Yeah," I said, thinking about the youth club. And then I told her what had happened today.

"That's no problem. My Mum always picks me up, and I only live about ten minutes away from you. Only I stay late on Thursdays for dance."

"Cool," I said.

November 29th

So I've been getting a lift to school with George all week, and a lift home with Erin's Mum. All a bit weird really. Erin's Mum works all night at the petrol station on the Peter Cross road, and George says he's chatted with her a few times. I've been invited round to her place a couple of times, but I'm still catching up with school. Next week, perhaps.

As I expected the party tonight was quite girly, and a little bit silly. It's funny really, but I've always thought of my church family as my real friends. They're OK, this bunch, but they're always fussing about how they look, or what someone said on *Facebook*, or who's got the most hits on *YouTube*. I haven't really got time for that sort of thing, but I pretended to know what I was talking about, and everyone seemed really pleased to see me. Certainly, no-one had a kind word to say about Barry, and by the end of the evening I even felt a little bit sorry for him – until, of course, I thought about the knife.

"So you're really going to be a footballer?" asked Poppy.

"Yes, I am," I said and for some reason she and some of her friends started to giggle. Maybe they'd just had too much lemonade, or maybe they'd just found their Mum's stash of cider.

Erin just rolled her eyes and smiled at me. "You want to stay much longer?" I whispered. "It's nearly half past ten."

"I'll go when you want," she replied. So we made our excuses and left, and I walked her home. It was a drizzly, damp night, but we didn't notice. Outside her Mum's flat I gave her a kiss and then turned for home. It hadn't been a bad evening.

Later on, I had a text from Alex. *Missed you tonight. You'd have enjoyed the band.* I probably would have, but I'd been busy.

December 5th

I've been round to Erin's a couple of times already this week. Her big thing is dance, and she's introduced me to her programme on the *Wii*. I think I'm starting to get the hang of it. At least, learning how to has been great fun.

As always, however, football training tonight brought me down to earth. I kept making silly mistakes and Stan shouted at me to focus. I tried harder and eventually I snapped back into the old habits.

"You've got to concentrate from the beginning, if you're going to make any progress," he said. "Learn to focus in the warm-up." I tried to explain that I usually did. "A professional always does that," he replied.

At least Erin won't be around to distract me at the weekend. She's involved in a big Christmas production at the theatre, so she'll be busy rehearsing all weekend. Bit of a relief, if I'm honest. Means I can go to youth club, focus on the match on Saturday, and then go to church on Sunday. And as Mum has been reminding me this week, there are end of term exams coming up.

December 14th

I finally caught up with Mark and Olivia today. After a scrappy 1-0 home win today, Olivia picked Kai up from her Mum and we all went round to the flat for tea. It was all neat and tidy, but there were toys everywhere.

"Bit of a squeeze, isn't it?" said Mark as he put Kai on his special seat. "That's why we're hoping to move in the new year. Maybe even have room one day for another addition to the family."

"But not yet," said Olivia firmly, slicing up a carrot for Kai.

"Don't worry, I didn't hear that," I replied.

"Oh, it's nothing," said Olivia. "It's just we both have to work so hard to make ends meet. 'Cos this little one is growing and growing, and we always need new stuff."

"But we wouldn't have it any other way," said Mark.

"No, we wouldn't," said Olivia as she gave Mark a kiss. "Which leads me to ask – can we get Kai christened at your church?"

"Of course. Why are you asking me?"

"We don't go to church, not sure even if we believe that much. But it just kind of seems the right thing to do."

"I agree," said Mark, as Kai experimented with his carrot.

So I gave them John's phone number. "And you'll be a godparent?" asked Olivia.

"Yeah, that would be great," I replied.

So as Kai's future godparent, I helped with tea, read him a story, and told him some funny jokes. Not that he understood the jokes, but he has learnt to laugh. And I mean, laugh. Then he did an enormous poo, and it was time to hand him over to Mark and Olivia.

As for me, I was going to the theatre. I'd been talking with Erin this week, and it turned out I'd never been to the theatre before, and she'd never been to church – except with the school. So we agreed: I would go to watch her perform tonight, and she'd come to the carol service. When I mentioned it to the youth club, it turned out they wanted to go too, except Daisy. So we all met outside at seven.

It turned out to be a musical production of *A Christmas Carol.* Erin was playing one of the street children, and also was in the chorus. It was hard to recognise her with the make-up and the lights, but Alex and I agreed she looked fantastic. I don't think she could see us, as we were right up in the cheap seats. The whole place was packed, and the time fairly flew by. Alex I could see was making some notes, but I don't think that lad is ever satisfied. KT and Sian were just singing along. And as for Claire, she seemed to disappear at half-time, or as Alex would insist on calling it, the interval.

I only had a chance to say a brief word to Erin afterwards. I told her she was fantastic, and she gave me kiss. Then as she slipped away again, she put something in my hand, and I realised it was a programme signed by the whole cast.

December 24th

The day of the carol service. This year John was holding two services as the event has been getting so big over the years. So before the main event, he was holding one specially for young families. The youth club had been asked to put on a small drama, so we arrived early to rehearse in the hall. I was one of the first there, because Dad had offered to go round collecting some of the older church members. Alex, then Sian, followed shortly afterwards and then Claire walked in with Tom! Apparently, she had bumped into him at the theatre, and they were now together again. There's clearly so much I need to learn about this boy-girl stuff.

Then KT turned up, and I noticed she was wearing a new leather jacket with real studs. Some kind of early Christmas present from Trevor. We hadn't really had time to learn our lines, but it seemed to run OK. As soon as the church was free, we wandered over there because KT needed to set up her drum kit.

Already the church was filling up fast. I was hanging around for Mark and Olivia, and they eventually turned up without Kai because they weren't sure they would be allowed to bring him. At the same time Erin turned up wearing this really smart jacket and skirt. I guess I hadn't told her how informal we were at Drumley Green. I introduced Mark and Olivia to Erin, and they talked about how frightening it was being first-timers. Then I said I was a first-timer only three years ago and it really wasn't so bad. I asked Olivia if Irina was coming as well, but apparently there was too much for everyone to do at home.

Finally Dad came in with the last of the regulars and with Gran, just as the procession was forming in the vestry. I wondered if I was doing the right thing, introducing Dad to all these people, especially Mark, but he didn't seem to mind. So there we were jammed in a pew, Dad and Gran on one side, Erin, on the other, with Olivia and Mark beyond. If anyone told me we'd be all sitting like this at the beginning of the year in church, I'd have thought they were mad.

As usual, the place simply rocked and even Erin eventually relaxed and took off her jacket. I noticed KT was looking at us a couple of times, but we only touched hands during the sermon. Later on, during the prayers, Erin whispered, "Do I have to pay for this?" and I had to explain, no, you just put in the collection what you want. At the end she got confused when everyone else remained standing for the blessing, but I reassured her no-one was watching.

"It was kind of fun, but I didn't understand a word the vicar was saying," said Erin, at the coffee.

At this point KT was walking past but she didn't stop to be introduced. "Yeah, it was all a bit weird," agreed Olivia. "But I'd like Kai to be baptised in a church like this. Don't you agree, Mark?"

"Right," said Mark who was checking something on his phone.

Then I told them about my birthday and the New Year's party in the church hall. Mark and Olivia couldn't come, but Erin said she'd look forward to it.

"She seems like a very nice young girl," said Gran when we got home. "I remember I was going steady with a young lad when I was just a little older than you. His name was Frank. I often wonder what happened to him. Last I heard he was out in the tropics, doing something with coconuts."

I'm not sure if she had meant to make us laugh, but at that point Dad snorted into his tea.

"Did you enjoy the service?" I asked, changing the subject.

"Oh yes," she said. "I wouldn't miss it for the world. Now I understand you're not going to be here tomorrow, so I thought I'd give you your presents before you leave."

And as always, Gran gave me some new clothes that fitted perfectly. Dad must have told her I was now over six foot, and bless her, she always finds the right thing to wear.

Sadly, the season of goodwill and peace to all men did not extend to Mum's. It was late when I got in – just after eleven. Usually the turkey would be cooked by now, but there'd been a problem with the oven and George was still hard at work in the kitchen. Carrie and Nina still hadn't settled, despite Irina's best efforts. And Harry had been very naughty at bathtime and smashed Mum's special candleholder.

"Glad you could make it," said Mum, still sorting out the Christmas stockings.

I was going to say something sarcastic in reply, but before I could say anything, George intervened from the kitchen, "Lay off, Nicky. From what I've heard, he was at a very special event."

And just as I was praying a quick thank you, Irina emerged downstairs, ever so quietly and whispered, "OK, I think they're settled."

"Praise the Lord," said George unexpectedly. "I think we could all do with a drink."

So we sat round till midnight, then Mum went upstairs to hang up the stockings, George checked on the turkey and found it was done, and we then wished each other a Happy Christmas. Sometimes family life isn't so bad, after all.

December 31st

A very special birthday today. It started out at Mum's. She gave me a load of age-appropriate DVDs. I'd seen most of them before, but it was nice to have my own copies. George bought me an electric shaver and Irina gave me a Bulgarian football shirt. Carrie and Nina had baked a cake, and Harry made me a special card with fifteen different animals stuck on it.

Then in the evening as usual I went over to Alex's to celebrate my birthday, before going over to the church hall. Erin was waiting for me outside, even though it was getting cold, and we went in together, just as the band was starting to play. *The Potential* weren't that used to playing dance music, but they played some really slow blues numbers, and Erin was an expert in teaching me the right steps. I don't think she even noticed who was looking on, but I could see Alex and the others watching us admiringly. KT was busy in the kitchen, getting the food ready. After a while, the band stopped for a break, and we all piled in.

"Quite a spread," I said to KT as I helped myself to a pile of pasties.

"Well, you must be hungry with all that dancing," she said and went off to find Daisy.

I don't know if I've upset her or something, but she hasn't said very much at all to me in weeks.

By the time I got back to my place, Erin and Irina were having quite a conversation, but I got the impression they changed the subject when I sat down. Then Claire wandered over with Tom, and so began the introductions all over again. In fact me and Erin barely had a moment to ourselves until the music started again. So we decided to stay sitting down, while others danced, until midnight struck, and Trevor played *Auld Lang Syne* on his guitar.

"Happy New Year," said Erin.

"Happy New Year," I replied and I followed her outside to where her Mum was waiting.

Yeah, I reckon it's going to be a good year. But it's nearly two now as I write these words, and I better get some sleep, because Drumchester City are playing tomorrow - and I'm taking Erin with me.

THE DRUMCHESTER DIARIES: VOLUME 5
KEEPING ON WITH DAD
THE DIARY OF KT LEE, AGED 15

January 1st

It's nearly two o'clock in the morning as I write this and although we've been home nearly an hour, I can't get to sleep. I'm still so cross with Ally, although I don't know why. As Daisy said during the party it's not like he's my boyfriend, or anything. It's just that we've been through so much together, especially last year, what with his home being flooded out and that incident with Barry. But now he's going out with Erin, it's like he barely notices me. Not that Erin has that much going for her. At least a foot shorter than Ally and spotty, and she doesn't go to church. But Ally just doesn't get it. That's boys, I suppose.

January 7th

Daisy's first day at school. I know she's been dreading this day for months. Her Mum, Elspeth, spent the last weeks of term coming into school having all those meetings and trying to get the right support. Daisy, I think, is worried everyone will think her stupid. I told her they'll soon learn differently. But I know Daisy won't stand up for herself. And she's worried sick about her Dad who's in hospital yet again with his depression.

So Doris and I decided this morning to go round to her place and walk with her to school. Her Mum, Elspeth, is renting a new place, out beyond *Asco's*, on the road towards Dulling St Mary. A little box without a garden must be such a shock after living on a farm, but Elspeth says she can't make any plans until she knows how much money she's getting from the sale. Still, Doris and I arrived early enough for her to make us both a nice hot chocolate, and did we need it. It was a bitterly cold morning, and I was glad Jacky had given me her old, padded jacket, even if I looked like a caterpillar in it.

Daisy wasn't eating any breakfast, despite Elspeth's best attempts. Doris and I looked at each other, and decided it was best to get going.

"How do I look?" asked Daisy as she paused by the mirror in the cramped hallway.

"As pretty as ever," said Doris.

"No, like seriously," said Daisy.

"Like seriously," I said. "I wish I had your skin – not that anyone's likely to get sunburnt this morning." As we opened the door, a cold drizzle began to fall, maybe in sympathy with Daisy's mood.

We hadn't gone too far before Daisy had to slip into *Asco's* to use the loo. I just had time to race to the bakery counter and buy her a doughnut. "Take this for later," I said, slipping it into her pocket. "Believe me, you don't want a school muffin."

We got to school just in time for registration and tutor group. Fortunately there was another new girl, Shakira, in the class who could talk for England, so Daisy didn't attract so much attention. Still, I noticed a few boys who couldn't help getting a look at her. Daisy is striking, after all, with her straw-coloured hair and dark brown eyes. But she'd be a lot prettier if only she could relax and smile.

Not that there was an awful lot to smile about the first day. Daisy was supposed to be having a specially trained teaching assistant, but her car had broken down somewhere north of Drumchester, and she wasn't going to be in for hours. In the first lesson, the laptop Daisy had been given suddenly decided it wasn't going to work. I could see Daisy wasn't going to say anything, so I motioned to the maths teacher, Mr Brown. After much scratching of heads, and a visit from the technician, another laptop eventually appeared. But by that time Daisy had already lost half the lesson.

The only upside as far as I could see was that Daisy was excused French and PE, so she could have some extra English tuition. As we got ready for the gym, I hoped she realised how lucky she was. You can never quite tell with the heating in the hall. Sometimes it doesn't work at all, sometimes it roasts us alive. Today the setting was definitely roast, and within ten minutes we were all dripping with sweat. It was disgusting. Cheryl told the teacher she wasn't going to do anything else, unless it was switched off. So the caretaker came with a ladder, fiddled with some switches high on the wall, and the heating switched off with a loud groan. By the end of the session we were now both wet and freezing. And there wasn't time for a shower afterwards.

The last lesson for the day was art. We'd been studying Gustav Klimt and we were supposed to think how we might draw a piece in his style. While we were still thinking about what to do, Daisy had already set to work with a set of crayons. We all watched amazed as within about ten minutes she came up with a perfect sketch of his drawing. "Well, that's what I was supposed to do," said Daisy afterwards. "You use words, I use pictures, that's the only difference."

January 12th

I saw Ally for the first time since the New Year party today. He didn't have Erin around, and he seemed genuinely pleased to see me. Turns out he's been asked to be a godparent for his stepbrother's son, or something like that.

"You'll make a good godparent," I said.

"You mean that?"

"Why wouldn't I?" I said, a little too fiercely. Then I blushed and added, "Yes, I mean you'll be wonderful. After all, you love little children, don't you?" And for the first time in ages he actually laughed at something I said. But at that point Alex came up and the moment was lost.

After church, as usual Dad and I went home to lunch. Lee had come over from the agricultural college where he's studying, and as it was well past one, we were all starving. But there was no lunch. Even more peculiarly, there was no Jacky. We knew she'd gone out last night. But ever since I was little, she had always cooked us Sunday lunch. Dad rang to find out if she was all right.

"Yes, I'm fine," said Jacky on the other end of the phone. "Just met a friend, that's all. I'll be home by tonight."

"And what about our lunch?" asked Dad.

"I'm sure you'll manage," she said, and we could swear there was a man in the background laughing as she hung up.

"That's not like our Jacky," said Dad. "More to the point, what are we going to do about lunch?"

"I'll cook something," said Lee immediately.

"Steady now," said Dad. "That's not like our Lee either."

"I've been learning at college. Just you watch me knock up a quick pasta."

"I think we'll let you get on by yourself," said Dad. "Just make sure you don't burn the place down."

As we shut the kitchen door, Dad made a face at me, and I laughed. Then I asked, "Dad, did you ever learn to cook?"

"Susan tried to teach me. I think we got as far beans on toast, before we gave up. I do a mean takeaway, though."

Actually, Lee's pasta dish wasn't half bad, even if he used a bit too much salt. He suddenly seemed a lot more grown up now he was at college – no longer the silent, slow type always picking his nose, but actually talking about what he was learning, and the friends he was making. It's taken three years, but I might just be starting to like him.

January 17th

It had to be Maxine. There's something about Maxine that means she just can't stop picking on people. I'd feel sorry for her, except I know what it's like to be at the end of her bullying. Up until now Daisy had been coping really well at school. She was getting incredibly tired, and more than once Doris and I had found her nodding off at lunchtime. But since that art lesson I guess we all respected the fact there was a special talent here, and her textiles weren't half bad either. Only Maxine doesn't see talent. She sees weaknesses to be exploited, little digs here and rude words there. Maybe one day she'll grow up. Or maybe she won't.

We'd all gone out for lunch, only Daisy remembered she had left her glasses' case behind. It was a pretty floral case she had carefully patterned herself. She knew she left it on the desk, but we hunted high and low, and we couldn't find it. The teacher came in and joined the hunt. Then I remembered Maxine's ways of old. Sure enough, the case was in the bin in the girls' toilets, carefully filled with wet paper.

"Leave this to me," said Cheryl, who was just fixing her make-up (Cheryl is always just fixing her make-up). I wondered what that meant, but if anyone knows how to get Maxine in line, it's Cheryl. I don't know what she said, but at the beginning of the next lesson, Maxine passed a note to Daisy with the word, 'Sorry' written on it. But I noticed Daisy was even quieter than usual that afternoon.

So Doris invited us both back to her place after school and showed us her pictures of Christmas back in Poland. It turns out Doris has even more family than I realised. And then she said, "Mum wants us all to go back in September. Dad has said no, but I'm not sure he'll get his way."

"But that's not fair!" said Daisy.

"What to do? Where could I live?" said Doris.

"We'll pray about that," I said.

"Thanks," said Doris. "You're a real friend."

January 25th

Jacky has gone away for the weekend with her new man. It turns out he's a travelling catering rep she met last year, and they've been chatting away online for ages. "Aren't you going a bit fast for this?" asked Trevor.

"Not if you've been waiting thirty-nine years for the moment," replied Jacky. "And I'm sure KT can cook you lunch."

That was news to me. So this morning I've been going round *Asco's* with a shopping list and some money Dad gave me. He did offer to come, but honestly, I can't see him pushing a trolley, at least not without frightening the other customers. I think I've got everything I need. Now all I need to do is to work out how to cook it and get to church on time. Doris' Mum, Agnieszka, has given me some advice. But I'm not totally sure it's going to work.

Then after lunch, I cycled over to Dulling St Mary to see Siobhan. Siobhan is one of those girls you don't see much of for ages, but then when you catch up, it's like you're really close friends again. She invited me over, because her Gran had bought her an incubator on *E-bay* for Christmas, and she was just hatching some eggs in one of the outbuildings. It was really sweet, watching the chicks struggle out of the shells and learn to find their feed.

"Just wait until some of them start to crow," said Siobhan. "Then you can come back and help me wring their necks."

"That's fine by me," I said.

And it is honestly. I still am aiming to become a vet one day, and it takes a lot more than that to gross me out. So Siobhan took me outside where her Gran was busy mending a fence for the current flock of chickens. Apparently, there was a fox around last night, and he'd taken the head off a couple of the old birds, before being caught in the act. We carried on talking about chickens for a while and then as we were going back inside Siobhan suddenly said, "You know, I'm really worried about Mum."

"Been maxing out on the credit card, again?"

"Too right. I told her I didna want anything for Christmas, but she still bought me loads of stuff. It was all so embarrassing. Gran told her off right there and then, and she even took some of it back, when Mum wasn't looking. But now there's a big court hearing next month, and her boss is threatening to sack her if she's found guilty."

"So what'll you do?"

"That's just it. I don't have a clue. I know I can always stay here with Gran. But I'm not sure Gran will keep letting Mum stay here."

"So where's your Mum now?"

"At work, doing some overtime. Either that, or she's out shopping. Sometimes it really is hard to tell."

And here I was fretting about Sunday lunch. Maybe once I've got it sussed, I could invite Siobhan and her Gran over. They could even bring the chicken.

January 29th

Jacky has started singing to herself. She says she doesn't even realise she's doing it, but you get up close, and there's definitely a tune. She's also had her hair cut short and dyed, so you can't see any of her grey hairs any more.

I went down to the café after school. The regulars were just leaving as it was coming on to rain, and they wanted to catch the town bus home. So Jacky made me a hot chocolate and I asked her about her man.

"Well, he's called Gerry," said Jacky, "and he has a daughter about your age. I think you'd like her if you met her."

"Would I like Gerry?"

"What's not to like? He's tall, with wonderful blue eyes and blond hair. And he's Irish, like me, even if he comes from County Cork."

"Where do you come from?"

"Ah, that's a complicated question, to be sure," said Jacky. "But I was wondering if I could invite Gerry over one weekend, show him the café that sort of thing."

"And introduce him to Dad?"

"Aye, and introduce him to Trevor."

"Could be an interesting meeting."

There was a pause for a moment and then I asked, "So where do you come from?"

"Another time, love," said Jacky. "Let's get this place cleaned and spotless for the morrow." With that she got up, cleared up the dishes and went into the kitchen, still singing. Sid the chef caught my eye and he winked at me, knowingly.

February 7th

Today I did something I've been planning to do for a long time. I invited Daisy, Doris and Siobhan to come for a walk with me after school. I didn't tell them where we were going, and I wasn't going to answer any of their questions. I don't think they remembered what day it was, but that was fine by me.

So we walked out of the school, past *Asco's*, through the new estate, over the railway bridge and the main road. "Is it much further?" asked Doris.

"We're nearly there," I said, as we approached the cemetery gates.

"We're going in there?" asked Siobhan.

"I'll show you why," I replied.

Daisy took my arm as we passed the children's cemetery just by the gates. A foil balloon fluttered limply in the breeze. We came up past the chapel and I headed down the pathway to the right. There was a new mound of earth covered with a green sheet, just by the bent oak tree I always used to find my way.

Five headstones up, there she was: Susan Lee died 7th February, '*Homeward bound'*. I could see Dad had already been up today as there were eight red roses on the grave, one for each year they'd been married. Doris and Siobhan crossed themselves – it didn't occur to me until then that Siobhan might also be Catholic. Daisy gave me a hug.

"It's all right," I said, breathing deeply. "I just thought this year I ought to share this moment with others."

"Thank you," said Doris. Then pointing at the headstone, she asked, "Was that your mother's favourite song?"

"Yes, I think so. At least that's what Dad always told me."

"Tell us more," said Doris. "At least once we've found somewhere warm."

So we all went back to Daisy's, except for Siobhan who had to go and look in on her chicks. So we crammed into Daisy's tiny lounge, and I told what little I could remember; what Dad had told me; what I learnt from Jenny. It was hard to be clear who had told me what, but it felt OK to be talking about her.

"You're very brave," said Daisy. "I don't know what I'd do without my Mum."

Just then Doris noticed a pile of CDs in the corner, and she put on Mum's favourite track. That's when I lost it for a moment, but then Elspeth came in and I just managed to pull myself together.

I didn't go to youth club tonight. Jacky stayed in to cook us tea and afterwards Dad and I did what we always did and looked through the family photo albums. Only this year Dad had managed to get them all onto a CD, and he gave me my own copy. "Thought you might want a screensaver, or something like that."

"Thanks, Dad," I said, and I gave him a kiss.

February 14th

Valentine's Day. Always a day of such fun and misunderstanding. I had half expected to get a card from Timmy Timms. He's sent me one for years – not that he's serious, more that's it a kind of joke between us. He's always been the class joker and I could never go out with a clown like him, even if he is six foot and is getting to be almost half the size of my Dad. Someone did put something into my bag when I wasn't looking, but I couldn't work out who it was from, and it was only a cheap card anyway.

I didn't think more about it, until Daisy came up to me in break all in a fluster. Apparently, Timmy had asked her if she'd like to go and see a film over half-term. "What do I do, KT?" she asked.

"Well, what do you want to do?" I asked, a little impatiently.

"I don't know. Nobody's ever asked me out before."

"I'll have a word with Timmy," I said and went to find him. He was eating an enormous pork pie just outside the gym.

"I've only asked her to watch a film. Nothing more," he said. "What's it to you anyway?"

"Just be careful with her," I said.

"Yes, ma'am," he said, and he saluted.

"And make sure you have a shower beforehand," I said, as I caught a whiff of male teenager. His mates all giggled, and he threw his pie at me.

"Go if you want to," I said to Daisy later. "But the boy's an idiot."

We'd agreed that Daisy would stay over at the weekend, so I went home with her to collect her things. Only when we arrived Elspeth was on the phone, and she motioned to us to wait. So we waited. And we waited. And we waited. Daisy got changed and packed her bag. Elspeth was still on the phone. Daisy made me a cup of tea. Still she was on the phone. Just as the clock reached five, Elspeth finally put the phone down and let out a little scream.

"Sorry about that, but I just need to check I'm not going mad. I'm going to talk at you very fast and you are not to interrupt. I just want to make sure I have got the whole story straight. Let me know afterwards if I am not making sense."

"Ready? OK, here goes. The good news, Daisy, is that Dad is well enough to go home. The bad news as you can see is that there's no room for his wheelchair here. I have rung around, and there is absolutely nowhere in Drummington-on-Sea for him to live. There are purpose-built flats in Drumchester, but I don't want to live in a flat in Drumchester, and besides, there is a six-month waiting list. And on top of all that, you are getting on so well at school here. So I rang back the hospital who suggested Dad might move into a home. I said I didn't want Dad to move into a home, and besides, where was there a suitable home? Apparently, somewhere down near Cornwall. So Dad is staying in hospital for the time being. Now all I need to do is talk to Joe and find out if there is any chance of getting any money, and just in case there is, find somewhere suitable to live. All by the end of the month. And by the way, I have an interview at the job centre on Monday to find out why I am not looking for work. Meanwhile I need to go up to Bristol this weekend and see what Dad thinks about the situation, without making him ill again. Are you with me so far?"

I nodded. Daisy burst into tears. "Come on," I said, "give your Mum a hug, and then let's take you home – I mean, round my place."

February 16th

It's been a funny weekend. Jacky was around for once, but she was in a peculiarly foul mood. Before she left for the café on Saturday morning, she had a row with Dad about the state of the house and said she wasn't his live-in keeper, whatever that means. I tried to ask her about getting some new clothes, but she only told me she wasn't made out of money. When she was finally gone, Daisy offered to help tidy up the house and go through my wardrobe. We scrubbed the bathroom and vacuumed through, and then we sorted out the huge pile of clothes sitting on the chair in my bedroom. Some were way too small, others needed a good wash, others I had simply forgotten about. And Dad? He was off somewhere practising for the next gig.

"Doesn't he ever help around the house?" asked Daisy.

"He means well," is all I could say as we started to put stuff away.

Jacky had a late-night party down at the café. I wanted to ask her if she was going to do lunch tomorrow. She simply texted back the word, 'No'.

"So I'm expected to cook as well as clean?" I asked Dad, who'd been out all day with the band.

"Well, you know what I'm like in the kitchen," is all he could say.

"Isn't it time you learnt?"

"Believe me, I've tried," he said.

"Perhaps you should try a bit more," I said and then wished I hadn't with Daisy there.

"Let me cook," said Daisy, as ever trying to be the peacemaker.

So, today after church, Daisy cooked lunch. It was very nice, and it would have fed three ordinary-sized people. But Dad is not an ordinary size. I think he was expecting seconds, except there weren't any. Shortly after, Jacky came in and started complaining about the state of the kitchen. I tried to point out that we hadn't had time to clear up, but she was having none of it. Apparently, Gerry is coming in three weeks' time, and she wants everything to be spotless.

"OK, I'll wash up," said Dad. "But lay off KT, OK? Especially when she's got a friend round for the weekend."

"I was coming to that," said Jacky. "We can't afford to have a boarding house for anyone who wants to turn up."

"That's not fair," said Dad, "and you know it."

At that point Jacky just picked up her coat and walked out.

"Is she usually like this?" asked Daisy.

I shook my head. "Ever since she started going out with Gerry she's been, well, different. It's as if everything is about him."

"I guess you'll find out what he's like when he comes."

"Won't that be fun?" I said rolling my eyes. At that point there was a loud crash in the kitchen, and I realised Dad needed a hand. "Come on," I said. "We've got work to do."

I was glad that Elspeth turned up before Jacky got back. I still don't know where Jacky went or what she was doing, but to be honest, I don't care. I called for Daisy to get her stuff, and I expected Elspeth to come up to the house. But she just stayed in the car. She didn't even seem to be looking at me, even though I waved. I thought I should tell Daisy something was wrong, but I decided I didn't want to upset her.

Later on Daisy gave me a ring. It turns out her Dad, Bill, has decided he doesn't want to be a nuisance to anyone and he would like to go into a home – even though the home is in Cornwall. The only thing he kept saying all weekend to Elspeth apparently was "I'm sorry" and "You deserve better."

"Oh, Daisy," is all I could say really. There was a brief moment of silence and then I heard the front door slam. I wanted to rush down and tell Jacky how selfish she was being, that there were more important things in life than making everything nice for Gerry. But I was in no mood for a shouting match. When Daisy had rung off, I put on my headphones and pretended not to hear her going on at Dad yet again.

March 1st

Ally was at youth group tonight. It was the first time I had really seen him since the New Year's party. He'd managed to dislocate a finger during a training session last week, and so he wasn't off playing anywhere. I wanted to say it was good to see him, but I only succeeded in making him cross.

"I thought you would be with Erin tonight," I said.

"Oh no, that finished a couple of weeks ago. She decided I spent too much time with the club."

"Like she noticed?" I asked.

"Shut up," said Ally.

I tried to say sorry but by this time Alex was about to interrupt the conversation as usual. Ally didn't say another word to me all evening. I tried to apologise again on the way out, but Claire and Tom wanted to have a word with me about something, and the moment was lost. I don't why but I want to get on with Ally. Even if he can only think about football, he's about the only normal boy of my own age I know. Having undiluted Alex for the past few weeks has, I think, been a strain for the whole group.

March 8th

Gerry finally showed up today. I disliked him from the moment I saw him. He was wearing a plain blue suit with a plain white shirt that had a ridiculously wide collar. I don't know what fragrance he was wearing, but it smelt like the stuff the school used to exterminate all those bees last summer. Jacky had been making our lives a misery up to the point he arrived, but as soon as he was in the house, she was, as I think they say, all sweetness and light. I think she had warned Gerry about Dad, but he still scowled as she introduced them.

"So this is the famous Trevor," he said in his broad Cork accent.

"Who said I was famous?" said Dad. "Someone been spreading rumours about me?" he said, looking at Jacky.

"Don't be daft," said Jacky, who was suddenly all giggly and not at all like the nearly forty-year-old she really is.

"And this must be KT," said Gerry, as he leant forward and actually kissed my hand.

"Got it in one," I said, trying to work out how soon I could escape and wash the kiss off.

"You're quite the scholar, I hear," he continued, "wanting to be a vet, or something?"

"When I'm not busy looking after the house," I said. Jacky coughed, all embarrassed.

There was an awkward pause. "So, Gerry," said Dad, "tell us something about yourself. I believe you are a salesman or something like that?"

"Mobile customer services representative," corrected Gerry in all seriousness. I so had to make sure I didn't catch Dad's eye at that point, otherwise we would have lost it. "Just waiting to take up a directorship with the company."

"He's been rep of the year three years running," added Jacky as if that was going to impress my Dad.

"Well, it's nearly quarter to five," Dad said, "and I'm going off to check the results."

"I'll join you," I said, and we escaped into the lounge.

"I always thought my cousin, Jacky was the sensible type," whispered Dad as we sat down. "Personally I wouldn't trust Gerry as far as I could throw him."

"You could throw him further than most people," I replied.

"Don't tempt me," said Dad with a grin. "But seriously, I wonder if Jacky isn't making a big mistake. But it's not up to me to tell her. Oh heck, Drumchester City has lost again. Badly."

At that point Gerry came into the room, sweeping his hand through his long, suspiciously blond hair. We weren't quite sure how much he had heard of the conversation, but to be honest, we didn't care.

"Where's Jacky?" asked Dad.

"She's getting ready – I have a surprise in store for her tonight," replied Gerry, "so don't wait up for us."

"Well, yer not exactly teenagers, are you?"

Gerry laughed, and his smile revealed that his teeth were almost as white as his shirt. "Talking of teenagers," said Gerry, turning to me. "Has Jacky told you about my daughter? 'Bout the same age as you, I think you'd get on. Her name is Chelsea."

I wasn't quite sure what to say, so for the next half an hour I sat watching the football results intently, as if they were the most interesting thing on earth. Just as the closing credits rolled, Jacky emerged with the most revealing outfit I'd ever seen her wear. It was the sort of thing Cheryl and her gang would wear if they were going on a date, but I'd always thought Jacky was more sensible than that. Gerry, however, was clearly enraptured, and soon the two, star-struck lovers left the house.

"What's the expression?" asked Dad. "It always ends in tears?"

"Oh, I hope not. I really hope not."

March 22nd

Dad went out early and came back with a huge box he dumped in the kitchen. "What's that?" I asked, still eating breakfast.

"Something Jacky would never let me have before," he replied, "but as she's not around as much, I thought, what the heck?"

I quickly guessed he was talking about a microwave. Once Dad unpacked it, he put on his reading glasses and spent the next quarter of an hour staring at the various buttons. Someone once asked me if my Dad was intelligent. I guess they can only see the tattoos and the huge muscles. Give him time, and he's as smart as the next person. After fifteen minutes intense concentration, he pressed a few buttons and the time appeared. Then he put a cup of cold coffee inside and a minute later it was steaming hot. "If only Susan could see me now," he grinned. "Right, what do you fancy for lunch?"

I didn't dare tell him I'd arranged to go into town that morning with Doris and the family. "Er, anything you like," I said.

"Right, I've always fancied jacket potatoes myself."

I did point out it was only eleven o'clock in the morning but that didn't put him off. He was rather upset when the first lot of spuds exploded, so I pointed out to him how you needed to prick the skins first.

"Where did you learn that?" he said, genuinely astonished.

"In school," I said.

"That explains it," said Dad, "no wonder I never knew nothing. Right, let's start again," and by half twelve we had a half decent meal on the table. Jacket potatoes, ham, cheese and onion.

"How did you get on?" asked Doris when she popped round later.

"I think we've made a breakthrough," I said.

"So have you talked to him about the other matter?" I shook my head. I was a bit embarrassed to bring up the subject. "You've got to, you know?" she said.

Sometimes I think Doris would make a very good teacher, but I wouldn't like to be told off by her. "OK," I said. After all, I still need some new clothes and Jacky isn't minded to help me any more. So after tea (which I cooked), I explained to Dad what Agnieszka had said to me about a clothing allowance.

I don't think Dad ever really thought that much before about how much clothes actually cost. When you live in jeans and T-shirts, you don't really have to worry what you're spending. And it's not as if Dad is still growing, at least I hope he isn't.

"Fine," said Dad, after he'd had a chance to mull it over, "if that's what you need, that's what you need. After all, you're all I've got, and I want you to have the very best."

"Thanks, Dad," I said, and gave him a kiss.

March 31st

Daisy finally went out with Timmy Timms last night. It turned out to be a complete 'mare. "He took me to a film I didn't want to see," she said on the way to school. "He insisted on sitting right close to me, and you're right, KT, he doesn't smell good. I could have kind of coped, but halfway through, he tried to put his arm round me."

"That sounds gross," I said, as Doris joined us outside *Asco's.*

"It was," said Daisy. "It was like, what do I do now?"

"So what did you do?" asked Doris.

"I asked to go to the loo. Only I didn't need to, you see, and I just walked straight out the cinema and phoned my Mum to get me."

"Good for you," I said. As far as I know, that's the first time Daisy's ever stood up for herself.

"Only, like, I feel so guilty. I haven't slept all night wondering what Timmy's going to say to me today."

"Leave it to us," said Doris.

"He may be big, but he's harmless," I said.

I kind of regretted those words later. Somehow Timmy has got it into his head I'm to blame for Daisy walking out, as if I put her up to it or something. "I really don't understand boys," I said to Doris at lunchtime, "somehow I keep winding them up, and I don't know why."

"Don't worry about it," said Doris, touching my hand.

Later on I found someone had posted a picture of a witch on my *Facebook* page. Well, it could have been worse. Much worse. I heard one of the sixth formers today got expelled for posting what the head called "something inappropriate" online. I don't think she was pleased when we all burst out giggling.

April 7th

Jacky has agreed I can start working in the café over the Easter holidays. Just a few hours towards the end of the day, when the families come in off the beaches, and the few people who still actually shop in Drummington-on-Sea are looking for a cuppa. So here I am, taking my first ever order. I feel very conscious in my low-cut white blouse and tight black skirt, and I am sure there are a couple of men in the corner looking at me. I take a deep breath and say a short, silent prayer, and give two fat, sweaty ladies a menu. They take for ages to decide what they're having. In the end it's a cream tea for one, but no cream (isn't that the point of a cream tea?) and black forest gateau with strong, black coffee – "strong, mind, and don't forget to bring two forks."

I write all this down and just about avoid bumping into a customer who's pushed back his chair as far possible to stand up. I get as far as the kitchen where Jacky is there, all cross handing me my mobile phone. "I told you to switch it off," she hisses.

"Sorry, I thought I had," I replied sincerely.

"Someone's been ringing you. Tell her to ring back later."

I do as I am told but realise it's Siobhan ringing. That's the first time Siobhan has ever rung me. Puzzled, I text her that I'll ring back at six. At least while I'm wondering what she wants, I'm not quite as nervous taking orders and clearing the tables.

It was about half six before I finally had a chance to call her. When Siobhan answered, she was talking at about twice her normal speed, and I had to tell her to slow down before I could make out a word she was saying. It turns out that her mother's court hearing has finally been set for next Monday, so today she did a runner. She took a suitcase with her to work, and then disappeared at lunchtime. Siobhan had a text to say she was going away for some time and she loved her. But that was it. Not even a word to Siobhan's Gran.

"Oh," I said, when Siobhan finally paused for breath. What could I say?

"Look, I know you're religious, and all that. Could you say one for me?"

"'Course," I replied.

I told Dad all this later. "Silly woman," was all he said. "You can try and run from the law, but it will always catch up with you sooner or later."

"I guess you'd know," said Jacky, who was looking something up online.

"Oh yes, I know," said Dad. "Anyone want to try a microwave pizza?" he asked. "My mate was telling me all about them today. Apparently, he swears by them."

Jacky and I just looked at each other. "No, we'll be fine," said Jacky, as he went out into the kitchen, "just make sure you clear up after yourself." Then when he shut the door Jacky and I just burst out laughing. It had been a long time since I had shared a joke with her, and for a moment I think I saw a bit of the old Jacky. "By the way," she said, "you did well today. I still remember the first order I ever took. I think it will haunt me for the rest of my life."

"Thanks," I said, and for once we had a brief hug.

April 18th

Good Friday evening. We wouldn't usually have a youth group tonight, but one way or another most of us are around. All except Alex, who's up in London with his grandparents, and Claire and Tom who are at some festival or other. John wanted us to think more about the Garden of Gethsemane and difficult situations where we needed to pray. I talked about taking my first order. Daisy very quietly talked about having to do something she knew would upset someone else. I don't think anybody else there guessed what we were talking about.

And then Ally shared something which floored us all. He knocked out a school bully last year who pulled a knife on him. I can't imagine what it must have been like for him. He's quite gentle and sweet really, even if he's still putting on more muscle every time I see him, and I don't want to think he could actually harm someone else.

Anyway, Erin and her friend Poppy told the police back then they saw the bully with a knife on the morning of the incident. Only now Erin has just told Ally they didn't really see the knife. They only said they did because they were on Ally's side.

"So what do I do?" asked Ally. "Do I go back to the police or what?"

"I guess you must've been really praying about that one," said John. "What do others think?"

In the end we decided Ally ought to challenge Erin and ask if she was willing to go back to the police. After all, as John said, one thing we can learn from Easter is about the cost of standing up for the truth, even if it causes us to suffer. I'd never thought about it that way before. But then John has this amazing way of making you think. I guess it's one reason why this group has been going for so long, and why we keep coming back.

April 22nd

I asked Siobhan if there was any more news of her Mum. She shook her head. Apparently there's now a warrant out for her arrest.

"How's your Gran taking it?"

"I daren't mention it. She says Mum's never going to be welcome under her roof, as long as she lives. Apparently Mum forged Gran's signature to get a couple of loans."

"That's terrible."

"Not as terrible as the language Gran used when one of the loan companies turned up on her doorstep. I don't think they'll be back in a hurry."

"And what about you? Do you have any money?"

I kind of regretted the question, but it sort of slipped out. I knew Siobhan was always having to beg and borrow to get by.

Siobhan began to cry a little. "It's so hard, KT," she said. "Gran showed me what she had to live on the other day. It's not a lot. She should have some money for looking after me, but of course Mum's taken the lot."

I talked over the situation with Doris later on. Usually sensible Doris has an answer or can say something wise, but she was just very silent. "That is very difficult," were the only words she said, as we slipped out of school.

We went shopping in *Asco's* and I spent some of the money I had earned at Jacky's over the holidays. I would have spent more, but I was still thinking of Siobhan, and thought perhaps I ought to save a little.

May 4th

I had a go at Dad yesterday. It's not like we argue most of the time, but this really was the last straw. Dad had been working in the morning, and he was out with the band in the afternoon. So like usual I did a few chores around the house. I don't even know if Dad actually notices whether I do them or not, to be honest. Then when he gets in, he puts his head round the lounge door and announces he's invited Pete Green and Ally to come to lunch tomorrow.

"And who's going to cook for them?" I asked.

I could see Dad hadn't really thought about that, or maybe he'd forgotten Jacky was having a long weekend away with her man. "I'm sure we could do something," he said cheerfully.

"Do you mean us, or do you mean me?"

Dad scratched his head.

"'Cos I've got my own life to lead, and I can't just step in when Jacky's not around."

"I know that, love."

"Do you know what I've done whilst you've been out today?"

"Calm it down, KT. I've been busy too, you know."

"Oh great. Like all the housework and cooking's down to me, is it?"

And I slammed the door and went upstairs at that point to watch my favourite programme.

I didn't see Dad until breakfast today. He was trying to clean the sink in the kitchen, but he wasn't making a very good job of it.

"Let me help," I said, "you need to do it like this."

"Perhaps we ought to get a cleaner," said Dad. "At least one that gets paid."

"And what about the cooking?" I was still cross.

"Well, for now, we're going to Pete and Ally's for lunch. I rang up and rearranged."

So today we went over to their new house after church. It was the first time I had been over there. After lunch, Pete and Dad went out into the garden, to see what they could do. It had all been covered with weeds when Pete first moved in, and they were threatening to make a comeback. That left me with Ally, which I think we both found awkward. I offered to wash up, and Ally said he would dry. We watched the two men start prodding around with a couple of forks and cracked a few feeble jokes, and then we fell silent.

Finally I asked him how he had got on with Erin. "Yeah, fine," said Ally.

"Just that – fine?"

"What's it to you?" he asked.

"Just asking, that's all."

"If you must know, I went round to see Erin. Only Erin had just split up with Phil 'cos Phil was wanting her to do stuff she didn't want to do. So we kind of like made up. Not that we're back together or anything," he added hastily.

"So she's not going to go to the police?"

"No," said Ally in such a way that I knew there was no point asking any questions. Then he put down his tea towel and said, "I'm going for a run. See how your Dad's getting on."

"OK," I said. Why do I always feel so awkward when Ally's around? I felt like I'd put my foot in it again, but I couldn't kind of work out why.

When I went out into the garden, Dad must have hit a stone or something, because the prongs of his fork just crumpled as he dug into the ground.

"Your Dad's not very good at being domestic, is he?" said Pete.

"That's not funny," I said, and I asked Dad when we could go home.

"But I've only just started," Dad replied.

"And a fine mess you're making as always."

"That's enough, KT," he said, and I bit my tongue.

But honestly, it was the most boring afternoon ever. I did help a bit, deadheading some daffodils and making mugs of tea. I tried texting a few people, but everyone seemed to be busy or away. Daisy was visiting her Dad and helping Elspeth make preparations for him to go into the home. Doris' youngest sister was having her first communion. While Siobhan, apparently, was mucking out at the stables Stacey and Cherie use, to try and earn something. "Could bring some over for the garden later when I'm done," she said. That was about the only thing that made me smile the whole afternoon.

May 9th

Jacky wasn't at all impressed with the idea of us having a cleaner. When she returned late on Sunday her only comment was, "I knew you wouldn't manage without me." Since then she has made a point of keeping the house clean throughout the week. She's twice told me off about the state of my bedroom. As I guessed, that could only mean one thing. Gerry is coming in a fortnight, and this time he is bringing Chelsea.

"And where is she going to sleep?" asked Dad over tea.

Jacky looked at me. I shook my head. "I've never met her before, and besides, I have all this revision to do for my exams."

"Since when has that been an excuse?" asked Jacky.

"Since I wanted to make sure I can do the subjects I want to do next year," I replied.

"'Cos you're going to be some kind of genius who's going to be a vet?" Jacky replied sarcastically.

"Well, I believe in her," said Dad, "and I want her to do the very best."

"OK," said Jacky with an unnaturally long sigh, "the sofa it is. So the lounge better be tidy. Tidy by my standards, I mean."

At youth group tonight there weren't many around. Ally had gone out with a friend, apparently – no guessing what that meant. Claire's brother had a birthday, and Sian had gone as well. So that left me and Daisy and Alex. John and Helen must have arranged something beforehand, 'cos John took Alex off into his study to discuss some book or other. That left us with Helen who sat with us in the vicarage kitchen and made us hot chocolate.

Somehow even though we were surrounded by all of Emily and Josiah's bits and pieces, and there was a huge pile of dirty laundry on the floor, Helen as always made the whole place seem peaceful and calm. She didn't say a lot really, tonight. She didn't need to. We both wanted to talk. Daisy about her Dad and how Bill was going to move finally at the end of the month. About her brother Derek who had come near the top of the shooting test and was going to pass out as an infantryman at the end of July. About Elspeth who was having trouble sleeping and missing her Dad badly.

"What about you?" asked Helen, after she had been up to check on Josiah.

"Yeah, all right, I s'pose," I said, taking a sip of my second hot chocolate. "It's just like everything's changing at home, and I keep on having these arguments."

"Go on," said Helen, passing me a biscuit. So I talked about Jacky and her man, and how I was struggling to cook and do the housework, and how I loved Dad, but he wasn't that much help around the house.

"Perhaps you ought to, like, stay over my place one weekend," said Daisy. "I could sure do with some help with my homework."

A thought crossed my mind. "Like in a couple of weeks' time?" I said.

"Yeah, great," said Daisy.

"In the meanwhile, if you want to come over and help entertain two lively little children, you'd be very welcome," said Helen. I gave her a hug, just as the study door opened, and John and Alex entered the kitchen, totally unaware of what was going on.

"That's men," whispered Helen, as she let me go, and we laughed.

I was going to tell Jacky about the weekend when Elspeth dropped me home, only this time Jacky and Dad were having an argument. It was about the car. I never realised Dad put in some money for it. The plan was for Jacky to use it during the week, and Dad to have it during the weekend. Only with Jacky away, Dad had to keep borrowing a van from work, and work wasn't happy about it.

"I shall be glad when I'm finally out of this place," was what I heard Jacky saying as I entered the hall.

"Be careful what you wish for," growled my Dad. "Hello, KT, did you have a nice evening?" he said as I entered the lounge. Jacky stood by the kitchen door with her arms crossed. Dad was right on the other side of the room. Jacky just turned and glared at me. Then she shut the kitchen door behind her and turned on the telly really loud.

"You all right?" I asked Dad, as I gave him a hug.

"I don't like what Jacky's turning into," was all he said, "even if she's madly in love." Then he gave me a kiss and said, "But, KT Lee, you're all right."

May 24th

As I predicted, Jacky wasn't that impressed with my idea to sleep over at Daisy's tonight. "You never said."

"You never asked," I replied. "And I do need to help her with her schoolwork."

"Yeah, right."

"I'm happy to meet her," I said (although happy wasn't the word I wanted to use), "and I'll let her use my room, but I have exams coming up in a fortnight."

"You and your excuses," said Jacky.

"Believe me or not, I don't actually care," I replied.

"Well, you f***ing well should," she answered.

I had never heard Jacky use the f-word before, certainly not at me. I stared at her not knowing what to say next. At that point my phone rang.

"Excuse me," I said, and went up to my room.

It was Siobhan. The police had just come round to say they had found her Mum. She was living in a caravan in Cornwall under a false name, helping out at a local hotel. And now she was in a police cell in Bodmin, being interviewed under caution, whatever that meant.

"So what happens next?"

"Gran says she can't afford to get to Bodmin, and she sure as hell doesn't want her back in her house. So I dunno. Keep praying for me, sister."

"I will. Catch up on Monday."

"Love you, sweetheart," she said in what one teacher recently called "her lilting Irish accent."

I sat on my bed and took a few deep breaths. I was in no mood to go downstairs and face Jacky. John had preached last week about blessing those who persecute you, but I wasn't ready to bless Jacky just yet. Dad had decided to work most of today, as well, which probably had made her mood even worse. I just wished she could see the damage she was doing to her family, just like Siobhan's mother was doing to hers.

I put on my music and turned to my revision. No way did I want to do combined sciences in September, and my form tutor told me this week I could get straight A's in each of the three individual subjects, if I put in just a little more effort. So I got online and for the next couple of hours immersed myself in my studies...

…until on the stroke of one the doorbell rang.

It was just as I feared. Jacky and Gerry were soon all over each other like a rash. Chelsea was as I imagined her to be. She was a bit like Maxine, except more spoilt. Her biggest aim was to become the next top model, or failing that, a beautician. So I told her about Siobhan's chicks and how we would have to start culling the roosters. Chelsea said that was gross and Jacky told me to change the subject. So I talked about Dad's band and the charity concert that was coming up. But she had never heard of any of the songs I mentioned, and only listened to boy bands. Gerry apparently was taking her to see *One Direction* at Wembley some point. Why wasn't I surprised? I offered to stay behind and clear up while Jacky and Gerry took Chelsea to see the café.

"You can wipe the tables," I said cheerfully, as they left. Chelsea just scowled at me. I'm surprised her make-up didn't crack at that point.

Fortunately, I escaped while they were still out. Daisy was really glad to see me, but both she and her Mum looked exhausted. Her Mum had some enormous form on the lounge table she was trying to fill in.

"I've reached page 11," she said, without looking up. "I need to reach page 48 before Bill can go into the home."

"I think we'd better leave her to it," said Daisy.

But there wasn't much place we could go. By now it was drizzling outside, and they only had a tiny garden which was mostly filled up with a shed. Daisy's bedroom was tiny, and there was only just enough room to put my sleeping bag between the radiator and the wardrobe. I perched with her on her bed and was just about to get out some of my books, when Daisy suddenly dissolved into floods of tears.

After I'd held for a few minutes, I took a good look at her. "You look a real mess," I said, and she did. I could tell no-one had made her feel special for a long time. So I brushed her lovely long, smooth hair and helped her put it up in a ponytail. We found her favourite dress, and she wound round the scarf I bought her a few years back. "Go and look in your Mum's mirror," I said. "That's better, isn't it?" She nodded and for a brief moment she even smiled.

"Now I think I can face the dreaded English," she said.

We were still working when Dad rang. "I want to go and live on a desert island," he said.

"Is it that bad?"

"Picture Jacky singing her favourite *Bananarama* songs, Chelsea dancing round the lounge and Gerry laughing like a hyena."

"That's so bad."

"That's worse than bad. Oh no, they're changing to *One Direction*."

"It's only for one night."

"That's still one night too long. Right, there's only one thing for it. *Van Halen* in my headphones. Very loudly."

"I love you, Dad."

"I love you, too," he said.

"Trouble?" asked Daisy.

"Don't ask," I said.

I was about to do some more stuff with her, when Elspeth called us down to tea. "Wow, you look amazing, Daisy," was her only comment. I think she'd forgotten just how beautiful her daughter could be. But with that form still lying there on the table, I couldn't blame her.

May 29th

As it was half-term, I went round to Siobhan's. Her Gran had already started on the first rooster and was sitting on a stool in the garden plucking the feathers. "At least we've got chicken to eat, if nothing else," she said.

"Do you want a hand?" I asked.

"Do you know what you're doing?" I shook my head. So her Gran explained how you first of all dunk the chicken in some hot water for a few moments to loosen the feathers, then pinch the skin and gradually work round the bird.

At that point Siobhan came round into the front garden with another bird. We sat for a good half an hour working on the young roosters silently. Presently Kathleen said, "To be sure, this makes a change from worrying about that flighty young girl of mine."

"You talking about me again?" asked Siobhan, half-jokingly.

"Eh, don't be daft. I mean your Mum," she said, as she picked up a knife and began to gut the now bare carcase.

"Where is she now?" I asked.

"She's got another man-friend," said Kathleen and I could tell she didn't approve. "He picked her up from the station and paid her bail. So I guess she's staying with him somewhere in Cornwall. Not that she's told us or anything."

"Do you miss her?" I asked, thinking of Daisy.

"Not that much," said Siobhan. "I've been worried about her for too long. At least we now know where she is and what she is doing." At that point a gust of wind got up and scattered the feathers that had escaped from the bag.

"Don't worry about those," said Kathleen. "The magpies can have those. Now who's going to get me another young bird?"

I reckon there can't be too many fifteen-year-old girls who think wringing a chicken's neck is their idea of a good time. Chelsea would be clean out of here, probably Cheryl too. Stacey would claim to know it all, anyway, and wouldn't be interested. Siobhan and I laughed as we imagined their reactions. She then got out her phone and pictured the dead bird hanging limply from my arms. I couldn't imagine why she wanted to do that, but I s'pose it takes all sorts. By the end of the morning we had five prime birds, which all went straight in their freezer.

It was about three o'clock when this enormous old estate car pulled up outside the cottage. We didn't pay that much attention at first, 'cos Siobhan was showing me the latest pieces she'd been learning on the bass guitar. Only when Kathleen came in and told us, "To shut up this bloody racket," did I realise this car in fact belonged to my Dad. He'd sorted it out with Jacky, apparently, and now he had a car of his own. Bought off a mate of Pete Green's apparently. It should have cost a lot more, but the electrics needed some work, or something like that. But Dad reckoned this bloke at work had a friend who could sort that out, and fix a few other minor niggles as well.

On the way home, we stopped by Daisy's so we could take her up to Doris, as Elspeth was going to be busy moving Bill that weekend. As Daisy got out, she thanked him for the lift.

"Not at all," said Dad.

"It's good to know there's now another taxi driver in Drummington."

June 6th

Daisy and me finally persuaded Doris to come along to our youth group tonight. Claire and Sian had already started their exams, and us year tens were getting pretty nervous about next week. So John decided we needed distracting from our studies, and he handed all of us a ten-pound note.

"Does he do that every week?" asked Doris.

"No, sometimes, it's twenty," said Ally and we all laughed.

Then John began talking about the parable of the talents, and he challenged us to think how we could best invest the ten pounds he had just given us.

As usual, Alex was the first to speak. Someone in Drumley Green was selling strawberry plants and he could buy a load for the fruit. Ally had seen a bundle of old football programmes in a charity shop window, and he wanted to sell them on *E-bay*. Claire reckoned she could hire the church hall for an hour and put on a gig with Tom. In fact everyone seemed to have their ideas, except me and Daisy.

"Don't worry," said John. "I'm sure you'll come up with something. You have until September, after all."

At that point Helen came down from seeing the children, and I introduced her to Doris.

"I've never met the wife of a priest before," she said later, "but I kind of like her."

"It's hard not to," I said. And I mean it. Thinking of all that's happened, she's been like a mother to me at times. Certainly more of a mother than Jacky at the moment. I bumped into Sid the chef today and he's seriously unimpressed by the amount of time she's taking off from the café at the moment. Especially with the holiday season approaching.

June 12th

I think I've had a brainwave! Talking to Siobhan today, I found out they have about twenty hens ready to lay. I explained the challenge John had set us, and I asked if me and Daisy could buy a hen. Siobhan texted back later to say in return we could half the money the hen gets for her eggs down the local shop. So that's sorted. Eighty pence a week – it's not much, but by September we might at least be able to pay John back.

June 20th

Our exams are finally over today. The last couple of weeks haven't gone too badly, I think. It's Daisy who's had the nightmare. There's been a big problem with all the school laptops, some kind of virus apparently. So every time Daisy has come to an exam, she has never known whether her laptop was going to work or not. Twice the laptop just died halfway through the paper. She's never been one to complain, but Doris and I have been keeping a special eye on her just in case. We wrote a letter of protest to the head this morning, which will probably mean we end up in trouble, but we figure someone has to speak out.

At least now it's over. So we do what we always do when we want a treat. We steam down to *Digby's* ice cream parlour and head over to Drake's point. Only I notice that Jacky's café next door is closed. There's a sign on the door saying, 'Sorry closed today. Back open tomorrow'. I don't know what's going on, but it's very odd.

"It's probably nothing," says Siobhan who has come along with us. "Come on, I'm going to have pistachio."

It was a good few hours later when I finally made it back home. It was a lovely warm evening. We all went for a paddle in the sea, and Siobhan even took her shirt off to sunbathe. A couple of boys from school noticed and whistled, but she didn't seem to care. Me, I was just glad to keep in the shade as my skin was burning as usual, and Doris and Daisy were too sensible to do anything like that. We just sat on a rock and chatted, as if school and home and everything else was a million miles away, and we were simply friends having a good time.

But now I'm home, Jacky is in a foul mood. It all came to a head with her and Sid today. Sid told her to look at the takings, and threatened to walk out, together with Betty, if Jacky didn't start "pulling her finger out." Jacky closed the café for the day and they clearly had a row. But I know Sid has been working with Jacky for years and there is no way Jacky can ever sack him. Sid is probably right as well. So Jacky's been on the phone to Gerry and cancelled their plans for this weekend. Me, I'm going to have to keep my head down. It's not going to be a lot of fun over the next few days.

June 25th

Daisy's birthday today. We wanted to go shopping with her after school, but apparently Elspeth had plans. So I went back home, made sure I did my washing like Jacky told me to, and started learning a new worship song for Sunday. I haven't been to the band practice for ages, and now exams are out the way, I need to brush up my playing. Dad gave me an electric drum kit for Christmas, so I was busy practising up in my bedroom when suddenly my phone rang. It was Daisy. What's more she was happy and excited.

When Elspeth meant she had plans, she meant she was going to show Daisy the place she was going to put an offer in on. The money from the farm was going to come through any day soon, and there was just enough to buy somewhere to live. So could Elspeth come and pick everyone up to give the guided tour?

That's how that evening Siobhan, Doris and me ended up jammed in the back of Elspeth's little car as she took us out along the back road to Dumpley Common. Just before we reached Dumpley End, she turned right down a little road I had never seen before. There was an old bungalow down there, with an enormous garden that had been turned into some kind of allotment. There was even a rather green and stagnant pond at the end, next to the wreck of caravan that hadn't been moved for ages.

"OK, it needs some work doing," said Elspeth, "but it's nothing compared to the farm, and it's lovely and quiet. And if Bill does ever come home to visit, it's all on the level for him."

"That's quite some present," I said.

"Thanks, Mum," said Daisy.

"Well, let's wait and see," said Elspeth, "I've had enough disappointments recently."

July 4th

Jacky has been working non-stop since that day with Sid. Today was the first time she had taken any time off. I thought she'd have a lie-in or something, but no, she was first out the house, even before Dad who was going off to do an overnighter somewhere in the depths of Yorkshire.

She still wasn't back when it was time for the youth group. Fortunately, Doris was able to pick me up. I don't think her Mum approves of her going, but she's starting to enjoy herself. Today she brought along her guitar and sang a song from something called a 'folk mass', whatever that is. When the time came for prayer, she even shared something for once. Apparently, her Mum is still planning to go back to Poland in September. But her Dad still has work here, and Doris doesn't want to return, so Doris is going to stay here with him, at least for another year.

"That's not easy," said Helen.

"I know," said Doris and as we prayed for her, she crossed herself three times. I don't pretend to understand her faith, but at least I know it's real.

I was still thinking about Doris when the front door opened. I was just getting ready for bed, and I started like a frightened rabbit. But it was only Jacky. "Can I come in?" she asked. I quickly got into bed, as she opened the door without waiting for my reply. I thought I might've done something wrong again, but she wasn't cross. Far from it. She'd been up to Bristol to have lunch with Gerry, and, "Oh, KT," she said, "he's asked me to marry him."

"That's nice," I said, trying to sound enthusiastic.

"It's wonderful," she purred, "after all those years. I've spent all this time thinking all men were the same, but now I know I'm wrong," and she showed me the ring. It was one of those large, flashy affairs you see in the windows of cheap jewellers.

"So will you be my bridesmaid? Will you?" she pleaded.

"With Chelsea?"

"Yeah, with Chelsea," she beamed.

"All right," and at that point Jacky gave me a big hug. I realised she smelt different, and I guessed it was Gerry's perfume that was all over her.

"We'll talk more when Trevor gets back. But just to let you know, we've already set the date and the venue. It's August 30th, up near Bristol. That's only seven weeks away! I can't wait."

I smiled. I wasn't sure what to say. But as Jacky wasn't listening, it didn't make any difference. "I love you, KT Lee," she said, and she gave me a big kiss.

"Goodnight," I said, and I rolled over pretending I was about to fall asleep.

In fact I spent the next half an hour wide awake thinking how quickly how everything had changed over the past six months. I thought Jacky would always be there, at least till I had grown up. Me, Dad, Jacky, we were family, or so it seemed. I found myself praying and then I wrote a long e-mail to my Aunt, Jenny.

July 13th

Ally's half-brother, Mark, had his little boy baptised today. There must have been fifty or more guests there, so the main service today was really packed. Most of them I reckon had hardly ever been in church before, and none of them knew the words to any of the songs. Quite a few were on their phones while John was preaching. When the time came for the parents and godparents to make their promises, only Ally seemed to be speaking. But at the end when Mark and Olivia stayed on for coffee, they said how much they had enjoyed the service. They'd left it too late to book anywhere for the party afterwards, so they decided to hold the celebrations in the church hall. We weren't quite sure who was invited, so in the end most of us stayed behind for lunch.

Little Kai was quite the star of the show. I remember Ally telling us what an awful start he'd had in life, but here he was happily toddling around, and generally enjoying the fuss. When he started wandering too far, Ally just scooped him up in his enormous hands, and passed him over to me.

"Can't get anything on me suit," he explained, "it's brand new, and Mum says it's dry-clean only."

"You look very smart in it," I replied, before realising what I was saying.

But he did. Ally just smiled and said, "You played well this morning."

At that moment, as always, Alex somehow interrupted us, and Kai burst into tears. I kind of knew how he felt.

July 18th

The end of term! One way or another I've managed to pass all my exams, with grades good enough to do all ten subjects next year. Usually I'd give the report to Jacky to read first, but I decided it was better to give this one straight to Dad. Daisy didn't do quite as well, but she came top of the year in Art. I was going to congratulate her, but she was even quieter than usual today, and wouldn't say why. Eventually, on the way home, she told me that someone else had put in a higher offer on the bungalow.

"It's just not fair," she said. "Nothing's going right at the moment."

I wasn't sure what I could say, so I changed the subject. "At least we got another £2.40 from Siobhan today. We should be able to pay John back in September."

She tried to smile, but I could just see she was really, really tired. Sometimes I forget just what hard work it is for her to get through the school day. I think the teachers forget as well. The head did reply to the letter which Doris and I wrote, but she just went on about "circumstances beyond the school's control." I thought about what John said the other day about everything being in God's hands. Tonight I prayed that somehow or other Elspeth and Daisy would get the bungalow. I think they both could do with a miracle in their lives right now.

August 3rd

Dad and I are going on our holidays. Jacky isn't too impressed, with the wedding being only twenty-seven days away. But I think we both need a break from her. She's decided to hand the business over to Sid in a couple of weeks' time –as if he needed that right in the middle of the holiday season. In the meantime she's working flat out to pay for the wedding, and when she's home, she's almost constantly online organising the wedding with Gerry. Gerry's done some kind of deal with a posh hotel near a place called Weston-Super-Mare. We're all going up the day before, and I think that when we get there Jacky expects me to be tarted up like a Barbie doll. Well, I've given her all the measurements she needs for the bridesmaid's dress – three times so far – and my shoe sizes. There's nothing more really I can see needs doing. Dad has bought a new suit and has even lost a few pounds to make sure he can fit in it. But he's refused to get involved any more than that.

So we are going on holiday. Dad, as always, has a week booked with his best mate Nick and his family. But first he has promised to take me up to Surrey where I'll be staying for a fortnight with my Aunt, Jenny.

Today was a baking hot summer's day. Dad tried turning on the air-con, but it didn't seem to be working, even though his mate had sworn to him the other day it was fixed. We tried rolling down the windows, but the noise and the fumes meant we thought better of it. Dad had put some bottles of water in a cool-bag which helped a little. But not much.

And then just as we thought our journey was coming to an end, the traffic on the motorway ahead of us ground to a standstill. From the police cars and ambulances speeding past us, there must have been a big accident, or something. So we finally wound down the windows and waited and waited. Dad turned off the engine for a while, as we were going nowhere. After what seemed an eternity, the cars in front began to crawl forward slowly. So Dad turned the engine on. Nothing happened. The engine made a funny noise, and then stopped. He tried again. Still nothing. The cars behind us honked.

"Best get out yer phone," said Dad, "and call the police."

Slowly the traffic made their way round us. It started to speed up. We were stuck in the nearside lane with our flashers on. It was a real relief when a patrol officer on his bike turned up. Soon the lane behind us was coned off, while we waited for the recovery truck.

In the end we were towed to some industrial estate where eventually Dad got hold of a hire car. By now it was getting late. We were hot and hungry, and Dad, I could see, was cross about the car. We pressed on to the hotel where Jenny was waiting for us, and Dad decided to spend the night there.

It wasn't ideal, but it gave the three of us time to talk about Jacky over dinner. After Dad and I had said our piece, Jenny turned to Dad and said, "So you're managing to look after KT, then?"

"Yeah, sort of."

"It can't be easy with a full-time job, and sometimes having to stay overnight."

"We manage, don't we, love?" I nodded.

"KT's always welcome to come and stay with us, you know, if things get difficult."

"What exactly do you mean?"

"It's not always easy having a teenager to look after, especially if, you know…"

"You know, what?"

I could tell from the way Dad was frowning he wasn't that happy about the way the conversation was turning. Jenny had done something with her hair since I last saw her, and she didn't remind me half as much of my mother as she had then. She picked up her spoon and said slowly, "You know, being a single parent, and all that."

"Yeah, I know. Being an alcoholic, and an ex-convict, and covered in tattoos. You've never really accepted that, have you?" and Dad looked hard at her as he put his spoon into his dessert.

"He's not done a bad job, you know," I said, getting more and more uncomfortable at the way the evening was turning out.

Jenny looked at me. "Yes, I suppose not. But the offer's always there."

"Thank you, I think," said Dad. But I could tell he was hurt. I'm probably the only person in the world who could see that, but then as he's told me before, I'm the only one he's got. I put my hand on his arm, and he closed his hand over mine, in that firm but incredibly tender way only Dad can.

Jenny didn't say any more, but she texted me later to say she was sorry it came out all wrong and hoping we could still have a good holiday together. We shall see. I gave Dad an extra big hug when he said goodnight just now. I think he needed it.

August 17th

Came home from holiday today. It wasn't easy the first couple of days, but I think Jenny was genuinely sorry for what she had said. And we did have a lot of fun together. As always, Jenny insisted on buying me lots of new clothes, and I've come back on the train with an extra suitcase. Jenny wanted to show me some museums and galleries in London, but honestly, it was too hot and crowded, and I've never been big on that sort of thing anyway. Most of the time, except when we were shopping, we didn't bother going into the capital but stayed near the hotel. We hired bicycles and rode along by the canal. We found a formal garden with a very posh tearoom, and a local nature reserve which was far more to our liking. We spent hours watching the dragonflies humming over the pond and trying to guess which fish might be hiding at the bottom of the water.

But the best bit of the holiday was on the middle Saturday. Jenny insisted we went back to the hotel for lunch but wouldn't tell me why. It was only when I found Arthur and Peggy arriving in the hallway that I twigged something special was going on. It was their fortieth wedding anniversary, and they had come down for the night for a show up in the West End, together with their daughter Suzanne. While everyone else was chatting about the weather, Arthur and I got down to the serious business, and began talking chickens. Sid the cockerel had apparently been taken by a fox trying to defend his ladies, but, as Arthur said, he was getting a bit old, anyway. So there was a new kid on the block, Junior. And he would have told me about him, except Peggy wanted the key to the room, and we had to make plans for the evening.

I always thought musicals were boring, but this was all about rock and roll, and the tunes were really good. Jenny had bought me a posh new frock and shoes the day before, and now I understood why. I felt really grown-up mingling with the crowds at the interval, and Jenny bought me an extra-large ice cream that I managed to avoid spilling down my front.

When Dad came to pick me up today, he was in a different car. Apparently, he had persuaded the bloke who sold him the estate to buy it back – how I didn't want to think. Instead I told him all about the musical, and when we got in, he played me some of the tunes on the guitar. They were the first songs he ever learnt to play, he said.

I was still happily singing along when Jacky came in. It was the last day of her running the café. It had been a mad day with any number of customers, and they had stayed open late. Even then, she had to go through everything with Sid and do a complete stock count. It was now ten o'clock and her mood was as black as the night sky.

"Pipe down, KT," she said, as she brewed herself a strong coffee. "I need all the peace and quiet I can get." Just like that. No welcome home. No "how are you?" I had bought her a little present, but I decided it could wait till morning.

August 29th

We travelled up to the wedding today. Jacky travelled in our car, 'cos as she said, she wasn't coming back. Last night for the first time she even got a little tearful and gave me a hug. But then Gerry rang about some last-minute detail and the moment passed. I was glad Dad had bought another estate as we had so much stuff. And this one didn't break down on the way.

The hotel turned out to be some kind of stately home, with an enormous dining hall. Jacky explained that would be where the reception would be held tomorrow. The actual wedding would take place in a small function room somewhere down the corridor. I asked if there would be any hymns or anything like that, but Jacky said you couldn't have that in a civil wedding. Doesn't seem to me to be much like a wedding then, but I held my tongue.

My room is enormous. For some reason I have a double bed, and a sofa, and the ensuite is bigger than my entire bedroom back home. I have this amazing view over to the sea, and to my right there is a field of cows. Mostly Aberdeen Angus, I think.

Jacky came up with my bridesmaid dress and insisted I tried it on. It was very pretty, but I wasn't comfortable with the idea it was off the shoulder. "I'll only burn," I said.

"Don't worry," said Jacky and she produced this ivory cream shawl to go with it. "There, don't you look lovely, especially with those shoes?" And then she then proceeded to give a long spiel all about what I was supposed to do and not do. Well, if it's her big day, then I better make an effort. And even if there aren't any prayers in the service, it doesn't mean I can't pray for Jacky and Gerry tonight.

Oh yes, and Chelsea too. I had to sit next to her at dinner tonight. I tried my best to be nice to her, and she seemed genuinely interested to hear about the musical. In return she told me all about *One Direction*. I still think I had the better deal.

August 30th

The weather broke overnight. I was woken by a huge thunderstorm. It was spectacular watching the lightning over the bay, and today the sea had turned from a brilliant blue to a heavy grey. There was a steady drizzle in the air, and a cool breeze as I opened the window. It was relief, though, not to feel so hot and know I wouldn't burn.

Jacky had arranged for her, Chelsea and me, to have our hair and make-up done in the morning. I protested though when it came to my turn. The lady wanted to cover over the scar beneath my left eye and no way was I going to let her do that. She couldn't understand why it was so special, so in the end she laid off the foundation altogether. I didn't mind at all. Jacky and Chelsea wanted me to try on some false nails, but I pointed out I was playing the drums later, and I needed to keep my nails short.

We then hung around for ages in this room that oddly seemed to have very little in it, apart from celebrity magazines and a large harp. Jacky and Chelsea were happy reading those, even if they kept nipping off to the loo. The minutes on the clock ticked slowly. I wished I had my phone with me, but of course I didn't have any pockets or even a handbag. The florist showed up, with gaudy bouquets of pink and purple flowers. They did smell fantastic, but I wasn't that sure about the combination. Then the hair lady came back to see if we needed any last-minute alterations. We didn't.

At last the clock rolled round to one o'clock. We walked down the corridor to just out of sight of the function room. Lee was there by the door. I hadn't seen him much recently, as he had been busy finishing his course at college. But he looked a completely different person to that snotty, smelly boy who turned up on my doorstep three years ago. He had a natty suit with a thin blue tie, and shiny brown shoes that looked uncomfortable and new. Then he would have not even bothered to look up at me. Now he gave me a grin and said, "You look fantastic." Then he got embarrassed as he realised he shouldn't let anyone know we were waiting there.

Finally, someone I didn't recognise put their head round the door, and said, "Ready?"

Jacky took a deep breath and said, "Ready." Jacky's favourite *Bananarama* song, '*Robert de Niro's waiting*' began to play and slowly we walked forward. Even if it was Gerry, not Robert de Niro, at the front.

The whole service was incredibly short. No hymns, no prayers. Just a woman in a trouser suit who gave Jacky and Gerry the words to read off a card. Without the fancy dress, it could just have been another one of Gerry's sales conferences, as Dad said later. Then on to the reception, where before we could eat a whole host of people gave some very long speeches with some very dull jokes. I was sat right at the front, and I was conscious there were all these strangers looking at me. Particularly a boy at the back, who was about eighteen.

Then we had to toast the couple as they prepared to cut the cake. Someone tried to give a glass of champagne to Dad. Dad politely declined, but the young waiter insisted. Dad tried again. In the end Dad had to take the glass, but he pushed it as far away from him as possible.

It was hard not to avoid the alcohol today. There seemed to be drink flowing everywhere, and no-one seemed to mind how much Chelsea was drinking. Dad and I were glad when we could leave to get changed and get on stage. Dad had invited his friend Nick down to play the bass, and it was good to finally meet him. Dad gave him a real man-hug as we walked up onto the stage, and then he signalled to me. We'd been practising those rock and roll numbers I'd heard up in London, and although I hadn't got them perfect, they were pretty easy to play. Then later, as the evening wore on, Dad and Nick began jamming the blues. I had never seen two people play so naturally and completely in harmony. I just had to give them a twelve-bar rhythm and they began improvising to their hearts' content.

Jacky and Gerry took centre stage, and whatever else you might say about them, clearly they were in love. They moved slowly and gracefully across the dance floor, even if some of the others were swaying rather more unsteadily. Someone dimmed the lights, and Dad and Nick played on. It was all getting to be a rather special evening. That is, until Chelsea suddenly began throwing up. Then Gerry's brother knocked over someone's drink and they had a loud argument. Jacky and Gerry took this as a signal to leave, while the staff mopped the floor, and Lee fetched a broom to sweep up the broken glass.

We packed up pretty quick after that. I heard later there had been a couple of fights, and the police had been called. But for all that, playing with Dad and Nick at the wedding was a very special experience I will never forget. Nick has invited me to come up with Dad next year and meet the family who are all musicians. I think I might just do that. For now, Nick has posted a video of us playing on *YouTube*. So here I am, finally tucked up in bed, going to sleep with our blues playing in the background. Life really doesn't get much better.

September 12th

Something pretty special has happened to Daisy over the summer, as well. I haven't had much chance to catch up with her as she's been away most of the time. First, it was Derek's passing out parade and then the whole family – except Bill, of course, went on holiday with Daisy's Gran, the first time they have ever been able to do that. Daisy's Gran had just inherited some money so they went round Paris. Daisy has come back with some fantastic ideas for her artwork, and she's even leading a group designing some new murals for the canteen. It's the first time she's ever taken a lead in anything.

And on top of that, Elpseth's offer for the bungalow has been accepted. The other bidder who wanted it is one of those people that knocks down old houses and puts lots of tiny new ones in their place, but the seller didn't want that to happen. Thank you, Lord! So all being well, Daisy should be moving out of her cramped little box in a couple of months' time. Derek has promised just as soon as he can, he will bring a bunch of squaddies down to sort out the house. So already Daisy is planning all the décor. That girl really does have a fantastic eye for colour. It's just a pity she has to take all these written exams.

But it's Doris I'm worried about now. Agnieszka isn't going back to Poland until the New Year now, but she's definitely going. Pavel has had a big argument with her and said he wants to stay here too. I'm not sure if Pavel is going to win that one. But Doris is spending a lot of time at lunch times with him and a couple of Polish girls in his class. They don't even speak English when they're together. I asked Doris if she was coming to the group tonight, but Agnieszka has said she doesn't like her going. "I'll see you there in the New Year," she said, as we left school today.

September 20th

Sid has let me work in the café on Saturday mornings, until lunchtime. He's taken over as manager and there's a new chef who is slowly learning the ropes. Usually the morning session is fairly quiet, but not today. Apparently, there's a big cycle race leaving Drummington today, and last night these huge trucks rolled into town. There's now a huge stage on the seafront, with crowd barriers and bunting all the way along. Sid asked me to come in at eight, and I can see why. There are huge numbers of folk wanting breakfast or just a cup of tea, and the whole place is heaving. Some of them are dressed in Lycra with the names of all the cycling teams, others had travelled from other countries just to watch this race. In Drummington of all places!

Gradually the noise outside grew louder. There was a PA system making all kinds of announcements. Motorcycles kept whizzing by the window. Up above we could hear a helicopter. Someone explained that was the film company and the whole race was going to be shown live on national television.

Then just before eleven, the whole place emptied. "They're just about to start," said Sid. "Let's just lock the front door for a few minutes and go upstairs to see proceedings."

At the far end of the promenade there were dozens and dozens of fit young men all dressed in Lycra on these impossibly thin racing machines. In front of them, a man with a microphone held a large flag which he slowly lowered. And they rode by, followed by any number of cars each with yet more bicycles on their roofs, and a large van at the back with a broom on its rear door.

I think I could get into cycling. It would be a lot more fun than doing PE, anyway. This week we were basically just running and running around a muddy field in the pouring rain. I can't run fast for very long, and it only seemed to be an exercise in making us all tired, dirty and sweaty. Everyone was grumbling by the end, and Cheryl's announced she's not going to do PE any more. We shall see.

Me, I'm going to save up my wages for a new bike. The old one's getting too small anyway, and according to Sid you need to be measured properly to get the right frame. Dad's offered to join me when I go out riding, but I think he was joking.

October 4th

It's been just over a month since Jacky got married. We haven't heard much of her since. She and Gerry posted photos of their honeymoon on *Facebook*, which mostly seemed to be of them singing karaoke on the cruise ship or bathing in the jacuzzi. Gerry's got his directorship now, so they have moved into a big new home on the edge of Bristol, and Jacky's been telling us about how wonderful it all is. There's a business hotel nearby, and she's working there as a receptionist for now. She says she couldn't be happier.

I don't think she's really stopped and thought how different things are for me. When Dad has to work away overnight, the house does seem quite lonely sometimes. There was a strange noise in the garden a couple of nights back. Siobhan reckons it was probably just a fox, but you never know. Dad does his best to text me, and he's just learning how to Skype but it's not quite the same. Pete's cleaner does come in twice a week but she's pregnant, so I don't know how long that's going to last.

Dad very rarely lets me go with him into work. It's a huge busy place with loads of lorries and forklift trucks, and it would be very easy to get in the way. But today he actually picked me up after school and took me there. I wasn't expecting him to be waiting by the school gate. Quite a few of the boys looked nervous as they passed this huge hulk of man standing there.

"It's OK," I joked, "he's my bodyguard."

He still wouldn't tell me why he had come, though. We came to the huge industrial estate between the station and the main road, and he parked the car carefully right at the far end away from all the traffic. "Come with me," he said. "I have a little surprise."

There was a kind of store room right by the fence. It was the sort of place where men keep tools and signs, and that sort of thing. "Quiet now," he added, as he carefully opened the door. He moved a few bits and pieces, and there right at the back, there was a mother cat, with these really cute little kittens suckling.

"She moved in a couple of weeks back. I thought I'd tell you, and then I thought no, I'd give you a surprise. I've spoken to the manager, and he says you can have one of the kittens. Maybe two, if you like. Once they're a little bit older. Would you like that?"

In the end I chose a black and white one, and a ginger tabby. Both boys apparently, although it is hard to tell at this stage. "Hope they'll make the house a little bit more like home," was all Dad could say, as he picked up a tiny, squirming bundle and held it ever so delicately in his huge palms.

Afterwards we had a cup of strong builders' tea in the tiny office above the warehouse. I met some of Dad's workmates, who all seemed a really nice bunch. It turns out that one of them belongs to a cycling club in Drumchester that meets on Sunday mornings and Wednesday evenings. It was hard to explain I couldn't manage Sunday mornings. But Dad has offered to take me on Wednesdays just as soon as I get my new bike.

Dad is trying to be a really good father at the moment, and I think I must let Jenny know about the cats and the cycling club. It's just a pity he can't shop and cook, though. Still, you can't have everything.

October 17th

John finally asked us for our money back tonight. He didn't want everything we made, he just wanted the original ten pounds. So we went round the group. Alex confessed he had forgotten to water the strawberry plants, so they didn't make any money. Ally sold the programmes and made an instant profit, as did Claire and Tom on their gig. But Claire had already given all the money to the church anyway, so that was all right. As for me and Daisy, well, I'd been keeping a little book. Our hen was still laying, and we'd had eggs for fourteen weeks now, so we had made precisely £1.20 profit. Siobhan has said that we could keep our share of the egg money until the end of the laying season, though, so there was still more to come in.

John then asked us what we could all learn. Alex said it was very well having a gift, but you had to use it. Ally said you get back what you put in. We all said a few more things, and then John said, "You know what's really interesting? Sometimes you can use a gift and you get instant results, just like Ally and Claire did. Sometimes you can use a gift and you only get gradual results, like KT and Daisy. Think about it."

"Well, at least I've made a cake for tonight," said Alex, and we all laughed.

As we shared what to pray for, it turns out Ally is training extra hard at the moment. Not only is the under-16 team harder work, but the under-18s have some kind of injury crisis, so he's going to be on the bench for their match next Monday evening. He's heard a rumour one or two bigger clubs are looking at him, but he said, "From what I've heard tonight, I'm happy to let my gifts grow slowly right here." And everyone else agreed that was a good idea. At least I did.

October 23rd

I went with Siobhan and her Gran down to Truro today. Siobhan's mother was going to be sentenced today for what apparently was called "obtaining property by deception." Kathleen wasn't sure whether she wanted to go, but in the end, she went for Siobhan's sake. As we went into the court, we noticed there were one or two reporters outside the building. We didn't think they were there for us, as least we hoped not. We were a little bit late, and Siobhan's mother, Niamh, was already in the dock. When we got into the gallery, she turned round and gave us a little wave. She didn't seem at all sorry for herself at all.

The judge accepted her plea of guilty and she gave her two years' suspended sentence and two hundred hours community service. We asked Kathleen what that meant. "Basically," she said, "she has to stay out of trouble for two years, or she goes inside. That could be difficult. In the meanwhile she has to work doing stuff like digging gardens or picking up rubbish. I can't imagine she's going to be too happy about that."

Kathleen offered to take Niamh out for lunch afterwards. Niamh gave her a hug but explained she was going out with her boyfriend to celebrate her freedom.

"That's not fair," said Siobhan. "We've come all this way to see you, and now you're off before we can even chat."

"I love you, Siobhan," replied Niamh and gave her a kiss, "but I'm a lousy mother. That's just the way it is."

And with that she walked off with the new love of her life, leaving Siobhan for a moment completely speechless. But not for long. If I'm honest, it was hard listening to what Kathleen and Siobhan were saying about Niamh. It all sounded plain nasty. But who am I to judge? It was a long, awkward journey back home.

"Thanks for coming, sweetheart," Siobhan said and kissed me. She invited me in, but I made some excuse about the kittens coming and left. Even if they won't be here for another fortnight, at least.

November 3rd

Something strange happened at lunchtime today. I was stopped in the corridor by a sixth-former I had never seen before and asked if I could play the drums in their band. They had a gig coming up in a couple of weeks' time, and their drummer had pulled out. I asked how he knew who I was and it turned out he's seen Nick's video on *YouTube*. I said I'd have to check with my Dad, but it should be all right.

"He's the heavy who plays the lead?" he asked.

"Yeah," I said. If only people knew what my Dad was really like, but I guess he can't help being the way he is.

Then over lunch Cheryl came up and asked if I was interested in joining a girl-band she was putting together. She's never asked me anything like this before, but it turns out that while all her band members look fantastic, none of them can actually sing. "So, like, I was wondering," she said. "We could end up on *X-Factor* or something like that."

"You were selling it to me until then," I laughed. "I've just joined a band, actually."

"Which one?"

I told them and it was her turn to laugh. "What's so funny?" I asked.

"You'll see," she said, and she skipped away, but not before nicking some of my chips.

November 7th

I went along to the rehearsal this lunch time. I met the lead singer who was called Groth, for some reason. It's hard to say what he looked like, because there was this curtain of hair over the top of his face, and a scraggly beard covering the bottom half.

"Is that our new drummer?" he asked. My contact, Greg, nodded. "She's a girl!"

"He isn't always that quick," whispered Greg to me.

"And she's wearing a uniform."

"Just like you did last year, Groth," replied Greg.

"I need someone who can play," said Groth.

"She can play," said Greg. "Trust me."

Groth gave out what sounded like a huge sigh. "OK, we only have thirty minutes. Let's see what we can do."

When I say Groth was the lead singer, I mean it in the loosest kind of sense. He had pitch and he could hold a tune. But the noise that came out sounded like he was in a lot of pain. He fancied himself as a bit of a songwriter. Groth, it turned out, was a mixture of 'Grunge and Goth' so there was a lot about dying, feeling sad and generally not wanting to live. If he wasn't quite so serious, it could have been funny.

Groth left us packing up, 'cos he said he needed a fag. Greg and the other guy Bart said, "Don't mind him. He's harmless really."

"Um, it's not quite my type of music."

"It's not mine, really," said Greg. "Don't tell him, but I prefer Indie."

"But it's good to keep the Groth happy," said Bart.

"Yeah, I can see he's really happy," I said, and they laughed.

I thought about Cheryl's girl-band and for a moment I was tempted to join in with her instead. Doesn't anyone do any decent music any more?

Later on Greg texted to say the gig was in a fortnight's time and asked if I was still happy to play. Dad said it was OK, but he'd be there on the stroke of ten to pick me up. So now I am officially in a band. I'm not sure if that's a good thing or not.

November 15th

We went to pick up the kittens today. Daisy and Doris insisted on coming along as well. They were twice the size since we last saw them, but they still looked so small in the carrier I had bought them. When I let them, one of them took one look at the litter tray and peed on the carpet instead, while the other climbed right to the top of curtain and then complained it was stuck.

"What shall we call them?" asked Dad.

"Pest and nuisance," suggested Doris. It was the first joke I had heard her crack in ages. In the end we settled on Bert and Ernie, I can't really remember why.

As we were playing with the kittens, I asked Doris how things were going. It turns out Agnieszka has booked the removal van for 3rd January. Pavel did get his way in the end and is staying. "But it's not easy when your parents live apart," said Doris.

"Like I know," said Daisy, rescuing Bert from yet another tight corner.

"Thing is," said Doris, "I'm not even sure Mum and Dad get on that well any more. It's not like they argue, or anything like that."

"So what's the problem?" I asked as Ernie sunk his teeth into my finger.

"It's just like they are never together. Either Mum is out on Saturday, or Dad is. And Dad's stopped going to church. Mum takes us all on our own."

We chatted a bit more, and then Dad called us to lunch.

Dad's been practising salad recently. Never mind that we had a hard frost last night, and there was a cold north wind blowing. He'd spent ages chopping up the lettuce and the cucumber and the tomatoes really fine, and he finally seems to have got the hang of jacket-microwaved potatoes. Even if there were far too many for us to eat.

November 29th

The evening of the gig. I invited some of the girls to come along, but they all seem to have other excuses. To be honest, I wish I was at youth club as well. Greg picked me up just after seven and we drove to this tiny little hall on the far side of Dumpley End. Groth was already there, dressed all in black, with his hair dyed to match. Bart was wearing this hideous flowery shirt and was busy tuning his bass to the keyboard he also played. Greg helped me set up my electronic drumkit and then we had a brief run through. It was all going very well, even if Groth sounded more miserable than ever.

By now it was quarter to eight, and the first few people turned up. My heart sank as I realised nearly all of them were boys. Most of them wore black, and some had almost as much make-up on as the few girls who were there. I recognised one or two faces from school and saw how surprised they were to see me there. I felt out of place in my stripy top and blue jeans.

Groth came on stage, with his fag still in his hand, to huge cheers. We began slowly, but after a few numbers he was busy pouring out what Greg called his angst. Just when I thought I couldn't cope with much more of this, we moved to a couple of numbers Greg and Bart had written. They were lighter and far more tuneful. Many of the boys shuffled for a pee or a fag at that point. Then back to Groth's own material, and soon there was this heaving, shuffling mass that I have to say didn't smell too good.

At the end there was a standing ovation, and we did a couple of encores by *The Cure*.

"Well played," said Greg, packing up. "Do this again?"

"Possibly," I said. By now the smell was getting pretty unbearable, and I think the toilets out in the corridor must have become blocked. The cigarette smoke was giving me a headache as well.

When I came home, I threw all my clothes in the wash. But this morning I can still smell that horrible stench all over me. So I have thrown all my bedding in the machine as well and run the deepest bath I can. If that's what being in a band is like, then I think I'll give it a miss.

December 3rd

My birthday! Today I am legally allowed to buy a lottery ticket or to fill up a car with petrol. I could also if I wanted to ask Dad if I could get married. Not that I am likely to. Greg texted me to see if I wanted to go with him to *Pizza Hut*. He's quite sweet, I suppose, and I didn't want to hurt his feelings, so I told him, not this side of Christmas.

Dad took the day off today and he said he'd meet me after school. I told him not at the gates this time, and he took the hint. We had hot chocolate down at the café which Sid let us have for free. Then he took me into Dewglass, into a part of the town I had never seen before. I only guessed what he was up to when I realised we were heading for a bike shop.

"I was saving up myself," I protested weakly.

"Yeah, well, save up wages for when you really need them," he said. "Besides, I did a job for the owner a while back, and I've arranged a special deal."

The bike was just what I wanted. The owner took ever such a lot of trouble to make sure it fitted me perfectly. Apparently, the cycle club only meets on Wednesday evenings in the summer, but that's all right. I'm not planning to ride it in the dark, anyway.

Later on that evening, Siobhan, Daisy and Doris came round with their presents. And of course they wanted to see Bert and Ernie who wanted to play with the wrapping paper. Daisy made the mistake of putting her cup of tea down on the floor, so Bert started drinking from it, and then Ernie knocked it over, chasing Bert's tail.

When we had sorted all that out, I talked about how good Dad had been to me recently and wondered out loud what I could do for him.

"What's the one thing your Dad can't do?" asked Doris.

"That's easy," I said.

"Cook!" everyone said.

"So why don't you cook him a special meal?"

"Like at Christmas?"

"You couldn't see him cooking a Christmas dinner, could you?"

"But it'll be really strange just cooking for him and me."

"We could come round," said Siobhan, "and I'd give you a hand. I'd like to say thank you to me Gran somehow."

I wasn't too sure about this. I hadn't spent that much time with her since we'd been down to Truro. There was an awkward silence.

Presently, Daisy spoke up. "Come round to our new place. My Mum says she wants the biggest Christmas ever and says I can have some friends round. Dad will be there, and Gran, and Derek, but I'm sure there's plenty of room for more. And Mum will want all the help she can get with the cooking."

So that's Christmas sorted, I think. Siobhan left early. She said she had a headache, but I wasn't too sure. Still, she said she would be there on Christmas Day, if her Gran said yes. Of course, Doris can't be there, but as she said, there's always next year. Assuming she's still in the country. As Daisy and Doris got up to leave, Doris gave me an extra big hug. "Stay over in the New Year," I said.

"I will," she said. "I'd like that very much indeed."

December 11th

Maxine finally turned up at school today. No-one has seen her for a couple of weeks, but there's been all kinds of rumours flying around. Still, she looked awful when she walked into the classroom. At breaktime, Daisy and me found her retching in the toilets. I realised at once what the problem was. "You're pregnant," I said.

"Leave me alone," she said, "this is grown-up stuff."

I could have pointed out that I was two months older than her, but she has never been that hot on logic. I found a member of staff and she left soon afterwards.

Although everyone's guessing, none of us have any idea who the father is. Apparently, though, there is plenty of footage online showing how she had got pregnant. Cheryl offered to show it to me at lunchtime, but I refused. I asked how her band was going and she said, "Don't ask. You still won't sing?"

I thought for a moment. I thought about the gig with Groth and Greg asking me out on a date. "Oh, all right, I said, "it could be fun."

So now I am in a girl-band. And while we are singing soppy love songs, one of our number is pregnant. It all seems as if suddenly we are growing up very fast. I'm not totally sure I like it.

December 24th

The carol service at Drumley Green is always the best service in the year, and I have been practising really hard with the worship band. It's not that the songs are any different, but we want to make sure we play them as well as we can. There's been a group at church making candles and another practising a drama. Everyone has been making mince pies and mulled wine for afterwards, and the heating has been left on in the church hall all week to make sure it actually gets warm.

Dad and I were just about to get ready to go, when there was a ring on the doorbell. "It's for you," said Dad, as he answered it. It was Doris and she had been crying.

"It's Mum and Dad," she said, "they have finally had that big argument."

"I'm so sorry," I said, as I took her in my arms.

"It was all so silly, too, about which stuffing they would have for the turkey."

"If they hadn't argued about that," said Dad, "they'd have ended up arguing about something else."

"I guess so," said Doris. She put her hand through her hair. "I must look a real mess," she said. "Can I use your things, KT?" she asked.

"Yes, but we need to go soon," I said.

"That's OK, I'm coming with you. I told them I would be back later, but they didn't seem to be listening."

On the way to church Doris was on the phone texting her Mum, Dad, and Pavel. We had arrived early, just as the service for the little children was ending. I wondered what to do with Doris while we were setting up. But she made her way to a back pew, knelt before the Communion Table and hid in a corner, obviously praying.

Soon the church started filling up. When Daisy came in with Elspeth, I pointed Doris out, and they went and sat on either side of her. Then Claire and Sian noticed her as well, and soon she was surrounded by a crowd of familiar faces.

As always, the place was packed and John was on top form, even if he was starting to lose his voice. When the lights went out, the light from candles filled the whole church with this magical atmosphere. Dad picked up his acoustic to play Silent Night unaccompanied, and this sense of God's presence was everywhere.

We dropped Doris off afterwards. She said very little on the way back but just before she got out, she said, "That was very special. It is good to know Jesus and all the saints are watching over us at a time like this."

December 25th

This Christmas was different. For a start, it was just Dad and me. Jacky had sent our presents, but I wasn't sure about the skimpy skirt she had sent me, or the aftershave she had sent Dad. Chelsea sent me a *One Direction* calendar that I have to say went straight in the bin. Jenny, though, was really thoughtful and generous, and sent us both tickets to another musical in London and told Dad this time he had to come too.

At ten, as we agreed, we took the back road to Dumpley End, and made our way to Daisy's new bungalow. There was still a smell of new paint, and the colour scheme was, as I imagined, fantastic, fully co-ordinated with the carpets and sofas. Some of Daisy's pictures were hanging on the wall, and there were vases of dried flowers everywhere.

Both Dad and I had been a bit nervous at going, but we needn't have worried. Dad spent a long time chatting with Bill, all the while kneeling down by his wheelchair. I went to help Daisy and her gran prepare the dinner, while Derek and Elspeth set the table. We just wondered where Siobhan and Kathleen were. Eventually I had a text from Siobhan, *Sorry. We're still hung-over from last night.*

As Daisy said, "If that's their idea of fun, I'm glad they're not here."

At half twelve John and Helen came over with children, and a cousin Daisy had never mentioned also showed up, with a little one Emily's age. The turkey took longer to cook than we expected, but no-one really minded, and I was allowed to take some scraps back for the kitten.

All in all, it was a very special day, and we got home late.

"You know," said Dad, "when I was in prison, this was always the hardest day of the year. No-one visited, and I didn't get any presents. When I heard other people talking about what a lovely time they were having, I used to get so angry, and all I wanted was to drink. If I could have seen then how things would have turned out, I would have just laughed. I am still amazed how the Lord has seen fit to bless me."

"But that's what Christmas is all about, isn't it, Dad?" I said.

"You're right there," he replied. "Now would you like a slice of Christmas cake, I'm sure there's one in the kitchen somewhere?"

"No thank you," I said. "I've been blessed enough already today," and we laughed. But tonight, as I look back over the year, I'm so grateful for the blessing Dad has been to me. I'm not sure how to tell him, and it would sound very cheesy. But it's true. Maybe, just maybe, tomorrow I will be able to find the way to say the words. 'Cos I do mean them from the bottom of my heart.

THE DRUMCHESTER DIARIES: VOLUME 6
PARTING GIFTS
THE DIARY OF ALEX ANDREWS, AGED 16

January 1st

It may be the New Year, but things are still pretty much the same in dear old Drumley Green. At least, most things. Ally didn't come round my house last night to celebrate his birthday. I can understand why, with all his new football friends. But it would have been nice to be invited to his party, all the same. Of course, I could have gone with the rest of the family to the traditional party in the church hall, but I've decided I don't like the music, and, even worse, what my Dad calls small talk. There have to be better ways of spending your time than standing around chatting about what colour you're going to paint the lounge or dye your hair, or whatever else folk at church talk about. Although as far as I can see, Mum and Dad, Sophie and Mitch have no such trouble talking about such trivial things.

So I spent a quiet evening on my own listening to the Diabelli Variations and working on a story I showed my English teacher, Mr Maxwell, just before Christmas. He said it was well written, but the characters lacked emotional depth. I couldn't work out what he meant. I read it a couple of times and made a few alterations, but it seemed fine to me. I even began to map out in my head the plot for the sequel.

About half past twelve everyone came back. "They were all asking after you," said Mum, as she took off her coat.

"I don't think everybody was," I said.

"Well, happy New Year to you," said Sophie, as she put on the kettle. "I loved seeing everyone again. It's just a shame I have go back tomorrow, I mean today."

"Must you really, love?" asked Dad.

"Sorry, but that's how it is."

So today Sophie left soon after lunch. She's landed some high-powered job at a firm of international lawyers, and she only just managed to get enough leave to see her through Christmas. When she came down on Christmas Eve, she was still dressed in her sharp business suit with high heels and expensive leather briefcase. As my Dad says, she's come a long way from being a student digging toilets in the depths of South America.

Mitch spent most of today asleep, or playing on his *Xbox*, while Mum spent the day going through the freezer. So this left me and Dad to go out bird-watching.

It was a beautiful, if chilly, winter afternoon as we crossed the centre of the village out onto the track that led down by the river. It used to be a muddy little path that cut past an old farm, but now that *Morbury's* have nearly finished building their supermarket, it's become a smart, busy cycle path leading all the way from Drummington to Drumchester. They wanted to rip out the old hedgerow alongside it that protected the farm from the river, but the pressure group I joined managed to stop them doing that. So at least you can't see the shop from the path, although you can just make out the top of the mound that I helped to excavate a few summers back. It was once the site of a medieval church, but it looks like it's going to be covered now with a play area and hard steel benches.

"The march of progress," said Dad. "You really don't like it, do you?"

I wasn't sure if he was teasing me or not, so I remained silent, at least until we turned right to go to the bird hide. We'd fought long and hard for *Morbury's* to do something for the environment and they had promised to build a new one. Perhaps they are, but at the moment there is just a bare slab where the old one once stood surrounded by lots of ugly fencing and cold, disgruntled bird-watchers unprotected from the breeze along the estuary.

Dad and I managed to stay there for about half an hour. There seem to be plenty of avocets there this year, and quite a few widgeon and teal. We counted about fifteen different species before the cold got to us, and we turned for home. Mum tried to sound interested in our observations, but she's never had much enthusiasm for that sort of thing. Perhaps she thinks it is just 'small talk'.

January 9th

Our Friday evening group started again at the vicarage. Joe introduced us to an American couple who have come to help out with the youthwork, Ted and Bobby Nadgett. Ted is apparently over here doing a doctorate on something to do with the

Protestant Reformation. I could see that most people's eyes glazed over when he briefly explained what he was studying, even if I found it fascinating. But he left most of the talking to Bobby who we quickly discovered could do enough talking for both of them. They were quite a contrast, Ted, slight, with round glasses and a short goatee beard, Bobby, large with tangled blonde hair, and a definite Southern twang.

We spent the rest of the evening introducing ourselves. Bobby had prepared some kind of activity which was more suitable for the younger group that had met earlier so that didn't work. But it was fun explaining who we all were, and how long we had been coming to the church. At the end Bobby asked what we wanted prayer for. Ally asked for prayer for his Dad who was having a routine cancer check. Doris mentioned prayer for her Mum who had gone back to Poland. Daisy said her Dad, Bill might have to go back to hospital soon, while KT said the police were investigating some explicit pictures that had been circulating around her school.

We've been together so long now that I don't think any of us were that surprised by our requests. But I could see that Bobby was genuinely shocked by all that we shared, even if she was apparently a trained youth worker. "My," she said, "you sure have a lot to deal with." Then for once she fell silent and there was this awkward pause until Ted took off his glasses and began to pray in a very quiet, soft-spoken voice. I can't remember what he said but his words seemed to make perfect sense for the situation. It was a very special moment until Bobby, rather too loudly said, "Amen," halfway through.

January 19th

Our mock GCSEs began today. To be honest, I hadn't even given them much thought until Ally turned up on our doorstep yesterday afternoon. As usual, with all his football, he'd left most of his revision to the last minute. For a moment, I was tempted to mention his party, but I thought better of it, especially as he was hobbling after yesterday's match. A whack on the ankle as he smothered the ball in the penalty area, apparently. Once you stop him talking about the football, though, he can be good company and he certainly appreciated all the time I spent with him. Perhaps I will get an invitation next year. If I want to go, that is.

So today we had our first couple of exams. I don't understand why everyone seems to stand around afterwards talking about the questions.

"As far as I'm concerned," I said, talking to Phil over lunch, "what's done is done."

"It's easy for you to say that," replied Phil, "but you know you're going to pass."

"Yeah, it's not like you have got to make much of a choice what you're going to do next year," said Poppy, who is apparently now Phil's girlfriend.

"I haven't totally decided on my A-levels," I said, and for some reason they both giggled. When I got up to leave, I could hear them repeating that sentence in a fake posh accent to each other and laughing loud enough for everyone else to get the joke.

February 1st

Mum and Dad invited Ted and Bobby round for lunch today after church. I couldn't say I was looking forward to it, and as I feared, Bobby did most of the talking. But she was more interesting than I expected, talking about her grandfather who had fought in Vietnam, and her Pop who was the pastor in a small town in the Deep South, where nothing ever really changed.

"Bit like round here," I said.

"Best go sit on the rocking chair on the veranda, then," said Dad, as it began to hail outside, and as usual everyone laughed. Why does everyone else find what I'm saying so funny?

After lunch, Ted volunteered to wash up and I went with him. I asked him a bit more about his doctorate and he seemed surprised that I was the least bit interested. "You're a serious kind of guy," he said, handing me a plate.

"Mum says it's just the age I'm at."

"Moms know best, eh?" he smiled. "I would guess you get teased a lot at school."

"How do you know?"

"'Cos it's hard work being the high school nerd, that's all."

I wanted to talk to Ted more but just then the phone rang and there didn't seem to be anyone else to answer it. Mum and Bobby were chatting in the study, Mitch was practising the piano as usual, and Dad was seeing one of his clients who as every year had failed to send in his tax return on time. So seeing it was Grandpa ringing, I picked up the phone. Granddad sounded older somehow, but I couldn't work out why. He wanted to ask if it was all right for him and Grandma to come to stay for February half-term and to leave a message for Dad to ring him back.

My grandparents haven't stayed for years, in fact I can't ever remember them coming here before. Grandma has lots of things wrong with her, and she doesn't travel much. So I assume it must be for something important, only I can't work out what.

Ted and I never resumed our conversation after that, and we soon finished our jobs in the kitchen. But Ted did suggest we meet up at Drumchester University during the half-term vacation, and I said I would go. He sounds like one person at least who's on my wavelength.

February 14th

Mitch has been doing his best to wind me up this week. He knocked on my door early this morning and demanded to know how many Valentine cards I'd received. I couldn't be bothered to rise to the bait, though. While Mitch had been out with friends or practising the piano, I had been helping Mum and Dad this week get ready for the visit. Grandma's been having trouble with the stairs, apparently, so we've been working late into the evening to clear out the old playroom behind Dad's study we don't really use any more and turn it into a bedroom. Talking to Dad, I could see he's really quite worried about her.

And when Granddad eventually turned up in his old *Rover*, it was immediately clear that the journey had worn her out. Dad gently helped her up the front steps, along the corridor and into the bedroom for a rest, while Mitch and I helped Granddad with the luggage.

"Been a bit of a struggle?" asked Dad as we sat in the front room drinking tea.

"Yes," said Granddad, taking off his spectacles and polishing them. There was a moment's silence and then he continued, "Well, I better come straight to the point. Phyllis isn't really coping any more at home, and to be honest, our house is far too big. It would be different, of course, if you were round the corner, but you're not, and I'm not expecting you to move." He gave a little nervous cough at this point.

"Go on," said Dad, passing him a biscuit which he politely declined.

"Well, I've finally persuaded Phyllis to think about selling the house. We've talked and talked about where we could go next. We don't want some pokey retirement flat, and I'm certainly not ready for a home. So we talked some more, and I started thinking about the stables out the back here."

It was Dad's turn to take off his glasses and polish them. At this point Mum looked at me and Mitch, as if giving us permission to leave. Mitch took a handful of biscuits and disappeared upstairs. But he's never been that close to Granddad like me, and I sensed it was important for me to be there.

Slowly, methodically Granddad set out his plans, how he would sell the house and pay for the work on the stables. He reckoned it shouldn't take more than about six months, and that would give them the chance to move in the summer, while it was still warm. He could auction many of his rare books, and if he was honest, he would be glad to give up the garden.

The mantelpiece clock ticked slowly, evenly as Granddad continued. "And what about Paul?" asked Dad. "He's still pretty sore about the fact you gave me this house."

For the first time that afternoon Granddad smiled, even if it was only a weak smile in a tired, grey face. "We've already spoken about that. He can have the rest of the money from the house sale. Might help to make him settle down."

Dad made a face. "Honestly, Joe," said Granddad, "he's a different person since his girlfriend left him last year. He's sold his business and got a regular job. In fact, I said he could come down this week, if he managed to get some time off."

At that point Grandma began calling, so Granddad got up to leave the room.

"Do you need any help?" asked Mum.

"I'll let you know," he said.

Dad went and looked out of the window. Outside the evening was drawing in, and the bare poplar trees by the drive were swaying in the wind. Mum went up and gently put her hand on his shoulder.

"I'll make some more tea," I said, aware that now was a good time to leave.

Half an hour later Grandma came into the room, rather steadier than when she first got out of the car, but already breathless by the time she came to sit down. I had never really thought much before about what it must be like to watch your own parents get older and frailer. I tried to imagine what the situation would be with Mum and Dad in thirty, forty years' time, and whether it would be me sitting there, polishing spectacles of my own as Dad told me something I needed to hear.

As I set down the tray, Mum whispered that now would be a good time to get supper ready, so I disappeared back into the kitchen to get out the cold meats and salad. I then went to fetch Mitch, but he was more interested in slaying dragons than coming down to his grandparents, so I left him to his own devices. Coming down the stairs, and hearing the gentle buzz of conversation, I felt this was a day when past, present and future had somehow come together, and as we said grace, I became aware of an overwhelming need to pray.

February 20th

Grandma hasn't been up to much this week, although we did manage to take her down to see the sea yesterday. Mostly she's been in the front room, wrapped in her shawl, knitting a scarf for Granddad, or simply dozing in front of a cup of tea. At first Mitch was nervous about practising when she was sitting there, but he soon realised she was pleased to hear him play.

Granddad has spent a lot of time with Dad in the study drawing up plans and discussing costs. Dad is supposed to be writing his last essays for his ordination training, so he's working late into the evenings after everyone else has gone to bed. I came down a couple of nights ago to fetch a bottle of water and the light was still on in the study at two in the morning.

Mum ran me up to Drumchester University this morning so I could have a coffee with Ted while she went to the library there. Ted is clearly a history man like myself, and I soon found myself fascinated by his accounts of obscure religious wars in the sixteenth century. I was going to tell him about the lost medieval village of Upper Drumchester, when I suddenly realised Professor Smith was sitting at a table near us. They hadn't actually met before, but soon they were having their own academic discussion which I didn't really understand but found fascinating. If that's what being at university is like, then I definitely want to go.

They were still going strong, when Mum came to pick me up. The professors asked us to stay, but we had to get back, as Paul was coming down for lunch.

"Did you have a good time?" asked Mum.

"What do you think?" I said, and we both laughed.

Paul had already arrived when we got back home. But instead of a flash wedding automobile, there was a smart, grey hatchback sitting on the drive. To our surprise, it was Paul sitting with Grandma in the front room, and they were looking through an old photo album Paul had brought with him.

"He's a good boy," she said, holding his hand, "I just wish my boys could get on like you and Mitch."

The funny thing was, my father and my uncle did seem to be getting on. I even found myself sharing a joke with them over lunch, and later that afternoon, after they had spent a couple of hours in the study with Granddad, they seemed to come out with some kind of agreement.

"Miracles do happen," whispered Mum. She invited Paul to stay the night, but he said he had to get back. Before he left, Grandma got up and gave him a big hug. I don't think I've ever seen her do that before.

"Travel safely," said Dad, as the grey hatchback started off, and I knew he meant it.

February 22nd

Granddad left Grandma at home while he came with us to church this morning. John preached a really good sermon on God who can do immeasurably more than we can ask or imagine. I thought about Paul's visit; I thought about Grandma; I also thought about school. I realise I haven't written much about school recently, but to be honest, I haven't been enjoying it that much. I still love the lessons and most of the teachers are great, but Phil and Poppy still have it really in for me. Ally tells me not to worry when I hear others laughing at their impressions of me, but sometimes it is hard, and I'm not looking forward to going back tomorrow.

When we got home, we found that Grandma had somehow managed to peel and roast the potatoes, although she was now dozing by the stove in the kitchen. We gently woke her up, even if she denied being asleep, and she insisted on helping set the table. It was a special Sunday dinner, all in all, and over pudding Granddad asked us all to come up after Easter and choose whatever books we wanted, before they went off to auction.

"I could be a little busy," said Dad, who was still worrying about his essays.

"Nonsense," said Mum. "You'll need a break by then."

"And what about me?" asked Mitch who seemed to think he wasn't included.

"Oh, you're coming too," I said, and I wondered why everyone seemed to be so ungrateful. "E-mail me some dates," I continued, turning to Granddad who was proud to have mastered the technology.

"I will," he beamed. "Right, old girl, shall we get ready for the off?" And with that Granddad helped Grandma into the bedroom to pack, while Mitch reluctantly cleared the table. As they got into the old *Rover*, I wondered if this was the last time they had come to visit like this. At this point I began to frame some words for a poem, so I asked to be excused and went upstairs to see what I could compose.

March 6th

My sixteenth birthday. I thought it would feel like a special occasion, but for most of the day, it was just the end of a very tiring week. Dad finally got all his essays done, and he only has to spend a couple of weekends away before he has finished his vicar training. But in the meanwhile his accounts have built up, and he's been developing a nasty cough. He finally went to see the doctor on Wednesday and was signed off sick for a week. At the same time the Ofsted inspectors turned up at Mum's school and so she has been working late into the evening in front of the computer and leaving first thing in the morning. I've been getting in from school and cooking tea, while Mitch has decided the best way to cope is to stay out late with friends.

So I wasn't too surprised that Mum asked last night if we could celebrate tomorrow, at the weekend. I guess we didn't have a lot of choice. She was still out when I went off to the youth group, and by then I had only opened my cards. Dad had already gone back to bed after tea, and Mitch was out yet again.

I was feeling well fed-up by the time I got to the youth group. Phil and Poppy were holding a big bash tonight and most of the class were going for a sleepover. I hadn't been invited, of course, and I wouldn't have gone. But for no-one even to have time for your own birthday, well, that was a bit much.

I was still in a gloomy frame of mind when I arrived at the vicarage. What I hadn't bargained for was the fact Ally had told Ted and Bobby. Ted had brought along his squeezebox and Bobby had turned the occasion into some kind of excuse to bring as many puddings as possible. To be sure, I still didn't have any presents, but there was pecan pie, which I had never tasted before, banoffee pie, Mississippi mud pie, in fact most pies I could think of. While everyone was tucking in, Ted slipped me a book about medieval history he'd been talking about. I know some people think it's weird I've been going to the same church group for years, but if they only knew, they'd want to be part of it too.

And to round off an unexpectedly happy evening, Sophie was waiting when I got back home. "Thought someone ought to be around to give my little brother a proper birthday," she said, as she gave me a kiss.

"Where's Mum and Dad?" I asked, as she made me a cup of tea.

"Oh, they're fast asleep."

March 20th

The youth group met at our place tonight as Emily and Josiah had caught some kind of bug. As I was waiting for Ted and Bobby in the front room, I saw the lights on our drive come on, and someone huddled in a thick coat running up towards the house. I expected a ring on the door, or a loud knock, but there was silence. Cautiously, I let the winter evening in, and I saw a figure all curled up on the doorstep. It was the new Polish girl, Doris, who had started coming recently.

"Oh, it's you," she said.

"What's the matter?"

"I knew it was early, so I decided to wait."

"Out here? In this weather? Whatever for?"

Doris got up slowly, as I held the door open for her. She took one look at me, and she suddenly burst into tears. I didn't know what to do, but very gently I took her in my arms as she rested her head on my shoulders. This was definitely the first time I had ever held a girl like this before.

"What's going on?" asked Mum, coming down the stairs.

Doris stepped back and said in sobs, "My father... I just find out... He's having an affair."

"I can take it from here," said a familiar voice, who was presumably unaware of my mother standing inside. It was KT Lee. Doris turned to her and this time she collapsed on her shoulder in floods of tears.

"Come on, girls, into the kitchen," said Mum, holding out a hand.

We didn't see KT and Doris until the end of the evening. Ted had prepared some good material but to be honest, the whole group was rather distracted. I was still thinking about Doris. Ally was focused on tomorrow's match as it could decide whether he was going to be selected for the under-16s. Claire and Tom had clearly fallen out just before the meeting, as they kept making faces at each other, while Sian kept getting distracted by her phone. In the end Bobby told us all to take five, whatever that meant, and then hastily rounded off the evening in prayer.

March 30th

Something happened to Dad over the weekend. On the Friday he was grumbling about having to go away on this silent retreat, even if Mum said it might do him good. He was still very tired and coughing from time to time, as he tried to catch up on his day job. But when he came back yesterday, I think we all noticed the change. Dad had spent most of the weekend asleep. "The best form of meditation there is," he said. At the final Communion service someone had laid hands on him, and he said it was like a huge weight had lifted from his shoulders. Dad has never been one to show much emotion and even now as he described his experience he could just as easily be explaining a set of accounts to a client. But he's stopped coughing, and there's this gentle, relaxed smile I think I've rarely seen before.

So today, in the warm spring sunshine, we walked down towards the new hide *Morbury's* has finally put up in place of the old one. On the supermarket site the store stood almost ready to open. We had managed to delay it by about six months, but it was definitely opening at the end of April.

"That's the end of your campaign, I guess," said Dad.

"We can still organise a boycott or something like that."

"And drive across town to shop at *Asco's* instead?"

I hate it when Dad has a point, but he definitely had a point. There aren't any shops left in Drumley Green. The Post Office closed about five years ago, and for all the talk of a community shop no-one had actually come forward to run one, and they certainly weren't going to now.

"Well, I'm definitely never going to work for them," I replied defiantly, thinking of all the students at the academy who were going for jobs there.

"Fair enough," said Dad, who clearly wasn't in the mood for an argument. At that point we were completely distracted in our argument by a large group of people with telephoto lens who were making their way to the hide, some on their mobile phones. "I think we have a spot of twitching going on," remarked Dad, and he was right. There was something called a little crake in the reed beds just up river, and everyone was straining to get a look. As we peered through our scopes, the sound of a pneumatic drill echoed forth from the site. "I expect you will be writing a poem about this," said Dad as we made our way back from the heaving throng. "Let me see... They went to *Morbury's* to buy a cake, but no-one stopped to see the little crake." He laughed, as I gave him a nudge. "No, I better leave that to the expert, I suppose."

But by the time I got back I had already had a phone call from Ally who as usual wanted to come round to have some help with revision. When he came, I tried to tell him about the little crake. But he was more interested in me helping him with our core English texts. His Mum, apparently, has grounded him until he has done at least a week's revision and he knows better than to mess with his Mum.

April 3rd

Usually on Good Friday we would all go off to our local church, but Dad has been asked this year to lead a simple meditation in the church up at Drummington Marsh. It hasn't had a vicar for a couple of years, and John reckons he will soon be asked to take it on. As if he hadn't enough to do in Drumley Green!

The church in Drummington Marsh is a small, medieval building just above the river, squat and grey on the outside, dark and damp on the inside. It is apparently famous for its wall paintings, but the only thing I could see on the walls was the blown plaster and green mould. There was a congregation of about twelve elderly ladies, who did their best to offer a warm welcome. But even with the sunshine outside, the atmosphere inside was chilly, and I noticed Dad started coughing again once or twice during the service. We sang a couple of Passiontide hymns but so slowly it was hard to hold the tune, and after the service the electrics cut out so we couldn't have a cup of tea.

Over the past three years Dad has spent a lot of time in his vicar training discussing and writing about the future of the Church of England. My one thought, as I sat in that building wrapped in my thick anorak, was that whoever built the church never intended services to be like that.

"We should knock the church down," said one of the ladies as she fiddled with the fuse box, "but of course the authorities won't let us."

"Hear, hear," said another, as there was a worrying flash and the tea urn groaned back into life.

April 6th

As a thank you for all the help I had given him last week, Ally bought me a ticket to watch Drumchester City. I had only been once or twice before. It's not that I don't like football, and I enjoy playing, but I have never been one for crowds. But there wasn't much problem with crowds today. Even though a few thousand were there, quite a few of the terraces were empty. We were playing the league leaders and I think most people assumed we were going to get thrashed.

It turned out instead to be a rather enjoyable 2-2 draw. Ally literally followed every kick of the ball, and it was fascinating to hear him commenting on the goalkeepers' performance. It was rather less enjoyable hearing him join in with the singing, but at least he stopped himself when the crowd began to question a player's size and parentage.

Ally's made the under-16s team now and he reckons he will soon be offered an apprenticeship. As I met up with some of his team-mates after the match, I soon realised quite a few were gutted not to make the next level. I never realised before how much a dream could mean to some people. But then I am still not sure what I want to be. Some days I want to be a writer, some days an archaeologist, some days a historian.

"You could be a vicar like Dad," said Mitch the other day. But I don't think so somehow, although I'm not sure why.

April 11th

We've been spending the last few days up at Granddad's, although Dad insisted on us staying at a nearby hotel. Dad and Mum have been making quite a few trips to the charity shop, while I helped Granddad tidy up the garden and clear the shed. Most of the time Mitch has been playing the piano for Grandma, who has been sorting out drawers and cupboards. The architect and the man from the council are looking over the stables on Tuesday but as Dad already has permission to do the work, he reckons it will only be a matter of sorting out the details.

Today before we left, Granddad kept his promise and let us all choose the books we wanted to keep. Sophie came over for a few hours, and Paul joined us as well. Dad picked out some ancient Bible commentaries by someone with the strange name of Lightfoot, Mum found some classic French novels, Mitch selected some old spy thrillers, even though I know they are not really his thing, and I went for a series of English poetry. The one thing we couldn't touch was the collection of rare first editions Granddad is loaning to the local museum. Even so, after everyone had taken their turn, the shelves barely looked emptier than when we started.

"You've still got a fair bit of work to do," remarked Paul.

"Oh, he'll enjoy it," said Grandma who had been dabbing her eyes with a handkerchief. "Fifty years and a life's work to sort out all in a few months."

Sophie went over and held her hand. Mitch went off to play the piano.

April 24th

Ted and Bobby are making a habit of surprise birthday parties, although Bobby insists it's only for special cases. And I think we all agreed Doris was a special case. Ever since she found out about her father, she and Pavel have been living at Daisy's until the end of the school year. Derek is apparently serving overseas somewhere, and he isn't due back until the end of July, and Bill isn't planning to come home any time soon.

So this evening we all piled over to Elspeth's huge bungalow beyond Dumpley End and with the exception of Ally, we all fitted in easily. We had agreed we all wanted to give Doris little gifts which she could take back to Poland. Daisy had drawn a sketch of the church, KT had made a recording of a song, and Ally made everyone laugh by presenting a signed Drumchester City programme. When it came to my turn, I gave her a carefully written poem about life on the river. KT laughed, but Doris said, "I like poems," and folded it carefully in her bag. Later on, when no-one was looking, she said, "Thank you," and gave me a peck on the cheek.

May 9th

I had a couple of interesting e-mails this morning. One was from Mr Maxwell, my English teacher who had read my poem, *Parting Gifts* and asked if I would like him to get it published? The other was from Professor Smith inviting me to a young archaeologists' camp in the summer. It turns out the dates coincide with Mitch's summer school for pianists, and that means at least we won't have to trail round France this year.

After lunch, Dad and I went over to the stables to have a good look round before the builders moved in on Monday. This is when I confessed I had found the newspaper in the hayloft three years ago, even though I know I shouldn't have been there. Dad seemed fascinated more than angry. I showed him the spot in the corner, where the plaster had come down. Dad reckoned there was a void between the ceiling and the roof, and he promised that the builders would show him anything they found there.

In the original plans, the hayloft was going to be the upstairs bedroom, but as Grandma couldn't manage stairs, this was going to be Granddad's study. When I asked whether Granddad wouldn't have to be looking after Grandma, Dad said he had made sure carers would come in twice a day.

"My mother wasn't always frail," Dad added, as he wiped the dusty, cracked window that obviously hadn't been opened for years. "She used to take Paul and me for long, long walks and when I got tired, she would sometimes even piggyback me home."

May 18th

It's only one school week to GCSEs and the pressure is starting to tell. Phil and Poppy have officially split up, although I reckon it won't be long before Phil has another girlfriend. Poppy apparently has been trying to knuckle down and do some serious revision over the past couple of weeks, but Phil has been getting in her way. Something like that, although I never pay that much attention to gossip.

At lunch time Poppy even found me out in the lunch hall and asked for some advice about the history exam. "Only if you promise not to make fun of me," I said. She promised, and soon there were a group of about five gathered round me, including Ally and Erin. Maybe, just maybe I'm going to get some respect, although I still remember what Ted said about being the class nerd.

When I got back home, the builders had moved in on the stables. There was a huge skip outside and a big lorry delivering a Portakabin. I went to see if there was anything in the skip but there were only a few empty plastic bags, and a pile of plaster.

I was just settling into my revision when Mitch came in with the glad tidings that he was now officially taller than me. I couldn't see the big deal - when you're five seven, most boys are taller than you, but he just wouldn't leave me alone. In the end we fought a kind of wrestling match until Dad told us to stop. I don't know what's got into Mitch recently, but he's doing his best to be annoying. He skipped church for the first time on Sunday and announced from now on he would be having a lie-in. Well, if he wants to go his own way, that's fine. Just so long as he stays out of my way.

May 29th

I'm not the only one feeling the pressure of exams. Mum has been working non-stop for the past few weeks trying to get her classes ready for their GCSEs. I always knew this was a busy time of year for her, but it's only really this year I've understood why.

But today Dad announced we were all going to take a day off. "After all," he said, "I've learnt a lesson recently about not working too hard." When Mum pretended to protest, Dad said he had already packed the picnic. Mitch, of course, wouldn't come, but to be fair he does have his grade 7 coming up in a few weeks.

Dad refused to say where we were going. But he drove up through Drumchester, onto Drum Moor and almost over to the other side. How he found his way through all the twisty lanes I will never know. Almost two hours later, he parked up in a space overlooking the head of a deep, leafy valley.

It was a magical walk. The dappling light among the trees was warm, but not too hot. We heard woodpeckers and chiffchaffs, and we thought we saw a buzzard hastily take off as we neared a clearing. Mum showed a surprising knowledge of the wildflowers, and we even found a patch of small, sour strawberries. We were descending down to the point where two rivers joined, and there Dad set down the picnic blanket and our lunch.

"How did you know about this place?" asked Mum.

"A vague childhood memory that came back to me the other day. Do you remember, Alex, I told you about the long walks my mother used to take with us? This was one of them we took on holiday when I was very young. I asked Paul the other day exactly where it was. You see that rock over there? That's where I was standing when he pushed me in. I was lucky the river isn't very deep on this side. Granddad had gone off to take a photo of something, so Grandma had to haul me out. She wasn't best pleased when he returned."

We sat silently for a while eating our lunch. A dipper flew downstream and perched on a nearby pebble, bobbing up and down in the way only dippers do.

"And what about your family?" I suddenly found myself asking Mum.

"Well, as you know my parents split up when I was very young. My father moved out to Canada, and I wouldn't be surprised if I had family out there. Last I heard he had married again and had children. Oddly enough, the only thing I have from him is also a book. He thoughtfully left Mum with the car, and the maintenance manual inside. So if you want to know why I have the instructions for an Austin 1100 in the back of my wardrobe, it's because my Dad left his signature inside it, along with directions to the local garage. I've tucked a few photos into the back as well, but I don't really remember him. I was only four at the time."

Dad held Mum's hand at that point, and I turned my attention to the dipper who seemed quite oblivious of us, until suddenly another flew downstream and the two disappeared together as if they had never been there.

When we got back, Mitch wasn't around. He had left his bedroom window open, which didn't please Dad. We never found out where he had been. He'd just been doing 'stuff'. But I was more distracted by the bundle of old newspapers the builder had left in a plastic bag on the doorstep.

"Keep them until after the exams," said Mum. I'll try, but it won't be easy.

June 10th

Halfway through the exams today. The school have tried to help by providing a chill-out zone next to the library. The only problem is everyone has their own way of chilling out. No-one goes round listening to the music I listen to, for example. The last time I was in there Phil and his mates were playing a loud video game until the librarian came in and told them to shut up.

I have had a flick through the newspapers. A lot about the diamond jubilee of Queen Victoria; the shocking crimes committed by thieves and vagabonds; betrayal of masters by their servants. I even found myself dreaming halfway through a physics exam about the plot for my next story, until I saw the time and realised I still had four questions left to answer.

I haven't seen much of Ally lately. When he's not sitting in front of a script, he tends to be up the gym or out for a run. He's insisted on staying at his Dad's during the exam season which has gone down badly at home. I told him I was praying for him. He'll need all the prayers he can get when he finally returns to his Mum.

June 27th

To mark the end of the exam season, Ted and Bobby have arranged for the group to go away for the weekend to an old manor house somewhere in the wilds of Dorset. There's a larger group from a huge church in Drumchester going as well. So this afternoon we managed to cram into Trevor Lee's huge estate, and Pete Green's 7-seater and were driven for a couple of hours almost due east. I found myself sitting next to Doris and she slipped me a poem she had translated herself for me. It's such a pity she's going back to Poland in a few weeks' time. I will miss her.

When we arrived, there were already a couple of smart minibuses waiting outside. We've spent the evening playing silly 'getting to know you' games with the Drumchester crowd. Both Ally and myself were surprised we already knew a couple of them from school, Megan and Tyson. We never knew they went to church, and they certainly didn't know about us. It made us all wonder how many more there might be in our year.

At the end, we went outside to a huge bonfire where we toasted marshmallows and drank hot chocolate. Ted introduced us to some authentic Midwest camp songs, and then one of the Drumchester leaders finished with a prayer. However, none of us wanted to go inside. The sky above us was warm and clear, and there was a full moon set in a sheet of stars. I expected to find Doris next to me, but in fact Daisy was sitting there.

"Quite a picture," I said.

"Yes," she replied, "I'm just working out how I can draw it."

We sat silently for another quarter of an hour gazing up into the heavens, maybe longer. The time somehow wasn't that important.

June 29th

It has been a very special weekend. We had been staying near an old railway line, so yesterday a group hired some bikes and went off for the day. A few of us didn't want to cycle that far, so we just went as far as we could on foot. That's how I found myself with Daisy, Doris, Ted and Bobby, and a few of the Drumchester crowd. Even just a couple of months back I would have found the idea of chatting all day tedious as anything, but we all had interesting stories to tell. I shared the history of the house where I lived, Doris talked about her home town, and Daisy described how the farm came into her family four generations ago. Everyone else had a fascinating story to tell as well, and when we weren't busy talking, Ted would tell us one of the tales of his settler folk way along.

In the evening we had some kind of musical night, with everything from Ted's squeezebox to someone from Drumchester demonstrating the art of beatboxing. Daisy went round sketching everybody and later on I made sure I put her sketch of me in a safe place, next to Doris' poem. I didn't have much chance to speak to either Daisy or Doris, because KT was making sure they stayed close to her, I'm not sure why. The only person who wasn't there was Ally, not only because he isn't musical, but also because pre-season training starts tomorrow. He had special permission to go for a run, and he only turned up at the end, having covered an impossible number of miles.

Then this morning we had a time of worship. I say worship, but it was nothing like at Drumley Green, even at the carol service. There weren't many of us, but the singing just flowed on and on and on. Somebody shared a vision, another a testimony. A few were praying quietly in tongues, something I had never heard before. When it comes to emotions, I'm a bit like my Dad. I believe because I took a chance on God, that's all. But today was something else. I know I'm not describing it very well, but you really had to be there to know what it was like. We finished with an enormous outdoor picnic out on the lawn and Ally said, the world of exams and school seemed like a million miles away. I think we all began to understand what Jesus meant when He talked about a heavenly banquet.

July 10th

We had some good news today. Granddad and Grandma have definitely sold their house. We've been promised that the stables will be ready by the end of August, so the timing is perfect. One way or another, ever since that weekend, I keep finding prayers being answered.

But I'm still not sure what to do about Mitch. Tonight was the school prom, and he kept teasing me that I had no-one to go with. I had for a few weeks, been nervous about going, especially as Ally would be away somewhere in London at a tournament. But I was looking forward to seeing Megan and Tyson again. In fact the three of us spent most of the evening in a relatively quiet corner catching up with each other. We were only disturbed by Phil who kept pestering Megan for a dance until she flatly told him to go away. By the end he had his arms round someone else, so I think he was happy.

July 17th

Doris' last evening with us. She and Pavel were flying back to their mother tomorrow. They had spent the previous evening with their father and his new partner, but I gather the meeting was not a success.

We thought for ages what to do as we had already celebrated her birthday together. In the end we settled on a barbecue on the beach, and we told Doris and Pavel they could bring whatever friends they wanted. So there were some Polish cousins, a few friends from their school and the youth group. But somehow it didn't matter we didn't know each other. We all learnt some Polish folk songs, and both Doris and Pavel received signed shirts from their classes. John and Helen turned up halfway through, and the party could have gone on all night. But at ten Elspeth arrived.

Doris went round giving everyone a hug, and as she came to me, she said, "Keep in touch," and gave me a kiss. But as she kissed a lot of people and told them to stay in touch, I am not sure if she said those words specially to me. I still have her poem though, even if tonight was just goodbye.

When I got in, I picked up a message from Sophie asking if I wanted to go and stay with her for a few days. She had a couple of days leave due and she wondered if I wanted to see the museums. The dates were just after my archaeology camp, but that didn't matter, did it? Mum said it was fine, so I accepted on the spot.

August 8th

A week ago we all set off on our holidays. Mitch was going to a summer school in Manchester, while I was due to dig a Roman villa somewhere in Leicestershire, so Mum had this bright idea of putting us on the same train. We both managed to ignore each other until I got out at Birmingham. Mitch spent the journey slaying dragons while I was listening to some obscure Romantic composer I had recently discovered on *YouTube*.

I would like to say I have enjoyed the first week of camp, but actually it's been fairly miserable at times. For the first couple of days it rained relentlessly, and we all got bored hanging around. Then everyone went down with diarrhoea, until the chemical toilets began to stink.

I was with a small team investigating a rubbish pit to the south of the site. We thought we might make some interesting discoveries, but so far we have mostly been digging up animal bones. Someone found a small fragment of a burnt pot, and another a lump of metal, but that's been about it.

But it's been in the evenings I've really missed being with my church family. The activities and the lectures have been quite fun, and I have got to know a few people. But there's a small group who are actively smuggling cider onto site, and boys trying to get into girls' tents and vice versa. The leaders have tried to take some action, but I don't think so far I've had a single good night's sleep.

I had a message from Ally today saying that his Dad was starting to feel unwell again. He wouldn't contact me usually on the day of a big game unless it was serious, so I just texted back that I was praying. Later on he told me that he had kept a clean sheet in a 3-0 victory and then he added: prayer works! But I don't think he was talking about his father.

It seems really weird to me that tomorrow will be just another day of digging. There is a trip out organised for Monday, and it will be good to go, but for once in my life I find myself wondering what is happening back home.

August 15th

As I stepped off the train, Sophie took one look at me, and said, "See what the cat's dragged in!" To be honest, after two weeks under canvas I was aware I was smelling a bit rank. Sophie immediately took me back to her flat for a shower and a shave while she threw my clothes into the washing machine. "Do you have any decent clothes with you?" she asked as I emerged wearing her old dressing gown. I shook my head. "Right then," she said, "just as soon as you have something dry to wear, we are going clothes shopping."

That's how two hours later I found myself in the local shopping centre while Sophie bought me a pair of smart trousers and leather shoes, and a pile of short-sleeve shirts. As she did so, I realised that even her off-duty clothes were impeccably smart, if not designer. She was clearly going up in the world and having a scruffy brother in tow was not going to win her any street cred.

We went back to the flat for me to get changed, and then we went out again. Sophie had arranged to meet some of her church friends at a nearby restaurant. I thought they might look a bit more relaxed than Sophie, but they all seemed one way or another to be power-dressed. Still, they were all very friendly. One of them, a fellow lawyer, had read history at Cambridge. Another was a journalist who was interested in the poetry I'd been writing. The only person I didn't get on with was the journalist's sister called Lavinia who was about to take a degree in the history of fine art. Her main topic of conversation seemed to be the number of foreign places she had spent time in, and the galleries she had visited. By this time we had already consumed an ample first course and I was starting to feel shattered, so I felt quite justified in yawning.

August 20th

I am right. Drumley Green is quiet, especially after you have spent a few days in London.

I went with Sophie to church on Sunday. The minister didn't wear robes or a dog collar but looked quite at home in a smart suit and tie. Everyone I met seemed to be a lawyer or accountant or banker, although there were also a group of less well-dressed asylum seekers in amongst the congregation, and Sophie explained how much work the church did amongst refugees. I tried to join in with the worship, but I was amazed at the amount of technology and the quality of the music. There were obviously professionals at work with every note highly polished, every chord perfectly arranged. Still, I wasn't sure if I preferred them to our home-grown band at Drumley Green. There was no way Trevor and KT would end up playing with them.

Then after a quick lunch out Sophie started on a whirlwind tour of the museums. So much to see, so little time. I have brought home so many guidebooks and leaflets just so I can go through all that I have seen. But even so, I reckon I have only covered a fraction of what's there and there are some things I simply must go back and see again.

But the best bit was actually spending some time with Sophie. We had never been on our own together before, and once she had organised my wardrobe, she treated me like a fellow grown-up more than her kid brother. We ate out most of the time, partly because her flat is so tiny, and she asked my opinion on what to eat, how it tasted, even wanted me to sip her wine and let her know what I thought about it.

She seemed genuinely sorry to see me go yesterday. I know that if I get the chance, I'd like to live in London, even if you have to dress posh. But for now, while Sophie is preparing for her first foreign trip to South America, I am back home. And for now, that's fine. Dad is making every effort to make sure the stables are finished on time. Mum is planning lessons for the new school year. And Mitch has come back from summer school, realising, I think, just what hard work and practice actually looks like.

September 6th

The removal van arrived today, almost as soon as the builders had handed the keys over to the stables. Dad had gone up to fetch Grandma a few days before, so she didn't have to cope with the stress of the big day. She seems a little brighter than I last saw her, and yesterday even managed to help with the washing up.

"So, Joe, where do you want us to unpack?" asked Trevor Lee as he stepped out of the cab. (Granddad was staying overnight with a friend before making the long trip down in his Rover.)

I thought it would take ages for the men to empty the van, but with the speed Trevor and the gang were moving, it was all done within the hour. Joe invited Trevor in for a cuppa, but he had to get back to the depot. So Dad woke Grandma up and showed her round the new home. She didn't realise he and Granddad had spent ages e-mailing about carpets and curtains, and all that sort of thing. She spent ages admiring the fitted kitchen and insisted on being shown how the dishwasher worked. Then Dad showed her the wetroom, specially designed so she wouldn't have to step in and out of the shower. And next door was the large bedroom cum sitting room, with the special bed Granddad had ordered to make getting up in the morning easier.

"You are so good to me, Joe," she said and gave him a kiss. "But I can't sleep in my new place until Bob's here as well. And don't forget," she added, "it's our fifty-fourth wedding anniversary a week on Tuesday."

September 12th

Ally only comes into school two days a week now, as he has started his apprenticeship at Drumchester City. He's attempting to do two A-levels in economics and maths, on top of all his football training and jobs around the ground.

"It keeps Mum happy," he explained over lunch, "and I guess she's got a point. Only two or three of us each year get a professional contract, and I know I still have to improve. The scary thing, as someone pointed out to me last week, is that I am now officially the club's fourth-choice goalkeeper. Should there be a run of freak injuries, I might just end up out on the pitch on Saturday afternoon."

"You'll do fine," I said, as I gave him the last of my pasty, reasoning he needed it more than me. "And what about your Dad?"

Ally looked around, seeing the crowds of people on either side of him. "It's not good. Tell you more tonight."

The news about Pete Green indeed isn't good. He's starting to be in a lot of pain, but no-one can quite work out where the pain is coming from. He's due to have a whole host of tests at the hospital the week after next. In the meanwhile he is keeping on driving, because he needs to pay the bills. Ally said all this while looking down at the carpet in the vicarage front room. KT gently laid a hand on his shoulder, and then Ted suggested we should all lay hands on him and pray.

What we didn't expect as we prayed was that Ally would suddenly start singing. He only uses his singing voice on the terraces usually, and it's how loud you sing that matters there. But in a shaky voice, he began singing, "Come, Lord Jesus, come," over and over again, and soon there were a whole group of us adding our harmonies. I have no idea what was going on, but after we had all finished, we had a powerful sense God would be in this, whatever lay ahead.

It was hard to know where to go after this. Ted had some material, but he said it didn't feel appropriate somehow. There were a couple of new girls who had joined the sixth form at Drummington Comp and they spent a while quietly introducing themselves. Then I explained the arrangements for Dad's ordination at the end of the month. There wasn't going to be room for everyone at the cathedral but the whole church was planning a surprise party after a special evening service. At which point the evening picked up, and we all began to discuss what we could bring. All, that is, except Ally who had slipped out to have a word with John.

September 16th

John came round to see Granddad and Grandma on their 54th wedding anniversary and to bless their new home. He didn't stay long, apparently, but Grandma kept going on about that nice young vicar we have. If she's up to it, she might even join the Mothers' Union next week. She's definitely brighter and less tired now the carers are coming in, and she doesn't have to worry about the house. She even walked over to our place all by herself after tea to bring us a plate of home-made cookies for pudding.

Which was just as well, because everyone had come home late that day. Dad had been down to Cornwall to see a client. Mum had a staff meeting, and Mitch had got his first ever detention for not doing his homework. "You'll all wear yourselves out," she said.

"Yes, Mum," said Dad and then he laughed. "I haven't said that for years, have I?"

September 27th

The day of Dad's ordination. He left us all on Thursday to go on his retreat. Just before he left, he tried on all the various robes he had ordered. "This all feels strange," he muttered as Mum made sure they all hung properly.

"Do you really have to wear them?" asked Mitch.

"Good question," said Dad. "Hopefully not too often. I could always wear my Hawaiian barbecue shirt instead."

"OK, that all looks right, now," said Mum. "And, Joe, I'm proud of you." Mitch and I looked away as she gave him a big kiss. "Now have you got everything?"

"I think so. If you're asking whether I'm ready, that's quite a different question."

"You'll be fine," said Mum. "Now just imagine me as a vicar's wife." We all laughed at this point. "Come on, or I'll be late for parents' evening."

So this morning instead of going to Drumley Green, the whole family went up to the cathedral, including Sophie who had come down for the weekend. Grandma decided she probably couldn't sit in such a large service for such a length of time, but we parked her in a very friendly teashop nearby and Granddad showed her the button to press on his mobile if she needed to speak to any of us. We couldn't invite the whole church, but John and Helen were there of course. He'd left the regular Sunday service to Ted and Bobby, with Trevor leading an open time of worship.

It was hard to imagine that combination, but of one thing we could be certain, the service would be nothing like the one in the cathedral. The ancient Gothic edifice was full to overflowing as suddenly the organ sprang into life like a foghorn, and we all stood for some long Victorian hymn none of us could quite remember. Dad trooped in with a whole line of new vicars, and I was surprised to see there were quite a few older than him. At the rear came the bishop who had come to our house three years ago, no longer in a black suit but what Mitch called a gold and a green carpet, with all kinds of strange symbols all over it.

"That's a cope," whispered Mum.

As we came to the end of the hymn, the organist carried on playing for a few bars and did a crescendo into the loudest chord I had ever heard.

Then there was silence apart from the wail of a small child who had obviously been frightened. There shouldn't have been silence, but the bishop's microphone wasn't working and there were a couple of minutes of hasty toing and froing until a man in a blue gown and white gloves produced a new one. But apart from that hiccup, the whole service was very special. As Dad knelt before the bishop, I think I realised for the first time what God had chosen him to become. Mum was even a little bit tearful, in a way Mitch and I had never seen before.

Eventually we all came out into the bright midday sunshine where the bishop stopped to take pictures with the vicars (curates as I learnt they should be called), both individually and as a group. He came over to shake hands with Mum, and he surprised us by remembering all our names.

"That's because I've been praying for you," he explained with a twinkle in his eye.

Then Granddad went off to fetch Grandma and we all went off to a picnic on the moor. The church had offered to put on lunch, but Dad insisted he needed a break somewhere in the day. I think he suspected something about a surprise party later on.

We had just got up onto the moor when my phone rang. It was Ally. He had been with his Dad to the hospital this morning, and he sounded very shaky. "I need to talk to someone," he said.

I found John and handed over the phone. He went over to the far side of the car park and spent what seemed like ages in conversation. When he finished, he beckoned me over. "Six to nine months, they reckon," he said. "But don't tell anyone here. Let's get today over with, and I have promised to spend tomorrow with the family."

At that point we were distracted by Paul turning up. He had come in late right at the back of the cathedral and had somehow missed us, until someone told us where we were heading.

"Thought I would surprise you," said Paul. "I haven't been to a church service for years, but that was something special."

"You ought to go more often," said Grandma who was still inside the car wrapped up in a rug.

"Well, yes, maybe," he replied, which was probably his way of saying no.

I was still thinking about Ally when the evening service started. By this time Sophie had left as she was preparing to travel this week, and Paul agreed to take her back as far Ealing. Grandma had fallen asleep in the car, and she and Granddad had gone home for a lie-down. When they left, Mum whispered in my ear, "Bad news about Pete, then?" I nodded, and she gave me a hug.

But even as I was worshipping tonight, I still couldn't get out of my head Ally singing at the youth group a few weeks back. If someone asked me where God was in all this, I couldn't give an answer. I just know He is there somewhere.

October 1st

Ally turned up briefly at school today. He'd had a long chat with his Mum and stepdad, George, and they agreed it was best for him to postpone his A-levels for now, with everything else going on. When he spoke to the head, the only reply he received was, "Well, maybe you can do them next year."

"That's charming," I replied as we sat together in the far corner of the sports field.

"At least Mum is starting to soften a bit," he went on, picking a blade of grass and running it through his fingers. "I shouldn't know this, but she's given Dad some money to pay the rent until next Easter. And she's said I can stay with him as much as I want."

"What about the football?" I asked.

"That's the one thing Dad wants me to carry on doing. You can either worry about me or you can do me proud. That's what he's always said." Ally looked away at this point and wiped his eye. "So, yeah, I'm playing on Saturday and I'm going to win." With that he stood up and kicked an imaginary football into the far horizon.

"Shall I come?" I found myself asking.

"Not unless you fancy standing on a training pitch somewhere in Swindon," he replied, smiling.

"Let me know how you get on," I replied.

"Promise," he said.

At that point Tyson came over and gave him a man-hug. "Praying for you, bro'," he said. "By the way, the head has just turned down our request to form a Christian Union. It goes against the school's policy of equality and diversity and tolerance."

Ally spat onto the pitch. "Well, that's what I think of that. You just keep meeting here, then." The buzzer was going for the end of lunch time. "I better clear off. Have fun," he said, and we watched him jog off through the back entrance.

October 3rd

Ally did text me. His team had won 2-1, and he had saved a last minute penalty.

Sophie Skyped as well. She had safely arrived in South America and was staying in some impossibly posh hotel. She wasn't allowed to say exactly what she was doing, but it involved something to do with oil.

October 9th

We don't usually pay much attention to the news headlines in the morning, as most of us are trying to get out of the house, and Dad is making sure we haven't forgotten anything. But just as I was about to switch it off, the newsreader announced there were reports of a major earthquake in exactly the same country where Sophie had been working.

"Try to get hold of her," said Mum to Dad. "I know the capital is supposed to be all right but let me know as soon as you hear from her." With that she picked up the car keys and left.

Dad was meant to be writing his first sermon today, but I don't think he got a lot of work done. He spent most of the day trying to get through, but the mobile network was unavailable. He finally forwarded a text from Sophie at three saying, *Everything fine here. Will Skype as soon as.*

We finally established a connection about nine o'clock at night, well past midnight over there. Sophie looked drawn and tired. "Most of the damage is in the north," she said, "where I was helping to dig latrines a couple of summers ago. No-one has been able to make contact with the town there. I wondered if I should stay on a bit, but as my colleague said, what actually could I do? Still, my firm has promised me they will make a large donation to the relief effort. I guess that's something."

"So you're flying home tomorrow?" asked Mum.

"Yes, before the airport fills up with the relief effort."

"Take a break."

"I can't. There's so much to tie up from this week, and I think I need to be working."

"Let me know when you hear from your friends."

"I will, I promise." She was about to send her love when the connection went down.

Mum and Dad looked at each other, and then Dad said, "I think we need to pray." It was the first time we had ever prayed as a family and even Mitch joined in.

October 17th

Sophie has finally heard from her friends. Most of them are fine, but one has been seriously injured. She needs to be taken to the capital for urgent medical treatment but can't afford it. Sophie is researching ways of funding the treatment herself, even as she is putting in the overtime on her current project.

We decided at church to hold some kind of fundraising event. Pete Green was there again this week. He had skipped the last couple of Sundays because he wasn't quite sure what to say to people. Actually, he needn't have worried. Apart from one insensitive question from someone who should have known better, everyone just welcomed him warmly and treated him as if he was another member of the congregation. The new pain medication he has been given is working well, and as Ally said, to look at him you wouldn't know there was that much wrong.

Dad led the service as John had been called away at short notice to cover at Drummington Marsh. Helen sat next to Mum muttering something uncomplimentary about the Church of England, until Dad said, "No talking in the front row!" and everyone laughed.

October 29th

Today Dad received a phone call from Paul. It turns out that his accountant was arrested a couple of weeks ago on charges of fraud and now the tax authorities are investigating all his clients' books for the past six years including Paul's.

"So what do I do?" asked Dad. "I've just sorted out my work for the next few weeks, when suddenly I am asked to get involved in something extremely time-consuming. I dread to think what I will find when I start digging around. My head says I should stay well clear. But my heart says he is family, and I doubt he can afford another accountant to do a proper job."

"And you have that essay to write on the nature of the diaconate," said Mum.

Mitch looked at me blankly, but I passed as well. Sometimes the language of the Church of England defeats even me, and I am studying English A-Level.

In the end Dad agreed to invite Paul down in a couple of weeks, and they would spend three whole days going through everything he had. I could see Dad wasn't looking forward to it. He spent the rest of the afternoon rearranging his diary and starting work on his dreaded essay.

As for me, seeing as it was half-term, I decided to walk on my own down to Drummington and visit Drake's point. I realised the other day that most of my poems have recently been about people rather than places, and I wanted to see what inspiration I could get from sitting on the beach. Unfortunately quite a few other people had the same idea, and although there was a dramatic weather front obscuring the setting sun, somehow I found I couldn't concentrate on the landscape. There was a young child trying to protect his sandcastle from the inrushing tide, another shooing a seagull away from his bag of chips, while on the bench a very elderly couple were tightly holding mugs of tea, talking about something that happened just after the war.

Still, it gave me the inspiration for a short story which maybe one day will get published. My poem *Parting Gifts*, has recently been re-published, and Mr Maxwell says he'd like another contribution sometime soon.

November 13th

Paul and Dad emerged in total silence after almost three solid days in the study. They disappeared first thing in the morning and carried on late into the evening. We never heard Dad's voice when we were home, just occasionally Paul venting his frustration or protesting loudly. I could imagine Paul pacing up and down while Dad just sat there, methodically going line by line through the accounts in front of him, asking probing questions as he did so.

We had invited Grandma and Granddad over for our evening meal before Paul went on his way. They tried to get us to talk, and Granddad spoke at length about this literary society in Drumchester he had recently joined. But it was hard to keep the conversation flowing with Dad and Paul sitting there, motionless apart from the act of putting food into their mouths.

As soon as he was able to, Paul said he had better leave. Dad nodded and helped him load all the boxes of records into the back of another, newer, smart grey hatchback.

"That bad?" said Mum, as the taillights disappeared down the drive.

"A large five figure sum, I would reckon," replied Dad. "I am going to write my report to the taxman next week."

There was a lot of talk about money at the youth group tonight. Ally's Dad has decided to give up his airport run at the end of the month. He is still trying to work out what benefits he might be entitled to. At that point Daisy shared how her Mum was trying to fill in all the paperwork for Bill who was being reassessed yet again for care. Sian and Claire then started talking about the costs of going to university next year. At which point Ted pointed out that while we might be feeling poor tonight, we still had promised to raise some money for the earthquake fund.

"We could always do a concert," I said trying to brighten up the evening. "You could ask Tom to come along," I told Claire. But she just glared at me, and I realised I had put my foot in it yet again. Eventually one of the girls suggested a sponsored car wash after church next Sunday. No-one had any better ideas, so in the end we settled on that.

November 29th

No-one in the end owned up to the bright idea of a carwash in November. It wasn't pouring with rain, for once, but the number of waders arriving on the river should have told us that winter was on its way. So while the rest of the congregation were inside sipping coffee, we were out in the car park with buckets of freezing water.

"This is like so not good for my hands," said Daisy who was wearing at least three scarves, and KT agreed.

There were nine of us, including Ted and Bobby, and KT's brother Lee who had come over for the weekend. By the end we had raised the princely sum of £85. We went into the hall, only to find the tea ladies had already emptied the urn, washed up and gone home.

A miserable day got worse when Grandma had a fall in the stables this afternoon. She insisted it was only a minor bruise, but we insisted on the paramedics coming to take a look at her. They helped her into a chair and decided she needed to go into hospital for tests.

"I don't know what all the fuss is about," she kept saying as they wheeled her into the ambulance. Dad, Granddad and myself all followed on, but there had been some major accident on the motorway and Grandma was left on a trolley for over three hours before anyone saw here. They decided that apart from some rather large and colourful bruises there was no reason to keep her in. Only there wasn't a doctor available to discharge her so she would have to stay in overnight.

"I need cheering up," said Granddad as we came home. He disappeared into the front room and began playing a tune on the piano. I had never realised before what a fine pianist he was. Even Mitch was impressed. "That one is called, *Moonlight over Alabama*, Phyllis' favourite tune. In our case, it should be Bognor Regis, but I don't think anyone's ever written about that place. Come on, Mitch," he said, "let me teach you to play it."

December 3rd

In the end Grandma stayed in three days as the doctors decided to change her medication. I went round to the hospital to meet Granddad who had come to collect her. On the way in, we bumped into Pete Green. "Don't worry," he said, holding up his hands. "The pills I've been taking are giving me a rash in an extremely unusual place." He was trying to laugh but I noticed he was looking more tired, and his face had swollen up because of the steroids he was taking.

Grandma was already sitting by the bed with her coat on, although the heat in the ward was almost unbearable. She was just waiting for a prescription to give to the pharmacist. So we waited with her and waited and waited. At one point Grandma even dozed off.

"This is really too much," said Granddad and he marched off to the nurses' station. But no-one seemed to know anything about a prescription. It was nearly six o'clock before we left, in heavy rush hour traffic, in streams of torrential rain.

December 13th

The last youth group of the year. We had a party which gave Bobby an excuse to bring out the pies yet again. We all began to discuss what we were doing for Christmas. Claire's eldest brother had just got engaged and he was bringing his girlfriend down to stay. KT Lee was going to see Jacky and her new husband, although she wasn't looking forward to it. Daisy's father was coming home for Christmas, and Derek had some leave at the same time.

"And what about you?" asked Ted quietly, when we realised Ally had been silent.

"Well, Gran's coming down and she says she's not going back for a while. I think I know what that means. I can't imagine what it's been like for her. She said she would pay for Dad to go anywhere he wanted, not that she's got the money, really. But he just wants to be here, and he's told me I must spend some time with Mum, and with Mark and Olivia. Oh, and our third-choice goalie, the first-year pro, has just busted his ankle ligaments so there's a lot more football on the horizon. But to be honest, I don't know what I'd do without you guys, so let's hang together through this."

And then he raised his glass and said, "To the future, whatever that might be."

"He's so brave," Daisy whispered in my ear, and I had to agree.

December 24th

The carol service was different this year. The music was as special as ever, and there was a powerful sense of the Holy Spirit. But the atmosphere was quieter, had a kind of static electricity about it. John asked me to read my poem, *Parting Gifts*. I was really nervous about standing up in front of so many people, but somehow, I got through it. Then he talked about the parting gifts the wise men gave to Jesus. And then he talked about the gifts Jesus gives us which never leave us - hope, faith and love. Usually he preaches from notes, but tonight he was just standing there, with his arms outstretched, as if issuing an invitation. You could hear a pin drop at the end. Trevor had his arms round

KT, who was holding her cross to her lips. Daisy had her hand on Bill's lap. And Ally, well he and Pete were holding hands, with eyes closed as if they were lost in prayer.

December 31st

Last year I was cross because Ally didn't invite me to his birthday party. That seems so trivial, now. This year Ally, his Dad and his Gran came over in the afternoon, and those in the youth group who could make it. Ally's Gran and my grandparents were soon getting on like the proverbial house on fire. Dad and Pete were soon talking about sheds and gardens, and Pete explained what he was planning to plant in the spring. Daisy gave Ally a drawing of some sunflowers because it was the brightest thing she could think of, while KT had bought him a pair of silly socks. None of us really noticed the time, and we even decided to give the traditional church party in the hall a miss.

At midnight we joined hands and sang *Auld Lang Syne*. "Parting Gifts," said Ally.

"Faith, hope and love," I replied.

Then for the first time ever he gave me a proper hug and placed his enormous hands on my back. "Love you, brother," he said. And I knew he meant it.

Parting Gifts

The time has come for me to say goodbye,
That little word I'll never say again.
I cannot rightly tell what lies ahead,
But these three things, faith, hope and love remain.

Sometimes to live means that we must lose,
And nothing I can do will ease your pain.
My time of earth has run at last its course,
But these three things, faith, hope and love remain.

A day shall come when we will understand,
And you and I no longer need explain,
But till then, when all our tears are wiped away,
– These three things, faith, hope and love remain.

THE DRUMCHESTER DIARIES: VOLUME 7
FROM LIFE'S FIRST CRY TO FINAL BREATH
THE FINAL DIARIES

January 13th (AG)

I played my first game for the reserves today. Artur, our first-choice, picked up a knock on Saturday and needed a couple of days' rest, while Paul, our faithful reserve goalie, had a cold and so the boss decided to leave him on the bench.

"I've watched you in training and I like your attitude," he said to me during training. "Believe in yourself and you'll do fine."

Just before we went out onto the pitch, our centre-half warned me to watch out for their forward. I already knew his name and reputation, and just by looking at him, you could see he was the lazy kind of bully that gave football a bad name. It was barely five minutes into the game, when I came to claim a cross. He was a yard away as I caught the ball, but he still ploughed on straight into me, and knocked me to the floor. Whenever there was a corner, he was always nearby, and he seemed more intent on attacking me than the goal. I can still feel the bruises in my ribs.

As for the game itself, our mixture of young pros and first-teamers returning from injury played really well. The fact they didn't seem bothered by a kid just turned 17 between the sticks certainly gave me confidence. If only someone could put the ball in the back of the net. I knew a counterattack would come, and sure enough it came from their speedy left-winger who ran through our defence as if it wasn't there. Just a pity he shot straight at me. In the end we won 1-0 and I was so proud to keep a clean sheet.

I got home really late that night and everyone else had gone to bed. But with Gran staying, I don't have to worry about left-overs. She's trying to get Dad to eat and he does his best. Even so, some meals he hardly eats at all and he's still losing weight.

January 27th (AA)

I went up with Mr Maxwell and a couple of fellow students to look round his old college in Cambridge yesterday. The moment I saw the crenelated gateway and the cloisters I knew this is a place where I really want to go. I've sat in on a real history lecture and been given the syllabus for next year. So much choice, I don't know what to choose, but the possibilities are endless. At the faculty I found myself sitting next to a grumpy lad with a long beard called Istvan. His grandfather escaped from Hungary in 1956, apparently, and he wants to study the history of Eastern Europe in the 20th century. He couldn't understand anyone who's fascinated by the Middle Ages and digging old bones out of the ground.

February 7th (KT)

Dad and I went over to Pete and Ally's after church today. Dad moved Pete's bed downstairs. He's trying to remain positive, and he says he's put on two pounds. But I noticed he only ate a little of his Mum's scrumptious roast chicken dinner. I asked Ally afterwards how it was going. I don't see much of him now as he finds it hard to get to the Friday group on time, and often has to leave early. "Some days are better than others," he replied. "But I think we are all getting very tired. Gran's nearly eighty, after all."

We finished washing up in silence. I wished I could say something, but I wasn't quite sure what. Then Ally went out with Dad to help put up a greenhouse in the garden. "It's for the seeds Pete's going to plant in the spring," explained Gran who was knitting in the front room. There was an awkward pause so I asked what she was making. "It's a scarf for Pete," she replied, "he does feel the cold so." Then she smiled and said, "But so much for me. You know our troubles and our worries. Tell me something to brighten my day." So I told her about my cats Bert and Ernie and their ongoing battles with their arch-rival Marmaduke from across the street. I told her about my dreams of becoming a vet, and if that didn't work, becoming an ecologist. I told her about Dad's band and the mini-tour *The Potential* were taking next week in aid of cancer relief.

At that point Ally and Dad came in from the garden, cold and dirty, but obviously having achieved their work. "Come and have a cup of tea," said Ally's Gran who bustled off to the kitchen before they could say anything. She returned with a tray loaded with biscuits, even though we hadn't long had lunch, which the men soon devoured. "I've been finding out all about your lovely daughter, Trevor," she said. "You must be very proud of her?"

I could have died of embarrassment there and then, especially with Ally there. But Dad just winked at me and said, "She's all right. Most of the time."

"Only most of the time?" I said pretending to be offended, and we all laughed.

At that point Pete came in all bleary-eyed, having just woken up. "Don't stop laughing on my account," he said, "just tell me who ate all the biscuits?"

February 19th (AG)

Gran had to go home this week as another member of the choir had died, and she wanted to sort out something to do with the gas meter. She was really worried about leaving Dad and myself on our own for a few days, but with the number of meals she left in the freezer, we wouldn't have starved. Besides, Helen has organised a rota of church folk to come in each day, so it's not as if Dad is lacking in company.

Dad said I should take the opportunity to go back to Mum's for a few days. This was a good idea, except that she was away at a sales conference most of the week. Still, when George told her I was at home, she decided to come home early. "After all, I know who has won the golden mobile award this year," she said.

So today, as it was the last day of half-term and I had managed somehow to get a day off training, I dutifully went with Mum, the twins, Harry and the au pair to an indoor play park. They romped around and screamed to their hearts' content, while Mum and I tried to find a quiet corner over a hideously overpriced cup of instant coffee.

"If you need anything, let me know," she said. "I know Pete finds it hard to take anything from me, but I haven't forgotten I was married to him once."

"Thank you," I said.

"It was the lack of money that drove us apart, really," she continued. "Everything we had worked for had gone, bankruptcy looming, I just couldn't cope. Sometimes you have to just get out of a situation and take a break."

"And I guess you'd say it worked out well for you?"

"Perhaps," she said, stirring the dregs of her coffee. "But when I met George, he had only just started his own business. We counted every penny, especially once the twins arrived. That's when I decided I needed a career as well. You can't just live on fresh air and prayer."

"Certainly not fresh air," I replied. I wanted to say how many prayers we had seen answered recently, but I felt she wouldn't understand.

At that point the au pair brought Harry across who was crying. As so often happens, he had ended up in an argument with another little boy who didn't understand he couldn't hear him. He made a rapid series of signs which none of us could understand. Mum got him to slow down and eventually realised he wanted to go back home and play on the computer. It reminded me that life was sometimes hard for her as well.

March 4th (KT)

I spent most of this afternoon helping Daisy with her English work. For some reason the school have cut back hard on the extra support she has been getting, even though they insist she needs to retake her GCSE. With a major art exhibition coming up, and a textile project to finish, she's beginning to feel the pressure. Her Mum would help more but since the start of the year she's been working all hours for a mental health charity.

To cheer her up, I took her down to the cafe for a hot chocolate. Sid wanted to know if I could do extra hours on Sunday, but I said Saturday morning was enough. We were chatting away when we suddenly heard the sound of someone effing and blinding in the street. It was Maxine who seemed to be having difficulties getting her toddler to sit in the buggy.

"Do we think we should help her?" asked Daisy.

"I don't think she'd appreciate it," I replied. "But who would be a teenage mother, eh?"

In the evening Ted and Bobby had this idea of getting us to start leading the group in turns. As I might have expected, it was Alex who volunteered first, and he wanted us to look at poetry in the Bible. We all groaned when he announced the topic, but it was more fun than I imagined. I later learnt he had borrowed the idea from his Dad, which probably was just as well. He wanted us to think what images of God we would use if we were writing psalms today.

"God is my referee," immediately suggested Ally. No surprise there.

"God is my designer," volunteered Daisy. We all had our own ideas, and then Alex read out some modern versions of Psalm 23 he had found on the Internet.

"Your turn next week, KT," said Ted. I groaned inwardly.

"I'll lend a hand," said Daisy, who had worked out by now how best to avoid her stint.

"Next week?" I said unenthusiastically. "Seriously, me lead a group?"

"Don't worry," said Ally as he made his usual early exit, "you'll be good at it, you'll see."

March 16th (AG)

I've been playing in the youth team again, as City have signed a short term loanee, because our young pro is likely to be out for another few months. This afternoon we travelled a long way across the South Coast to the league leaders. It was going to be a tough match, but we've been working really hard on our defensive play as a team. In the end we came away with a 1-1 draw. I could have been slightly better positioned for the goal, but I did make a double save in the last few minutes to keep out the winner.

I was just getting showered and changed when someone said, "Your phone's ringing." It was Gran speaking from the hospital. Dad has been struggling for a few weeks now, but today he had some kind of fit.

"I didn't know what to do," she said, "but Bob and Phyllis were with me, and Bob knew all about the recovery position."

I spoke to the reserve team coach who told everyone to leave on the double and promised to drop me off first at the hospital.

It was a long coach drive back in gathering darkness. We were all on our *iPads* or listening to music. KT had given me some worship music she and her Dad had recorded with his friend Nick last summer, and that sort of calmed me down. I just wished the driver could go faster. We were stuck at a set of roadworks for what seemed like ages, even if it was probably only a couple of minutes.

Eventually, just before seven, the coach arrived outside the hospital. I gave everyone a high five as I got off and collected my kitbag. I had texted John who was away somewhere, but he had passed my message on to Joe, who was waiting for me in the foyer with his dog collar on.

Dad was lying in a cubicle on his own. He was in what I learnt was called a medically induced coma which was going to give the brain time to recover. He looked like he had shrunk from the father I had known and loved for the past seventeen years, and I guess he had. The doctors were also worried he might have contracted pneumonia, and there was a drip feeding all kinds of medicines into his arms. I gave him a kiss. I wanted to sit down next to him but after so many hours on the coach I needed to stretch and warm down.

"Anything you need?" Joe asked.

"Just stay for a while," I said. So he stayed, as the minutes and hours ticked by. I never knew a night could be so long. Eventually, at around midnight, he persuaded me to go home.

So here I am scribbling in my diary. Part of me is desperately tired, part of me is cramped, and part of me is wide awake. I think I will put a DVD on. Maybe that will help.

March 18th (AA)

Ally wasn't at youth group tonight. Pete had woken up today, although he was very sleepy and groggy. John came into the group and led a half night of prayer. We prayed for all kinds of things, and although of course our prayers were focused on Pete, we covered every kind of topic. My sister Sophie has been given paid leave by her firm to go out for a month and help rebuild the community affected by the earthquake. KT's brother, Lee, has lost his job as a stockman, something to do with falling milk prices. Sian needs to have her wisdom tooth out, which she doesn't want just before her A-level exams. And so the list went on. John and Ted simply and gently led us, focusing all the time on the cross.

March 26th (AG)

I can't quite believe what's happened today.

Dad is gradually getting better, but it could be another week or so before he can go home, and there needs to be big meeting about his nursing care. Throughout the week, various people from the church have popped in, and have been keeping me informed when I've been at training sessions. The club have offered me time off, but Dad tells me he wants me to stay focused on my football.

So that's what I've been doing. I don't have a match today, and I can follow the game on the hospital TV. But just after lunch time, KT Lee dropped by, having caught the first train up after work. Dad wanted to sit up and we ended up having a silly argument about his pillows.

"You're acting like an old married couple," he said, angrily. "Now leave me for a bit, so I can get a kip before the game."

So we went out into the corridor heading towards the cafe. "Sorry about my Dad," I said, "he's been a bit moody recently with all his meds."

"Not at all," KT replied and she slipped her arm into mine.

"I mean, that bit about an old married couple, so embarrassing."

"You think so?" she said, turning to me and smiling. Then she reached up to give me a kiss. I think she only meant it to be a small kiss, but somehow we got caught up in each other.

As we walked towards the cafe hand in hand, she said, "You know I will always be for there for you. You can call me any time."

I don't know exactly what we talked about when we got there, but as we spoke I realised for the first time what wonderful clear blue eyes she had. Probably because she had never looked directly into my face before, as she was doing now.

Before we knew it, it was three o'clock. "You go back to your Dad," she said, "I'll get going. But call me tonight," she added with a lovely, warm smile.

"I will," I said and gave her a kiss.

March 26th (KT)

There. I have done it. I have finally admitted to myself something I have known all along. Completely the wrong time, of course. But if I can just be there for Ally, maybe he can see how much I do genuinely love him.

April 2nd (AG)

A week like no other has ended up with the second greatest surprise of my life - I actually got to sit on the first-team bench today!

I haven't had time to write down in detail all that has happened. I couldn't sit next to KT on Easter Sunday, of course, as she was playing in the band, but I saw all the surprised looks as we held hands in the hall afterwards. She has promised not to be a distraction, but to be honest, it has been so good to have her company. I have been trying to concentrate on my training and spending most evenings up the hospital. Sometimes Dad has been asleep, so KT and I have had a couple of evenings just to catch up and chat, and I can make sure she gets on the last train home. Dad has always got on well with KT, and so far at least he hasn't commented, although I can see he is pleased.

But back to today. Our loanee goalie returned to his club at the end of March but with two fully fit goalies the boss thought we had no problems in that department. He didn't reckon with Paul eating a dodgy Thai green curry last night. By this morning he was apparently green all over, and the last thing we needed was a sickness bug in the camp. If we win our last three matches, and if other results go our way, then possibly, just possibly we might sneak into the play-offs.

So early this morning I got the call. KT was just on the way out to work, but she promised to be there at the match. I don't usually get nervous, but as I entered the dressing room an hour before kick-off and to see my shirt on the peg, alongside some of our stars, that was very special.

"Is it me or are goalies getting younger these days?" asked one of them and everyone laughed.

"Don't forget, you've still got a job to do, even sitting on the bench. Be focused, be alert, and if needed, be ready," said the manager. "Got that?"

"Be focused, be alert, be ready," I repeated.

"Good lad." Then he gave his team talk and made it clear only a victory would do.

Lee the goalkeeping coach then warmed me and Artur up on the pitch. Every time I touched the ball it seemed like someone in the crowd was cheering. I wondered where KT was, but it was impossible to tell. Then we disappeared back into the changing room, for one final word, until it was time to walk out onto the pitch. The roar as each name was announced was deafening, and my heart leapt when my name was announced. "Number 42, Ally Green." At that point I wished more than anything for my Dad to be there. But I knew he was watching me in his hospital bed, and Trevor told me later how proud he was of his son.

I wasn't needed, of course. But we played really well and ended up winning 4-1. It was well after half five when I emerged from the changing room, and I could, as they say, have walked on air. I wondered where KT was, but I needn't have worried, she had hooked up with Mark and Olivia at Kev's burger van.

"The au pair has Kai for the evening," Olivia said, "and I think we have a lot to celebrate," looking at KT and me.

"There's this great little restaurant not too far from the hospital," KT added, "and Joe has said he will stay with your Dad until we arrive."

Who could argue with a plan like that?

April 15th (KT)

Pete came out of hospital a few days ago, and there are now nurses going in every day. I've been trying to catch up on all my schoolwork, and Dad is really concerned I don't fall behind. So I haven't seen a lot of Ally this week, but we have been in touch every evening. If I understand correctly, and Ally has been over this several times, if Drumchester City win by three goals, and their only rivals lose at home, then miracle of miracles, they end up in the play-offs.

And Pete has insisted on going to the match. There will be a nurse with him, and I will be there as well. He's not too sure about buying a season ticket next year, however. Ally would join us, but he's now part of the matchday squad, in case anything happens.

April 16th (AG)

Paul is definitely not getting the luck. As everyone was warming up for the final match, he felt something click in his back. He hobbled off gingerly holding the lower part of his spine. "You're on," said the boss, as someone else went off to give my name to the referee.

The team we were playing had already been relegated from the league, but we still knew we needed to beat them well. There was no problem there. They were desperately short of confidence, and even the simplest pass went astray. By the interval we were 4-0 up. But our rivals weren't doing much worse. They were cruising to another comfortable victory.

After eighty-five minutes, it was clear we weren't going to make the play-offs. We had added another goal, but a three point difference is a three point difference no matter what the score line. The manager whispered to his assistant, and then he turned to me, and he said, "Is your Dad here?" I nodded. "Best warm up," he said. "You're going on."

So two minutes later the fourth official held up the board with the number 42 on it. A huge cheer went up and everyone stood and applauded as I ran onto the pitch. Although the press haven't commented on my story, apparently most fans know what's been going on.

You can either worry about me or you can do me proud. Those were the exact words of my Dad going through my mind as I staked out my penalty area. He was probably saying them even now. So here's a cross from the left-wing. That's mine. A header back from our centre-half. I'll claim that, thank you very much. A weak shot dribbling towards the corner. There's no way it's slipping through my hands.

I can't actually remember much of the last few minutes, but at the final whistle the whole team did a lap of honour and stopped exactly where Dad was sitting. They held their hands above their heads and began to applaud and everyone joined in. There was no way KT could speak to me, but as I'm a pretty good lip-reader I could see her saying, "Love you so much." Dad himself was in floods of tears, as the nurse had her arm around his shoulders in the wheelchair.

"Thank you," I said to the boss back in the changing room.

"I lost my Dad to cancer, you know," he said. "Now warm down properly, take a few deep breaths and get ready for the interviews."

"What interviews?"

"Just a wee word at the post-match press conference."

That was news to me. I texted KT and she said, *praying*.

The boardroom is behind the rickety old stand that should have come down years ago. I've cleaned it a few times, and the post-match conference is usually two reporters from the local paper, a stray dog and a manager not saying very much. But today the place was absolutely packed.

"Give the lad a break and respect his privacy," said the manager. Everyone started asking questions all at once. I looked at the boss nervously. "Just a few words," he whispered, "then you can go."

"I've always dreamed of playing for City," I stammered nervously, "and I'm so grateful I had the chance." I felt the tears well up, but I was damned if I was going to cry in front of the camera. I coughed, "And for my Dad to see me play was very special."

"Thank you, lads," said the manager. "Now let him go." I went out followed by what seemed a whole rugby scrum.

Mark told me later what all the headlines were about: *Young goalie plays for dying Dad*, that sort of thing. *Brave son takes a bow*.

"You lie low now," said the manager, "and don't worry about the upcoming youth tournaments. I don't want to see you around before the pre-season training. Is that understood?" I nodded.

Dad was completely worn out afterwards and couldn't eat anything at all that evening. The nurse put him straight to bed and he was almost immediately sound asleep. Gran had cooked me my favourite tea and then disappeared into the kitchen.

"You two deserve some quiet time all to yourself," she said. "Don't mind me."

But KT and I were pretty shattered ourselves and by the time Trevor came to pick her up, we were both dozing off in each other's arms.

April 29th (AA)

I have felt rather left out at the youth group, the only lad who's on his own. Perhaps for this reason, or perhaps because I am the only one willing to volunteer, Ted has got me more involved in leading. Tonight I wanted us to talk about something that had been on all our minds but none of us had dared mention, and that was heaven.

Last week Grandma started talking about her childhood in a tenement in Plymouth. I had never really heard her talk about her father who worked long hours as a victualler and died young, or her mother who used to go out and clean for others. Dad did offer to take her down there to see her childhood haunts, but she had no desire to go back. "I like to look forward," she said, "even now."

I told that story to the group and although it was a painful discussion, we had a really good time of what my Dad calls sharing. Ally didn't say much, but sat on the floor, resting against KT.

Then to change the mood completely I had arranged to connect up a Skype chat with Sophie who showed us photos of some of the work she had been doing. There was still rubble everywhere, but where the diggers had got in and cleared, the whole community was coming together to rebuild.

"That's what heaven is like," said Ally suddenly, "a sort of rebuilding project. Except there it actually gets finished and there's no-one to knock it down."

There wasn't a lot to say after that, except KT shared a long e-mail from Doris thanking us all for her birthday card. Not one of us could quite believe it was only just under a year since she left. So much has happened, and I do wonder what she would make of it all.

May 10th (KT)
When the end came, it was unexpectedly quick.

For the past few days Pete had been getting weaker and weaker, and he had barely eaten. He refused any more morphine saying he wanted to stay clear headed. I sensed Ally wanted to be alone with his Dad and with his Gran, so I have spent the last week cramming in as much work as possible, while drowning out other thoughts with my music.

In the morning Nicky came to see her ex-husband. We will probably never know what they talked about, but she stayed an hour. In the afternoon, Ally looked in on his Dad to check that everything was all right. Then he went out into the garden which over the past month he has been transforming into a mini-allotment. He found the first crop of radishes was ready to pick, and a lettuce big enough to eat as well. He called his Gran who suggested washing them and taking them into his Dad. But his Dad had already slipped away - so typical, as Ally said later. He never wanted to be the centre of attention, and to the end he didn't make any fuss.

I was just finishing revising the joys of differential calculus when the call came, and I didn't really need Ally to tell me what had happened. The school day was ending in any case, and nobody minded that I slipped out five minutes early.

I caught the first train up to Drumchester and then the bus out to the Octopus and Trumpet. There was already a small black ambulance outside, and John's car. I felt I ought to wait outside even though it was beginning to rain. I put up my umbrella and stood and watched at the end of the drive. Getting wet was a minor inconvenience at a time like this. Eventually the small black ambulance drove away, and somewhat uncertainly I walked down the drive.

There wasn't any need for words at that moment. Ally just held onto me for what seemed like ages, out in the hallway while his Gran and John talked quietly in the living room. Eventually his Gran came out for a refill. She didn't say anything. I could see she had been crying, but when she saw me, she smiled warmly and made sure she came back with an extra cup.

We sat drinking tea for a while, and I wondered what I was doing there. But then as news began to spread, the phone started ringing and I played receptionist for the next few hours. There were folk from church, fellow taxi drivers, even people who used to go to his shop. I never realised just how many people Pete knew, and everyone seemed genuinely shocked by his passing.

It was almost eight by the time I left. His Gran offered to cook, but nobody had any appetite.

"Call me when you need me," I said to Ally.

"Of course." Then for the first time he added, "I love you."

May 23rd (KT)
The day of the funeral. I haven't seen Ally that much and he's still in a state of shock. He's been doing a lot of gardening and he's been going to the gym every day. Dad and I invited him back for lunch yesterday, but he decided to leave it to next week.

Typically, Pete had requested no long funeral procession, and for everyone to meet the coffin at the church. I helped Ally to get ready, and then Dad took us down early to the church. Already there was a small group gathered by the lychgate where the first bouquet had already been placed. Ally held onto my arm so tightly as we walked into the church and looked around. Clearly the cleaning team had put an extra shift in, and the flower ladies had changed the display, although it was only Monday.

Ally wanted to show me the order of service. It showed Pete standing by his taxi, with his hand on the open door, as if welcoming us to get on board. "We've done 200," he said. "I hope it will be enough."

By the time the coffin arrived, it was clear more could easily have been printed. The whole church was jampacked. Ally, Dad, Joe and the one known as Steve's Dad, carried Pete into church for the final time. John welcomed everyone and the service began. Ally never let go of me for one moment, except when he stood up and read the lesson from the end of Revelation. I was so proud of him at that point. He had apparently spent all last evening rehearsing it. One of Pete's taxi driver mates shared some funny stories, and then John began to talk once again about faith, hope and love, and how Pete found all three when he came to the church and was baptised in the sea. At the end the coffin was carried out to one of Pete's favourite songs: *The presence of the Lord* by Eric Clapton.

I let Ally and his Gran go on their own to the crematorium, while I went over to the hall to see if I could help with the catering. Ally had asked me to ask Sid to put on a spread, but I think even he was taken aback by the sheer number of people.

"Don't worry," I said, "it's amazing what you can do with five loaves and two fish." And somehow the food didn't run out, even though people were spilling out into the car park and beyond. John managed to be everywhere, moving from one group to another with ease.

Ally found me again, and whispered, "Come back to the house afterwards." Then he was swept away again in a sea of people wishing him well and sharing their memories.

In the end his Gran simply had enough and wanted to go home and rest. The funeral director took us all back, and Dad promised to pick me up at ten. While his Granny was resting, Ally found the trashiest film he could find, while I made popcorn, and we pretended for the next couple of hours just to be a normal couple.

May 30th (AG)

KT's exams start tomorrow, so I won't be seeing her much for the next fortnight.

"Will you be alright?" she asked last night.

I laughed and said, "You know what my Dad would say." But I did confess I needed a break before the pre-season training. But I didn't know where to go and I didn't want to go on my own.

"Leave that to me," she said mysteriously. And tonight she Skyped to say everything had been sorted. In view of her "exceptional attendance record" the school would give her a week's compassionate leave in the last week of June. She had spoken to her aunt, Jenny and we are all apparently going walking somewhere in Wales. I really do like it when she has a plan.

I've been thinking a lot about the house. Although Dad had quite a few debts, he had massive amounts of insurance which more than covered them, so I don't need to move out just yet. But Gran is going back and I'm glad about that. She needs her church and her choir and her nosy neighbours over the fence. So what to do? Mum wants me to move back permanently but I am not sure I am ready just yet.

In the end I've had a brainwave, or maybe it was just answered prayer. Mark and Olivia would be delighted to come and take on the house, provided the landlord agrees. Kai can enjoy all the stuff I've been planting, and there's enough space for me to live there, if I choose.

July 2nd (KT)

It's been a brilliant week away, and Jenny has got on so well with Ally. We've finally had a chance to do what Jenny calls normal "boyfriend-girlfriend stuff" and I am starting to see the old Ally with his sense of humour, and a twinkle in his eye. Of course, there have been moments when he's been very quiet and most mornings he's got up early to do a long run on his own. But we have been on a boat trip and seen the dolphins. We've photographed each other among the ruins of an ancient castle, trying not laugh too much at the guided tour Alex would be giving at this point. We've eaten fish and chips on the harbour wall, and we've danced to a live band at a folk festival we found going on. Ally has even put up with Jenny taking me on the traditional clothes shop run on the final day and told me exactly which top I looked better in.

I have a lot of catching up at school on Monday, and Ally starts his pre-season training. As he says, it's like one year is ending and another beginning. That's exactly how I feel.

July 8th (AG)

Tonight marked the last ever meeting of our youth group. Sian and Claire have done their A-levels and are about to go travelling. I will often be preparing for the big match from now on, and there aren't really enough left to keep this group going. They can always join the slightly younger ones if they want.

So this evening John opened up the church, and Joe and Ted and Bobby all came too. We had a simple service of Holy Communion where we all gave thanks for the extraordinary times we had shared together. We had a very special sharing of the peace halfway through where everyone hugged each other, and when it came to the actual Communion, we all knelt in front of John who prayed for us by name. Then we went back to the vicarage where KT had left the most enormous chocolate gateau she had blagged off Sid, and Helen had made the most wonderful fruit punch.

Before it got dark, Ted took us all out into the garden for a group photo. And tonight we promised that wherever we went, whatever lay ahead, we would all look at that photo and keep praying for each other. Come what may.

July 17th (AA)

With all that's been going on, Daisy and myself have been feeling quite left out. We were hanging around at the end of church, not really knowing what to say to each other. I started to say something and stopped. Then she said something and stopped. Finally I blurted out, "Would you like to come for a walk this afternoon?"

"Why not?" she said. Just like that.

So this afternoon I met her outside Jacky's on Drummington seafront. We had agreed to walk along the coast path to Dewglass and then follow the old railway line to Dumpley End. She was wearing a very pretty floral dress with a matching blue cardigan, and she had tied up her hair into this most elaborate bun. I can still see her standing there now, waiting for me.

As we made our way towards Dulling St Mary, I told her about my accident all those years ago and how KT had found me at the top of the cliff. I think I managed to find the exact same thornbush. But she was more interested in the view than the bush, and I began to appreciate what I had failed to see back then. On either side the soft white cliffs arched away, with the sea lapping onto the pebble shore below. Beyond the cliffs the sea rose and fell in a tapestry of blues until the horizon melted into the sky.

"Do you mind if I stop and draw a sketch?" she asked.

"Be my guest," I said, and watched fascinated as within a few minutes she had a rough pencil drawing of the whole scene.

Soon she was talking about her love of art, and how she enjoyed trying to capture the spirit of wildlife and of the natural world. That led me to talk about my poetry and I showed her the notebook I always carry around with me. She asked me to recite some of my poems and she said they were very special. She told me she still remembered the poem I read out at the last carol service.

I had never had a conversation on my own with Daisy before, but it was more than a conversation. It was a meeting of two minds. As we came towards Dewglass, Daisy took my hand and asked if I would buy her an ice cream. I must have said something funny at this point because she laughed, and I saw she had the most gorgeous and most natural smile I had ever seen. We ate our ice cream and then we paddled in the sea, until we realised the time. Then we made our way up the old railway line, until we came to the turning for home.

"Thank you for a lovely day," she said.

"We must do this again," I said, and I realised at that point I was probably in love.

"Yes, let's," she said, and she gave me a kiss.

"I was starting to wonder where you two had got to," said Elspeth as she set out the plates for tea. So Daisy told her about the ice cream and the paddling. After we had eaten, Daisy took me up to what she called her studio. It was in reality an enormous bedroom with a skylight, but most of it was given over to her painting stuff and her easel. I had never realised before just what a talent Daisy possessed. We seemed to spend ages looking at her work, until Elspeth called us downstairs and said it was time for me to go.

On the way back I calculated the distance between home and Daisy's at about six and a half miles and decided I needed to get a bike. I mentioned this to Daisy tonight and she laughed that same wonderful, sparkling laugh I heard earlier. "Oh do," she said. "I hope you come here often."

July 18th (KT)

Alex and Daisy? Seriously?

At school today, Daisy rushed over to me as soon as I entered the form room and took me off into a corner. I wanted to say something, but she just couldn't stop talking. When she eventually paused, she looked at me with her large, dark eyes, and I think she was waiting for me to express my delight at the wonderful news. I hesitated for a moment, wondering what to say. She was still looking at me. Eventually I said, "Like, are you sure?"

Daisy smiled her widest smile and said, "Oh yes."

August 3rd (AG)

KT has gone off with Trevor to stay with Nick and his family for a week. Mum and George are also away, so Mark is working hard at the garage, and Olivia is busy with

Kai. I've been getting ready for the new season, and the training is going well. Today we beat Dewglass Town 3-0 in a friendly, and I played the whole match. But coming back to an empty house has been hard. I still expect Dad to be waiting there, wanting to find out how the game went, offering me a word of wisdom or making me a cup of tea as I told him the news. I wanted to tell him I was probably going to make the bench for the season opener on Saturday, and I wanted him to tell me I'd done him proud. I was about to ring KT, but then realised she had told me she was going to be out until late this evening.

I went out aimlessly into the garden. Dad had bought some runner bean seeds before he died, which KT had helped me plant out. I noticed they were suffering in the heat, so I filled up the watering can and set to work. Anything to keep me busy. The whole vegetable patch needing weeding really, so I fetched a fork. I found several snails which I crushed beneath my feet. Then I saw the grass wanted cutting. I cleared away Kai's toys and got out the lawnmower. I didn't hear Mark and Olivia both come home. When I turned off the lawnmower, they were watching out of the kitchen window. I wiped the tears from my eyes, took a deep breath and gave Kai a big hug as he came running towards me as fast as he could.

August 14th (AA)

Mum and Dad went off on their annual trip to France today. Mitch was as usual away at his summer music school, and apparently if he does really well, he will get the chance to play with an orchestra next year. I promised to stay behind to keep an eye on Granddad and Grandma. Grandma has been slightly better with the fine, dry weather we've been having recently, but she is still sleeping a lot, and Granddad is often glad of the company.

This afternoon I went over to Daisy's. I have bought that bike, and it's been getting a lot of use over the past few weeks. Daisy and I do have just so much in common. I love the way she is able to capture the beauty of a flower or the colours of a sunset or the texture of a tree trunk. We've spent a lot of time just going out for walks in the countryside, she with her sketchpad, me with my notebook. It's as if we were made for each other.

Today Elspeth put on a proper cream tea for us in the garden. As we ate her delicious home-made scones, eaten the proper way with jam on top, she announced she had to go away next weekend to see Bill. She glanced nervously at Daisy and asked, "You will be all right on your own, won't you?"

Daisy and I had just had a silly argument about who was taller. Eventually we had measured each other standing barefoot against the doorframe of her bedroom. It turned out she had the advantage of a full extra half inch. She looked at me still triumphant and said, "Oh, yes. I'll be just fine." Whenever she smiles at me like that, she is absolutely irresistible. I think she was going to say something else but at that point a wasp landed on her plate, and our conversation was cut short. At least it gave me the chance to play the gallant hero.

September 17th (KT)

Last Monday Ally and I had our first proper row. He's been finding it tough being around the first-team squad and I'm convinced he's carrying one or two knocks, even if he won't admit it. As for me, my hormones have been all over the place and to cap it all, my form tutor told me what I already knew really, that I wasn't going to get the grades to become a vet.

When I Skyped Ally later, I told him the news. "I'm sure something will turn up," he said, in a way that seemed to me like he hadn't really been listening. He was still sitting in his chair, flexing his left shoulder.

"It's all very well for you to say that," I replied crossly, "but then you're living your dream."

"Don't you ever say that," he snapped, and for some reason we ended up arguing the next few minutes over the silliest of things, until one of us hung up.

I've been low and miserable for most of the week. Dad had to ask what was wrong – as if it wasn't obvious! Daisy's been trying to cheer me up, but I sense something is up with her, I'm not quite sure what. Eventually, I texted Ally last night that I was sorry and missed him so much. Which was true.

Miss you too, babe, he replied. *Let's catch up after the match tomorrow.*

So today I went down to the match where I was sitting behind all the players. As the team came out onto the pitch, Ally was there. I managed to catch his eye and gave him a little wave, before feeling all embarrassed.

We were playing one of the top teams in the league. They seemed to have an extra player on the pitch, and we kept giving them the ball. It was only a matter of time before they scored, and sure enough, that's what they did after about half an hour. Then just before half-time, their massive centre forward cut into the penalty area unmarked. Artur rushed out to stop him and as Ally explained later, "Took one for the team." Result: centre-forward on the ground, Artur heading back to the changing rooms.

It was then it dawned on me that Ally was actually going to come on. As I watched him warming up and stretching, I suddenly realised how young he looked, and I wondered how on earth he was going to manage for the rest of the game. Slowly he jogged over to the goal which now looked twice as big. The massive centre-forward who a few minutes previously had been rolling around as if he had been shot, got up and smiled a big ugly smile as he approached the penalty spot. He didn't exactly run. He just reckoned he had to stroke the ball past this boy, which he did – except he hit the base of the post.

So slowly, slowly, the ball trickled back along the goal-line. My heart was in my mouth as this ruck of players all descended on it with Ally somewhere underneath. Eventually, I could see him lying on the ground with all these legs around him. For a split second I thought he wasn't going to move. Then he gingerly got up with the ball firmly clutched to his stomach and we all burst out in applause. At least I did, and I think then I realised just much I cared for him, and how much he needed caring for.

In the end the team lost 3-1 but Ally made some great saves along the way. I hung around for ages after the match to tell him how proud I was of him. "I'm sorry for what I said," I blurted out as I took his arm.

"Me too," he said, as he gave me a kiss. "Let's go somewhere and talk."

"Guess you've seen what the dream's like," he said over a pizza. "Sometimes I think I must be crazy to do what I do."

"But you're good at it," I replied. "I wish I knew what I was going to do."

"You really aren't going to be a vet?" I shook my head.

"The thing is," I went on, "I was always going to work outside with animals."

"You could try my job," Ally replied, and for the first time in ages we actually laughed together. I don't think we sorted out my future this evening, but I am looking forward to seeing him at church tomorrow.

October 7th (AA)

I was just finishing my history essay so I could spend the weekend with Daisy when she rang. At first it was hard to make out what she was saying because she was crying so much. I told her to take a breath. She paused, blew her nose and said, "So it's like this – I'm pregnant."

"Are you sure?" I asked, and then cursed myself for such a daft question.

"The last few mornings I've been feeling pretty sick. Mum didn't say anything, but she came home today with these strips and told me to take the test. So, yeah, I am. I really am." I wondered what to say next. "We don't have long to talk 'cos like, my Mum is phoning your Mum," she said in her own quirky way that always sounded like a question.

I found myself repeating a line I'd heard in countless songs and films before. "I will always be there for you." My mind was too numb to think of anything original to say.

"I love you, too," she said.

"So can I see you?" I asked.

"What do you think? Quick… my Mum's just got off the phone."

"Well, I can still talk to you, can't I?"

"Please. I really want you to."

At that point I heard my Mum's steps coming up the stairs. "Love you, darling," I said. At that point the door opened.

I won't put down in writing all my Mum said. There are times when I am reminded just why she is head of department at Dewglass School. She was calm and controlled all the way through, making sure I understood every word she said and cutting off any argument I tried to make. Again and again she talked about "abuse of trust," of Daisy, of Daisy's Mum and Dad, of her and my Dad. When she was through with me, she walked out in silence.

Mitch then popped his head round the door with a dirty grin on his face. "So what was it like doing it?"

I literally threw him out of the room. But I was confused. How could something that seemed so right end up so wrong? I tried to listen to my music, but for once it just annoyed me. I looked at some of the poems I had been writing over the past few months (the ones I hadn't given to Daisy) and I threw them in the bin. I even tried praying, realising I hadn't been thinking about God at all since we'd started going out. But I wasn't sure what I was praying for, and God didn't seem to be giving me any clues.

Dad had been out on a visit and didn't come back till late. I have never seen Dad lose his temper, and I wondered what he was going to do and say. I think he reckoned Mum had said all that needed saying. He just stood in the doorway and said, "So you're still going to Cambridge then?" That was the last thing I needed to hear. I hadn't even thought about that, but of course how can I go away if Daisy has a baby? My baby?

Daisy and I chatted long into the night. I kept trying to be strong for her, to encourage and to reassure her. Even if on the inside I felt like I was falling apart. Eventually she rung off, but not before I had promised to be with her every step of the way – whatever that means. And to be honest, I don't have a clue what that means. Me, Alex Andrews, the one with the clever answer for every situation, the boy who found the lost medieval village, the student going to get straight As in all four subjects.

It's already three o'clock in the morning now. The house is still, and I can only hear the soft fall of a grey drizzle outside. I wish I could sleep. I wish I could have a single constructive thought. But I can't. Daisy's pregnant. That one phrase keeps repeating in my head. And what the next line in the story might be – I don't have a clue.

October 15th (AA)

Elspeth relented and let me see Daisy today, for just two hours while she went shopping in *Asco's*. When Daisy saw me approaching, she ran and gave me an enormous embrace, which lasted for what seemed like hours. "So, what shall we do?" she asked. I looked at the sky which was getting darker and darker by the minute. We decided on a coffee somewhere – but where? We could hardly go to *Asco's*. KT was working at Jacky's and Daisy knew girls working in at least three of the coffee shops. Eventually we found ourselves at the small *Pumpkin* café at the railway station. No-one ever goes in there 'cos of the hard plastic orange chairs and the rubbish on the floor. But the drinks were surprisingly good.

"So how are you?" I asked (I still can't seem to think of anything original to say).

She smiled and brushed a strand of her yellow hair from her cheek. "Yeah, not too bad. I had a long chat with my Gran who told me to take it one day at a time. So that's what I've decided to do. I think I'd go mad trying to work out the future. As the good book says, each day has enough troubles of its own."

"You're really all right?"

"Yeah, I think so, I hope so. So many people have asked me that question already, and I think I've given a different answer every time."

We paused, and then she put her hand on mine. "And what about you?"

"What about me?" I replied. "You're the first person to ask me that question. Well, I've had plenty of messages telling me just what people think of me. I seem to have committed the crime of the century. I've been trolled, spammed and generally unfriended. Although I don't feel any more evil than I did a couple of weeks ago."

"It wasn't entirely your fault," she said, smiling warmly. "It was, like, I was there too." She was still holding my hand at this point.

"I still love you," I said without thinking.

"I know," she said, smiling with those gorgeous brown eyes I find so seductive. "Come on, we have just over an hour left. Let's go for a walk."

"But it's chucking it down out there," I said.

"So? I just want to do something wild."

"I think you've already done that," I replied, and she just laughed. So we spent a mad hour going down to the beach, walking into the gale, watching the seagulls hunkered down and letting the rain soak us right through to the skin. I don't think Elspeth was impressed when Daisy turned up bedraggled and five minutes late.

When I got in, Dad was waiting for me. He wasn't impressed with my general state of appearance either. "There's something I need to say," were almost his first words as I dripped on the hall carpet.

"Can't I get changed first?" I pleaded.

"I've been talking with Joe. We both agree it's best if I only serve at Drummington Marsh for the next few months."

"I didn't think what I did would make that much difference," I said inching to the stairs.

"Listen to yourself," said Dad. "You didn't think!" And then I heard him shout for probably the first time in his life. "You didn't think!" I ran upstairs and hid in the shower. What on earth have I done?

We had all gone to bed tonight when we were woken by the sound of gravel hitting our front windows, and someone shouting from the driveway. I ran to the end of the corridor and looked out of the window. It was Derek, back from the army, I think he had been drinking. He was bawling out something about filthy rich people and the things they did to children. Dad phoned the police, but by the time they arrived he had gone away again, and Dad told them not to take any action.

"I didn't think, did I?" I said to Dad.

He shook his head. "Sorry I shouted at you earlier," he mumbled. "But remember this – whatever you start you need to see through. You can't, you mustn't walk away. Understood?" I nodded and suddenly felt as if I was about six years old again.

I tried to get back to sleep after that but couldn't. So as I looked through my shelves for something to read, I found that old novel I had so proudly shown to my English teacher. At the time I couldn't understand what he meant about it "lacking emotional depth." Now I felt deeply embarrassed by the drivel in front of me. Perhaps it was time to admit I really didn't know as much about life as I thought I did.

November 3rd (AG)

I went to see Joe this evening. The club had laid on a course about personal finance, and tax, none of which I really understood. And somebody recommended me to get an agent, just in case another club makes a bid for my services, and, to be honest, it's all been very confusing. There are times when I wish I had been able to do my business studies course.

So tonight I went to talk to someone who knows. But before we got down to business, Joe gently asked how I was doing, asked about Dad, about Mum, about me and KT. That's the thing I like about Joe. He may not be the world's most interesting person, but he takes time to listen. And somebody has to do the boring things in life. So after checking I was all right, he started to go through all my financial affairs piece by piece. He didn't know much about agents or sponsorship but he reckoned he knew a Christian who could help me out. By the time he started on his third mint, I realised that whatever happened to me, I could always trust Joe to sort things out.

We were just about wrapping up, when there was a knock on the door. Alex apologised for interrupting, but his Grandma had taken a turn for the worse, and could Dad come over at once?

"I think we're just about done, here," said Joe, getting up. "My door's always open, if you need it."

"Thanks," I said, getting up as he passed out the room.

So for the first time in months there I was standing in front of Alex, mano a mano, as they say. I looked at him, and he looked at me.

"You've been a f***ing idot," I said. I have no idea where that language came from. I only swear when I'm on the pitch, 'cos that's the language everyone seems to understand out there. "That, at least, is true," said Alex with grin. So typical of him to make a clever joke out of a situation.

There was a brief pause. "So how you doing?" I asked. Alex just shrugged his shoulders. This was definitely not typical Alex. I expected the usual clever response – but he just stood there, looking at the carpet, obviously uncomfortable at my question.

"You've helped me through some tough times," I said, "so I guess it's my turn to help out now."

"How?" he asked, looking up at me.

"Dunno," I said, facing him down, "but you're still my friend."

"Thanks," he mumbled.

I later repeated this to KT.

"That boy has always been an idiot," she said.

"Yes, but he's our idiot," I replied. "I think you and I ought to get together with Daisy and Alex some time. I think they need us."

"Possibly," said KT, but she was wrinkling her nose in a way that told me she didn't agree. We dropped the subject after that.

November 12th (AA)

Grandma caught pneumonia last week. Granddad tried to persuade her to go into hospital, but she said she had had enough. No-one could blame her, really. She has been ill for years now, and none of her many treatments have seemed to make much difference. The carers have come in morning and evening to make her comfortable, and Granddad has never left her side. Two days ago, as her breathing worsened, he sent for John. Grandma seemed pleased to see him, but as far as we could make out what she was saying, she thought he was Father Michael, whoever that might be.

I saw Grandma for the last time last night. She was propped up in bed, gasping for air, even with the oxygen mask on. Granddad had put on his best suit and was holding her hand which felt icy cold. He looked up at me and simply said, "The Lord gives, and the Lord takes away. Blessed be the name of the Lord." On the shelf by their bed, he had arranged photos of the entire family, and right at the centre was their wedding photo, all in black and white, taken nearly sixty years ago.

"She was a right looker then, wasn't she?" said Granddad, and I nodded.

We didn't talk after that. Eventually the door opened, and Sophie came in, straight off the train from London. "Oh, Granddad," she said and gave him a kiss. Then she fussed about how Grandma was lying and tried to make her comfortable.

Granddad simply put his hand on hers and said, "Let her be. There are some things we just can't fix."

Grandma slipped away just as the sun was rising on a clear, cold autumn morning. Over the trees from my bedroom window it rose in all its glory, greeted by a cacophony of rooks and crows who were circling the bare branches of their roost. We wouldn't all have fitted into Grandma's bedroom, so I waited until I was summoned. Somehow after months of silence it felt as if God was somewhere in that moment, and that one day all would be well.

Ally warned me how everybody suddenly becomes so busy when there's a death. We had the doctor and the funeral director, of course, plus a few friends from the village. Eventually, at around eleven, Paul turned up. He had seen Grandma the previous weekend, and I think they had said their goodbyes then. For the rest of the day he and Dad would sit together, drinking tea, sharing memories, starting to make plans.

There was one more visitor I wasn't expecting. About three I saw Daisy walking up the drive. I rushed up to meet her, and she gave me a kiss.

"I said to Mum I had to come," she said. "She said, like, I would be in the way, but I insisted."

"It's a bit crowded in the house," I said, suddenly thinking of all the people in there.

"It's just you I came to see, actually," she said suddenly aware they could be watching us from the house. "I wanted to know you were all right."

So we went into the orchard where Miss Watson's chickens came rushing up to see if we had any tasty treats for them. When they went away disappointed, we spent an hour walking among the old trees, just chatting. There were still just a few apples worth picking, so we collected those and slipped back into the kitchen.

"Hello, Daisy," said Mum and Sophie as they bustled about inside with cups of tea.

Daisy looked shyly at me, "Perhaps I should better let my Mum come and fetch me."

"Have a cup first," said Mum touching her hand. So we sat in the kitchen, as people came backwards and forwards with trays and teapots and cakes, until Mum volunteered to drive Daisy home.

"I know this has been awkward for you," said Mum on the way back, "but I'm so glad you were brave enough to turn up. After all, what's done is done, and of all days, today is a good day to be reminded that new life will come." I realised at that point she too had tears in her eyes, and after I said goodbye to Daisy, I gave my Mum a kiss.

22nd November (AA)

The day of the funeral. Mum insisted that Daisy travel with me in the limousine. She went with me to pick her up. As she came out of the house, I couldn't help noticing how stunning she looked all dressed in black.

"How do I look?" she said nervously.

"Absolutely ravishing," I replied, squeezing her hand.

We were still holding hands as we walked into the church. It was the first time I had been inside for a couple of months. The contrast with the dreary, damp atmosphere of Drummington Marsh struck me at once. There was a kind of warmth about the place I had missed, and not just the fact we had central heating that worked. The Sunday School had put up a display of their artwork, bright banners adorned the pillars, the altar cloth had a rainbow with the words, 'God is love'. One or two people frowned as they saw Daisy and me holding hands, but more than that came up to us after the service and wished us well.

Dad insisted on taking the service, as always in the same quiet, unhurried style of his, although I noticed he glanced once or twice at Mum and Paul. And once again Granddad led the tribute, just as he had at his aunt's funeral all those years ago. His theme was "Blessed are the poor" and he talked about how his Phyllis had escaped from the poverty of her childhood by taking a job in London, how he had met her at a jazz club, and instantly known she was the girl for him, how she brought two wonderful sons into the world, and how she never stopped working throughout her life.

Then it was me. The family insisted I read my poem, *Parting Gifts* again. I hesitated in my seat. "You can do this," Daisy whispered in my ear. And I did. As I made my way back to the seat, her smile told me she was so proud of me.

Daisy never left my side for the rest of the day. Mitch, Sophie and myself fielded questions from cousins, second cousins and relatives we never knew existed, as usual taking it in turns so one of us could get a chance to eat. Granddad made a point of slowly going round each table in the church hall, thanking everyone for coming. Although he was clearly very tired, he made sure he had a special word for everyone. When it came to Daisy, he told her she was a very special young lady, which made Daisy blush.

But she is, and I can sense she is becoming part of our family. I just wish I knew what the future held. She keeps telling me to take it one day at a time, but I can't help wondering.

December 3rd (KT)

My 18th birthday today! For the first time ever Jenny and Gordon came down to Drummington-on-Sea last night. We offered them Jacky's old bedroom but they preferred to stay in Dumpley Manor, the poshest hotel in the area. Ally was getting ready for the big match, and I knew I wasn't going to see him until the evening. I suspected he and Jenny had been plotting, but they weren't going to let on.

In the morning, after I opened my presents, Jenny and me hit the shops, as usual. This left Gordon with Dad. I can't imagine what they could possibly have been doing together, but they were deep in conversation when we got back, stopping only when they saw the number of bags we were carrying. Then off to lunch and on to the match at Drumchester City. I am not sure Jenny and Gordon had ever been to a game of football before, and it must have been a strange sight watching us all, with Dad in front and me behind making our way to the seats.

"Reminds me of my old West Ham days," said Dad as he saw the teams warm-up. "Mind you, I had more than water bottles with me, then." At that point I could see a steward eyeing him nervously. Dad just smiled back with his widest, toothiest grin.

I had never been to a football match with Dad before. It was so embarrassing. He followed every kick of the game, argued with every decision of the ref and when Drumchester City scored the winning goal, he let out a roar so loud I guess the players down the other end of the pitch could hear it. Certainly Ally in the dugout below us had no problem identifying the voice. He wasn't playing, of course, but every time Artur went down in a heap, I couldn't help wondering if he was going to come on.

I was expecting to be taken out this evening to some fancy restaurant or other, but Jenny said she needed to go back to the hotel. Ally said he had invited one or two friends to join us, and it was then I twigged what was going on. When I protested I didn't have anything to wear, Jenny just smiled and said it was all sorted. Which indeed it was. She had left me a beautiful slate grey dress and matching shoes in her bedroom, which was certainly an improvement on the Drumchester City top and hoodie I'd been wearing.

When Ally came to fetch me, he led me down a couple of flights of wide, plushly-carpeted stairs, down a corridor full of mirrors towards the door of a function room. I knew what was going to happen next, even though for the moment everything seemed to be quiet.

Everyone was there. There was Ally's entire family, there were folk from church and a few from school, John and Helen with the kids, Elspeth and Daisy, even Alex and his parents. And right in the middle the most enormous buffet you could imagine. I've been trying to lose weight recently, but *what the heck?* I thought.

"Happy birthday," whispered Ally and I gave him a kiss.

It was fascinating to see how everyone somehow all mixed together. Jenny had never met Nicky before, but soon they were having a long and involved discussion about marketing techniques and sales strategies, all the while keeping an eye on Carrie and Nina and checking with Mark and Olivia that Harry and Kai were all right. Gordon and George were chatting about cars, of course, while John remembered Siobhan and somehow said something that made her laugh.

I was focused mainly, however, on Alex and Daisy. I hadn't seen them together since the first silly few weeks of their affair. They seemed to circulate independently, but from time to time would just come back together as if to make contact with each other, Daisy gently laying a hand on his arm, he resting his hand on the small of her back. I still don't understand what they see in each other, but they appear to be genuinely in love.

Eventually they came over to us and for the first time we sat together as two couples. It felt kind of weird, and I'm not sure any one of us knew what to say. So it was Ally who broke the ice with the obvious question, "So, Daisy, how are you?"

"Yeah, I'm OK," she replied and squeezed Alex's hand. "We're having a scan next week."

"I didn't know Alex was pregnant as well," I replied without thinking.

Everyone laughed, but I felt I'd put my foot in it. Still, it was a shock hearing Daisy talking about "we." Then Alex asked about the football, and Ally started explaining the match in great detail... until he caught Daisy and me rolling our eyes, and he saw the funny side of what he was saying. That finally broke the ice, but I couldn't help thinking we were no longer four friends, but two plus two, if that makes sense?

"Yeah, it does," said Ally at the end of the evening as we were saying our goodbyes. I wondered if I needed to return the dress and shoes, but, while Ally was helping Nicky with the kids, Jenny just put my old clothes in a carrier bag and told me to keep them.

"He's a good lad, Ally," said Jenny. "I'm sure if Susan were here, she'd tell you to stick with him."

"I will," I promised.

"Happy birthday," she said, and she gave me a big hug. "And when I see the way you've turned out," she added, "I'm pretty proud of Trevor too."

"It's just a shame about the tattoos, isn't it?" I said.

"Yeah, but they're only skin deep."

December 13th (AA)

Daisy had her scan today. I didn't want the whole school to know why I needed to take the afternoon off, so I just told the office I had a medical appointment. The first bus to the hospital didn't turn up, so by the time I reached Daisy and Elspeth at the entrance, I knew we were cutting it fine. Elspeth accepted my apology tersely, then told Daisy to tell her all about it later.

"Isn't she coming with you?" I asked.

"She says she needs to work late tonight. Besides, this is, like, a you and me thing, isn't it?" she said smiling and took my arm.

I have never liked hospitals. Long corridors, no fresh air, little natural light. And it was so confusing finding out where we were supposed to be. Eventually we were shown a large waiting room, where there were plenty of other mums-to-be sitting around, some with young children, some of them with their partners. All of them were much older than Daisy and me. One looked at least as old as Elspeth.

"This makes it all a bit real?" I whispered to Daisy, and she nodded, too shy to say anything. Several gave us glances which were less than friendly, while all the while the big round clock slowly counted off the minutes. A baby came crawling over to us and tried to pull himself up on Daisy's lap. The mum shouted at the baby, so Daisy simply scooped him and handed him back. I realised soon we would have one of our own we couldn't hand back, but I knew it wasn't going to be helpful to say that.

At last the name of Daisy Dawkins was called, and we were ushered into a small cubicle. The nurse looked at me quizzically, but Daisy said simply, "It's, OK. This is Alex – he's my boyfriend."

I sat at the top of the bed and watched as she put this funny jelly-like substance on Daisy's tummy and carried out the scan. Eventually these strange fuzzy pictures began to appear on the screen. The nurse explained what we were seeing and asked if we would like to keep the photographs. I looked at Daisy and she nodded.

"Well, Daisy, it looks like you are carrying a perfectly normal, healthy child and I expect the child to make an appearance into the world some time at the end of May. So I don't know what your plans are, Alex," she said turning to me, "but it would be good to keep your diary free around then."

I instantly thought of my precious A-levels. How on earth was I going to take them with Daisy giving birth? But I looked at Daisy, and understood that come what may, she was going to have to come first.

"I can if you like tell you what sex your child is going to be?" the nurse added. Again Daisy nodded. I could sense she was completely overwhelmed at this point. "I could be wrong, but it looks like you are carrying a little girl. We can check again in a few weeks."

Daisy didn't say anything until we were outside and were walking down towards the station. It was a miserable December afternoon, with a cold drizzle and a gusty wind that caught you when you turned a corner. We cut through the park and sat for a little while in a shelter to gather our thoughts. Daisy took the photos out of her handbag and just stared at them. "I wonder what we should call her," Daisy wondered.

"Fuzzy," I replied, and she laughed.

"I just can't believe we made her."

"Neither can I," I said. We looked out onto a bare flower bed and the imposing statue of some long forgotten general on which a pigeon sat miserable and hunched. "But I will look after her. I will look after you," I said. "I mean that. I don't know what that means, but I mean that." I took Daisy in my arms and for a moment as I felt her warm body snuggling up against me, I remembered that August weekend we spent together, like a shaft of summer sunlight on a cold winter's day.

"Come on," said Daisy, "Your Mum and Dad have invited us for tea, and we don't want to miss the train."

When we arrived home, Granddad was in the front room, playing the piano. We paused wondering if to say hello, but he just smiled at us and ushered us to come in.

"Did I ever tell you, Alex, I once played at that jazz club for two weeks? The regular pianist disappeared, and his understudy got sick. So I filled in one summer, until I was found out and the manager found someone who could actually play." Then he turned back to the keyboard and played a slow, haunting piece that perfectly matched our mood.

"Play another one," said Daisy as he finished. So for the next half an hour we sat , hand in hand, listening to him play while outside the gusty wind strengthened into a gale. Then Dad came in, complaining that no-one had shut the curtains and the spell was broken.

At first, tea was a fairly awkward affair. Daisy was tired, and she wasn't feeling at her best. Sitting round a table with my family I could see was a bit of a strain, and she didn't want to eat that much. Mum had come in late after another hard week of school, and she clearly had something on her mind. So it was just Mitch and Dad who did most of the talking. It was only over pudding that Mum finally said, "So, Daisy, do you have some picture to show us?"

Daisy blushed and handed round the photos of our baby. Mitch didn't seem interested and barely looked at them. Dad handled them more thoughtfully, "I didn't think I was going to become a grandfather so soon. I feel so old."

"Less of the old," said Granddad. "Phyllis would have loved to see the baby. She was always good with children, better than me." Then he put his head down and concentrated on the rest of his crumble.

There was a brief lull and then Daisy suddenly asked Mum, "Can I ask when you found out you were pregnant?"

Mum looked at Dad, and Dad smiled straight back. "Come on," she said, "help me with the tea things, and we can have a proper chat." I don't know what they found to talk about, but I have never known the tea things take a whole hour before. They were still talking when Elspeth came to pick Daisy up. "You can call me any time," said Mum.

"I will," said Daisy. "Coming, Mum, just let me say goodbye to Alex..." And in the hallway right in front of everyone she put her hands on my cheeks and kissed me full and hard on the mouth.

"Wow," said Mitch as she left. "Just wow."

"Shut up," I said, "you know nothing."

December 25th (KT)

It's been a strange, strange Christmas. About eleven o'clock yesterday morning, I had a phone call, of all people, from Doris. She was at Drumchester Central, and could I come and meet her? I dropped what I was doing and rushed into town. We found a crowded coffee shop just off the High Street and she explained what was going on.

"I came over to see my Dad and his new wife," she explained. "But she didn't like me and I didn't like her. We have a big row the first evening I arrive, and then I listen to them grunting and groaning all night, and I think to myself, *'What am I doing here?* But there are no seats back to Poland. So very early this morning I write Dad a note and leave him my present, and I catch the first train here. So can I stay here a few days?"

What could I say? I had so wanted to see Doris, but I never expected her just to turn up. "Of course," I said, "I'll clear it with Dad but we don't have anyone else to stay."

On the train back Doris asked me how I was and then she asked where Ally was. "He's in a match somewhere up north today. He won't be back till late."

"But you and him, you're fine?"

This was the Doris of old, always so wise and supportive. "Yes," I smiled. "It's not your usual relationship. He works so hard at the club, and training on his own. He wants me to use the time to study and I do. But sometimes I miss him so much. Then he rings or *Skypes* me and every night we have so much to talk about. We can spend half the night chatting. And he makes sure that Saturday evening and Sundays are our time together."

"He sounds like he's really grown up."

"He's had to, fast," I said and told her about his father.

We didn't have time to talk much more because I was going to be busy with the carol service for most of the rest of the day. The service was packed as usual. Doris helped out with the refreshments, and we only got back about eight o'clock. "And now you wait for Ally to get in touch?"

Ally's coach had a flat tyre on the way down the motorway. It was nearly midnight when he finally *Skyped* me. "That was a horrible journey," he said, "and I get back home only to learn Mum and the family have some kind of chesty bug, which I really don't want to catch. So here I am on my own at Mark and Olivia's, 'cos they're staying with her Mum and Dad. I really didn't want to spend my first Christmas without Dad on my own, but there you go," he added sighing.

"You could always come and kip on our sofa," I said.

"I think it's too late tonight. But tomorrow, yes, I'd love to. Still, I've got plenty to think about. Artur picked up a knock late in the game, so I'm playing on Boxing Day. That means I have to spend Christmas Day preparing for the match." I must have made a face 'cos he said, "I'll be over as soon as I can, I promise."

So Christmas morning began with Dad, me and Doris at home – something I never expected. At eleven Lee turned up with his new Romanian girlfriend, Alina, who he'd met at the meat packing plant where he's working. It turned out Alina had spent some time travelling in Poland, so we all listened as Doris and Alina chatted about places they had in common. I went with Lee to get the dinner ready, and we just decided the turkey was cooked through when Jacky and Gerry turned up. They were on their way down to Cornwall for what they called a "romantic retreat."

Lunch was difficult 'cos I was the only person who linked everybody together. I made a few introductions, but Jacky obviously didn't think much of Alina, and Gerry didn't think much of Lee. Jacky remembered Doris, of course, but she didn't show any interest in the answers Doris gave to her questions. So Dad chatted with her, and Jacky and Gerry, Lee and Alina kept themselves to themselves. Me, I just made sure everyone was served, and dutifully ran to and from the kitchen.

Jacky did offer to wash up with me. She showed more interest in me and for a while it seemed like I was talking to the old Jacky as she made sure I was eating properly, was looking after my money, watching my weight, all that sort of thing. Then she turned to the subject of Ally. "He's become quite a fit young man," she said. "You are being careful?"

"Careful about what?" I asked.

"Do I really have to spell it out?" she said smiling.

"Our relationship is not like that," I replied, getting cross.

"That's what they all say," she replied in her lilting Irish accent.

I took a few deep breaths, tried to keep calm and rushed out of the kitchen. I was so angry, I ran straight up to my bedroom.

Dad came up eventually and asked what was wrong. When I told him, he gave me a hug. "I sent Jacky and Gerry packing a few minutes ago. They were going to open a bottle of whiskey, and I told them not here you don't. Jacky protested it was as much her house as mine, but I pointed out I was the one making the rules here now, seeing as I lived here."

"Thank you," I said, and I told him what Jenny said about him at my birthday party.

"I always knew I wasn't that bad," he said. "Now, come on, Lee and Alina are about to leave, and it dunna seem right, just me and Doris."

I washed my face and went downstairs. Dad, Doris and me played on the *Wii*, and clearly they were enjoying themselves. Me, I couldn't concentrate. I couldn't just help wondering when Ally was about to turn up.

He appeared about five. He was still in a tracksuit, although he had clearly just had a shower and a shave. He gave Dad a high five, and Doris a peck on the cheek which made her blush. Doris took one look at him and said, "He will not fit on the sofa."

"Oh, I'll sleep anywhere," said Ally, "just not in an empty house."

In the end Doris offered to sleep on my floor, while Ally slept in her bed. "It will be just like old times," she said.

But of course this Christmas is nothing like old times. So much has happened over the past year, and where we all will be next year, as Dad says, the Lord alone knows. But for now, Ally is here, even if he has to leave early for the match tomorrow, Doris is here, and I think I've learnt not to take Dad for granted.

31st December (KT/AG)

After a clean sheet on Boxing Day, Ally kept his place in the team today. Drumchester

~ 318 ~

City were playing away in a local derby, and I was nervous about going. Fortunately, I was able to travel with Mark and Olivia. We all packed the away end, separated by the police from the home supporters. Every time Ally got the ball he was booed, and I couldn't help hearing some of the chants about him. The whole ground seemed to know it was his eighteenth birthday.

"Don't let it get to you," said Olivia, but that was hard.

When he was pushed off the ball by one their forwards, the crowd just cheered. But Ally responded by playing a blinder. I couldn't see anything of him in the first half, but in the second I could see he was completely focused by what was in front of him, not what was behind. It was ages since we won this particular match, but despite a late penalty we came away with a 2-1 win. Well, we would have done, if the police hadn't kept us in the ground for half an hour, until they were able to safely escort us to the car.

I thought I might meet up with Ally afterwards, but Mark and Olivia insisted on taking me straight home. "He's got something planned?" I asked.

"Just wear something smart," smiled Olivia, "and be ready for seven o'clock."

KT was wearing the leather jacket I gave her for Christmas, with a sleeveless blouse underneath, and an ankle-length black skirt with a really pretty border. She looked at me in my new suit and said, "Are we going somewhere special?"

I grinned. "You just wait and see."

The manager had recommended the restaurant on the edge of Dewglass. "Reservation in the name of Green?" asked the waiter, surprised at our ages. "Follow me." We were led to a table with a glittering white cloth and more cutlery and glasses than I had ever seen. "This is on me," I said. By now KT was beginning to suspect I was up to something, but I told her to wait until our main course came.

I could see Ally was nervous, but I couldn't work out why. He kept fiddling with the end of his tie and making sure it wasn't anywhere near his food. At last, as we tucked into our steaks, he looked up at me and said, "As you might expect, there are several championship clubs who are getting seriously interested in me. City need the cash, and I am apparently a hot prospect for the future."

I wasn't surprised by the news, not after the way I'd seen him playing.

"But it's hard," he went on, putting his knife and fork down for a moment. "Am I ready to say goodbye to Drumchester? To my family? To my church? To you?"

I reached out for his hand. "I've been doing a lot of thinking and praying," he went on, as he put his fingers in mine, "and I want to give you this."

He fished a small box out of his suit pocket. "It's for you," he said.

I didn't know what to say. "I found it when clearing out Dad's stuff. Gran's never seen it before, so I reckon it must have come from my grandfather's side of the family. Go on – open it."

Inside was a simple, slender diamond ring. "I don't understand," I said.

"It's just a gift, 'cos you are the most wonderful and most special person I have ever met. Look, I don't know what the future holds. But I want you to have this ring so you know I am always thinking of you. You need to pass your exams, go to university, I know all that. Maybe one day our paths will go so far apart you will want to give the ring back. Or maybe one day you will decide you want to wear that ring for good. There's no hurry. Just keep it. It's yours." At this Ally fell silent, clearly embarrassed by what he had just said.

"You are going?" I said.

"Only if I know you're behind me with this. I will still talk to you every night, I promise."

I was filling up fast by now. He gently brushed away my tears with his napkin. "I... I... don't know whether to feel happy or sad," I eventually said. "This is a beautiful gift. I am going to put it on my chain, next to my cross. Thank you so much."

I never meant to make KT cry. I had rehearsed my speech hundreds of times, but somehow the words when they came out weren't quite as I planned. I could see I had shocked her, but I wasn't sure how to put it right. I picked up my knife and fork, and eventually we started talking about the future. KT is aiming to go to university somewhere near London, and I know at least one club not too far away from there that wants me. So that helps make my decision easier. "I will be waiting for you," I said.

"Can you really promise that?" she said looking at me straight in the face.

"Yes," I said gazing back into those wonderful blue eyes that were still brimming with tears. And by God's help, I added silently in my heart, I am going to keep that promise, come hell or high water.

By the time the dessert came, it was still only half past nine. We were meant to go on to the New Year's party at the church hall. "I don't think I can face it right this moment," I said.

"Me neither," said KT. For all we had been talking, I think we were still very aware there were plenty of other people in the restaurant. We needed some time to be alone and private, before we were ready to face the crowds.

The taxi came at ten. "Where to?" asked the driver.

I looked at KT and she looked at me. She gave her address. "We can always get a taxi back to the church."

"Not tonight," he said. "This is the last free taxi."

"OK, we can walk," I said.

My hands were trembling as I unlocked the front door. While I went into the kitchen to make some coffee, Ally switched on the TV and found some live gig or other, with bands we both liked. "Come on," he said. "Let's dance."

So we cleared the lounge floor and we danced. It seemed an eternity since we first danced at that folk festival in Wales. Then the music was loud and energetic. Tonight there were slower numbers among the ballads, and I just let Ally gently take me in his arms. I wished he could hold on to me forever, and I suspected he felt the same too.

Before long it was nearly half past eleven and I realised I needed to put on something warmer if we were going to walk up the river. When I came back from getting changed, Ally was already holding my coat, and insisted on helping me on with it. At that point it almost hurt to realise just how much I loved him.

In the films, winter scenes always feature glittering snow under a clear moonlit sky, with barely a puff of wind. But then nobody ever filmed the Drum estuary on New Year's Eve. The moon was playing hide and seek behind fast moving clouds, and there was a keen wind with a hint of rain that cut straight through you. We had to walk briskly to keep warm, but all the time I had my arm around KT.

There were a surprisingly large number of people taking the same path; crowds of partygoers; a jogger ("Why?" asked KT – I couldn't answer that question) and a drunk on a bicycle who was having trouble keeping a straight line. We hoped he would get home safely without falling into the river, and at least we didn't hear a splash.

It was almost midnight by the time we arrived outside the church hall. "Ready?" asked KT.

"Not quite," I said and gave her a kiss.

"I hoped you'd do that," she said beaming. "Right, deep breath."

Dad was just about to break into Auld Lang Syne when we walked through the doors. Everyone had gone quiet, but I didn't mind all the glances as we walked up to the stage.

"Everything all right?" whispered Dad, looking worried.

"Oh yes," I said.

Then he stepped up to the microphone with his acoustic and soon we were all singing.

Later I spent a long time talking with Dad. I showed him the ring, which he said was a real beauty. I told him about Ally's promise. "Well, he may find that hard to keep once he's away, but if I know Ally, he'll try. The question is – will my little KT be happy?" I nodded. "Then," he said, "that's good enough for me. Come on, I'm all done in. Let's get some sleep and see what the morning brings."

January 8th (AA)

The four of us met for the last time – or it so seemed – at Sid's this afternoon. There wasn't anyone else in the café, but Sid was happy to keep the place open for us. We could have been any group of ordinary teenagers having a chat. Daisy and KT were talking about a new cookery show on TV. Ally was talking about how his mother made him watch Carrie and Nina prepare for their ballet exam. Then Daisy talked about her Gran who might finally be retiring soon, and Derek who was serving somewhere secret. The old me would have kept interrupting and trying to top everyone else's stories. But as for the new me, I was just enjoying listening to everyone else.

It was only at the end that Ally got serious, talking about how he was going off to London tomorrow to meet his agent for the first time face to face, and then be interviewed by the manager and have a medical. He reckoned his signing would be announced about Wednesday, if all went well.

"I'm sure it will," said KT, putting her arm round his considerable shoulders.

At some point in the conversation KT let slip something about a ring. I don't think she was meant to say anything, because Ally gave her a hard stare and she started blushing. But as we said our goodbyes, a thought came into my mind. But I need to talk to Mum and Dad, and to John first. I can't work out at the moment whether I'm being stupid or inspired.

January 22nd (AA)

Last Wednesday I finally plucked up the courage to e-mail Elspeth. Before pressing 'send', I made sure Dad read it, to check he was happy with the contents:

Dear Elspeth,

I know you find it hard to forgive me for what's happened between me and Daisy. I am sorry for the hurt I have caused you, but I want you to know I intend to look after my new family and provide for them as best I can. I have had a long chat with my father, and he is willing to offer me a flat he owns in Drumchester to live in, probably from the start of August. I would have to pay for all the bills and so I am planning to find work just as soon as I finish my exams. I am willing to do anything to make ends meet, and I will try and give Daisy and our baby the very best.

I have thought long and hard to try and work out how I might show my commitment. If Daisy is willing to have me, and to live with me, then the best way I can think of doing this is by offering to marry her just as soon as we have the flat. But I do not want to do anything without your blessing, and if you can see some better way for me to provide for her, then I will do whatever you ask.

I have talked through all this with Joe and with Mum and Dad, and they have told me this is a very big step to make, but that if I am serious, they will support me as best they can. So now I am writing to you to ask for your support as well, and permission to speak with Daisy.

Even as the message went, I still wasn't sure whether I was being stupid or inspired.

Almost exactly two hours later Elspeth responded: *I have read over your e-mail with Daisy. Daisy wants to talk with her Dad. Come round on Sunday at six o'clock, and we will talk further. Please give Daisy the time she needs to make a decision.*

Since then, I have hardly slept. I have tried to get ahead in all my subjects, but I find my mind wandering in the midst of my essays and my teachers have all noticed I've been distracted. Everyone keeps asking if I am all right, but what can I say? I just nod politely and apologise I haven't been paying attention.

This morning in church KT wasn't playing the drums. For the first time ever she came over and sat next to me. If she had been talking with Daisy, she would have said something. But she didn't, and I didn't need to say anything to her because we both understood each other. Ally is in touch as much as he can, but he's found it tough stepping up to a higher level. KT's worried for him and missing him, and even though it's only been four days, I am worried about Daisy and missing her. Both of us missed the end of the prayer time, and even as the next song started up, we were still lost in our own private thoughts, deep in the presence of the Lord.

The rest of the day dragged slowly. Five o'clock came, then five fifteen, then half five. "Do you want me to come in with you?" asked Mum, as we got in the car. I shook my head.

It was dark and cold as I walked down the drive to the bungalow, and I felt very alone. It took an age, or so it seemed for Elspeth to answer the door, and I jumped when she suddenly appeared before me.

"Do come in," she said, showing me into the lounge. "Daisy's upstairs," she went on, "I think the two of you need to have a conversation." Then she smiled slightly and said, "Off you go, you know the way." So, slowly I walked up the stairs. Daisy's bedroom door was shut, so again I knocked.

"Come in," said Daisy, giving me a kiss. So I sat on the end of the bed, while she stood facing me by her easel. Neither of us spoke for a long time. Then she said, "You know, I always say take it one day at a time. But at night, I worry about the future as much as you. Can I have the baby? Will I be able to look after her? I don't like to share my fears with you, 'cos I know how afraid you are." I was going to say something, but she just raised her hand. I could see she had tears in her eyes. "But, like, the biggest fear of all is bringing up baby on my own. And then Mum gets that e-mail. I don't know how you managed to send that, and I don't think you know how confused I was when she read it out to me. Mum told me there and then to write down a list of pros and cons, but I don't think like that. I knew I had to speak to Dad, and to Gran. Dad wasn't well when I saw him, and the only thing he said was, 'You know, Daisy, what you want to do'. Gran was working nightshift, so I just got a text saying, 'Don't just feel – think'. So I've been thinking, I've been praying." She paused at this point, and she came towards me.

"So, Alex, are you ready to do something wild? Something so wild everyone will think we're mad? Are you? 'Cos I need to know the answer, and I need to know it now."

I cleared my throat. "OK, then, Daisy, will you marry me?"

"I think we'd better call your mother in," said Elspeth, making us tea a few minutes later. "She must be freezing outside."

June 5th (AA)

It all started as one of Mitch's jokes a few weeks ago. One teatime he announced that *Morbury's* was opening a new local shop in the middle of Drumchester and were looking for staff. I looked at Dad and Dad looked at me. "You can't afford to be choosy, son," he said.

"Perhaps you might be able to persuade them to stock some decent books," observed Granddad.

"OK, OK," I said, "but after all my efforts to stop them building their store, they're hardly going to consider me, are they?"

They considered me. They interviewed me. And to my great surprise, they offered me a job this morning. It is just the other side of the river from the flat so it's in an ideal location. Who says God doesn't have a sense of humour? But I didn't have too much time to reply, because today I had my French literature exam. I've been so glad over these past few months that I read all the texts last year, what with schoolwork, and ante-natal classes, and counselling sessions with John and Helen.

I was just about to go into the exam hall when I got a text from Elspeth: *Daisy has gone into labour. Come when you can.* Fortunately, the questions on the paper were all fairly straightforward. I answered them in half the time allowed, and then got a taxi over to the hospital.

Daisy was in a side ward by her own. She was so relieved to see me, but I could see she was scared and in pain. Nothing of the preparation we had done had actually made us ready for this occasion. For the next few hours it felt like a bad dream, as Daisy laboured and laboured, attached to drips and monitors, being carefully supervised by the gowned and gloved medical staff. I hoped that at some point I would wake up in an exam hall, and all would be peaceful and still, but, no, this was actually reality. I could only pray that everything would be all right, as I held her hand, and from time to time mopped her brow. She was being told constantly she was doing fine, and everything was all right, but it certainly didn't look like it to me.

Eventually Daisy gave one final push, and our daughter was born at just after four in the afternoon. We had both decided early on we would like to name her after our late grandmothers, so as the medical staff cleaned the baby up and carefully placed her in my arms, I explained she was called Ruth Phyllis Andrews. Then very gingerly I passed her over to Daisy who smiled at me and wept.

"She's perfect," she whispered, "absolutely perfect."

"Well done," I said, and brushed her damp hair out of her eyes. All this time Elspeth had been waiting outside, but I invited her in to come and see her granddaughter. I sensed Daisy and Elspeth wanted to be alone for a moment, so I went outside and let my family know.

Oh, and I have a history exam tomorrow. But as someone once said, all history is selective, and to me today has been as much history as anything else. I was going to wait until Daisy's birthday to give her the ring, but to mark the occasion, I think I'll give it to her just as soon as she's home.

August 20th (KT)
Today was Alex and Daisy's special day. When Ally asked me this morning why they had chosen this date, I reminded them it was their anniversary. I could see Ally was

about to ask me what anniversary and then he suddenly twigged. But I couldn't really blame Ally for being dopey. He got a boot in the face yesterday and he still had a headache when I met him off the train late yesterday evening. I just hope the stitches over his eye won't show up too badly on the photos.

So in the service today the two of us stood as godparents for baby Ruth. John preached a really powerful sermon on the birth of King Solomon and how despite everything the boy was still loved by God. I could see Daisy and Alex holding hands at this point, with Ruth snuffling and yawning in her sling. We all had cake in the hall afterwards, and it seemed like the whole church came up and wished them both well.

As I saw everyone milling around and chatting, it struck me how much I will miss the folk at Drumley Green when I go to university. It's not that I don't want to go. Dad is so pleased that I got my first choice, and I am happy Ally is living not too far away. But he has looked after me ever since Mum died, and maybe it's just with all these changes I'm missing her more than ever.

I must have been daydreaming or something, 'cos Daisy surprised me, when she came up and asked if we were ready to go back to her place. I nodded and told Ally I'd see him later. The idea was that we would have enough time over lunch to get changed, but by the time Daisy had fed Ruth, changed and settled her, she was in a rush to get changed and pin up her hair. Twice Derek came in and asked if we were ready, and we had to shoo him out of the room. Eventually we both emerged in these amazing ivory-coloured dresses that Alex's Mum had bought us, and we set off back to the church.

It was Ally's idea to hold the ceremony on a Sunday afternoon as he couldn't see any other time of the week to come down and be the best man. That suited everyone fine, because right from the beginning Daisy and Alex insisted they wanted a quiet family affair. So as we finally arrived outside the church, there were only about the usual number of cars outside, even though we were already five minutes late.

Lee had taken it upon himself to be the photographer, so that took another ten minutes, but I kind of sensed time wasn't too important on this occasion. Finally, Daisy was ready to walk down the aisle with Derek, and me following on behind as the single bridesmaid. I have to say she looked absolutely gorgeous, even though I knew on the inside she was feeling as nervous as anything. When she reached the front of the church, she handed her flowers to me and gave her Dad a kiss, before stepping forward next to Alex. They looked at one other, and I could tell at once that despite everything (or because of everything?) there was still a very deep and real bond between them.

When John finally declared them man and wife and a huge round of applause echoed round the church, Daisy's self-composure finally cracked. At this point Alex gently held her in his arms, as she sank her head onto his shoulders. Then he whispered something soothing in her ear that made her laugh and soon, after Daisy adjusted her hair, they were ready to kneel down at the communion rail for John's blessing.

We had already had cake after the baptism, but Joe and Sarah had prepared one more surprise for the new Mr and Mrs Andrews after the service – an ice cream van parked up in their garden, with a marquee for all the gifts. It was a beautiful, warm, late summer afternoon, with Mitch, Sophie and their Granddad Bob forming a kind of impromptu jazz trio - Mitch on keyboard, Sophie on guitar, and Bob singing in a surprisingly strong, low voice. Soon everyone was relaxed, even Elspeth who sat quietly to one side holding Bill's hand. I was just wondering whether to go over to them when Ally reminded me that unfortunately we had a train to catch, and he wasn't sure if I wanted to go in that dress.

Saturday 26th (KT)

It's been a wonderful, truly wonderful week. Ally's landlady had a spare room in the attic over the summer, and she agreed for me to stay for the week, provided I helped out in the church holiday club during the week. A few hours each day dealing with screaming children was no real hardship, because at the end of it I knew I could look forward to seeing Ally each day. The wound above his eye is gradually healing, even if the bruise has by now turned a most peculiar colour.

I began to appreciate over the week just how hard Ally is working to develop as a goalkeeper. Most days he has come back from training exhausted, at least until he has eaten what seems enough for both of us. I've had a chance to take him round the university where I'm studying, and we've worked out the best route to get across town to see each other. He's shown me the stadium, and I've met some members of his youth team, who now accept he has a proper girlfriend, and not just some random babe back home. But most of the time we've just been chilling, watching a DVD together, and curling up together on the sofa. It may only be just over 150 miles from Drummington-on-Sea to London, but sometimes it's felt like we've been on different planets.

But of course no holiday in London would be complete without seeing a show, and with the wedding, there hasn't been much time to celebrate my exam results. So yesterday Jenny and Gordon came up to stay in a posh hotel, and they bought a special room for my Dad as well, who arrived late after work. I wanted Jenny to take me shopping this morning, but she insisted on seeing the university and where I was going to be staying, and I'm glad she did, 'cos she thought of loads of things I needed to sort out, which I hadn't even considered.

After a brief lunch, we met Ally at the stadium for the big match. He isn't anywhere near the first team yet, so he was going to sit with us. As we took our places, he introduced me to the wife of the reserve goalie, and she chatted all about what it was like being married to a professional sportsman. If Ally could hear us, I think I could have been embarrassed. But he was off getting a pie, and on the way back he was talking to so many people he barely made it back in time for kick-off.

I had already made it clear that if I was going to be watching the match, I didn't want Ally commentating, and especially I didn't want Dad embarrassing me. They were generally both as good as their word – except when the winning goal went in. But I just gave Ally a kiss and he got the message.

The show in the evening, to be honest, was a bit of a disappointment and none of us liked the music much. But I was content just being next to Ally and we amused ourselves by watching the audience – the large lady in front who bought two tubs of ice cream, just for herself, the couple who were singing along so out of tune to the songs and the girl a few seats along who looked uncannily like Siobhan. Neither of us wanted the evening to end or think about me going home tomorrow.

Somehow Dad could read our minds. As the lights went on, and the audience thronged towards the exits, he slipped me a bunch of notes and said, "Go on, enjoy yerself – without the old folk," and he winked at Ally, and Ally took me by the arm and led me out to the taxi rank.

"Where are we going?" I asked.

"Anywhere you want," he said, and as he opened the taxi door for me, I couldn't help thinking of the photo on Pete's order of service.

Outside it was a still, warm, summer evening, and the last thing either of us wanted to do was to be indoors. So we just found a takeaway and walked along the river talking about everything and nothing in particular. We got as far as the Tower of London where Ally took a selfie of us, and then we meandered back. At midnight we reached Westminster Bridge where we heard the chimes of Big Ben.

"Guess folk will be wondering where we've got to," said Ally.

"Guess so," I said, as I felt his arms close around me.

It's now about two o'clock in the morning as I write these words. It's hot up in the attic room, and when I open the window, I can hear the traffic and smell the fumes. But that's not the real reason why I can't sleep. I have just said good night to Ally and in about eight hours' time Dad will come to take us both to the station. As I turned to go up the stairs, Ally gently kissed the back of my neck, and I can still feel that kiss right now. Yes, I know Ally told me to wait, but the more time goes on, the harder and harder it gets to leave. So here I am, holding his ring between my fingers, half wondering about the future, half praying. I think if I still feel this way by Christmas, I will definitely tell him I want to keep it. But somehow that seems a very, very long away, and I just hope I'm not taking too long to decide.

June 22nd – nearly two years later (Extract from John's diary)

Today I had the most immense privilege of marrying Ally Green and KT Lee. This has been a fitting end to my ministry here, and in some ways, I am sad to be moving on. The church at Drumley Green is a truly special one, but it's been a strain taking on Drummington Marsh, and now there's talk of working with the church in Drummington-on-Sea as well, and I really don't think I can cope with that.

Yet this day has not been the day for church politics. I had expected Ally and KT to marry next year, but KT said she wanted to be able to focus on their finals. And they have had so much to cope with recently. Ally was injured for a while and sent on loan somewhere in the Midlands while he got back to match fitness, while KT hasn't found it easy to settle at university. But theirs is such a close relationship, it's hard to imagine anything could really separate them. They have both grown up so early and so fast, and only they truly understand what the other one has been through.

Of course, as they've both been living away, they haven't been around much to organise the wedding. So they've left a lot of the preparations to Alex and Daisy. I can't say that I will ever fully understand their relationship, but somehow it works. Alex has made sure Daisy has finished her A-levels and arranged for her to start an art degree at Drumchester University. Daisy was a little uncertain of this at first, but that's only because she has turned out to be a wonderful mother, and finds it so hard to be apart from Ruth. I'm sure Alex and Daisy would have more children, if only they could afford to move from their flat. But that is still a few years off. In the meanwhile,

Alex is turning into a junior version of his Dad at work – quiet, dependable and thoughtful, and he's been selected for a management course sometime soon. I don't know if he's still writing, but he hasn't mentioned anything like that since the baby was born.

Ally and Alex arrived about noon at the church, and I was struck by the complete contrast between them. Ally tall, well-built with the muscles of a professional sportsman, Alex, short, wiry and as KT once said, "a bit of a weed." But again, for reasons I don't understand, their friendship has lasted. And they worked so well together with me, helping to make all the last-minute preparations needed for the big event.

And it truly was a big event. Most of the church family turned up, of course, but then so did loads of people from Drumchester City and Ally's current club. They hung around in the churchyard for ages, quietly chatting with each other, not quite sure what they were doing there, too embarrassed to go inside the church. Then Mark and Olivia arrived, and I stopped to have a rather longer word with them. They're getting married here in a month's time and they've even started coming along from time to time on a Sunday.

I was still chatting with them, when Nicky and George turned up. It's been clear Nicky doesn't hold much time for the church, but she managed at least to smile politely at me this time. Then Jacky came, clearly flustered. KT warned me that she and Gerry had had a big row, because Chelsea was upset she hadn't been asked to be a bridesmaid, and now Gerry wasn't coming to the wedding. I got the impression that it wasn't a big loss as far as KT was concerned, but I could see I was the last person Jacky wanted to speak to. She hurried past, just as Claire and Sian arrived, and I promised to catch up with them at the reception.

By now the tide of familiar faces was turning into a torrent, but I had to excuse myself. I invited Alex and Ally into the vestry for one final prayer with the churchwardens, got myself robed and waited, all the while listening to the conversation in the church get louder and louder. Then I got the nod, and I slipped out of the back door, down through the churchyard to where the limousines had arrived. Trevor helped KT out of the car, and for the first time in my life I saw his hand shaking. KT squeezed his hand and stepped confidently towards the lychgate where the photographer was waiting. She looked absolutely stunning, and her dress perfectly matched her mother's headdress with pink roses that her aunt, Jenny had given her a few years back.

"Ready?" I asked.

"Ready," she whispered, and for a moment I thought of the scared little girl I had first seen lying in a hospital bed.

As we reached the church doors, the churchwarden announced for everyone to be upstanding. I walked briskly to the front of the church, while behind, KT walked slowly on Trevor's arm, followed by Daisy and Doris, and Carrie and Nina, as bridesmaids, and Harry and Kai as the page boys.

I am not sure what kind of wedding the visitors were expecting. But I am sure the service was nothing like they had in mind. They wouldn't have imagined modern worship songs played by a mixture of our church regulars and members of *The Potential*, or Trevor's best mate Nick playing a solo set during the signing of the registers. They wouldn't have imagined me giving a simple gospel message straight from the Bible. And they certainly wouldn't have imagined Ally and KT giving their testimony. But right from the start of their wedding plans, they insisted that's what they wanted to do. So just before the solemnization of their marriage, quietly but confidently they talked of how the Lord had been at work through the good times and the bad, and at the end they both lit a candle in memory of absent parents.

You could have heard a pin drop at that moment. It was one of so many occasions I have experienced in this church when you could feel heaven touching earth. I don't know why it happens here and not elsewhere. It just does, and for that I continue to be so grateful. The sense of awe and wonder continued throughout the service, and the atmosphere was only broken right at the very end when I asked everyone to greet the new Mr and Mrs Green. And Ally looked at KT, and KT looked at Ally, and with a deep breath they walked down the aisle, towards whatever future the Lord has in store for them together.

www.ingramcontent.com/pod-product-compliance
Lightning Source LLC
Chambersburg PA
CBHW031155020726
47499CB00002B/372